The
Nature
of
Fragile
Things

Novels by Susan Meissner

The Nature of Fragile Things

The
Nature
of
Fragile
Things

Susan Meissner

Berkley
New York

BERKLEY
An imprint of Penguin Random House LLC
penguinrandomhouse.com

Copyright © 2021 by Susan Meissner

Library of Congress Cataloging-in-Publication Data

Names: Meissner, Susan, 1961- author.
Title: The nature of fragile things / Susan Meissner.
Description: First edition. | New York: Berkley, 2021.
Identifiers: LCCN 2020022072 (print) | LCCN 2020022073 (ebook) |
ISBN 9780451492180 (hardcover) | ISBN 9780451492203 (ebook)
Classification: LCC PS3613.E435 N38 2021 (print) | LCC PS3613.E435 (ebook) |
DDC 813/.6—dc23
LC record available at https://lccn.loc.gov/2020022072
LC ebook record available at https://lccn.loc.gov/2020022073

Printed in the United States of America
10 9 8 7 6 5 4 3 2 1

Jacket images: 1906 San Francisco earthquake © Everett Collection Inc./Alamy Stock Photo; figures © Tanya Gramatikova/Trevillion Images
Jacket design by Emily Osborne and Colleen Reinhart
Book design by Nancy Resnick

For Claire

Surely something resides in this heart that is not perishable—and life is more than a dream.

—Mary Wollstonecraft

The
Nature
of
Fragile
Things

INTERVIEW WITH MRS. SOPHIE HOCKING
CONDUCTED BY AMBROSE LOGAN, U.S. MARSHAL
CASE NUMBER 069308
Official transcript

San Francisco, CA
November 6, 1906

QUESTION: Thank you again for coming. Could you please state your full name, age, birth date, and the city where you were born, for the record, please?

ANSWER: Sophie Whalen Hocking. August 24, 1884. Donaghadee, County Down, Ireland. I'm twenty-two.

QUESTION: Whalen is your maiden name, correct?

ANSWER: It is.

QUESTION: Thank you. Now, if you don't mind, I've a few questions for the record, since you and I have not had an opportunity to speak before now. You emigrated from Ireland to the United States in 1903 and spent your first two years in this country in Lower Manhattan, New York City. Is that correct?

ANSWER: Yes. Nearly the first two years. Not quite that.

QUESTION: So you were nineteen when you emigrated?

ANSWER: Yes. So why is it you and I have not spoken before? Has the other detective moved away?

QUESTION: No, Detective Morris is still on the case. I was brought in only recently. I'm a U.S. marshal.

ANSWER: I don't know what that is, sir.

QUESTION: United States marshals serve at the federal level of law enforcement rather than local.

ANSWER: Oh. So . . . so you are also a detective, then?

QUESTION: I investigate federal crimes, yes. May we continue?

ANSWER: Yes.

QUESTION: Can you confirm for me that you married one Martin Hocking on March 10, 1905, at the courthouse here in San Francisco?

ANSWER: Yes. Yes, I did. Do you have news of my husband? Is that why you've called me in?

QUESTION: Possibly. Again, for the record, did you report your husband, Martin Hocking, missing six weeks after the earthquake that occurred on April 18 of this year?

ANSWER: I did, yes.

QUESTION: Can you tell me why you waited six weeks to notify the police that your husband was missing?

ANSWER: He travels for his job. I didn't know for sure he was missing at first.

QUESTION: You've stated previously you fled your home on Polk Street with your stepdaughter, Katharine Hocking, in the minutes following the earthquake. Is that correct?

ANSWER: Yes.

QUESTION: And the house on Polk Street was still standing when you left?

ANSWER: It . . . everything was broken and shattered inside, and the chimney had fallen off, but, yes, it was still standing.

QUESTION: And when you returned six weeks later was it still standing then?

ANSWER: I told the police before. It had burned. Every house on the street had burned. Every house in our neighborhood burned. Beggin' your pardon, sir, but do you not know what happened in this city? Have you not looked around?

QUESTION: I assure you, I'm not here to mock the loss of your home, Mrs. Hocking. I am only establishing the facts for the record. *My* record. I apologize for asking questions you have already answered. But I must ask them. You returned to your home six weeks after the earthquake and found it had burned? There was nothing left of it?

ANSWER: Nothing but ashes.

QUESTION: And you would have no way of knowing if Mr. Hocking returned to the house after the earthquake but before it burned?

ANSWER: How could I? I was not there.

QUESTION: Yes. Now, if we may go back to the day of the earthquake. You have said that you and Katharine found your way to the refugee camp at Golden Gate Park when the fires began. Do I have that right?

ANSWER: Yes.

QUESTION: And during your four days at the refugee camp you didn't hear from your husband, correct? He did not join you there?

ANSWER: No. As I said before, he was away on a business trip. He travels for a living.

QUESTION: So, to be clear, your husband left on his business trip before the earthquake and you have had no contact with him since?

ANSWER: I have not. Have you come by some new information about where he is? I think I have a right to know.

QUESTION: I believe I have come upon some new information, yes. But I'm not sure if this new intelligence aligns with what we know already. That is why I need to revisit some of the details you provided from the initial investigation into his disappearance, to see if what I've recently learned is consistent with the previously reported details. May we continue?

ANSWER: If this will assist you in finding my husband, then of course.

QUESTION: Thank you. Now, for the record, then, you married Martin Hocking the same day you met him, is that correct?

ANSWER: Yes.

QUESTION: And can you tell me why you did that?

ANSWER: Why I did what?

QUESTION: Married Mr. Hocking the same day you met him.

ANSWER: It is not against the law to marry someone you've just met, is it?

QUESTION: Indeed, it is not. I am curious, you see.

ANSWER: I married Martin because he asked me.

QUESTION: You had answered a newspaper advertisement that he'd placed in the *New York Times*? For a wife and mother. He had advertised that he was a widower with a young child. Do I have that right?

ANSWER: Yes.

QUESTION: And then you traveled to San Francisco from New York to marry Mr. Hocking, even though the two of you had not yet met?

ANSWER: I did.

QUESTION: Because?

ANSWER: Because, what?

QUESTION: Mrs. Hocking, are you declining to tell me why you married a man you'd only just met?

ANSWER: I am not declining, sir. I married him because I wanted to.

2

March 1905

The sun is dissolving like an enchantment as I stand at the ferry railing and look out on the San Francisco horizon. The day will end jubilant. *Jubilant.* This is the word I chose this morning from Da's book of words, and I've been keen to use it since breakfast. My father wrote that *jubilant* means you feel as though you finally possess everything you've always wanted, you are that happy. I like the way the word rolls off my tongue when I say it. I want to believe the day will end on a jubilant note. I am counting on it.

Most of the ferry's passengers aren't on the deck watching the golden sun fold itself into the western rim of the sky. They are seated inside, out of the bracing wind, but I don't want to be tucked indoors after six long days on a train.

I close my eyes as the heady fragrance of the ocean transports me as if in a dream to Gram's cottage in Donaghadee above the slate Irish Sea. I can see the house in my mind's eye just as it was when I was young, back when life was simple. I can see Gram making me a cup of sugar tea in her kitchen while a harbor breeze tickles the lace curtains she made from her wedding dress, two days after marrying my Anglican grandfather. On the kitchen table are shortbread cookies arranged on the daisy plate, and still warm from the oven. She is humming an old Gaelic tune. . . .

But no.

I've spent too many hours pondering what I wouldn't do to go back in time to Gram's kitchen, what I'd be willing to give up. What I'd be willing to give. I open my eyes to behold again the nearness of the San Francisco docks.

Backward glances are of no use to me now.

I move away from the railing to the shelter of an overhang and tuck loose strands of hair back into place. I don't want to step off the ferry looking like a street urchin. Not today.

I look down at my skirt to see how bad the wrinkles are. Not too noticeable in the day's diminishing light. My journey from New York to California took place on a second-class seat, not in a private sleeping car, hence the creases. I'd not expected anything different, as Martin Hocking had written that he is in good financial standing, not that he is rich. That he has means of any amount is miracle enough. I would have ridden in the baggage car all the way to get out of the umbrella factory and the tenement, and especially away from young Irishwomen just like me who reminded me too frequently of what I left back home.

If my mother could see me now, she'd no doubt put me on the first train back to New York. But then, Mam doesn't know how bad it was. I didn't want to worry her, so she doesn't know that the room I was subletting with four flatmates was no bigger than a kitchen pantry and that a single spigot in the back alley provided the only water to drink, bathe, and cook with for the entire building. She doesn't know everyone dumped their chamber pots out their windows because there were no indoor toilets—despite city ordinances requiring them—and that the stink of human waste hung on the air like a drape. The tenement wasn't a place to come home to at the end of the workday. It was just a shared room with sagging mattresses, a place where dreams for a better life could unravel faster than your threadbare clothes, and where girls like me from Belfast and Armagh and Derry and other Irish towns laid their heads at night.

"I had a neighbor lady in Chicago when I was growing up who was from Ireland," a woman seated across from me said hours earlier, as our train chuffed through the Nevada desert. "She came to America as a young girl during that terrible time when there was nothing to eat in Ireland and nothing would grow. That was years ago. I wasn't even born yet, so that was long before you were alive. She told me it was something awful, that time. Whole families starved to death." The woman shook her head in pity.

There isn't a soul back home who hasn't heard of those long years of scarcity. Everyone in County Down called that time the Great Famine. Gram, who defiantly spoke Gaelic until her dying breath, called it An Gorta Mór. The Great Hunger, as if to say it wasn't the lack of food that is remembered but how that stretch of years made people feel. Ravenous and empty and wanting.

"Yes. I've been told 'twas a terrible time," I replied.

The woman then asked if I'd immigrated to America with my whole family.

I thought of Mason, my brother who came to America first

and sponsored me, and who is now living somewhere in Canada with a woman he fell in love with. "No. Just me."

"You came all by yourself?" the woman said. "I think that's very brave. And you're so young!"

I smiled at this because some days I feel as though I've already lived several lifetimes and others as though I haven't lived any kind of life at all, that I'm still waiting for it to start. Or waiting for it to start over.

I answered I was twenty, nearly twenty-one.

"What lovely cheekbones you have, and such beautiful black hair," the woman continued. "I didn't know Irish had black hair. I thought you were all redheads and blonds and auburns."

And then the woman asked what was bringing me all the way from New York to San Francisco.

So many reasons. I gave her the easy one. "I'm getting married."

The woman offered me her congratulations and asked what my future husband's name was. As she did so, I realized I was itching to have someone older and wiser tell me I was making a sensible choice, an understandable one, considering how hard and complicated the world is.

"His name is Mr. Martin Hocking. Would you like to see his picture?"

The woman smiled and nodded.

I reached into my handbag and pulled out the photograph Martin had mailed to me. He was dressed in a vested pinstripe suit, his wavy hair gelled into place and his trimmed mustache partly covering his lips. He wore a fixed, charismatic gaze that I'd gotten lost in every time I looked at it. I'd had the photograph for less than two weeks but I knew its every inch.

"My, oh my! But he is handsome," the woman said. "Such striking eyes. He looks like he could see into your very soul."

"He's . . . he's a widower, newly arrived to San Francisco from Los Angeles. He has a little girl named Katharine. He calls her Kat. She's only five. Her mother died of consumption and the child has had a rough time of it."

"Oh, how sad! Aren't you a dear to take on the role of mother and wife all at once." The woman reached for my arm and laid her hand gently across it in astonishment, empathy, and maybe even admiration. And then she wished upon me every happiness and excused herself to find a porter to get a cup of tea.

I wanted the woman to ask how I met Martin so that I could gauge her response, but even after she came back with her cup, she didn't ask. While she was off to look for the porter, I imagined how I would've replied. I withdraw the photograph now from my handbag and remind myself of that answer as the pier grows ever nearer.

I've not met him yet, I would've said to the woman. *I answered his newspaper advertisement. He was looking for a new wife for himself and a new mother for his little girl. He didn't want a woman from San Francisco. He wanted someone from the East, where he is from. Someone who doesn't need coddling. Someone who is ready to step into his late wife's role without fanfare. I wrote to him and told him I didn't need coddling. I wanted what he could offer me—a nice and cozy home, someone to care for, a child to love.*

The woman, surely wide-eyed, might've replied, *But . . . but what if you are unhappy with him? What if he is unkind to you?*

And I would've told her that this is what I'd contemplated the longest in my tenement room before I left it, while rats scurried back and forth in the hall, while babies cried and men drank their sorrows and women wailed theirs, while the couple in the room above banged the walls while they fought and the couple in the room below banged the walls while they pleasured each other, and while my stomach clenched in hunger and I shivered in the damp.

It can't be worse than what I've already known, I would've said. *Besides. He doesn't look like someone who would hurt people, does he?*

I look at the portrait now, at this visage of a man who looks as near to perfection as a man could.

Would the woman have tried to talk me out of what I am about to do? Perhaps. Perhaps not. Half of my flatmates thought I was crazy, and the other half were jealous I'd found the advertisement and they hadn't. Mam does not know what I will do when I get off this boat, and I'm not writing her of it until it's already done.

Even after I finally tell her how miserable the tenement was, Mam will still want to know what possessed me to marry a man I don't know. This was not the plan when I left Ireland to come to America. This was not what she'd wanted for me when she helped me pack my one travel bag. I had pondered what answer to give to that question, too. I'd already started the letter I would send to my mother.

I want a home, I'd written in broad terms, so that if another reads the letter—perhaps one of my two older brothers still in Ireland—they, too, will understand. *I want what I had when I was a little girl. A warm house and clean clothes and food in the pantry. I want to sing lullabies and mend torn rompers and make jam and cakes and hot cocoa, like you did. And I want to have someone to share it all with. I just want what you had, back when you had it.*

But what above love? my mother will want to know, because

even though Da has been gone for too many years, Mam still loves him. She still feels like she is married to him.

What about love?

What about it?

The ferry is closing in on its slip, easing its way to the dock and the men who stand ready to tie up its moorings. Beyond the ferry building, the spread of the city beyond looks like an aspiring snip of Manhattan, with towers and multistoried structures lifting themselves skyward. The sun is beginning to dip below the buildings, casting a rosy glow that tinges everything with haloed light. The passengers in the main cabin behind me are already making their way downstairs to queue up to disembark.

I slip Martin's photograph back inside my handbag and straighten my hat. It was Mam's years ago, and made from the prettiest blue velvet and satin trim, both of which still hint at their original luster. Even slightly out of style, the hat pairs nicely with my dove gray shirtwaist, the only good dress I own, and I'd written Martin that I'd be wearing it. I reach for the travel bag resting at my feet.

Every step toward the ramp to the pier is taking me farther away from who I am and closer to who I am going to be. As I step off the ship and join the throngs moving toward the ferry building, I look to see if Martin Hocking is outside it studying the crowd of passengers, searching for me. Is his little girl with him? Is Kat wearing a pretty little frock to meet her new mother?

I don't see him in the sea of faces awaiting the arrival of passengers. Maybe he is waiting inside.

Dusk is descending like a veil and the electric lamps surrounding the ferry building are hissing as they come to life. The crowd starts to thin.

And then I see him. Martin Hocking is standing just outside the entrance, in a pool of amber light cast by a lamp above him. His gaze is beyond me and to the right of where I stand. Even from many feet away I can see he is as stunning as his portrait. Not merely handsome, but beautiful. He wears a coffee brown suit and polished black shoes. His hair, as golden brown as toast, is perfectly in place. He's tall, nearly six feet, I'd wager. He is not overly muscular and yet he has strength in his arms and torso, I can see that. He looks like royalty, like a Greek god.

And those eyes.

My seatmate was right. Martin Hocking's eyes look like they could peer into my very soul.

Time seems to stand still as niggling questions that I've ignored for days again needle me. Why does such a man want a mail-order bride the likes of me? This man could probably court any woman in San Francisco looking the way he does. He wrote to me that his desire to secure a new wife was for practical purposes—he needs a mother for his daughter—but also because he needs to be viewed as a fortunate businessman rather than a pathetic widower and father. Appearances matter when you work for a life insurance company and interact with their wealthy clients. And yet why send away to the East for someone, a stranger no less, and why choose a bride as uncultured as myself? And why doesn't he want the intrigue of romance? I know why I'm not keen to wait for it, but why isn't he?

Unless he is so grieved over the loss of his first wife that he can't imagine ever loving another. Unless he wants companionship and hot meals and a clean house but not romance. Not love.

Perhaps Martin Hocking wants—more than anything else—a Cinderella of a girl precisely like me, with no family, no background, and the simplest of desires. After all, what do I bring to this arrangement except my willingness? My emptiness? My *gorta mór*—my great hunger for everything Martin already has and which for me has been so elusive—a secure home, a child to love, food and clothes and a bed that doesn't smell of poverty.

If this is true, I am practically perfect for him.

And then he turns his head in my direction. Our eyes meet. Martin's closed mouth curves into a relieved, welcoming smile, and it's almost as if he'd indeed read my thoughts.

Yes, that half smile seems to say. *You are exactly what I wanted.*

I step forward.

3

Martin Hocking is alone.

I hadn't realized how much I wanted his daughter to be waiting there with him until it is clear she isn't. Perhaps Martin had asked Kat if she wanted to accompany him and she'd said no. Or maybe he'd asked and she'd said nothing. Martin had written me that his daughter had withdrawn into near silence following the death of her mother, speaking only an occasional word here and there. Maybe he'd invited her to come along and gotten no response at all.

"Welcome to San Francisco, Sophie," Martin says as soon as he is close to me. His voice is a little deeper than I'd imagined, a little softer. He doesn't seem nervous, not even a little. And he called me Sophie, not Miss Whelan. My first name fell off his lips as though we've known each other for years. He takes my hand and clasps it like we are old school chums.

"Thank you," I say, and then, in an attempt to match his relaxed tone, I add, "Martin."

He lets go of my hand. "I'm glad you're here," he says, without visible emotion, and yet he doesn't sound insincere. He sounds satisfied, relieved perhaps that I didn't change my mind.

"Yes, I'm happy to be here as well."

He reaches for my travel bag. "Do you have a trunk that needs to be sent along to the house?"

I own nothing else and my cheeks warm a degree. "I don't."

But Martin doesn't seem concerned or amazed that the entirety of my worldly possessions fits into a single travel bag and the handbag I am clutching. "We've only a few minutes before the courthouse closes, and they are expecting us." He speaks the words as though we might merely miss the opening lines of a play if we don't hurry. We leave the dock and enter the expansive and busy ferry building. We walk through quickly to the street entrance on the other side.

Delicate wisps of fog are just starting to swirl down upon the city, gauzy as gray silk and so very much like the approach of evening on the northern coast of Ireland. The street bustles with end-of-workday activity. A few automobiles sputter and cough as dozens of horse-drawn carriages and delivery wagons skirt them without much notice or fear. A streetcar full of riders rattles past.

"I've a carriage for us just here." Martin leads us to an ebony-hued buggy hitched to an even blacker horse that waits curbside. The driver opens the door for me and I step inside. Martin climbs in to sit across from me.

As the carriage begins to move, he asks if my travel was acceptable.

"Yes, thank you. It was."

He nods.

"Is Kat waiting for us to return after . . . after our errand?" I ask.

"Yes."

And then, because I must, I ask Martin if he has changed his mind about anything we'd agreed upon in our previous corre- spondence.

"I have not," he replies. "Have you?"

"No."

"Then we're settled."

"Yes."

And then, since we are apparently all set, Martin casts his gaze out the carriage window.

I had expected nervous conversation in the carriage or a string of questions politely thrown in my direction or perhaps a steady stream of information from him about his daughter or maybe even his dead wife. But Martin doesn't speak as the carriage makes its way to the courthouse. Perhaps he is shy around women? Or maybe he is choosing to mask any nervousness with silence, just as I am. Some minutes later the carriage comes to a stop.

"You can leave your travel bag," Martin says as he reaches for the handle. "The driver is going to wait." Martin steps out and then assists me. The combined courthouse and city hall looms in front of us like an opulent palace, with great columns of carved marble and a sparkling dome that is half-blanketed in light mist and twilight.

Inside, we walk swiftly through the echoing foyer and toward the offices of the justice of the peace, the heels of my shoes click- ing on the marble flooring.

We enter a courtroom where another civil ceremony appears to have just concluded. The black-robed judge, graying and portly, is shuffling papers behind his tall desk, and at a table next to him a woman in a dark blue dress is showing the newlywed couple's witnesses where to sign the certificate of marriage. A photographer is taking a portrait of the bride and groom. The bride is wearing a canary yellow shirtwaist, and her new husband a gray suit the color of thunderclouds. The two of them look like sunshine and rain, but they are beaming—joyful and clearly in love. A trio of lilies rests in the crook of the woman's arm.

"Next couple, please?" The clerk of the court—a lean, bespectacled man—looks past the freshly married couple to where we stand. "Mr. Hocking and Miss Whelan?"

"Yes, we're here." Martin reaches for my hand and leads me forward to stand in front of the justice's immense oaken desk.

"Stand right here," the clerk says. "If you have rings, get them ready. The judge will address you in just a moment."

"Thank you," Martin replies, without a hint of uneasiness.

"No witnesses of your own?" the clerk asks in a bored tone.

"No. It's just us."

The man turns to the woman in the blue dress. "I'll need you to stay and be a witness for this last one, Mrs. Farriday."

The woman nods as she gathers back her fountain pens and the document from the previous two witnesses. The happy couple in yellow and gray walk away arm in arm.

The photographer turns to Martin. "I'll take your photograph, as well, if you'd like, sir. I do nice work. Only a dollar for a nice portrait for your mantel. And I'll set you up for a set of cabinet photographs for giving away. Only two dollars for a dozen."

"No, thank you," Martin replies, not even looking at the man.

But I want a photograph of my wedding day. I want Mam to see this refined gentleman I am marrying, and how content I look on his arm. I want her to believe it will be different for me this time. I want to believe it, too.

I touch Martin's arm. "Please, may we have him take a photograph?"

Martin swivels to face me.

"I would like one for my mother. And one for us. Shouldn't we have one for us? And maybe one for your parents back east?"

He considers this for several seconds and then turns to the photographer. "We won't need a dozen. Just two. One for the mantel and one for her mother."

Martin hands the photographer the money and gives him an address. He then fishes out of his pants pocket two gold rings. The smaller one is set with a tiny glittering sapphire. He hands the larger one, a plain gold band, to me. It is smooth and warm in my palm.

And then the clerk is in front of us, telling us the judge is ready. The vows are simple and short. In a matter of mere breaths, it seems, the judge is finished and the rings are exchanged. The judge pronounces us married and then he stands and bids us good night.

There is no kiss to seal our vows. Our words did that, and the certificate will bear witness that we indeed said them.

I am led to a long table, handed a fountain pen, and told where to sign my name. Martin signs next, followed by the woman in the blue dress and the clerk. The judge, gone now, has already signed it.

"All right, then," the photographer says to us. "If you'll just turn toward me, folks. Sir, if you'll just slip one hand into your pocket there."

Martin and I stand as directed and the photographer takes the shot in a burst of bright light from his flash lamp.

The clerk and Mrs. Farriday are leaving by another door, and the photographer is hoisting his camera and flash pole on his shoulder and heading out of the emptying courtroom. I look down at the ring on my finger. Under the amber light of the ceiling lamps, Martin's little sapphire sparkles like a tiny moonlit ocean.

Night has fallen soft and ghostly when we emerge from the courthouse. Swaths of denser fog now hug the streetlamps and obscure the sky like a never-ending bridal train. We climb back into the waiting carriage.

Martin is again quiet as we ride. The silence doesn't seem to fit the occasion, even one as unusual as ours. I clear my throat. "Thank you for allowing that photographer to take our portrait."

Martin turns his gaze from the window to look at me. "You're welcome."

"So . . . are you sure you don't want to send a photograph back home to your parents as well?" I am wondering if he, like me, is hesitant to inform his family of what he's just done. When he doesn't answer me, I add, "I understand if you're anxious about telling your parents. I . . . I actually feel the same way about telling my mam."

He hesitates a moment. "My parents died when I was little," he finally replies, his tone betraying nothing of what it might've felt like to say those words to me. "I was raised by an aunt and uncle back east. We're not close."

My heart instantly aches a little for him. "I'm so sorry."

"It's all right," he says easily. "I don't remember my parents."

"Still, I'm sure it was very difficult for you losing your parents so young like that. How did it happen?"

"They were coming home from an event in the city but were caught in a blizzard no one knew was coming. They lost their way and froze to death in their carriage."

"Oh, Martin."

"That was a long time ago. I don't think about it anymore."

I wonder if this man has spent his whole lifetime telling himself it was just a small thing that he grew up without his mother and father. How does someone school himself to believe losing parents at such a young age doesn't matter? I can't imagine it. I lost my father when I was sixteen and it was nearly my undoing. I wait a moment to see if Martin will query me about my own parents.

"My mam likely won't approve," I say when he doesn't. "I'm not sure what my father would've thought." I turn my head to look out the window. I see only mist and other carriages and the hulking shapes of buildings in the undulating fog. "He probably would've said it was imprudent or preposterous, what I've just done. My da liked using fancy words. He collected them in a book like some people collect old coins. He wanted to go to university and become a professor, but there was no money for that. He became a roofer just like his father had been. But he taught himself what he could on his own. He was always borrowing books from the rich people in the village who had libraries. He'd read the books out loud to me and my brothers, and he'd find so many words he wanted to remember. He wrote them in a little ledger. He fell from a roof a few years ago. He never woke up from the fall and died a few days later. He was such a gentle soul." I turn to face Martin, my mouth suddenly agape. I hadn't intended to share that much with him. I don't know why I did.

Martin is studying me, however, with what seems to be intense interest. Something about what I said has drawn me to him an inch or two. And then the moment passes.

"How unfortunate," he says.

We are quiet as his reply, sincere but distanced, settles about us. The clopping of the horse's hooves outside the carriage is the only sound.

After a few more minutes the carriage comes to a stop.

"I'm afraid we will have to walk the rest of the way to the boardinghouse where Kat and I have been staying. The hill here is too steep for carriages and the cable car doesn't go up this street. San Francisco is like that."

"I don't mind walking."

"You can leave your bags inside the cab. We're coming back to it."

We exit the carriage. Ahead of us is a steeply inclined street packed on either side with three- and four-story townhomes, and whose end, if there is one, is concealed in mist.

We begin to ascend the hill like a seasoned couple who have strolled it a thousand times already.

"Kat and I have been staying at Mrs. Lewis's the last four months, and she's been looking after Kat for me when I've been working," Martin says as we walk. "But I've just taken ownership today of my own place. We'll collect Kat and then make our way there. I need to get back out to my clients, so I want you and Kat to get settled in right away."

I had momentarily forgotten that Martin works for a life insurance company on the road, not from a downtown office. "Of course," I say a second later.

We pass a few people on the street who nod their "good evenings." The steady incline is making me short of breath. I fairly whisper my own greeting in return.

We arrive at a large, four-story structure with forest green windowpanes and trim. Martin withdraws a set of keys from his pocket and slips one into the lock, and we step inside. The foyer opens to a hallway of doors to the first-floor rooms and a staircase to the second floor. Martin raps at the first door on the left.

The door opens. Mrs. Lewis—gray-haired, matronly, and plump—looks me up and down. Martin apparently told her who it was he was fetching from the ferry terminal and for what purpose. The woman looks deep into my eyes, as if wanting to divine how I became acquainted with Martin when she has never seen me with him. Not once. And yet here I am newly married to the man.

"This is my wife, Mrs. Lewis," Martin says. "Sophie, this is Mrs. Lewis."

"How do you do," I say, as confidently as I can.

"Pleased to meet you." But Mrs. Lewis is clearly something other than pleased. Flummoxed, perhaps. Baffled.

The woman turns to call out over her shoulder into the depths of her front room. "Katharine, your father and . . . your father's here." She holds out her arm for the child to come. The little girl appears and stops at the woman's side.

Kat is wearing a dress of pale blue that is too small for her, and in her arms is a black-haired doll whose porcelain face has a cracked cheek. The child's tawny eyes, so like her father's, seem bright and knowing, as though there is great knowledge behind them—impossible, I know, for a child of only five. Kat's heart-shaped face is framed by straight hair the color of cinnamon. She stares up at me in neither annoyance nor curiosity nor delight.

"Let's go, Kat." Martin motions with his hand for Kat to come. The child moves to stand by her father, but her gaze stays on me.

"I baked you folks a little wedding cake," Mrs. Lewis says. "Since you're not honeymooning or anything." She reaches behind her to a pedestal table and a small wicker basket covered with a paisley cloth.

"Thank you, Mrs. Lewis." Martin takes the basket from her.

I'm touched. And a little taken aback. A wedding cake? For Martin and me? I don't feel much like a bride. "Yes, thank you," I manage. "That's very kind."

"You're English." Mrs. Lewis's gaze is full of questions.

"Irish."

"Oh."

The woman seems loath to let me leave, as if there is something else she wants to ask me. Or tell me. But Martin is ushering Kat away from Mrs. Lewis's door, and as he does so, he introduces his daughter to me.

"Kat, this is your new mother," he says, nodding toward me as we turn for the front door.

Kat, whose gaze has stayed on me, blinks slowly.

"I'm so very happy to meet you, Kat."

The child says nothing.

"Thank you again, Mrs. Lewis," Martin calls over his shoulder. "Just add what I owe you to my final bill. Oh, and here are your keys." He stretches out his arm and the woman takes a step forward.

Mrs. Lewis looks fondly down at Kat as she takes the key ring. "Good-bye, Katharine. Come back and visit me?"

The child says not a word as Martin reaches for the doorknob.

Mrs. Lewis turns her attention back to me. "Please do come back and bring the child for a visit," she says, her gaze like steel. "Anytime."

"Thank you again for the cake," I reply, unnerved by the woman's stare.

Mrs. Lewis only nods and watches us leave. She is still standing at the threshold of the open door as we turn to begin the hill's descent.

Her image is lost in a swirl of fog as we walk away.

4

The carriage will take us as far as the Hyde Street cable-car stop a mile away, Martin explains. As we ride, Martin tells Kat that I've come a long way to be her mother and that he expects her to be a good girl for me. He doesn't want to come home from any of his travels to the news that she hasn't been on her best behavior.

"I'm sure we'll get along fine," I say reassuringly, very much wanting Kat not to be afraid of me. "There were dozens of tots where I lived back home in Ireland, Kat. I used to help my mam mind some of them for the mothers who worked with their husbands with the nets. I lived in a fishing village."

I was thinking Kat might warm to me a little knowing that, but the little girl says nothing. And Martin, who doesn't seem concerned or surprised that Kat remains silent, says nothing, either.

Martin pays the driver after we step out of the carriage, and a few minutes later the three of us are boarding a red cable car trimmed in yellow and packed with other riders. Half of its benches are sheltered from the elements and half are open-air with only a brightly painted roof over the seats. A gentleman who'd been sitting offers me his place on a bench that is unprotected from the night air. I take it and then hesitantly pull Kat onto my lap. The child doesn't object. The cable car begins to climb a long hill, stopping at each leveled block to take on new passengers and let off others. I can't discern how the car is able to move with no motor or engine and no overhead wires. I ask Martin how this is possible.

"It runs on the steel rail underneath," he says disinterestedly. "On a track. There's a slot between the tracks where an underground cable runs at a continuous speed. The car grabs hold of the cable like a pair of pliers and gets tugged along."

"But how does the cable run, then?" I ask.

Martin is too slow to reply. The man who gave up his seat and is standing near me is charmed by my interest and answers my question.

"The powerhouse over on Mason does the work," he says proudly, as if he'd invented the cable car himself. "Large wheels spin the cable all day long with hydroelectric power. Quite an impressive thing, isn't it?"

"Yes." I've never seen or heard of anything like it. Such power, so easy to go unnoticed.

After a few stops, we get off and walk a few more slightly ascending blocks. The homes, some amply spaced apart and with views of the matrix of streets below, are nicely appointed with paned windows that are aglow with electric lights. The people who live in these houses are a world away from the tenement dwellers of the Lower East Side. For a fleeting moment I wonder why Martin didn't pay the extra money for a sleeping car if he can afford to own a house in this neighborhood.

"Here it is," Martin says, as we arrive at a three-story house on Polk Street. It is not as imposing as some of the other homes around it, but it is freshly painted a deep blue with ivory trim. Black ironwork adorns the railings and window boxes. As we walked, Martin told me the house is situated a few blocks from Russian Hill, so that I would know which part of the city we are in. It had lately been the home of a doctor and his wife and their two young sons. The doctor had taken a director's position at a hospital in Argentina, and he and his family had left with only their personal belongings and a few housewares. Martin had bought the home fully furnished.

We step inside to a foyer lit by a chandelier of incandescent lights. My bag is set down by several other travel cases and trunks filled with Martin's and Kat's belongings from Mrs. Lewis's, which had been sent over that morning.

"I'll take all of those up later," Martin says, nodding toward the collection of possessions. "I'll show you the house first." He begins to show me the place, room by room. Kat trails behind us and I'm fairly sure she's seeing this house for the first time, too.

The downstairs consists of a sitting room, dining room, kitchen, and library. In the large kitchen there are hot and cold taps at the sink, an ample icebox, and a cast-iron cooking range piped for gas. There is a butler's table and chairs with a view of the back garden and a pantry full of odd nonperishables that the doctor did not take and a few staples that Martin arranged to be delivered earlier that day. Next to the pantry is a door to a short staircase that leads down to a low-ceilinged boiler room. The back garden has been bricked in and there are empty terra-cotta pots awaiting attention and a painted wrought-iron garden table and chairs. A long and skinny flower bed, perfect for rows of daffodils, lines the tall wooden fence at the property's edge. Over the top of the fence, I can see the upper back sides of homes on Van Ness, the next avenue over.

In the sitting room, upholstered sofas and chairs and ottomans in shades of rose and cream are situated in front of a gas fireplace framed in carved marble. A desk, chair, and matching book-shelves with volumes already tucked inside grace the library. The dining room table and breakfront are of the same warm-hued wood, which Martin tells me is redwood stained to look like cherry. Redwood is as plentiful here in this part of California as water in the ocean. The three upstairs bedrooms are furnished with bedsteads, bureaus, and wardrobes. The water closet on the second floor has indoor plumbing, glory be, and is tiled in black, white, and red. The third floor, with its pitched ceiling, contains two rooms. One is empty and looks as if it had perhaps been used for a maid's room. The other room was painted along one wall with the images of farm animals. It has the look of a former play-room. Each second-floor room contains a gas fireplace framed with mantels and hearths of marble or onyx, and which Martin turns on with a key before we head back downstairs.

Though it is not the most spacious home on the street, to me it is a palace. I don't know how much a house such as this one costs. I can't help but wonder if Martin has sunk himself in debt to acquire it and that is why I'd not been sent a train ticket for a sleeping car. It is more beautiful than anyplace I could ever have hoped to call home.

Martin had also arranged for a cold supper to be delivered just before he came to the ferry terminal for me. It had been laid out in the dining room on plain white bone china plates that the doctor's wife likely thought would not survive passage to Argentina. When Martin is finished showing me the house, we arrange ourselves at the table, choosing chairs that I suppose we will continue to sit in for every supper thereafter—Martin at the head, me on his right, and Kat on his left. Under the cloches are cold roasted chicken, pickled beets, and sweet peppers stuffed with rice and currants and capers.

No one says anything as we begin to eat.

"My gram used to make chicken like this," I say after several long minutes.

Martin looks up from his plate. Meals for Martin and Kat have likely been very quiet of late. He smiles slightly, and it is not a bona fide invitation to continue but I simply cannot eat an entire meal in silence. I begin to tell Martin and Kat about Ireland. I tell them about Gram's cottage on the hill, and my own family's little house closer to the water, and the thousand shades of green on the hillsides and in the fields. I tell them about my favorite dishes that Gram used to make, like smoked eel with apple glaze and cinnamony sweet barmbrack.

After we finish, we move to the sitting room by the fireplace to eat slices of the little spiced cake Mrs. Lewis made. I tell them how my brothers and I would walk along the harbor wall when we were young, while little waves licked the slippery stones on one side and brightly colored fishing boats pulled on their mooring lines on the other, and that ahead of us would be the lighthouse, tall and as white as snow with its steady, fiery light. I tell them how the bells at the Donaghadee parish church would ring out on Christmas morning and that I never tired of hearing them. I speak of only happy things, the things I miss.

When the hall clock strikes eight, Martin says it is time for Kat to go to bed.

"I'll start bringing up the trunks and bags," he says, and he starts with Kat's things, taking them to the first room off the second-floor landing. She and I follow him. The child enters the room almost like a sleepwalker, slow and uncertain.

"Might I tuck you in, Kat?" I ask.

Kat hesitates before nodding a wordless consent. Martin leaves to attend to the rest of the luggage.

The room had been the bedroom of the doctor's sons; this is obvious by the matching bedcovers adorned with a pattern of toy soldiers and the two rocking horses in the far corner. I am going to have to do something with this room. No five-year-old girl would be at home in it. I help Kat with her buttons and get her into a nightgown, which also seems tight and short. The child needs new clothes; she has grown since her mother's illness and death, and Martin perhaps has not noticed.

"I think we need to get a few new frocks for you." I hang the dress in the closet as well as the half dozen other dresses that are in her trunk—all the same too-small size. At the bottom of the trunk is a photograph in an oval frame of a beautiful woman with golden hair and fair skin, and whose nose is the same shape as Kat's.

"Is this your mother?" I pick up the frame to look more closely at the image and then glance at Kat, who is sitting on one of the beds, watching me.

The child nods and a veil of sadness seems to fall across her face. Oh, how I want this child to talk to me.

"I know what it is like to miss someone you love." I come to Kat's bedside, still holding the frame. "It's the worst ache in the world. My da had an accident some years back and went to heaven, too. Just like your mother. I miss my father very much."

Kat is still looking at me, but the look of sadness has merged with one of slight interest.

"Perhaps you want to sleep with her photograph under your pillow? It will seem like you're resting your head in her lap. Would you like to do that?"

The child nods, climbs into bed, and lies back on the pillow. I slide the frame underneath.

"Do you say prayers at night?" I ask as I tuck the quilts up under Kat's chin. It is chilly in the room despite the gas fire throwing an orange glow around the room. The child shakes her head.

"How about if I say a little one for both of us. Will that be all right?"

Kat blinks and says nothing.

"My mam used to say this one with me. Close your eyes, now."
Kat obeys.

I close my eyes, too, and then speak the memorized Anglican prayer from a thousand bedtimes in Donaghadee. "Lord, we beseech thee mercifully to receive the prayers of thy people which call upon thee; and grant that we may both perceive and know what things we ought to do, and also may have grace and power faithfully to fulfill the same; through Jesus Christ our Lord. Amen."

When I open my eyes, I can see that Kat's eyes are already open. She is staring at me, wide-eyed, in what nearly looks like wonder. Unexplainable tears are pricking at my eyes.

"Good night." I kiss the child's forehead and rise from the bed quickly. When I reach to turn out the light, I see Martin standing in the doorway with his arms folded comfortably across his chest as he leans against the frame. He's been watching.

"Good night, Kat," he says, and he steps into the room to turn off the fireplace. I follow Martin to the door and he pulls it shut behind us.

"Should we not leave the door cracked a little?" I ask. "Might she be afraid of the dark in a new place?"

"No," he says simply.

We head back downstairs. The foyer is now empty of travel bags and trunks. In the sitting room we retake our places, my new husband and I—Martin in an armchair and me across from him on the sofa closest to the fireplace.

"Watching you with Kat I would've guessed you've been a mother before," he says, in an almost complimentary tone. It pierces me nonetheless.

"I helped my mam mind neighborhood children, like I said earlier."

We are quiet for a moment.

"Kat has outgrown her clothes," I tell him.

"We'll buy her some new things tomorrow." He glances at the worn shirtwaist and skirt I'm wearing. "I take it you need new clothes, too."

"I don't need much. Just a dress or two."

A few more seconds of silence.

"We've a lot to take care of tomorrow. We should turn in." He reaches for the gas key at the side of the fireplace and turns off the flame. The coziness of the room fades a bit.

We ascend the stairs. On the second floor, the door is open to the bedroom where my bags are; I can see them by the bedstead. Everything in the room that is visible from where I stand on the landing is cast in a peach radiance from the gas fire that has been turned on to chase away the chill.

I turn to Martin.

"Good night," he says, without any hint at all in his voice that he is displeased with my one condition to marrying him. He'd wanted a façade of a marriage, and that was fine with me. I know what that word means: *façade*. It's in my da's word book. It's how you describe something that appears to be one thing from a distance but is something else when you look closely. An illusion is what Martin said he wanted and I'd replied I would see to it that he had it, which is why I asked if we might keep separate beds until we developed at least a small degree of affection one for the other. He had—surprisingly—agreed.

I wish Martin a good night, too. And then I walk to the bedroom next to Kat's, and he to the one across from it.

He doesn't look back at me, not once.

5

Sleep comes to me in fits and starts my first night as Mrs. Hocking. I awaken every five minutes, it seems. At some point during the night I think I hear Martin moving about and perhaps even the click of the front door latch, but I don't rise to investigate. I don't want him thinking I've already changed my mind regarding which room I want to sleep in. I haven't. Martin is stunning and the thought of him taking me to his bed makes my insides ache, but I won't be giving myself over to a man—body and soul—until I truly know him. I won't be making the same mistake twice.

Dawn's light is spilling onto the floor through a thin opening between window blind and glass when my eyes flutter open at daybreak. San Francisco is not as cold in March as other places I have lived, but there is a distinct chill in the room that reminds me of Donaghadee, and I half expect to catch a whiff of a peat fire and Mam's hot soda bread wafting up from downstairs.

I fumble for my gram's watch pin, which I'd placed on the

nightstand next to my bed. Twenty minutes past six. I push back the covers and dress in the shirtwaist and skirt I've worn for the past six days, thankful the garment doesn't smell sour. The only other dress I own is a plain wool frock suitable only for house-work. I braid my hair quickly and wind it into a circle at the back of my head. When I open the door, I see that Martin is also up; his bedroom door is open and there is a peep of light downstairs spilling from the sitting room. Kat's door is still closed.

I use the water closet and then venture down the staircase. Martin, bent over a writing tablet, sits on a sofa edge. Newspaper pages are strewn over the top of a little table between the sofa and armchair. The nib on the writing pen is making delicate scratch-ing sounds as he works. He is wearing a dark blue suit this morn-ing and his hair is neatly coiffed and his face shaven.

He looks up when I enter the room.

"Hello," he says, in a quiet but congenial tone.

"Good morning. You are up early."

"I've never been one to sleep past sunrise."

I notice he already has a cup of coffee. "I'll have to rise a little earlier, then, so I'll have a kettle on for you." I had seen the drip pot on the back burner of the range the evening before. My land-lady at the tenement had a drip pot like that. I've only ever made coffee once, when she was ill and she asked if I would make a pot for her. She'd told me how to pour the hot water from her kettle onto the ground coffee beans in the top of the pot, and I watched as the filtered beverage dripped down through fine mesh into the pot below. She said I could have a sip for my trouble. I didn't hate it, but I wondered why anyone would prefer it over tea.

I sit down in the armchair by the fireplace that Martin sat in the night before. He doesn't ask if I slept well.

I glance down at the tablet and newspaper but can't read either one upside down. "Are those working papers? For your job?"

"Yes. I'm heading out tomorrow."

"And how long are you usually gone when you go, if I might ask?"

"It depends," he says, casually, easily. "Sometimes two days, sometimes three or four. Occasionally a week."

"I see."

Several seconds of silence pass between us.

"You take the train when you travel?" I ask.

"I've purchased an automobile. I keep it garaged south of the pier when I'm not out on the road. I don't bring it into the city."

"An automobile?" I make no effort to cloak my surprise. I know no one who owns an automobile. Not a soul. Will he take me on a ride sometime if I ask him? Isn't that what people with autos do on lovely Sunday afternoons? I wait for Martin to notice my amazement, but he says nothing.

A few minutes slide by with the only sounds in the room being those of the ticking of a wall clock and the faint scraping of the nib of his pen.

"May I ask you a question about Kat?" I say.

"What about her?"

"Did she stop speaking straightaway after her mother died? I'm only asking because you are leaving tomorrow and she'll be alone with me and I want to understand better how to care for her. I don't want to do the wrong thing while you're away."

Martin caps the pen and sets it down on the table. I fear I've said too much, and all while he'd been trying to work. But when he opens his mouth to answer, his tone is calm.

"Candace was quite ill before she died," he says. "The more her condition declined, the quieter Kat became, and she'd been a quiet child to begin with."

"She must have loved her mother very much." I watch Martin carefully to see if he will react in a way that will clue me in to his own level of grief. His beautiful face is unreadable.

"Yes."

"And Candace's parents? Were they of help to you with Kat during this terrible time?"

"No."

He says the word effortlessly, as though it doesn't pain him to say it. As though he'd not been surprised his in-laws hadn't helped him and Kat walk that hard road since surely they were traveling it as well. "Whyever not?"

"We were not on friendly terms."

"Why is that?"

He studies me for a moment, as though he is now watching *me* carefully, gauging how much he will tell me about the intricacies of his first marriage. "They'd planned for Candace to marry someone of substantial means—someone like them—and instead she married me. That was a disappointment to them."

"But . . . but even so, surely they cared about their grand-daughter?"

"Kat has never been an exceptionally sociable creature. Even before she stopped talking, she was a sober child who kept to herself. Her grandparents, the few times they saw her, found that behavior bizarre."

"Are you saying they don't have affection for their own grand-child?"

"Didn't."

"Didn't?"

"Candace's mother died of pneumonia last year. And I hear her father is not well."

Poor Kat. Poor Martin. Poor dead Candace. My heart strangely aches for all three of them. How wounded Martin must be inside, and how hard it must be for him to pretend he isn't.

As if he can read my thoughts, Martin gathers up the papers and the tablet and places them in a leather satchel resting at his feet. He closes it in a gesture that seems to bring the gavel down on the conversation. "Why don't you rouse Kat and we'll have breakfast?" He rises from the sofa with his satchel in hand and I follow him out of the room. He heads for the library next to the room we have just left. As I pass by the open door, I see him open a drawer in the doctor's old desk and flip through some papers. He glances up, sees me, and waits for me to continue on up the stairs.

When I open Kat's door, she is sitting on her bed, already dressed in a too-tight, too-short dress of pale pink and holding the broken doll against her chest. Her cinnamon-brown hair is a tangled mess from sleep, but her eyes—so very like Martin's—are bright pools of topaz with not a hint of slumber clinging to them. Has she been awake for a while? Was she able to hear the conversation taking place directly below her on the first floor? It is impossible to tell from the blank expression on the child's face.

I reach for the hairbrush that I placed atop the bureau last night, and then I sit down beside Kat on her bed. "Did you sleep all right in your new room, love?"

She looks at me, her eyes communicating an answer that I can't decipher.

"I think today we should buy some new bedcovers for you in a color that you like. Do you have a favorite color?"

The girl looks down at her lap. I wonder if her gaze is drawn to the hazy pink hue of her dress.

"Pink, maybe?" I say.

She nods, and it is almost like hearing her voice.

"I love that color, too. Would you like one braid or two?"

Kat slowly holds up two fingers.

"Two it is, then. Can you turn a bit toward your pillow, love?" She obeys and I put the brush to her head and begin to gently loosen the tangles. "My best friend growing up had hair this color. So very pretty."

To fill the silence as I attend to Kat, I ramble on about how my mother used to braid my own hair too tightly and how my midnight blue hair ribbons had been my favorite.

"There," I say when the plaits are done. "You look very pretty. And we're getting some new clothes for you today. Won't that be a treat? You're getting so tall. You've outgrown all your dresses."

Kat looks down at her too-small dress and then raises her head to look at me again. The child looks troubled, as if the thought of parting with the constricting dress she's wearing is too painful a notion to consider. Perhaps Candace bought the dress for Kat before her illness sent her to her bed for good. Surely she had. Of course she had.

"You like this dress, don't you?" I say in a more empathetic tone. Kat says nothing. "It's very pretty. I can make some clothes for your dolly with the material from this dress if you like." I point to the doll Kat clutches. "I can make a frock for her just like this one. My gram taught me how to sew. I can make her some pantalets to go with it. Would you like that?"

Kat gives her assent in one slight nod. I want to pull her into my arms.

Instead I tell her she can help me make breakfast. We make her bed quickly and then head downstairs.

It takes me a bit of time to familiarize myself with such a well-equipped kitchen. The meal last night I did nothing to prepare, and Martin wanted to leave the plates to soak overnight, so everything about its appointments is foreign to me. It takes me several tries to light the stove, and then I'm opening cabinets right and left to find a skillet. Martin had boxes of staples delivered, so there are eggs and sausage, but there is no bread to make toast. And no yeast or lard or vinegar. I shall have to make a list. As I find my way around, I decide we will eat at the butler's table in the kitchen rather than in the formal dining room, and I give Kat the table settings to place at our seats. I am nearly pinching myself again at my fortune, strange as it is, as the room begins to take on the scents of cured meat and fried eggs. It's been such a long time since I've been in a warm, happy kitchen making a meal that is setting my mouth to water. At the tenement there was only the hunk of bread in the morning, the watery soup at the factory cafeteria at noon, and at night, the cold sausages shared among the other young immigrant women I roomed with. There was no table and no conversations around the meal, except for when there was an occasional pilfered bottle of whisky to pass from one to another to another.

After breakfast, we take Kat to a children's clothing store in the heart of Union Square, where Kat submits to trying on several ready-to-wear dresses in different colors and styles, some for every day and a few for special occasions, the clerk says, like a party or for churchgoing. I ask Martin if he and Kat attend church.

"No. But if you wish to go and take Kat with you, I've no objections. There are plenty of Catholic churches here."

"I'm from the North, remember? I'm . . . Protestant." I say this with a light laugh, a bit surprised he's forgotten that. I mentioned it in my letter to him.

Martins shrugs. "There are plenty of the other kind, too." He turns to the salesclerk and points to the Sunday-best dress Kat has on. "We'll take this one as well."

It's odd to me that he doesn't care if I decide to take Kat to an Anglican service, if I can find one, but empowering, too. He trusts me with her.

Next we step inside a dressmaker's, where I am measured and fitted for three new shirtwaists and undergarments.

We take a streetcar to the Palace Hotel on the corner of Market and Montgomery to have lunch in one of its lovely dining rooms. The multistoried palatial building has an open center entrance that until recently buggies could drive into to unload their passengers. The open court is overlooked by all seven stories and framed with white-columned balconies and decorated with exotic plants, statuary, and fountains. The American Dining Room, with its linen-topped tables and golden high ceilings, has just begun to serve the midday meal when we arrive. We lunch on consommé, duckling croquettes, and endive salad, with glazed peach tarts for dessert. It is the finest meal I've ever eaten and it's a challenge to pretend it is merely an ordinary lunch on a busy day.

After our meal we make our way to the Emporium to outfit Kat's new room with proper toys and décor for a little girl.

On the ten-minute walk to the Emporium—a multilevel department store that carries everything—I see more of the city's bustling retail area. I take note of a shoe repair shop, a milliner, a stationer's, a grocer, a bakery, and a hair salon.

The outside of the immense Emporium is as large as many of the buildings I'd grown used to seeing in New York, taking up nearly a whole city block on Market Street. We take an elevator to the fourth level and walk past displays of sporting goods and bicycles to the children's toy section. The display cases are laden with dolls and doll carriages, miniature tea sets, train sets, boxes of colored wax crayons, and paints. There are dollhouses and little wooden barns with carved farm animals and books and puzzles and looms and jointed stuffed bears and armies of toy soldiers.

Kat is drinking in the sight of all those shelves, I can see that, but she makes no move to walk toward any of them. Martin just waits for her to do so. I reach for her hand and lead her to a doll carriage upholstered in robin's-egg blue fabric, with chrome and rubber wheels and a collapsible hood trimmed in wide white lace.

"How about if we try out this carriage with your own dolly," I say, convincing Kat to lay down the doll with the cracked cheek inside the satin-lined bed of the miniature buggy. A glimmer of a smile tugs at Kat's lips.

"I'll find a clerk to help us," Martin says, and off he goes to find an employee to tally Kat's choices.

I help Kat select a second doll so that her first one can have a friend, and some dresses for them and one of the doll-sized tea sets. We choose wooden beads with string and the wax crayons and a tablet of paper, and sets of children's picture books and three jigsaw puzzles meant for older children, but which Kat is clearly interested in.

"She likes figuring them out," Martin says of these, after he returns to us. "She's good at those. You'll see."

Our last stop is a grocer's, where I am able to get the things for the kitchen that Martin did not think to buy. Martin arranges for all our purchases to be delivered to the house. The day has been a stretch of satisfying hours so foreign it is almost as if I am watching another person's day unfold. We leave the grocer's and walk to the cable-car stop.

"Kat is tired," Martin says, as the cable car clacks to a stop and people start getting off and on. "And all those deliveries are coming. You need to be there to receive them. Here you go." He lifts Kat onto the open car and then holds out his arm so that I can board. I turn to face him once I'm standing on the car's polished floorboards. Martin's arm is outstretched; he is handing me the key to the house. Our house. I encircle my gloved hand around it.

"I've got details to see to before I leave tomorrow. I'll be home later," he says.

I nod, draw Kat toward me, and take a seat on one of the benches. The car clangs as it grasps the cable deep in the slot, and we begin to move forward and up. Martin turns from us and walks away. I watch him until he is gone from view.

Back at the house, Kat and I explore all the cupboards and closets, discovering a great many things the doctor and his family decided to leave behind. The china cabinet still holds a good supply of dishes and glassware, and the linens closet is half-full. I imagine the doctor's wife had to choose just her most favorite items to take, perhaps only those things that had been given to them as wedding gifts. I wonder if Candace was given beautiful linens and dishes when she married Martin, and if she was, where are they? Did Martin abandon everything that was theirs when she died? Did he sell them to pay for the move from Los Angeles to San Francisco? I wonder how long it will be before I can ask him a personal question like that.

In the boys' room I take off the toy soldier bed linens as we await the delivery of the new pink bedcover and linens we purchased at the Emporium.

"Do you want that extra bed in here?" I ask Kat, who is silently watching me. Kat looks at the second bed and then back at me. She slowly shakes her head.

"That's what I would do, too. You'll have more room for your new doll carriage in here if we dismantle it and take it upstairs. Shall we?"

With minimal help from Kat, I drag the frame, the posts, and finally the mattress upstairs to the empty maid's room and lean them up against one of walls. We head back downstairs, and I make tea for us—sugar tea for Kat like my gram used to make—and we sip our drinks as we await the first of the deliveries and also Martin's return.

The groceries arrive first, then the Emporium goods, and then the undergarments and corsets and hosiery from the ladies' clothing store. The new clothes for Kat arrive last.

Dusk begins to fall and I am anxious for Martin's return. I set about turning on the electric lights in the house, and then the gas fireplace in the sitting room, as the day's warmth is leaving the house. As we wait, Kat and I sit by the fire and work on one of the puzzles she chose—a tableau of sketched butterflies of every shape and color. When darkness falls completely and Martin is still not home, I light the stove and place pork cutlets that I rubbed with butter and dried sage into a roasting pan alongside potatoes and carrots so that supper will be ready when he finally returns.

But he is still gone when the food is ready, and Kat is yawning. I fix her a plate, which she eats, and then I take her upstairs and draw her a warm bath, all the while expecting to hear Martin's footfalls on the stairs. But I don't. After her bath, I tuck Kat into bed.

I kiss her good night and close her door nearly all the way, but not quite, despite what Martin said the previous night.

Back downstairs I don't know what else to do but sit in the dining room with our now-cold meal and wait.

When Martin finally arrives home, it is after nine o'clock and I have fallen asleep at the dining room table, slouched in my chair with my chin at my chest. I awaken to his touch on my arm as he says my name. I startle, nearly knocking over a goblet of water. Martin catches it. Relief mixed with anger races about inside me as Martin sits down in front of his cold supper.

"Where were you?" I say. "I was worried."

"I told you," he answers calmly. "I had details to take care of."

"But . . . you were gone so long."

"There were a lot of details."

He doesn't sound angry or defensive or even conciliatory. I can't name the tone with which Martin is answering me.

"I was concerned. I didn't know . . . I didn't . . ." My voice drops away as the right words don't come.

"Did you need something while I was out? Did all the deliveries arrive? Was anything amiss?"

"No. Everything is fine. Everything arrived. I put it all away.

I made supper. I fed Kat and I put her to bed. And I waited for you."

"Then what is wrong?"

He is looking at me with those eyes that still nearly take my breath away.

"Your supper is cold."

"It's easy enough to warm up, isn't it?"

I stand to take our plates. Martin bends down to retrieve a newspaper from the satchel he placed by his chair leg.

Martin works as he eats, and I wonder if this is how he was with Candace the night before he left for a spell on the road, absorbed in his preparations. How did Candace sit through a meal like this one with their daughter already in bed and the scraping of tines on plates, the scratching of Martin's pencil, and the rustling of a newspaper being the only sounds at the dinner table?

After five minutes of watching him work and eat, I break the silence.

"The pork tastes good, I trust?"

He looks up briefly, chewing a bite. "It does."

His tone is sincere, but the next second he is back to his work.

I hesitate only a moment. "May I ask you a question?"

"What is it?"

"It's about Candace. If you don't mind."

I thought he might glance up at the mention of his first wife's name, but he does not. "Yes?"

"Was it . . . was it hard for her when you were out on the road so much? Was this kind of life one that she got used to rather quickly?"

He looks up. "This wasn't the kind of life we had."

"No?"

"I didn't work for an insurance company in Los Angeles. I worked at a riding club."

"A riding club? Do you mean . . . with horses?"

His gaze is back on his work. "Yes."

He doesn't seem the barnyard type. Not at all. "Were you raised around horses?"

Martin answers without looking at me. "No. I worked as a ranch hand in Colorado when I was younger. I met a man while I was traveling west who saw I needed someone to teach me a skill. I stayed at his ranch for a few years, learning to ride and care for horses, break them, and herd cattle with them."

"Oh. And then . . . then how did you come to California?"

"When that man died, he left me a little money in his will, and I decided to come out to the West Coast. I got a job at a riding club in Los Angeles where highbrow families send their daughters to learn to ride."

"And that's where you met Candace."

"Yes."

"But then how did you switch to working for a life insurance company?"

He pauses and I wonder if he is annoyed I am asking so many questions. But then he answers me. "One of the men who brought his children to the club for lessons sold insurance. He liked to talk, especially when he was doing well at his job. I knew I didn't want to work in a stable the rest of my life, so I listened."

"And now you sell insurance, too?"

"I assess risk for potential clients."

"Oh."

"I must get back to work here."

49

We eat the rest of our supper in silence.

When Martin is finished, he stands and thanks me for the meal. "Good night." He gathers his papers and leaves the room.

I watch him cross the foyer, enter the library, and close the door. I catch the merest whiff of women's cologne on him as he walks past me. It is so faint I question whether I detected it at all after he is gone.

I awaken the next day before daybreak. While the house is still quiet, I dress and make my way downstairs. I find it easier to strike the match and put my hand inside the stove to light it. I prepare the coffee and set about making cinnamon scones. As I'm rolling out the dough, I'm joined by Kat, inexplicably dressed in her old, too-tight pink dress. She quietly helps me cut the dough into triangles and then place them onto a baking sheet. I soft-boil some eggs and fry a rasher of bacon. I ask Kat if she'd like to set the small table there in the kitchen by the back garden window, and she does so without a word.

I am just pulling the baking tray out of the oven a few minutes before seven when Martin appears in the kitchen, shaved, dressed, and clearly ready to be off. He is wearing a heather gray suit that he looks particularly striking in.

Martin sets down his satchel, grabs a coffee cup, and reaches for the drip pot.

"You have time to eat something before you go, don't you?" I ask.

"You can wrap up one of your biscuits for me." He takes a gulp of coffee.

"They are scones, and if that's all you want, I can do that."

"I need to be on my way." He sets his cup down and reaches into his suit pocket, pulling out a few dollar bills. He places them on the countertop. "Here's some money if you need anything while I am gone."

Martin takes another swallow of coffee.

"I'm off," he says. "It will take a little while to get to the automobile and then out of the city. Even on a Sunday."

I follow him into the foyer and Kat trails behind me. "And if I should need to reach you, is there an office or person I should ring up who will know where you are?"

He is shrugging on his coat. "We don't check in with the office when we're out."

"But what if something should happen?"

"Like what?"

I blink back my surprise. "What if . . . what if Kat should get sick or the house catches fire or I fall and break my leg?"

Martin smiles easily. "I am confident in your abilities to see to any circumstance, Sophie. And what could I do from miles away if any of those events should occur?" He turns to get his hat off its hook on the hall tree, setting it on his head as he reaches for a packed valise on the floor. "I should be home in four days, maybe five. Be a good girl, Kat."

He doesn't seem to notice Kat is wearing one of her old dresses, or he doesn't care. Or maybe he believes I am better suited to getting Kat to relinquish the dress and therefore it is better if he says nothing.

Martin turns to me. If we were a normal husband and wife, he'd lean in at this moment to kiss me good-bye. But we are not a normal husband and wife.

He looks eager to go, as though he is about to embark on an

adventure that he is keen to begin. Perhaps this is another way he deals with his losses: by looking to the open road and the beckoning horizon as an escape from the reminders of all that has been taken from him.

"Have a good trip," I tell him.

Martin opens the front door and steps out into the cool mist of a quiet Sunday morning.

6

March 30, 1905

Dearest Mam,

You're surely wondering about the return address on the
envelope that brought this letter to you. I have married a
man who lives in San Francisco. His name is Martin
Hocking and he's the one pictured with me in the enclosed
photograph. Martin is a widower with a little girl named
Katharine. She's five years old and we call her Kat. I hope
to send a photograph of her to you sometime soon.

It truly doesn't matter how I met Martin; I will just
say that our paths crossed at the right time for both of us. I
know you thought I could begin a new life for myself in
New York, and I appreciate so very much everything you
did to get me to America, but I couldn't stay in Manhattan

any longer, for many reasons. It was no place where you'd want me to be, Mam, and all that you truly wanted for me, I now have. Martin makes a good living, he has a beautiful house here in the city, and I lack nothing. I even have my own bedroom, which is what I wanted, and he did not object. I think he still grieves his first wife's passing. He doesn't talk much about her, and I'm glad he doesn't. He travels most days for his job; he works for an insurance company.

I wouldn't say that Martin and I are good friends yet, but I think we could be someday. What Martin and I do have in common, aside from old wounds, is our wanting to provide a good home for sweet Kat. She has taken the death of her mother so very hard. The wee thing doesn't speak more than a word or two. I can see the pain of her loss in the way she looks at me, at everything. It is my hope that in time, the ache of her grief will lessen and she will want to again hear her own voice.

Kat and I find things to do while Martin's away and when it's not cold and rainy. There are many parks here, and a library and shops. The ocean is nearby and I can always get fresh fish. Occasionally the earth trembles here in San Francisco. There was a shuddering just a few days ago that lasted only seconds, and yet alarmed me greatly. But Martin assured me it is the nature of the earth to correct itself from time to time. This is how it does it. I will get used to the quaking, he said. Everyone who lives in San Francisco does. I'm sure he is right.

There is a lady who lives across the street with a baby. I have seen her coming in and out of her house and I hope to meet her soon. The other people who live on our street are older and are cordial enough when we pass one another on walks. They seem a bit wary of me and I mentioned this to Martin. He said people here are wary of all immigrants. We live not too far from Chinatown, which I don't visit, but when we are downtown I see the way some people glower at the Chinese men with their long braids trailing down their backs.

I think I can be happy here in San Francisco and I don't want you to worry. Martin is a rather private person but it's possible that in time affection may grow between us, and as you know, I am in no hurry. If you hear from Mason, please tell him I do not hold it against him that he left me in New York like he did. It was hard after he left, but I'm happy now being Kat's mother, especially since she will likely be the only child I will ever be a mother to.

Give my love to the brothers and their wives and all the wee ones. I miss you and think of you often and I'm so very glad you let me take Da's old word book with me. I know how much you loved it. Every morning I peek inside and choose a word for the day. Today I chose the word renaissance. *It means to be reborn. That's how I feel, Mam. I finally feel like I've been given a chance to start over.*

I've often wished I could turn back time and do things differently, but maybe it's better to start anew than to go back in time and hope you have the courage and wisdom to make different choices.

Please be happy for me, Mam . . .

Kat and I return from posting my overdue letter to my mother—one that I'd rewritten half a dozen times—just as a steady rain begins to fall. That we had to venture out under threat of showers was because I had no postage stamps and Martin keeps the desk in the library locked. I know this because I have tried its drawer pulls before—not to pry but because the days are long when Martin is away and there was a day when I thought Kat and I might pay a visit to Mrs. Lewis, since she made it clear to me she wants us to, but I didn't know how to find her place again. I had hoped to come across her address in Martin's papers, but the desk was locked. On another day I'd wanted to use one of Martin's fountain pens, as mine had run out of ink, and the desk was locked. At the time, I'd sat back in the chair wondering why Martin felt the need to lock every drawer in the desk when he was away. If he keeps money inside I could see where he might secure that one drawer, but all of them? It seems he doesn't want the contents of the desk safe as much as he wants them secret. What could he have in the drawers besides files for his job, ledgers maybe, a bank book or two?

I had asked him about the desk when he was home again, told him I'd needed to use a fountain pen while he was gone because I had no ink for mine, but instead of seeing it as a problem of access he told me I didn't need approval from him for every little purchase. If I needed ink, he trusted me to use the money he gave me to go to the stationer's to buy whatever kind of ink I wanted.

Today when I realized I needed a stamp to at last post the letter to Mam, I again tried the desk, on the off chance there were stamps inside and he had left it unlocked. He hadn't, and Kat and I ambled down to the post office under the grayest of gray skies.

I suppose Martin's wanting to have his desk all to himself is just how some men are with their desks. I wouldn't know. Da didn't have one.

In any case, we are back from our postal mission and are taking off our wraps when I notice a small envelope that was dropped through our mail slot and is now resting on the entry rug. Kat actually sees it first. She is at last wearing her new clothes after my telling her I would make dresses for her dolls from her old, too-small frocks. She bends to pick up the envelope and the crinolines under her skirt sound like they're whispering, *What's this?*

"Why don't you open it up, love, and we'll see who it's from." I hang up our capes and watch as Kat carefully opens the letter, sealed with just a bit of wax and a monogrammed letter *E*. She unfolds the single sheet of paper inside and hands it to me. At the top of the paper is the name *Elizabeth Reynolds* in embossed ink that shimmers like bronze. I read the note aloud.

"My dear Mrs. Hocking, If you are receiving guests, Timmy and I would very much like to stop by this afternoon at half past two to welcome you to the neighborhood. We shan't stay long! If it's an inopportune time, just send a note over to the house directly across the street from you and we will look to schedule another day. Cordially yours, Libby Reynolds."

I look down at Kat. "Are we receiving guests?" I ask her, unable to rein in the smile breaking across my face. Finally meeting the woman across the street after living in this house for nearly a month is too delightful a thought.

Kat just blinks up at me.

"We're going to have company, love!"

For the next hour I go from room to room making sure there are no cobwebs, no dull tabletops, no dusty surfaces. I have little to do all day but keep house and entertain Kat, so the house is clean, but I scurry about the rooms with a feather duster anyway. A few minutes before half past, I put a kettle on low, hoping Mrs. Libby Reynolds can be persuaded to stay for tea, and then I straighten Kat's hair ribbons and smooth back the hair from my face.

I am thinking we probably shouldn't hover at the door. I turn to Kat. "How about we look at some books while we wait for the lady across the street, hmm?"

We settle in the sitting room with our books and wait. Kat, like me, keeps an alert ear for steps on the stoop. The bell rings and I force myself to rise slowly like a lady who is *receiving guests*. Kat gets to her feet, too.

"Ready?" I ask her, and she nods.

We head to the door and I open it wide. The skies have cleared a bit and the street and every leaf on every tree are glistening.

The woman from across the street is standing there in a beautiful pea green shirtwaist with cream trim, with her little boy resting on one hip. In her other hand she holds a plate with a linen napkin over the top. Her eyes widen slightly, as if she's surprised Kat and I are at home.

"Hello," I say in the most cultured way I can muster, but I sound just like I always do.

She seems to recover from whatever it is that surprised her.

"Hello, I'm Libby Reynolds," she says cheerfully. "And this is Timmy. We've been wanting to welcome you and your husband to the neighborhood, and here I finally send a note to you and the weather nearly kept us from meeting. I'm so glad the rain stopped."

She's a bit shorter than me, rounder, with honey blond hair, full lips, and wide straight teeth. Her little boy looks to be a year or so.

"And I'm Sophie Hocking. Please, won't you come in?"

"If it's not an inconvenience?" she says politely.

"Not at all."

She steps inside and I close the door.

"How strange and wonderful it is to still see Mrs. Kincheloe's furnishings!" Libby says, looking all around the foyer at the hall tree, the chandelier, the Oriental rug at our feet, the little table by the stairs where I put the day's mail.

"Mrs. Kincheloe?" I say.

"The doctor's wife. This was her house."

"Yes. Yes, of course." I lead us into the sitting room. "Won't you have a seat?" I gesture to one of the sofas. Libby sits down and positions her son on her lap. I sit across from them in an armchair and Kat retreats to her book on the floor by the hearth.

"From your accent I would guess you're not from around here," Libby says congenially.

"No. I'm from Ireland originally. The North."

"And this is your little girl?" She nods to Kat, seated on the rug near my feet.

"Um. Yes. This is Kat."

"Kat?" Libby grins.

"It's short for Katharine."

Libby looks down at Kat. "What a pretty thing you are. And how old are you, Kat?"

Kat stares at the woman for a moment and gazes up at me.

"She'll be six in June," I say quickly.

Libby raises her head slowly, understanding, it seems, that something is a bit amiss with Kat. "Well," she continues. "It's a pleasure to welcome you. You and I are the only young mothers on the block! I was sad to hear Dr. Kincheloe had taken that fancy job in Argentina. His wife, Margaret, was a dear, always willing to take in Timmy if Chester had a nighttime function that I was suddenly expected to attend. My husband's the assistant headmaster of a private academy and they're always putting on plays and concerts. And I'll miss those two little Kincheloe boys, too. Timmy loved watching them run and play. It was quite a nice surprise to see you and your husband moving in and that you have a little girl. Is she your only one?"

"Y-yes," I answer clumsily.

"And where did you move from? Somewhere else here in the city?"

Again, I stumble over my answer. "Ah, well . . . My . . . my husband had been working in Los Angeles and then . . . ah, he came up here to begin a new job."

Libby stares at me with curious eyes. Answers to easy questions like these should fly off my tongue.

"How nice," Libby says. "And what is your husband's job?"

Finally, an uncomplicated question. "He does work for an insurance company. On the road, though. Assessing risk."

"I have a cousin who sells life insurance. In Portland," Libby says. "Which insurance company does your husband work for?"

My face warms with embarrassment. I haven't asked Martin the name of the company he works for. I haven't cared. And until Libby asked this question I hadn't considered that maybe I should care. Martin had said it is important for prospective clients to see him as a fortunate family man—because no wealthy man wants to be confronted with the actual proof that tragedy could befall him, not even when buying insurance, which is why he sent for me. But in the month I've been married to Martin, I've not met one client, not answered one work-related telephone call—the thing never rings—nor have I taken in any mail related to Martin's employer. I can't even look for an envelope and guess who my husband works for.

Libby is waiting for my answer. "He . . . that is, it's a new job and I'm not . . . I don't . . ." My voice falls away.

Libby cocks her head in a gesture of concern. "Is everything quite all right, Mrs. Hocking?"

Here is a question with such a bizarre answer, I can't help myself. "That might depend on how you look at it," I say with a laugh, and then immediately wish I could snatch the words back.

My neighbor's eyes widen in alarm. "Is your husband involved in some kind of illegal activity?" she whispers.

"No!" I gasp. "No. It's not that. It's . . ." Again, I let the words die on my tongue.

Libby regards me for a moment, and then she leans forward and lifts the cloth off the plate resting on the table between us. Lovely petits fours are arranged like little bud-topped houses. "I say we have something sweet and a cup of tea and a long chat. Shall we ring for it?"

Ring for it?

Libby looks behind her, as if expecting someone to enter the room. She swings back around to face me. "Does your maid have the day off today?"

My maid. This is why Libby looked so surprised when I answered the door. She expected my maid to do it. Never did I think I'd be getting a maid when I married Martin Hocking, and apparently he didn't think so, either. He's never spoken of it.

"We haven't hired one," I say, as delicately as I can.

Libby stands, hoists her son to one side, and grabs the plate. "It's hard coming to a new place and not knowing anyone. I know people who know where to find a good maid. I can ask for you. Here. You and I can make the tea, can't we?"

I want to tell her I make it all the time. I want to tell her I don't think I want someone else keeping this house. Besides Kat, it's the only thing I have that feels like it belongs to me.

"Of . . . of course. Right this way." I lead her to the kitchen, where the kettle is already simmering. She smiles at me.

"Well, look there, thinking ahead like that. You've already got the water going!" Then Libby asks if Timmy can play with some pots, pans, and wooden spoons so that he won't grow fussy. I ask Kat to find the makeshift playthings and she readily complies, sitting down on the floor with Timmy as he bangs away on a copper pot. Libby leans up against the pie safe and crosses her arms across her chest. I turn up the heat under the kettle.

"Let's start at the beginning. What's your husband's name?" she asks.

"Martin." I pull a tin of tea out of the cupboard.

"And he's from Los Angeles?"

"Not exactly. He's originally from back east but he came to Los Angeles a few years back."

"So you met him in Los Angeles, then?"

I am either going to tell my new friend the truth or I'll have to concoct a mountain of lies that I will forever have to remember. The truth will probably come out eventually, won't it? Maybe it makes sense to watch what it's like for someone to hear what I've done. Then I'll know if mine is a story that other people can listen to and not judge me a fool after hearing it. The only other option is to fib.

I glance down at Kat, who at this same moment looks up at me. Kat is aware enough of the truth. I don't want to lie in front of this little girl who is just beginning to trust me. I want Kat's trust more than I want Libby's friendship, and I know I always will. I turn my attention back to Libby as I set the tin on the countertop.

"I didn't meet Martin in Los Angeles. I met him here in San Francisco a month ago. At the ferry terminal."

"You met him a month ago?" Libby echoes, her eyes wide.

"And then a few minutes after I met him, I went to the court-house and married him."

For a second Libby says nothing.

"Did he make you do this?" she asks a moment later, with obvious alarm.

"No. He didn't make me, he asked me. In a letter, a few weeks before. And I said yes."

"But . . . but you had never met him!"

"No. Not in person."

"Good gracious! Why would you do that?"

The kettle starts to whistle and I turn off the flame. As I make the tea and then carry it to the little table, I tell her the barest minimum about having immigrated to America. I tell her about the horrible job and tenement in New York, and that I had seen Martin's advertisement and had been very keen on having a new life and a child, because doctors in Belfast had told me I'd never have children of my own. As we begin to sip from our cups and share the little cakes with the children, I tell Libby that Martin has his own list of woes, with a tragic upbringing, in-laws who did not approve of him, and a sick wife whose wasting disease had stolen her from him and left him a widower with a five-year-old daughter.

"One of my brothers was already here in America when I

came. Mason had written me that there were jobs in New York. But I had only been in Manhattan for four months when Mason fell in love with a woman from Montreal, and he moved to Canada to marry her. I thought maybe he would ask me to come with him, so that maybe I could rent a little corner of his home with his new wife, but he didn't ask. I had to find my own place. It wasn't the best situation. It was awful. And then one day, I read Martin's advertisement. I answered it."

"I'll be damned," Libby murmurs, and then quickly adds, "Beg your pardon. I just . . . I've never heard such a story."

I smile lightly. "Nor I."

Libby fingers the delicate handle on her teacup, her brows knitted. Then she looks up. "So. Is Martin . . . kind to you?"

I know what she means. It's the language of women, I suppose.

"He's been a gentleman. In every sense of the word."

Libby can tell my answer means something different than what those simple words suggest.

"Are you saying the two of you haven't . . ." Her voice drops away as her face flushes.

"We both feel strongly now is not the time for that," I say, which is not exactly the truth. I don't know what Martin would have done if I'd said nothing about wanting my own bed in my own room, but I barrel on. "I think he still misses his first wife. She was sick for a long while, but she's only been gone five months."

"Yes, but . . . but then why did he marry again? Why did he not just hire a nanny for the child, if that's all he wants?"

"It's not all he wants. He needs to maintain his image and how potential clients look at him and his employer. He needs to look successful, not tragic. He told me people purchase insurance in case something terrible happens, but they don't want to see the evidence that it can. He needed to look fortunate. Smiled on by Providence. So he needed a wife."

Libby ponders this for a moment. I can tell there is so much more she wants to ask me, but it's highly improper, I'm supposing, to discuss what we're discussing. In front of children, no less. She takes another long and thoughtful sip of her tea and then sets the cup back on its saucer. She glances down at Kat and then back at me. "The child's not said a word the whole time I've been here," she whispers.

I know Kat surely heard the softly spoken remark.

"Kat may be quiet, but she's also smart and strong and brave, and she misses her mother very much. I know she is thinking about what she wants to say, and when she's ready, she'll say it."

Clarity falls across Libby's face as she realizes those words were for Kat's ears. She looks from Kat to me with a mix of chagrin and a bit of admiration.

"She's very lucky to have you," Libby says.

"As I am lucky to have her."

Timmy, tiring of the pots and pans, toddles now toward the pantry.

"Well! We'd best be off. He'll be needing a nap." Libby gets up out of her chair to fetch her little boy, and I can't help but think she is ready to go home for other reasons. I am not like Libby's former neighbor, the doctor's wife. Not by any stretch. Libby and I are not the same kind of wife and mother.

"Must you go?" I ask.

"We've outstayed our welcome, surely." Libby scoops up her son. "And he truly does need his naptime."

We begin to make our way out of the kitchen, Kat following.

"I'm so glad you came," I say, in a bright-toned attempt to recapture the hopes I'd had for our meeting. "And thank you for the sweets."

"My pleasure," Libby says politely. "Just bring me the plate when you're through."

I like the thought of there being a reason to walk across the street and ring the bell at Libby's house on another day. "Certainly."

I swing the front door open and Libby turns around before stepping across the threshold. "If you need anything, anything at all, do come right on over." Her gaze is tight on me.

"I will, thank you," I reply, deflecting the concern. I don't want Libby thinking of me that way, as a troubled woman who's made a bad decision and who might need an escape route someday. "And please do the same if you should need anything. I would be happy to watch little Timmy if you ever need me to."

Libby offers a noncommittal smile, perhaps wondering, what would I know about taking care of babies when I've only been a mother to a five-year-old, and for less than a month? I watch as Libby, with Timmy in her arms, crosses the street and enters her own house—a large brick structure on a sloped, landscaped lot—before closing my front door.

I look down at Kat standing next to me.

"That was nice, wasn't it? Making new friends?"

Kat says nothing, but she is close enough to me to lay her head against my hip for a moment, as if to say the experience had been exhausting.

7

Not long after Libby's visit, Martin arrives home from several days on the road. He looks tired, out of sorts, and I ask him if he is feeling well. What should come across as simple concern from a spouse seems meddling somehow. He tells me in a clipped tone that he is fine.

I don't need to be told twice to mind my own affairs.

I make us a supper of roast beef and roasted turnips and carrots and serve the last of Libby's petits fours for dessert.

"Kat and I had company on Thursday," I say as I place two little cakes on a plate in front of Martin.

I tell him about meeting Libby and Timmy and that she brought the sweets and we had tea together. I wait to see if he will ask what Libby and I talked about. He does not.

Martin either doesn't care that I might've told the neighbor across the street how very strange our marriage is, or perhaps he assumes I would never divulge our personal business to a person I'd only just met. This thought makes me chuckle out loud because, of course, I'd married someone I'd only just met.

He looks up at me when I laugh.

"I just thought of something funny." He doesn't ask what it is. "She's very nice," I continue. "Perhaps we can invite her and her husband over for supper sometime?"

Martin swallows the bit of cake he has in his mouth. "I don't want you making plans for me when I'm not here to discuss them with you." The clipped tone from before is gone. He says this without a hint of anger. But with no kindness, either.

"I didn't suggest that to her. I am suggesting it to you now. I haven't planned anything."

My husband wipes his mouth with his napkin. "No." His voice is calm.

"No, we can't invite them over for dinner sometime?"

"I don't want to entertain guests during the little time I have here at the house."

He rises from his chair and heads to the library to work, as he does every night he is home. When it's time for Kat to go to bed, I bring her into the library so that he can wish her sweet dreams. He does so with his head bent over papers.

As I take Kat upstairs, I tell her that sometimes when fathers are unhappy they keep all their feelings wedged deep inside so that they don't have to talk about why they are sad. I figure she will understand that. When I tuck her under the covers I sing a little Gaelic lullaby my gram used to sing to me. The words mean nothing to Kat, and little to me. After all these years I can't quite remember the English translation. But when I am done, Kat murmurs the first word I have heard from her in several days.

"More?"

So I sing it again.

The next morning Martin packs his valise and is gone.

In the afternoon I decide to return Libby's cake plate. I dress Kat in one of her prettier frocks since this is to be almost like a social call—at least I hope it will feel like one—and together we leave the house.

"Perhaps we can stay for a little bit and you can play with Timmy. Would you like that?" I ask Kat as we walk across the street.

"Yes," Kat says in a quiet voice. The second word in as many days! I want to reach down and hug her for it, but instinct tells me to treat the response as unremarkably normal. Because it is.

Libby's front door opens a few seconds after I ring the bell. A trim older woman in a black-and-white maid's uniform stands on the other side of it.

"Can I help you?" the woman says.

"Is Libby at home?" I ask.

"Mrs. Reynolds is entertaining guests at the moment. Are you expected?"

For a second I simply stare at her. "No, not exactly," I finally say. "That is, I was just returning Lib—Mrs. Reynolds's plate. I live across the street, you see. She welcomed us to the neighborhood with some sweets a few days ago."

The woman looks down at the plate and seems to recognize it as one belonging to the Reynolds household. She looks down at Kat, too, wondering perhaps if she should in fact invite the two of us in. A second later she swings the door wide.

"If you could just wait here in the foyer a moment, I'll see if the missus will see you."

As I step inside the beautifully appointed entry—marble floors, a richly woven rug, and gleaming wood paneling—I hear women's voices, and it occurs to me that I should have sent a note first. That's what Libby would have done. Other people are already here.

Before the maid can leave us to speak to Libby, she appears from what is probably the Reynoldses' parlor, no doubt having heard the doorbell. Her face registers surprise and perhaps a little apprehension and then a sweet veneer of courtesy. She strides forward. Libby is wearing a beautiful dress of royal blue chintz with ivory lace tucked about the yoke and sleeves. It shimmers and swishes as she walks.

"Why, Mrs. Hocking," she says politely. "How good of you to drop by. I'm so sorry I can't visit at the moment."

"It's quite all right." I match the pleasant tone. "Kat and I were just returning the plate. Thank you ever so much for the cakes."

"Of course." Libby smiles graciously.

I extend the plate, but Libby does not reach out to take it. Instead, it is the maid who grasps hold.

Libby leans toward me a few inches. "I've some ladies from the academy over for tea. I'm so sorry."

Her words sound genuine enough, but I can't shake the notion that Libby is only sorry that I've come calling, not that she is unable to visit with me. I believe she has realized how very much I am not like her. I don't have a maid, I don't have women friends over for tea, I don't have a husband who comes home every night, I don't have a courtship to talk about or a wedding dress wrapped in linen in a cedar chest. I have a child but not the memory of bringing that child into the world or the joy of watching her first step or hearing her laugh or cry. I linger on the foyer rug when I know I should turn to leave.

Libby smiles sweetly at me. "Perhaps another time?"

"Yes, that would be . . . lovely." I finally turn to step out. "Thank you again for the sweets and your visit."

Libby smiles wide. "Good-bye!" The door closes.

Kat and I walk back across the street.

"I guess we will have to play with Timmy another day," I say with fake cheer. Kat seems to sense my disappointment. The child looks up at me with eyes that nearly gleam with perception.

"I'll be all right, love," I say. "I was just looking forward to a visit with our neighbors today. How about if we draw some pictures for Timmy instead? Would you like to do that?"

"Yes," Kat whispers.

And I squeeze her hand as tears prick. The morning's failed visit isn't a complete loss. Kat has spoken another word.

When I don't see or hear from Libby over the next few days, I decide to summon a bit of courage and drop a note through the Reynoldses' mail slot inviting Libby and Timmy over for lunch the following day. I am gratified when the maid from across the street comes by a few hours later and hands me Libby's reply that they would be happy to come.

Kat and I spend the better part of the afternoon making the back garden patio as beautiful as we can, pulling weeds, planting new bedding flowers, and polishing the scrolled iron chairs and table so that the garden is as pretty as a peek of paradise. We come into the house for refreshment and to clean up, and while we are having a drink the doorbell rings. Standing on the mat is Mrs. Lewis from the boardinghouse with a package in her hand and a half smile on her lips.

"Oh my! Mrs. Lewis!" I say. "Please, do come in."

She steps inside, warily it seems, as if weighing the decision to come to the house in the first place.

"How good of you to drop by," I continue. "May I take your hat and coat? Can you stay for tea?"

"No, thank you. I can only stay a minute," Mrs. Lewis says. "I've come with some hair ribbons that belong to Katharine. They've been at my place all this time. I've been meaning to return them to you."

She hands the package to me.

I fumble for a response. She came all this way to return a few hair ribbons?

"I'm so sorry for your trouble," I say. "That was so very good of you."

"Yes, well, I suppose I could've sent them by post, but I did want to see how you and the child were getting on."

"I'm so happy you've come," I tell her. And I am. There was a time not so long ago when I wanted her address so that I could see *her*.

Kat now wanders into the foyer to see who is at the door. She regards Mrs. Lewis with what seems half longing and half hesitation, as though she is afraid to let on that she is glad to see her.

Mrs. Lewis smiles at the child. "Hello, Miss Katharine."

Kat leans shyly into my hip.

"Mrs. Lewis has come to say hello to us," I say. "And bring you your hair ribbons that were accidentally left at her house. Isn't that nice, love?"

Kat nods slowly, never taking her eyes off Mrs. Lewis.

"Won't you sit down, Mrs. Lewis?" I ask.

"Only for a moment."

I show her into the sitting room and again I ask if she wants tea or coffee and again Mrs. Lewis declines. A bit of awkward silence follows, and I sense that Mrs. Lewis, who is looking from me to Kat and back again, wishes to speak to me alone.

"Kat, my love," I say brightly. "Would you be a dear and finish up watering the flowers on the patio?"

The little girl leaves the room without a word.

"I see not much has changed for the child," Mrs. Lewis says sadly.

"Actually, I see progress. 'Tis just a little bit at a time, but still progress. I think 'tis only a matter of time before she recovers from all that has befallen her."

"Yes, well. I hope you are right." She glances up at the mantel and sees my wedding photograph with Martin, the one I had to convince Martin to purchase. Then she looks back at me. "And you? Are you faring well with Mr. Hocking?"

"Indeed, I am."

"I'm relieved to hear that."

Another stretch of silence hovers between us. Mrs. Lewis seems unsure how to proceed.

"Is there something you want to ask me, Mrs. Lewis?" I say.

The woman visibly relaxes. Then she leans forward, as though the house has ears and might repeat back to Martin what she is about to say.

"Before you came I was so worried about that child and her father," Mrs. Lewis says softly. "Did you know he would leave her alone all day in their rooms, sometimes overnight?"

I stare back at the woman. Surely Mrs. Lewis is mistaken.

"Did you hear me? He would leave her alone all day and even overnight! I told him that was not safe and that I would look after her if he needed to be away. She's just a little girl!"

"Are you . . . quite sure?" I finally ask. "Are you sure he didn't take her with him?"

"She came downstairs for meals! And then she'd go back up again!"

I have no words in response. Mothers would know not to leave a five-year-old child alone all day long or, God forbid, overnight. Wouldn't a father also know?

When I say nothing, Mrs. Lewis goes on. "He doesn't hug or kiss her. He doesn't worry about her or wonder why she's not talking. It's not right."

I feel my mouth drop open as I realize I have also noticed this about Martin, that he doesn't hug or kiss Kat. He doesn't touch her at all. I'd decided it is because he is a man wrapped up in his grief, and maybe he is, but he is also a father. Even a grieving man remembers his child, doesn't he?

"It makes me wonder if she is his true child," Mrs. Lewis says. "I know I shouldn't wonder such a thing but I do, and you've only been knowing Mr. Hocking for such a short while. I just . . ." Her voice falls away. "The child whispered to me once that it was her fault her mother was dead. She said she made her mother sick. And of course I asked her why she should say such a thing. She wouldn't answer me. She never said another thing to me after that. Not one thing. I told Mr. Hocking she said that to me and he behaved as though he didn't care."

I stare at her, mute.

A second later Mrs. Lewis abruptly stands. "I shouldn't have come. I shouldn't have said anything. I'll leave now."

I rise, too, my mouth still unable to form words as I follow the woman to the front door.

"Thank you for bringing the hair ribbons," I say woodenly as I open the door. I, too, am wishing Mrs. Lewis hadn't come.

We stand in silence for a moment, and then Mrs. Lewis reaches out to touch my arm.

"I'm sorry if I've said too much, but you seem like a good person, and the child . . . It's not right that she's not speaking and that he does nothing about it. It's kept me up at night thinking about it, but I'm truly sorry if I should have said nothing."

I swallow hard against the knot of alarm that's taken hold of me. Mrs. Lewis is mistaken. Martin is just sad and flattened by his grief. He bought this lovely home for Kat and me to live in. He is good to us both in so many other ways. Mrs. Lewis is mistaken.

I clear my throat. "My husband and I believe the best thing to do for Kat is to let her recover from losing her mother without harsh expectations, Mrs. Lewis. She is in fact getting better every day, I assure you. And perhaps Martin did not realize Kat is too young to be left alone like that. But then you helped him see that it wasn't wise, and that is why he sent for me. And I'm sure as Kat matures I will be able to help her understand consumption isn't brought on by having to take care of a child."

Even as I say these things, it all seems to make sense.

"He's a caring father and a good husband," I continue. "He, too, is still recovering from the loss of his first wife. And you don't know all of the other heartaches he has suffered in his life."

Mrs. Lewis regards me for a moment. "Of course," she says, but I can tell she is not convinced. "Might I say good-bye to the child?"

It is on my tongue to tell the woman no, but that will only reinforce her strange notions. For both of us.

"Certainly."

We make our way through the kitchen to the back patio, where Kat is dutifully sprinkling water from a metal can onto the flower beds. She looks up at me.

"Mrs. Lewis is headed home. Come thank her for coming and bringing the ribbons."

The child sets down the can and walks over to Mrs. Lewis and blinks at her with beautiful eyes that are so like Martin's. So very much like Martin's.

Mrs. Lewis bends down to look at her at the level of those eyes. "I'm glad that you have this pretty house to live in and a new dear mama to care for you." She strokes the child's cheek and Kat does not flinch, but nor does she reach out to embrace the woman who had cared for her before I came, when Martin had been on the road. "You be a good girl, now, and mind your new mama, all right?"

Kat nods.

"Can you tell her good-bye, love?" I say, inwardly begging the child to please, please say the word.

"Good-bye," Kat murmurs.

Mrs. Lewis smiles, perhaps a bit reassured by hearing Kat speak. She rises to her full height and then turns to me. "If you ever need anything, come to me."

"Certainly," I say, as politely as I can; then I escort Mrs. Lewis back to the door and open it. "Thank you again for coming, Mrs. Lewis."

Mrs. Lewis says good-bye and I shut the door. Kat has a bevy of new hair ribbons, so it is easy, as I make my way back to the patio and my daughter, to toss Mrs. Lewis's package into the bin.

Libby and Timmy come for lunch the following afternoon. Kat and I made little sandwiches with the crusts removed and a tray of relishes and an aspic and a lemon chiffon cake. The day is sunny and the patio is pleasant and Kat and Timmy draw pictures on the patio stones with chalk after they've eaten.

Everything about the afternoon seems perfect. But I sense that Libby sees me not as her new neighbor but as someone who needs care and attending—a woman of misfortune who was so desperate to escape her lot, she married a man she didn't know. I am someone Libby should look after from time to time as is befitting a woman of Christian character. The lunch invitation was accepted because that was the charitable thing to do.

As they are leaving, I remind Libby that I am happy to mind little Timmy if she has obligations to attend. Libby thanks me sweetly for the offer and for the delicious lunch.

I tell her it has been such a pleasure having her and Timmy over.

"Let's do it again sometime very soon!" Libby says with her son in her arms and a benevolent smile on her face.

"Yes." I plaster the same smile on my own face.

I wait until Libby and her child are halfway across the street before I shut the door. I look down at Kat, standing next to me.

"Did you have fun today?"

Kat nods unconvincingly.

"Right. Me, too, love. Let's clean up."

As we put away the luncheon things, I decide I don't need Libby's friendship if every time we get together she will make me feel as if I am a charity case. I will find a new friend somehow. Maybe at an Anglican church, if I can find one, or maybe one of the other mothers I see in the park. And I won't tell anyone else ever again about how I met Martin. If people assume Kat is my own flesh and blood, I won't set them straight. If people ask why Kat doesn't speak, I'll tell them she's merely a quiet soul.

I am not a charity case.

I am not a woman of misfortune who married a man I didn't know.

I am a wife and mother who lives in a fine house and I wear nice clothes and I sleep in a warm bed.

When the kitchen is clean, Kat and I go into the sitting room to read and I see my wedding portrait in its gilded frame on the mantel. *That's who I am*, I say to myself. *I am Mrs. Martin Hocking.*

April slips into May and with it comes warmer weather. I manage to convince Martin one Sunday afternoon to join Kat and me on an excursion to the ocean side of the peninsula to walk along the beach and then have a picnic lunch in Golden Gate Park. Other families are doing the same thing and I am enamored of how much we look like them.

I am happy that evening, content. As we make our way home after a relaxing day, I look over at my husband. I feel a surge of desire for him and I decide I want him in my bed. He is my husband and I want him in my bed. It's been a long time since I've wanted a man to touch me, and I've even wondered if I would ever want it again. It's a scary, thrilling feeling, but a welcome one.

When I retire to my room after Kat is abed, I take extra care with my nighttime preparations. I brush my hair until it glistens, I apply a bit of rosewater to my neck, and I choose the nicest nightdress that I have. And then, just before I slip under the covers, I open my bedroom door wide.

Then I wait for him to come up the stairs. I listen for his footfalls, my heart pounding a little. It seems like a very long time before I hear him on the landing. I sense him pausing at the top. Looking at my open doorway, perhaps? A second later I hear him enter his own room and close the door.

My expectation flutters away. Perhaps he did not see the open door as an invitation. Perhaps it is too soon for him.

Perhaps he doesn't find me desirable. Perhaps it is a combination of all these things and more.

I roll over onto my side and leave the door open. I am disappointed and hurt. Let him think what he wants about the door being open. I am too tired to get out of bed and close it.

As the weeks roll on after Mrs. Lewis's visit, I watch Martin with Kat, and I conclude that he is no different from many of the fathers I knew back home in Ireland who didn't indulge in affection for their children. Some men just didn't lavish physical attention upon their wee ones. They showed their devotion by how they provided for them.

And while Kat continues to say little when Martin is home, she is saying more and more words when it is just the two of us in the house. With each passing week, everything is settling into its rightful place, except for the fact that I sleep with my door open every night Martin is home and he hasn't seemed to notice. I write my mother to assure her that in most every respect all is well, since her return letter to me expressed concern that I'd made a hasty decision in marrying Martin.

Martin is an excellent provider; I'll give him that much. I don't have friends per se, but I'm finding I don't need them. I like the quiet life that Kat and I enjoy.

In June, Kat turns six. Martin was away on the actual day of her birthday, but two days later he comes home with a dollhouse and a shiny red tricycle—both of which I had told him to get for her at the Emporium. The three of us attend the circus at the Mechanics' Pavilion for her birthday and Kat has her first candy apple. As she watches clowns perform their comic stunts, I see the first true smile on her face.

One night in August after Kat is in bed, I set about making some chamomile tea for myself and Martin. A light rain is falling outside and it taps the windows and gables gently. As I'm pouring the cups, Martin steps into the kitchen.

"I made us some tea," I say.

"Let's have it here in the kitchen," he replies. "There's something I need to discuss with you."

He doesn't sound angry, but I am concerned nonetheless. I can't help but wonder if I've done something he doesn't approve of. I bring our cups to the butler's table and we sit.

"I have a cousin who lives on my route, some miles from here," he says. "Belinda is the daughter of the same aunt and uncle who raised me after my parents died. Like me, my cousin wanted nothing to do with her family after she moved west. For a long time Belinda didn't even want to have contact with me. But I have been slowly rebuilding my relationship with her over the last few months."

"That's wonderful," I say, much relieved. "I would love to meet her."

Martin shakes his head. "It's much too soon to even suggest that to her."

"Oh."

"She's not had it easy in California, either. Her husband left her some years back for another woman. She's had financial difficulties and I've been able to help her out a bit."

"That's so kind of you," I say, and I mean it.

"Belinda's always been very good with plants and herbal concoctions, and she's come up with a tonic that stimulates hair growth for balding men. She's very unsure about how to market her tonic, so I'm going to help her with that."

"Oh. How?"

"I'm going to bring the bottles here to be properly cured. The tonic works best if it's cellared first. She doesn't have any kind of cellar at her place and we have the boiler room. I will take the finished tonic on my route, and when I'm not doing insurance business, I can take it to various stores and encourage the proprietors to carry it. Belinda would never be able to do this. She's a very private person and stays close to home. If her tonic begins to sell, she won't have to worry about her future."

I'm so touched by his care for this cousin that I want to reach across the table to squeeze Martin's hand. But the only time we touch each other is when he's assisting me in and out of a carriage. "I'm so glad you're doing this," I say instead. "I truly am, and I hope she will soon want to come see us, or perhaps someday Kat and I could go with you to see her."

"Perhaps someday," Martin says, and then takes a sip of his tea.

"Does Belinda know about me?"

He places his cup back on its saucer. "She knows I have recently remarried, yes. But the thought of engaging with more family does not suit her right now. It may be a long while before she will agree to that. It might not ever happen. I think we will just have to wait and see."

"All right. Well, is there anything I can do to help with the tonic?"

"No," Martin says quickly. "The tonic is a bit unstable at first, so the bottles mustn't be moved or jostled after I've placed them in the boiler room, or the cure will be ruined. And each batch takes a surprising amount of work to produce. The best thing you and Kat can do is to stay out of that room so that there's no chance of the bottles being knocked over."

"All right." I'm disappointed that I can't have more of a role in helping Martin's cousin, and at the same time so taken by Martin's good heart and generosity. For the first time in a long while, I feel a measure of fondness for him, and I wonder if this is how it will begin between us, a growing affection that is almost like love.

This fondness gives me the courage to come to his bedroom that night. He is sitting up in his bed reading from a slim volume when I knock on his door and then open it. If he is surprised to see me he doesn't show it. His expressionless face makes me stutter as I ask him if I can come in. He nods and watches me as I move across the room to the other side of the bed. I pull back the covers and I will my eyes to stay affixed to his as I slip in beside him. His eyes are still on mine with no hint of what he is thinking behind them.

"I told you the night we married that I wanted to wait to be with you until we had a bit of affection for each other because I didn't want to give my body to a stranger. I don't think of you as a stranger anymore," I say, as confidently as I can. "I would like to be with you tonight, if that's all right with you."

It takes courage to say those words because I'm risking that he might say that it isn't all right. He might say he still mourns his wife even though I'm sure he visits the Barbary Coast brothels. I've smelled the hints of cologne on him. The brothels are a place for mindless relations and nothing else. He surely doesn't think of his wife when he is with a prostitute. But letting me in his bed, his new wife who bears his name? I'm sure it will be different with me.

Or he might say he's not attracted to me.

Martin regards me for a moment, and then says without emotion, "If that is what you want."

"It is."

He nods once, places the book on his bedside table, and extinguishes the light. My heart is aflutter when he pulls me to him and pulls my nightgown up over my head. I chase away all thoughts of the last time this was done to me and focus instead on how it was the first time. I want Martin's kisses. I want them so badly. But he's not kissing me. His hands are moving across my body in every hidden place, and I feel a hundred thousand needles of delight, but he doesn't kiss me. He is on top of me and then inside me and it is wonderful and pleasurable, beyond any pleasures I have ever known. There is none of the violence of the last time I was with a man. But there is no passion, either. When we are finished Martin still does not kiss me. He has enjoyed my body as I have enjoyed his, and that is all. We haven't shared affection for each other; we have only shared our flesh. He doesn't ask me to leave and I don't want to. But I don't curl up into his embrace, either. When I awake in the morning, he is already up. And there is nothing in his morning greeting to indicate that anything has changed between us.

I find him in the boiler room at the far wall laying bricks one atop the other and setting them in place with a trowel. Next to him is an old washbasin in which he has mixed the mortar. The length of bricks is at least seven feet long and extends outward by perhaps five feet.

"The hair tonic needs to cure in a warm, dark place," he says, in answer to my stare, as though that was the only question on my mind. "I'm making a vault for it."

It seems such a drastic measure, disrupting the boiler room with such a permanent structure. And needless.

"Isn't it dark and warm enough down here anyway?" I ask.

"If it was, do you think I'd be going to all this work?" He doesn't say it unkindly, but I sense his displeasure at my question nonetheless.

"No, of course not."

He slaps on a layer of mortar and sets a brick in place. I wonder when Martin had the bricks delivered. While I was sleeping in the wee hours? While Kat and I were at the market yesterday? Some other time entirely?

"Are you wanting some breakfast?" I ask a second later, after deciding it doesn't matter. And I want to recapture a sliver of the intimacy we had last night. Martin is doing a kind thing for his troubled cousin. I am never in the boiler room anyway. So what if there is a brick crypt crowding one length of the room?

"Later. I want to get this finished so the mortar can set," he replies.

I watch him place a few more bricks and then I turn for the stairs and the light of day.

8

As August gives way to September, I continue to leave my door open, and occasionally Martin visits me at night. Sometimes I visit him. He never stays through until morning in my bed. I do in his, but he is always up before me and gone from the room when I awake. We never kiss; we never whisper sweet words to each other. We never give each other knowing looks across the breakfast table the following day.

I want to think Martin is finding comfort with me that is different from what he got at the brothels. I don't think he visits them anymore. At least I no longer smell the cheap perfume on his skin. But he doesn't have affection for me. I would know it if he did. He would kiss me if he did. And what little fondness I was starting to have for him is frozen in place now as I wait to see if he will begin to have any kind of likewise affection for me.

In late September Martin brings in the first bottles of his cousin Belinda's hair tonic. The unlabeled black bottles are the size of syrup containers, with white stoppers sealed with wax. I watch him the first time he sets them onto a little wooden shelf he placed inside the brick vault, which he keeps covered with a thick panel of solid wood. He positions the bottles like toy soldiers, like giant dominoes. By the time October arrives there are twelve bottles, the oldest ones on the far left of the shelf and the newer ones to the right.

I have only disobeyed him once. I reached inside the vault one day when he was home and the cover was off, noting that the temperature of the air seemed no different within the brick structure than outside it. I carefully lifted one bottle an inch or two off its straw bed. The glass was too black and the room too dark; I was only able to sense the heaviness of what was inside it. Whatever mixture was inside seemed dense with weight. I set the bottle back in place and went upstairs.

That same evening after supper I decided to speak to Martin about Kat's schooling. Another six-year-old child who we sometimes see at the park is attending school and learning to read and write. I had asked that child's mother about it and I learned that nearly all six-year-olds living in the state of California are enrolled in some kind of school.

"Do you think we should enroll her?" I asked Martin.

He did not seem to have an opinion. "I'll leave you to do whatever you think is best," he replied, sounding somewhat disinterested.

There is plenty of money, at least from what I can tell, and I asked him if I could check into the girls' school that this other child went to. This he seemed to consider for a moment before deciding that, yes, I could inquire about it.

The interview at that school, two days after Martin left for his route, was not successful. Kat would not engage with the head-mistress, did not answer any of her questions, made no attempt to show the woman what she already knew. The headmistress suggested rather quickly that Kat might be better off with a tutor at home.

"Some children have special requirements, and I think your daughter might be one," the headmistress said. "I've seen children like this before who are withdrawn. She wouldn't do well in a social environment like our academy."

Kat and I returned home. I was angry and hurt and annoyed, but Kat seemed unaffected. Perhaps a tutor was going to be the best thing, but maybe not until she was older. Perhaps for now I could teach Kat her letters and sums, I was thinking.

When Martin returned from his latest stint on the road and bearing three black bottles of hair tonic, I told him about the interview at the girls' school and what the woman had said.

"Do you think it would be all right if I taught her here at home for this first year until we can see better how she prefers to learn?" I asked him.

"Certainly," Martin said with a confidence that surprised me and with no surprise at all at what the headmistress had said about Kat.

So this is how Kat and I spend the autumn mornings. We work on her letters and simple sums. We string colored beads in different patterns and study maps of other countries and look at books with illustrations of animals and gems and plants. Some days I get out Da's book and I read off some of the words until we find one she likes and then she attempts to write it. Her favorite word thus far is *luminescent*. It has always been one of my favorites, too.

Kat, for all her oddities, was born to learn. Everything that I tell her she absorbs like a sponge, though she asks only a few questions now and then.

While I hunger to hear the child's voice more than just once or twice a day—and I do hear it at least once or twice a day—I do believe Kat has grown fond of me, perhaps even loves me. When Martin is home Kat seems no different than when he is away. She has nothing to say to him and he doesn't seem to mind that she doesn't. Mrs. Lewis's words haunt me a little then, but I imagine Martin feels he cannot change the way Kat is, and therefore what good does it do to worry about it?

The year comes to a close after a quiet Christmas. I make the house as festive as I can with my weekly allowance, bringing in armloads of evergreen branches and a little pine tree that Kat and I decorate with homemade ornaments and garlands. But despite the cheerful look of the house, Martin is his usual aloof self when Christmas Day actually arrives. I asked him a few weeks earlier if he wanted to exchange gifts and he simply replied, "No." I also asked him if he had any objections to my picking out our gifts for Kat, and he didn't. His only stipulation was not to give her too many; two or three were plenty. I complied.

Still, as 1905 becomes 1906, it is the first turn of a year since Da died that I am not unhappy with the New Year's prospects. I am grateful to have Kat to raise and love, and this fine house to live in, and I'm even content with my companion of a spouse. Martin has been hard to figure out, but he's a gentleman who provides adequately and who has never laid a hard hand on me. And he lets me mother Kat however I want to. I'm certain now that what I thought from the very beginning is true. Martin has decided he is finished with love. Perhaps even finished with love for his daughter, as Mrs. Lewis first suggested. He is done with loving anyone. This is his one major flaw, that he let what happened crush his willingness to love other people again. I don't know what guides his heart when it comes to his kindness toward his cousin Belinda. Perhaps it is duty or guilt. But it can't be love.

What a pathetic creature he is, I tell myself when I toast the first day of the New Year alone. Martin is away on business even though it is a holiday and surely no one will want him to come calling. I pity him. I do. And I pity my sweet Kat, who will grow up without the love of a father if Martin lets his grief keep him to his ways. I shall love her doubly the rest of my life to make up for it.

I spend January and February learning to fully embrace this truth that Martin has no emotional attachment to Kat and me, and perhaps never will. As March rolls in with its hints of spring, I know I must resolve to be content without any promise of Martin ever changing. I begin to remind myself every day of all that I have: Kat, this house, food to eat, nice clothes, a safe and warm bed, books to read, a garden to keep, a fine kitchen to bake and cook in, a view of the sea within walking distance, warm fires in the hearth, porcelain teacups, fountain pens full of ink, and a spouse who does not beat me.

All of this is enough, I tell myself, over and over. When I compare what I used to have to what I have now, surely it is.

As our first wedding anniversary arrives with barely a moment of recognition on Martin's part, I vow to wake up every morning—for the rest of my days—telling myself that what I have is enough. When Mam writes to me on the occasion of my first anniversary and asks how I am faring, I write back that I am as happy as I've ever been, because I am. We do not speak of the past. What is the point of it now?

March slides into April. Martin is away more than usual but I don't care. Kat and I fill the days on our own, and I am pleased to see that she is now speaking whispered sentences to me— whole ones—off and on all day long. It's as if she, too, has come to some kind of agreement with the hand she has been dealt and has reckoned me as an acceptable consolation for her other losses. She says things like "I don't want eggs" and "I like the blue carousel horse" and "I need new books." Martin is more phantom than anything else, and yet the house is calm and peaceful and warm.

It is mid-April now. Martin is away—as usual—and Kat and I begin this Tuesday afternoon with a trip to the library. Then we go for a long stroll down Market Street to have ice cream, and then to a butterfly house so that Kat can see the splendor of a chrysalis and its transformation from crawling worm to beautiful butterfly.

As we start for home in the late afternoon, I congratulate myself on how well I've settled in to my new perspective on my life. I've even begun to appreciate the singleness of my devotion to merely one person—Kat—instead of having to divide my affections between spouse and child as most mothers and wives have to do. As we walk down Mission Street to catch a streetcar, stunningly gowned women and smartly dressed men emerge from carriages to dine at the Palace Hotel prior to attending the opera tonight. Enrico Caruso is in town, as the posters declare, to sing the role of Don José in *Carmen*. Gaily dressed skaters readying for the masked carnival tonight at the pavilion are on the streets, too, boasting about which of them will win the thousand-dollar prize. The mood downtown is festive, alight with promise.

When we arrive home at dusk, Kat heads upstairs to her room and I decide to make a cup of tea before getting started on supper. Martin has been gone for two days and I expect he will be gone for two or three more. Maybe four. I have grown accustomed to knowing very little about his stints on the road or even about his occupation as a man who assesses risk for an insurance company. He has never talked about his work, never takes calls at the house related to his job. There has never been work-related mail delivered to the house because, as he finally told me months ago, he uses a post office box for that.

I am not expecting a caller when the front bell rings. As I go to answer it, I wonder if perhaps Libby is coming by for one of her charity visits, which she still grants me from time to time. But when I open the door, standing on the mat is a petite woman with strawberry blond hair and a decidedly rounded stomach. The woman has to be seven or eight months pregnant. She also seems out of breath and maybe even lost.

"Can I help you?" I ask.

"Yes," the woman says. "At least I hope you can. Is this the home of Martin Hocking?"

"Yes, it is. I am Mrs. Hocking."

"Is Mr. Hocking at home?"

How odd it is to have someone at the door asking for Martin. No one ever comes calling for him.

"I'm afraid he's not," I reply. "Is there something I can help you with?"

The visitor seems hesitant to speak her reason for coming.

"Would you happen to know my husband, James Bigelow?" she asks several seconds later.

I shake my head. "I'm afraid I don't."

The woman bites her lip, perplexed. "It's just that Mr. Hocking asked a favor of my husband and he's been gone on this errand longer than I expected. I'm . . . I'm getting worried."

I don't know how I can be of help and yet I feel compassion for this woman, who seems ready to collapse with exhaustion.

"Please come in and have some tea and I'll see if there isn't some way I can be of help to you."

The woman hesitates a moment and then steps into the foyer.

"I'm so sorry to be a bother," she says. "I'm only . . . I think something might have happened."

"'Tis no bother at all. I've already got the kettle on."

The woman exhales heavily, a hand resting on her abdomen. "You're very kind."

"It's truly no inconvenience, Mrs.—?" I have already forgotten her name.

"Bigelow. Belinda Bigelow."

I freeze in place with my hand on the door to close it. "Pardon? What did you say your name is?"

"Belinda Bigelow."

How extraordinary. Belinda isn't that common a name, is it?

"That's a beautiful name. My husband has a cousin named Belinda," I manage, as I push the door shut.

"It was my mother's favorite name. At least that's what my father always told me. I never knew her. She died when I was a baby."

"I'm so sorry to hear that. May I take your wrap?"

The woman takes off her shawl and hands it to me, and I hang it on the hall tree.

"Did you say Mr. Hocking asked a favor of your husband? James, is it?" I ask as I motion her into the sitting room.

"Yes, but I don't know what the favor was."

"Please have a seat," I tell her. "Does Mr. Bigelow also work for the insurance company?"

Belinda Bigelow gives me a puzzled look as she sits down on the sofa. "Pardon?"

"Does your husband also work for the insurance company?" I take the chair across from her.

"No. He's a land surveyor. Are you saying that's what your husband does? Works in insurance?"

"Yes," I answer, wondering what it was Martin asked this Mr. Bigelow to do for him. Is he thinking of buying some property? Maybe he is thinking of buying us a place in the country, perhaps in a town closer to his route.

"That's . . . that's strange," Belinda says. "James said your husband is in real estate development."

I stare at my guest for a moment. Perhaps there are two Martin Hockings in San Francisco. There have to be. This poor woman has the wrong one.

"I wonder if we are talking about the same man," I say with a smile. "Have you ever met this Mr. Hocking you're looking for?"

"No, I only know James said he had something important he had to do for him. He thought he'd be back two days ago. He . . . he had your address in his coat pocket."

The kettle in the kitchen begins to whistle slightly. I rise to attend to it, and as I do, my guest's gaze travels to the mantel, very close to where I am now standing.

Color drains from Belinda Bigelow's face and her mouth drops open.

"Are you all right?" I ask.

She lifts her hand and points to the mantel. "That picture . . ."

I turn to look at my wedding portrait. "That's me and Mr. Hocking on our wedding day last year." I turn back around. Belinda is rising on unsteady legs and then moving forward and reaching for the photograph, nearly falling over the hearth to get to it.

I reach out to steady her as the woman grabs the frame. "Whatever is the matter?" I ask.

Belinda Bigelow is now holding the photograph of Martin and me in trembling hands. She raises her head to look at me and her eyes are shimmering with alarm.

"What is it?" My own heart is pounding now. I can feel the collision of worlds—mine and hers—even before the next words are out of her mouth.

Belinda points to Martin's face in the portrait. "That's James," she says, her voice barely above a whisper. "That's my husband."

The teakettle in the kitchen begins to scream.

9

INTERVIEW WITH MRS. SOPHIE HOCKING
CONDUCTED BY AMBROSE LOGAN, U.S. MARSHAL
CASE NUMBER 069308
Official transcript

San Francisco, CA
November 6, 1906

QUESTION: Now, Mrs. Hocking, if we could return to the morning of the earthquake. You stated earlier that you and your stepdaughter, Katharine, were inside the house on Polk Street when the earthquake struck, but Mr. Hocking was away on business. You further stated that you did not see your husband that day, nor any day after that. Correct?

ANSWER: Yes.

QUESTION: And if the earthquake had not occurred, when would you have been expecting Mr. Hocking to return home?

ANSWER: Martin did not keep to a schedule I could rely on, sir. I never knew exactly when to expect him.

QUESTION: How long had he been gone on the day of the quake?

ANSWER: Two days.

QUESTION: Why was it your husband did not keep a schedule you could rely on?

ANSWER: It is the nature of his business. He assesses risk for an insurance company and he has to be out and about to do it. He doesn't know how long each appointment will take until he gets there.

QUESTION: Can you tell me the name of the insurance company he works for?

ANSWER: I'm afraid I cannot.

QUESTION: Are you saying you do not know the name of your husband's employer?

ANSWER: He likes keeping his work separate from his life at home, and that's fine by me.

QUESTION: I see. Mrs. Hocking, I need to ask you a very important question now. A man matching your husband's description was seen leaving San Rafaela twenty miles south of here late on the evening of April 17—that is, of course, the night before the earthquake. Your husband's automobile was found six miles north of San Rafaela on the morning of April 18, the day of the quake. The automobile had run out of gasoline on the road to San Francisco. I'm thinking he had to walk the rest of the way home, which would have him arriving here sometime during the early-morning hours. That being the case, I'm wondering if there's anything about your earlier statement you'd like to revise.

Interviewee doesn't respond.

QUESTION: Mrs. Hocking, do you want to revise your statement?

ANSWER: What do you mean by revise my statement?

QUESTION: I mean specifically did you in fact see your husband the morning of the earthquake?

Interviewee doesn't respond.

QUESTION: Your revised statement will help us make sense of your husband's activities and, more importantly, clear you of any knowledge of them.

ANSWER: What activities? What has Martin done?

QUESTION: No need to alarm yourself just yet, Mrs. Hocking. We are still in the process of gathering information, which is why your being forthright with me will be helpful. I need to know what happened on the day of the earthquake.

Withholding information from me will not help you, Mrs. Hocking. Not in the least. Did you see your husband that morning?

ANSWER: I've already said I didn't.

QUESTION: But you did have a houseguest the night previous, did you not? Did that person see him?

ANSWER: What do you mean?

QUESTION: There was someone else in the house with you and your stepdaughter the morning of the earthquake, wasn't there? A woman by the name of Belinda Bigelow?

Interviewee doesn't respond.

QUESTION: Mrs. Hocking?

ANSWER: Sir, why are you asking me questions that you seem to already know the answers to?

QUESTION: But I don't know all the answers. How do you know Belinda Bigelow? Why was she at your house on the morning of the earthquake?

ANSWER: She came to me the day before. She thought I could help her find her husband. He hadn't come home and she was worried about him.

QUESTION: Her husband being one Mr. James Bigelow?

ANSWER: Yes.

QUESTION: Did she know you? Did you know her?

ANSWER: No.

QUESTION: Can you please tell me, then, why she came to you for help?

ANSWER: Why does it matter?

QUESTION: I assume you have become aware that your husband, under the name James Bigelow, married this woman four months after having married you. Am I right about that? You know this to be true?

Interviewee doesn't respond.

QUESTION: Mrs. Hocking, the sooner we can clear you of having any knowledge of your husband's unlawful activities, the better for you. Now, I will ask you again. How did Belinda Bigelow know to come to you?

Interviewee doesn't respond.

QUESTION: Perhaps you don't understand how serious this situation is. For one thing, your husband's use of a false identity is a federal offense.

ANSWER: That is not the worst thing he has done.

10

Belinda Bigelow is as still as a statue with my wedding portrait tight in her hands. It's as if she believes if she stands there unmoving, the nightmare she's fallen into will dissolve and she will awaken. For a moment I remain motionless as well, wondering if I, too, am in a dream.

But the teakettle is squealing to wake the dead. We're not dreaming.

I hear myself say to her, "I'm sure your husband merely favors mine in looks, that's all. Surely you're mistaken."

Belinda, no longer a statue, shakes her head. "It's him." At the sound of her own voice the photograph slips from her hands and she falls back onto the sofa as if pushed. The frame hits the rug, and a corner splits and splinters off. The moment feels made of taffy, like it's being pulled and stretched and thinned. Part of me wants to reach for the fallen picture and part wants to reach for the woman who has collapsed onto my sofa, pale as chalk.

And then as I stand in that elongated moment, I see Kat at the doorway to the sitting room, watching. I don't know how long she's been standing there. Time seems to kick itself back into motion when I see my daughter.

"Kat!" I call out to her. "Wait right there!"

Kat obeys, but she is not looking at me. She is staring wide-eyed at the pregnant woman on the sofa, who has one hand on her swollen abdomen and another across her face.

Then, with a jerk, Belinda pitches forward and vomits onto the Oriental rug in front of her, and onto the portrait of Martin and me.

I dash over to Kat, put my arm protectively around her, and draw her away from the spectacle in the sitting room and into the kitchen.

I yank the kettle off the flame, and for a blissful moment there is silence. I place my hands on the countertop and lean my weight on my outstretched arms, letting the soundlessness wash over me.

I need a moment to think. Many moments. My thoughts are spinning madly and I can't seem to harness even one of them. Martin has another wife. She is pregnant with his child. He has another wife. He has another name. All those days and nights on the road while he's working, he's in another house. Another bed. He is sleeping with another woman. Having relations with her. Not just with prostitutes. Not just with me. I am married to a man who has another wife. Not dead Candace. Another wife entirely. One who is alive. A wife who cares for him. I saw it in Belinda's eyes just now, at that terrible moment she realized her husband has been lying to her in the worst possible way.

Kat leans against my hip. I look down at her and see fear. I put an arm about her.

"It's all right, love," I coo, but my voice sounds unsure. And even as the words leave my mouth I wonder which of us—Belinda or me—is rightfully married to Martin. Is Kat my stepdaughter or isn't she? In the eyes of the law, is she still mine?

I pull her even closer. I'll clobber Martin with an iron skillet if he tries to take Kat from me. I swear it. I don't love him, I don't want him, but I want this child. I love this child.

My chest is heaving with anger and rage and dread and other emotions I don't know the names of. Everything within me is pressing me to *do* something. Now.

I could escape San Francisco with Kat. I could do that.

But I don't have money and I don't have access to Martin's bank account. He only gives me what I need each week.

I could sell my sapphire ring and all the beautiful furniture in this house and take Kat back to Ireland . . . but, no, there are other complications there.

I need to know what happens next. What happens next? What do I do now?

First, that woman surely needs a drink of water. She has just thrown up on my rug.

Then we must talk.

I need to know who was married to Martin first. Who his legal wife is.

I grab a juice glass and fill it with water from the tap, all while keeping Kat close to me.

As she and I make our way back to the foyer, I lean down to speak to her. "The lady in the other room isn't feeling well. I need to give her a drink of water, love. Can you go upstairs and play with your dollies while I help her?"

Kat shakes her head. No. She will not go play with her dollies. Her eyes are still wide with apprehension.

I bend down close. "Everything is going to be all right, I promise. I need you to go upstairs and wait for me."

No.

I can't make her go. And I won't drag Kat up the stairs to her room. And, anyway, perhaps it is best if Belinda sees how much the child is devoted to me, just in case Belinda is Martin's rightful wife, and therefore Kat's rightful stepmother.

"All right," I tell her. "Just for a few minutes."

We enter the room. Belinda is sitting forward on the sofa, breathing heavily, eyes closed. I sit next to her. Kat, still standing, sidles up to me.

"Here," I say, extending the glass of water.

Belinda opens her eyes. She looks at the glass, at me. At Kat. Fresh tears pool as she stares at my daughter. Then she turns her gaze away and glances at the vomit at her feet.

"I'm sorry about the mess."

"It doesn't matter. Here. Drink the water."

Belinda reaches for the cup and drinks the water down.

I extend my hand for the empty glass. "More?"

She shakes her head and rubs at a tearstained cheek. "Who is that?" she says, nodding to Kat.

I put my arm around Kat's middle and pull her inches closer. "This is Katharine. We call her Kat."

Belinda stares at Kat for a moment as more tears puddle and then slide down her cheeks. "I don't know what any of this means," she says.

I regard her for a moment. "You're sure the man in that photograph is your husband?"

A weak sob claws its way out of Belinda's throat as she says, "Yes."

"You're quite sure?"

Belinda looks down at the portrait. The surface is vomit speckled, but Martin's image is clear. "No one has eyes like that but him."

Indeed, no one does. But then Belinda looks at Kat. No one else but his daughter, that is.

Belinda puts a hand to her mouth.

"Do you need me to call for a doctor?" I ask. "We have a telephone."

Belinda shakes her head. "I need to know what is happening. Where is my husband?"

I inhale and then let my breath out slowly. "I don't know where he is. There are many things I don't know right now, but I do know that you and I need to talk. There are things I need to tell you and there are things you need to tell me."

Belinda glances again at Kat. "Is she yours and his?"

"My . . . Martin was married before. To a woman named Candace, and he and she had a little girl. But Candace became very sick and now she's in heaven with the angels."

"He had . . . *another* wife?!" This fresh news seems to pierce the woman like a blade.

"Yes." I keep my tone even and controlled, for Kat's sake. "Kat is six; she'll be seven in a couple of months. She doesn't say very much, Belinda, but she's very smart. I think we should have that tea and Kat can work on some puzzles while we talk. You can tell me all about your husband, James, all right? Can you do that?"

Belinda glances from me to the child and back. "How will that help?"

I turn to Kat. "I need you to go up to your room and work on some puzzles, love. Mrs. Bigelow and I are going to have tea and talk for a bit. There's a good girl."

Kat, who hasn't taken her eyes off Belinda the entire time, lowers her gaze to Belinda's protruding stomach.

"All right, then, Kat? Off you go. I'll bring you up a sweet in a little bit," I say, when Kat makes no move to obey. "The adults need to talk."

A moment later, Kat turns from us and slowly leaves the room. I hear footfalls on the stairs.

I turn to Belinda. "When did you marry him? I need to know."

Belinda hesitates only a moment. "July of last year."

After me. He married her after me.

"When . . . when did *you* marry him?" Belinda nearly chokes on the words.

"March. Four months before he married you."

New sobs spring up from within this woman. "So I am not . . . I am not truly married?"

"I don't think that is our worst problem right now."

She shakes her head. "I can't believe this is happening. How can this be happening?"

At her words, my befuddled thoughts cease their racing and I realize the truth fully. Martin Hocking is not a poor soul shattered by grief. He's a scheming liar. A philanderer. He doesn't have a cousin named Belinda. He has another wife named Belinda. This poor woman and I have been duped, and surely the worst of it is we walked willingly into Martin's trap. At least I know I did. I was seduced by his subtle charms and ample provision because I wanted to be. I hear my da saying to me that it is no shame to find you've a grand hole in your roof, but it is to leave it that way. "It's happening because he wanted it to happen," I reply. "And we let him."

"But . . . but why?"

"That's what we need to figure out," I tell her, and then a new thought occurs to me. "Do you make and sell hair tonic?"

"What?"

"Do you have a knack for herbs and gardening? Do you make a hair tonic from what you grow?"

"Yes, I garden, and yes, I sell my herbs at my inn. But I do not make a hair tonic. Why are you asking me this?"

"You own an inn?"

"Just west of San Mateo in San Rafaela. It was my father's. Why?"

"Did Martin stay at your inn? Is that how you met him?"

"Yes. He came through town the first time in April of last year, and we were married in July. Why are you asking me all these questions?"

"Because he married you after marrying me for a reason. I don't know what it is, but I do know a person wouldn't do such a thing without a reason." Martin could have simply wed just Belinda if all he wanted was to appear to be a blessed family man. He wouldn't have needed to hunt for someone like me. There has to be a reason he married us both, and it can't be anything good. I pause and take a deep breath. "None of this will make sense until we know what that reason is. Come. We'll have our tea and you can tell me everything: how you met him, what he told you about himself. Everything."

We stand and make our way to the kitchen, where the water in the kettle is still steaming hot. I lead Belinda to the butler's table and to a chair facing the window. Outside, the sun has slipped below the horizon. Soon the sky will turn calming shades of scarlet and pink and then violet. Night will descend. This day began so very differently from how it is going to end.

Belinda stares out the window as I pull cups out of the cupboard. A moment later she begins to speak.

"Elliot warned me about James," she says in a dazed voice. "He knew there was something not quite right about him."

I am about to ask who Elliot is, but Belinda continues as if I am not even in the room.

"I told myself that Elliot was jealous. That's why he didn't like James. Because he was jealous. He'd been smitten with me since we were children. He is a good friend—my best friend. But I didn't think I was in love with him. Elliot had never made my heart pound or my gut ache with desire. But James? He made me feel hungry from the moment I met him. Elliot just made me feel safe. I liked feeling hungry after my father died. Hunger made me feel alive."

I turn from my tea making to look at her. I know the ache she speaks of.

"When did your father pass?" I ask, as gently as I can.

"Fourteen months ago." She answers like she's in a trance. "He fell down an abandoned mine shaft."

"My father died from a fall, too. He'd been working on a roof. I was sixteen."

But I don't know if she hears me say this. She just continues to speak to the panes of window glass. "The day before I married James, I walked over to Elliot's carpentry shop to ask him if he would give me away. I wasn't trying to be cruel; I thought it would help him let me go and pursue a life of his own with someone. But when I asked him, he just said, 'Don't marry him, Bel. Please.' I told him I loved James and why couldn't he just be happy for me, and he said I barely knew James and that all he's ever wanted was for me to be happy. He said it wasn't because of how he felt about me that he didn't want me to marry James; it was because of the way James looked at me, like he was looking right past me. Elliot said he knows how a man who loves me should be looking at me."

Tears are trailing down her cheeks again. She turns her head to look at me. I guess she was talking to me after all.

"I begged him to give me away anyway, and he just smiled and said he could never give me away. That he never will."

"He sounds like a good friend." I set a cup of tea in front of her that smells like wildflowers.

She dabs at her eyes with a napkin before taking a sip from the cup. I sit down on the chair next to her with my own cup.

We are both quiet for a moment. "How could I have been so stupid?" Belinda finally says.

"I've made plenty of decisions I wish I hadn't made," I say. "You weren't being stupid. You lost your father and were hurting. He made you feel better. You trusted him."

Belinda stares at me for a long moment. "You don't seem as devastated as I am about all of this," she says in a numb voice.

"I don't love Martin. I have never loved him."

Her mouth drops open. "But you are married to him!"

"Yes."

"How can you be married to someone you have never loved?"

I take a sip of tea. And then I tell her how.

11

As Belinda comprehends fully the arrangement I made with Martin, an unmistakable pang of pity crosses her face.

"Why didn't you want to marry for love?" she asks, incredulous.

I decide in that moment to tell her the barest minimum. "Because there was once a man I thought I loved and who I thought loved me. But I was wrong."

"What happened?"

"It wasn't love."

She waits for me to say more. But I don't.

And I won't.

Belinda seems to need a moment to make sense of this decision and the route the turns of the earth have taken me on. Have taken her on. How we have ended up in this same place together.

After another long moment she asks, "But . . . but you shared a bed with James?"

"That wasn't love, either. The man you know as James doesn't love me. I don't love him. It isn't love."

I can see how troubled she is by the fact that she had been spellbound by Martin's affections and I hadn't.

"Martin doesn't care for me, not in that way, Belinda. He never wanted me to love him. He must have behaved differently with you." I can't help but look down at her stomach.

"Yes," Belinda says, and I see pain etching itself in a sad half smile as she touches her swollen belly.

"Tell me how you met him."

She lifts her gaze and turns her head slowly to again stare out the window, as though she can see her past in the glass. "He came to the inn a few months after my father died. He arrived in an automobile, something I hardly ever see. I'd been in my garden and I had dirt on the hem of my skirt and under my fingernails, and there he stood, the most beautiful person I had ever seen."

I nod even though Belinda is not looking at me. I know the awe she is speaking of. I felt it, too, the moment I opened the envelope containing Martin's response to my letter and saw his photograph peeking out from underneath a one-way train ticket.

"He said his name was James Bigelow and that he needed a room for the next several nights, as he had business in the area. He told me he was a land surveyor and that San Rafaela and all the other nearby towns were being considered by wealthy investors for commercial development. The Loralei was central to all the places he needed to see. I gave him a room. My nicest one."

"How long did he stay?"

"Four nights."

"And how did he seem around your other guests?"

"I didn't have other guests. He was polite to me. Kind. He fixed a wobbly door hinge that I had been meaning to tell Elliot about without my even asking. And he was so easy to talk to. When I served James his supper I would sit with him. He said he enjoyed having someone to talk to while he ate. I enjoyed it, too. He asked me how long I had lived there and I told him that I'd been born at the Loralei, that my mother had died of an illness when I was still a baby and I'd only recently lost my father. He kept asking questions that no one ever asks me anymore, because everyone in San Rafaela knows all the answers. I . . . I thought he was genuinely wanting to get to know me."

She pauses a moment and I find myself baffled that the way in which Martin snared Belinda is so very different from the way he snared me. He'd never seemed interested in knowing me better. Not for a moment. It is as if Belinda is describing a different man altogether. A chameleon. But then again, Martin hadn't needed to woo me. He hadn't needed anything from me other than my willingness to marry him, and that had been so easily attained. Stunningly easy. "What other kinds of questions did he ask you?" I say.

Belinda turns to face me. "About my family. The property. At first I thought maybe he was trying to see if I would consider selling the Loralei. I told him I wouldn't, but he said he was interested in knowing why my family chose San Rafaela to make a home. He said knowing the reason would help him advise the investors."

"And so what did you tell him?"

"That my grandparents came out to California when my father

was just a boy, during the last year of the gold rush. My grandfather bought the property to build the inn because it was situated on the road to San Francisco and because there was an old mine at the far end that someone had long ago staked a claim upon but which had never yielded anything. My grandfather liked the novelty of that."

My ears prick at this. "A gold mine? There's a gold mine on this property?"

"It's abandoned, though. There's no gold in it. My grandfather and father poked about in it for years. They never found anything. And no one goes in it anymore. My father died in that mine. I hate it. I've always hated it. It was always dark and cold and full of bats. I thought the mine was dangerous. And in the end, it was. I was at the entrance when my father died; he'd wanted to show me something inside it and I didn't want to go in. I heard him cry out when he stumbled and fell. I will never forget that sound."

"And you told Martin all of this?"

"He is not Martin to me."

I say nothing and after a moment Belinda continues.

"He told me things about himself, too. It wasn't just me doing all the talking. He told me about life in San Francisco, where he had a room at a boardinghouse, about all the theaters and museums and restaurants. He told me that, even though he loved the city, he grew up on a cattle ranch in Colorado and that he missed it."

"Wait. He told you his parents had a cattle ranch?"

"Yes. Why?"

"He told me his parents were killed in a carriage accident back east when he was six, and that the aunt and uncle who took him in were cruel to him. He said it was a cattle rancher in Colorado who'd given him his first job and changed his life."

"Which story is true?" Belinda asks, though surely she doesn't think I know the answer. Either tale could be true. Or neither.

"It doesn't matter right now," I reply. "What else did he say about his family?"

"That his mother died of influenza when he was eighteen, and an older sister died in a riding accident the following year. His father passed away not long after that of a heart attack. He told me he sold the family ranch and moved to California to start a new life."

We are both quiet for a moment as our tea grows cool and we ponder what we thought was true of the man we'd married, and what are likely lies.

"How much time passed before he came to the inn again?" I finally ask.

"A week."

"Did you know he would be coming back?"

"He didn't say that first time, but I wanted him to come back. I missed him the minute he was gone. Each time he left I missed him more. By the sixth visit I knew I was in love with him. He seemed such an attentive, charming person. He knew how to coax my worries out and what to say to get me to laugh. Elliot had always been able to do this, too, but somehow with James, it was different. When he proposed after only three months, I said yes."

"And you . . . felt loved by him?" I ask, because I can't picture it. I can't picture Martin kissing Belinda, making her laugh, making her feel wanted—all behaviors I believed him incapable of because of his crippling grief over losing Candace.

"I did," Belinda says, but then a shadow seems to fall across her face. "In the beginning, anyway. But soon after we married I began to hope James would want a job that allowed him to be at home every night. I missed him when he was gone and wanted to believe he missed me. I thought the open road would loosen its hold on him, especially when I told him that I was expecting."

"But that's not what happened."

Belinda shakes her head. "When I told him I wanted him to find a job closer to home, he said that he liked the job he had. There was nothing about our situation that needed fixing. He said I knew what he did for a living when I married him, and that I fell in love with him when he was living that kind of life. I'd been happy then. I could be happy now if I wanted to be. I was choosing to be unhappy about it."

She pauses a moment, and I can see by the way she is staring down at her wedding band, plainer than mine, that Belinda was starting to see the cracks before she came to my house today. She came here to prove to herself the cracks were an illusion, that there were no cracks. But instead, her whole world has shattered.

"How did you know to come here?" I ask her gently. "How did you know the name Martin Hocking?"

She brushes away a couple of tears. "A few days ago when he was home, I saw an envelope half in and half out of his coat pocket. I pulled it out. It was addressed to a Martin Hocking at this address. The return address was from a bank here. I looked inside the pocket and saw another envelope addressed to this same man. James came into our bedroom as I was looking at them and he asked me what I was doing. I lied and told him I had wanted to launder his coat, because it was dirty from his travels, but that he had mail in the pocket."

"Was he cross with you at finding them? What did he do?"

"He merely put out his hand for the envelopes. I asked if Martin Hocking was a friend of his and he said no, a client. I asked why he had this man's mail. I hadn't wanted to sound meddlesome. I just wanted him to have a good reason for having someone else's mail in his coat pocket. He told me Mr. Hocking was out of town and that he was taking care of some business for him while he was away. I said that was very nice of him and he said Mr. Hocking was one of his best clients. Then he said that he would be gone on business for Mr. Hocking for the next two or three days. He took the coat from me and told me I could launder it when he returned, but that he needed to attend to Mr. Hocking's errand immediately."

"And he wasn't angry or upset with you when he left?"

"No. But I was sure something was wrong," Belinda says. "James had been planning to be home for a bit, and now he was off on an errand for two or three days? Just like that? I wondered if maybe James owed this Mr. Hocking money. Maybe Mr. Hocking was more than just a client. Maybe he was the reason James wouldn't give up his life on the road. I wrote down the address I had seen on the envelopes so that I wouldn't forget it."

"And when did this happen?"

"Four days ago. That's why I came here. I thought he might be in trouble. So I asked Elliot if he would mind the inn for me and give me a ride to the train station. I told him why I needed to go to San Francisco and that I would be back tonight. And then I arrived here. And rang your doorbell."

I sit in silence for a moment when she is finished, as the full weight of this predicament settles around me: I am married to a heartless fraud, and so is this woman sitting across from me. I am certain of nothing else except that this man has fathered a daughter whom I love as much as life itself. Whatever happens from this moment on, I must not lose Kat. I can't lose Kat. I can't.

I won't.

But how to proceed?

There has to be a reason Martin has done what he has done. What is it? What does he want? Why did he purposefully seek out a second wife right after marrying me?

Why?

I lean over the table and massage my temples as I contemplate. Martin didn't need to win me over with affection; he knew I wanted a child, stability, and a way out of New York. I wanted things he could provide, he wanted something I could provide, and we struck a deal. But he *had* won Belinda over with affection. Why? Martin isn't a land surveyor—I am fairly sure of that—and now I am beginning to believe that he doesn't work in life insurance, either. Belinda and I must fit into some larger plan of his, but what is it? Perhaps I do provide the look of normalcy to anyone who might wonder about Martin Hocking, but it's not so he can project a better image for an insurance company.

And how does Belinda figure in? It doesn't escape my notice that she and I have the same sad past, losing fathers we loved and who were good husbands to our mothers. Belinda had been specifically chosen—just as I had been—because she could provide something Martin wanted. What was it?

I don't know the answer to this because clearly Martin is a man of secrets.

The next second it occurs to me that I know a place where he keeps some of his secrets hidden. Two places, actually.

For the first time since Belinda looked at that photograph, I know what she and I need to do.

"Come with me." I rise to my feet.

Belinda must hear the urgency in my voice. She looks up at me in surprise. "Where are we going?"

"To the library first. And then the boiler room."

We turn from the table and toward the entrance to the kitchen and we both see Kat at the same time. The child is sitting on the floor leaning against the doorframe in the pose of someone who's been sitting there awhile.

Kat has been listening.

12

I don't remember what I knew of the ways of men and women when I was Kat's age—probably very little. But Kat is a smart girl. I know this because of the intricate puzzles she solves and the books she is able to read. And because of the way she listens. She doesn't just hear, she pays attention, and I can tell by the look on her face that she fully recognizes the situation Belinda and I are in. Kat knows that her father has another wife.

She surely suspected it after seeing pregnant Belinda pointing to the photograph and declaring Martin to be her husband. That was enough to entice Kat to tiptoe back down the stairs and position herself at the kitchen doorway to hear how it is that her father has two wives, one of whom is with child.

There is no point in scolding Kat now for having eavesdropped. I hadn't commanded her to stay in her room; I'd just assumed she would. Besides, what would scolding her accomplish? She cannot unhear what she has heard.

"Have you been sitting there the whole time, Kat?" I ask.

I see the barest glimmer of shame as she nods. She knew I meant for her to stay until I called for her, even though I did not say it. I cross the kitchen to her and kneel down. Belinda is still behind me.

"Were you listening to us? Did you hear everything?"

"Yes," she whispers.

I hadn't known how Belinda and I were going to proceed with Kat right there in the house, but now I don't have to worry about how much to tell her. She knows everything.

"Do you have questions for me, Kat?"

My daughter looks from me to Belinda and back again. She nods, and I don't care if she has a slew of questions. I hope we spend the next hour on the floor, she and I, as she asks me her questions in her sweet voice that I too infrequently hear.

Kat points to Belinda.

"There's a baby." Her voice is soft, just above a whisper.

"Yes, love."

"Our baby?"

I hesitate a moment before answering. "'Tis Miss Belinda's baby."

"And mine?"

I don't know how to answer her. I say nothing.

"My baby, too?" she asks.

I look back to Belinda, who seems to understand, just as I do now, the reason for Kat's intense interest. She understands in the simplest of ways that any baby that belongs to her father is her brother or sister. She has a sibling—something she didn't have before and which I see very clearly now she has always wanted.

Belinda stares back at me and reaches down to wrap one arm

around her middle as if to embrace her unborn child. I turn back to Kat.

"Sweetest, everything's a bit topsy-turvy at the moment. I don't have a good answer for you."

But Kat looks past me to Belinda, and I see only resolve on her young face. She already believes she is a sister to the baby that Belinda is carrying. The lack of full confirmation from me means nothing.

"Is that all, love?" I ask. "Do you have more questions?"

Kat slowly shakes her head. I can see that she has, in fact, more questions, but none of them matter like the one about Belinda's child.

"All right, then. To the library." I rise from my knees and reach out to help Kat to her feet.

The three of us cross the foyer into the library and I head toward Martin's desk. Kat lingers by the door. She's never liked being in the room Martin uses as his office.

"He keeps this desk locked and I don't know where the key is," I tell Belinda. "But we have to get into it. I think we might find some of our answers in here."

I remove a hairpin and insert the point into the keyhole of the main drawer, the largest one. I jiggle, jab, and jostle to no avail. Then I ask Belinda for one of her hairpins and try that. I try again with mine. I try with a darning needle, a buttonhook, and a hatpin. And then I try the hairpins again, only this time I use mine and Belinda's at the same time. The mechanism inside the lock turns at last and I pull on the handle.

The drawer is orderly, with folios of documents neatly piled upon one another. I pull out the first, lay it atop the desk, and open it.

On top is my and Martin's marriage license, followed by Kat's birth certificate, then the deed to the house.

I flip past these and there is the marriage certificate between James Bigelow and Belinda Louise Dixon of San Rafaela, California. Belinda stiffens next to me as she sees it, too, and I move past it. Next is his own birth certificate, one Martin Charles Hocking of White Plains, New York, son of Albert and Maureen Hocking. After that is the birth certificate for a James Wilder Bigelow, born March 12, 1873, near a town called Trinidad in Las Animas County, Colorado, and right past this is the death certificate for this same person in 1876. James Bigelow died of scarlet fever at the age of three. Martin was two years old at the time, which is why he was able to so easily use this person's identity. They were only a year apart in age.

"The real James Bigelow was just a little boy when he died," Belinda says numbly as she reads the document at the same time I am reading it.

"Yes."

"But how did he know about him?"

"I don't know." I keep at the task.

The next document is a marriage certificate between Annabeth Bigelow, apparently the older sister of the ill-fated James Bigelow, and a man named Percy Grover, who were wed on June 4, 1896, in Trinidad, Colorado. Next is Annabeth's death certificate a year after her marriage to Mr. Grover, the result of a riding accident. When I flip this certificate over to look at the next item in the folio, my breath hitches in my throat, as does Belinda's. There atop the rest of the documents is an unframed wedding portrait, small in size, but clearly of Martin and another woman. And it's not Candace. I've seen Candace's photograph. This be-gowned woman is plump and brown-haired and a bit older than Martin, I'd wager. I turn the photograph over. Someone has penciled in *Annabeth Bigelow and Percy Grover—June 4, 1896.*

"Good Lord," I whisper. Martin is not only masquerading as dead James Bigelow; he married under the name Percy Grover, too. It is falling into place now as I stare at a younger Martin in a wedding suit. I turn to Belinda. "That cattle ranch wasn't his father's like he told you, nor did it belong to a kindhearted rancher who gave him a job like he told me. The ranch was his father-in-law's. And then his wife's. Martin inherited it when this Annabeth died in a riding accident."

When I say this last bit, a cold thought prickles inside my head.

"She's a rancher's daughter and she died in a riding accident?" I mumble, and I should've left the thought unsaid. Belinda falters next to me. I grab the chair I'd pushed aside and pull it to her.

"Sit down." She doesn't argue with me.

"You can't be thinking he killed her?" Belinda says with a gasp, her eyes glittering with fear and dread.

I suddenly remember Kat was hovering at the doorway when I began working on the lock. I glance up and relief pours through me. She has wandered off, thank heaven, apparently having gotten bored with my efforts to pick the lock.

"We don't need to be wondering about that right now," I say. "Forget I said it."

And she nods, wide-eyed. But we both now know Martin is a coldhearted liar who can't be trusted. Everything in this drawer tells us we know that much.

I turn back to the folio, which seems to me now to be a grand collection of Martin's accomplishments as much as important personal records, or why else would he keep them all? I want to find Candace's death certificate; Candace, that young woman whose parents had enrolled her in a prestigious riding school where she met Martin Hocking. I want to see the cause of death as consumption. Martin could not have killed Candace outright to get an inheritance from her, not if she died of consumption. I need to know her disease killed her and only her disease so that I'll know if Belinda, Kat, and I must run from this house this very night and report Martin to the police.

I scan the documents that remain. An invoice for Annabeth's headstone. A bill of sale for the Colorado cattle ranch for twelve thousand dollars. A birth certificate for a Percy Grover, born in Cleveland, Ohio, in 1875. The bill of sale for a house in Los Angeles, dated four months before I married Martin; a marriage certificate to Candace, dated July 1897; two certificates of stillborn births—boys—delivered dead to Candace and Martin Hocking. The first in November 1897—which means Candace had been with child when she married Martin—and the second in March 1898. But there is no death certificate for Candace.

I rummage through the other folios. I find maps of California and Colorado, bank statements—only in the name of Martin Hocking; the largest balance is three thousand dollars. And then a collection of obituaries from different California newspapers. The obituaries are all for men. Martin circled the names of surviving daughters and where they lived. Some of the obituaries are from newspapers that were printed only a few weeks ago; others are older. Among the older pages is George Dixon's obituary, and there within it, in a penciled circle, is Belinda's name.

"That's how he found you," I tell her, though that fact is obvious to us both at the moment.

Belinda stares at her name as if she doesn't recognize it as her own.

"Why?" she finally says, several seconds later. "Why me?"

I leaf through the obituaries. The men had all been of means, and all had been preceded in death by their wives, so their surviving children had surely inherited from them. That being the case, what had Martin hoped to gain from a marriage to Belinda? A roadside inn is no great boon. He had to have chosen her for another reason, and even as I'm wondering what it is, I think I might already know where to go to puzzle it out. The boiler room will tell me if I am right.

But first I rifle through what I am able to of the rest of the desk. I find a locked strongbox the size of a jewelry case, the title to Martin's automobile and the agreement records for its garage, and receipts from the grocer and butcher and the Emporium. I find pay stubs from Martin's years as a stable hand in Los Angeles. I find no files at all related to his working as an assessor for an insurance company—not one—and nothing that tells me what Martin works on at this desk when he's home.

I decide to try the hairpins on the strongbox, and as I lift it out of the drawer, I spy an envelope that was resting underneath it.

The envelope is addressed to Martin at the Los Angeles address, postmarked six months before I married him. The return address is Las Palomas Sanatorium in Tucson, Arizona. I turn the envelope over and lift its broken flap. It has been opened. I pull out the letter inside and begin to read:

> *Dearest Martin,*
>   *Please don't be angry with my father or with me. I*
> *know it was not your wish that I come to the sanatorium,*

but Papa believes I will fare better here. I may even improve. That is why I allowed him to spirit me away like he did. It wasn't to anger you or conspire against you. He was afraid if he told you he was going to step in to care for me that you would prevent him from doing so. I have always taken your side with him, Martin. You know I have. But I feel he is in the right this time. Please, please try to understand!

They are taking wonderful care of me here, and I do feel stronger, even if it is only a little bit. Please come and see me as soon as you can and bring Kat. I know I haven't been the mother to her that I should've been, but I want to try to change that in whatever time I have remaining to me. I have made so many mistakes, Martin. We both have. But we do not need to keep making them. Please, my darling. I know it has not been good between us. I know now I took the losses of our sons too much to heart. I was not a good wife and I utterly failed Kat as a mother. I know I cannot be the wife for you that I should have been, but please, please let me attempt to be the mother I should've been to Kat. Please bring her to me. Let me see her.

Your loving wife,
Candace

My breath stills in my lungs. Here is the reason I can find no death certificate for Candace in Martin's desk. She's not dead. She's alive, or at least she was nineteen months ago. And since there is no death certificate and three thousand dollars instead of tens of thousands in Martin's bank account, she must still be at that sanatorium. Martin told me many months back that his dead wife had been bequeathed an inheritance from her grandmother and that that was what had allowed him to buy this house, but Martin hasn't inherited anything from Candace. She's not dead. He must still be living off the sale of Annabeth's ranch.

As I look down at Candace's letter, I feel my strength leaving me like blown dandelion wisps. Up to this point my mounting anger at Martin's deceit has felt like something to be harnessed and utilized, like a team of ready horses. But now I feel undone. Emptied of vigor.

This is surely how Belinda felt just an hour ago when she saw that photograph of Martin and me, as though her world was suddenly made of paper and she was made of thread. Her world was tearing into bits and she was unraveling as the pieces floated away on too swift a breeze.

Candace isn't dead.

Kat has a mother and it's not me.

13

There have only been a handful of moments when I've wished I could turn back time and make a different decision. I've never regretted coming to America and I don't regret answering Martin's advertisement—not even now—but in this moment, if I could reverse time, I'd back it up an hour or two, and when the doorbell rang at half past four I would not answer it. I'd leave Belinda standing there wondering if she's got the right house. I'd peer at her from behind the lace curtain at the sitting room window and I'd watch her walk away.

I don't care anymore that Martin is living an illusion and forcing all of us to live his lies with him. I don't care that he marries women because he wants something from them. And God help me I don't even care in this moment that perhaps Annabeth Bigelow Grover's riding accident wasn't an accident.

All I care about is that I woke up this morning the mother of a little girl who needs me and loves me. And now I am just another pitiful soul Martin Hocking has trampled upon. Maybe he didn't fiddle with the straps on Annabeth's saddle, but he certainly stole Candace's child from her. He told Kat her mother was dead. He gave Belinda a sham of a marriage. And now he's given me a child who isn't mine to keep. Candace is alive and living in a sanatorium in Arizona, wanting her daughter.

I feel Belinda at my side. She has risen from the chair to read the letter, too. I want to shove her out the front door, pretend I never saw her, never had any reason to pry open this desk today and unveil its secrets.

"Kat's mother is alive?" Belinda says a moment later, in a horrified tone. "But that child thinks her mother is dead!"

Whatever I might say in this moment is frozen on my tongue.

We are both silent for several long seconds.

"How could he do that to a little girl?" Belinda finally says, and her voice cracks with what I recognize as mother-love. She is not exactly a mother, and neither am I, I suppose, but we are both on the edge of being one. She on the inside edge, and me on the outside edge.

How indeed could Martin do that to Kat? Say her mother is dead when she is not?

"I don't understand why he would do that. Why would he do that?" Belinda implores, and she waits for me to answer.

"I . . . I wonder if he thought she would be dead of the consumption by now." My own voice sounds like it's made of air. "She's an heiress. I'm sure that's why he married her. And then lucky for him, she got very sick."

"But," Belinda says, staring down at the letter, "her father is still alive."

"She had money of her own. From a grandmother. Martin told me this."

"I still don't understand why he would tell Kat her mother is dead. Why tell her that?"

I can think of only one answer. I'd wager now it is the root answer for everything Martin Hocking does, now that I know the truth about him.

"Because it suited him. He *wanted* her to think Candace was dead. He wanted to live here in San Francisco as if she were."

"But *why*? Why did he do all these terrible things to us!"

"Because he wanted something for himself," I say, as everything I now know merges and assures me this is true. "He doesn't care about us. He doesn't care about anyone."

"Not even his own child?" Belinda says, incredulous.

"Not even his own child. I thought he was the way he was because he'd known too many sorrows. I thought he had decided to abandon love, even for his own daughter, because he didn't want to suffer any more because of it. But that's not it, Belinda. He's not paralyzed by grief. He's just a soulless, lying cheat. That's why he did all these terrible things."

"Stop it," Belinda whispers, wincing as if I've slapped her.

I soften my voice. The revelations swirling in my head are too hard for Belinda to hear. Too hard to hear all at once. But she has to hear them. Because we have to decide what happens next. "I'm sorry to have to say it. But it's true. He doesn't love you. He doesn't love anyone."

Again, we are silent for a few minutes.

Belinda casts her gaze over all the papers on the desk, at all the evidence of what Martin has done. Of who he is.

Of who he is not.

"What are we going to do?" she says, in a childlike voice.

"I'm fairly certain it's illegal in California to have more than one wife," I hear myself answer. "We can go to the police first thing tomorrow morning. We can have him arrested."

"And then?"

"And then . . . and then he goes to prison. I think. I don't know."

"What about that little girl?"

I know what I should say, but it takes me several seconds to say it.

"She will need to be reunited with her mother."

The clock in the foyer chimes half past six o'clock as I say this. Twilight has descended, and it will be followed by the heavy cloak of night. After we go to the police, everything will be different. The life I am currently leading will be over. I likely won't have a place to live and certainly no means. The police might take Kat from me straightaway when they realize my marriage to Martin is bogus and that Kat's mother still lives. They will take it upon themselves to transport Kat to Arizona. They will take that tortured child from me.

I can't let that happen. She has already been through too much.

I should be the one to take her.

But I am going to need train fare and money for food. Maybe there is cash in the strongbox. Maybe . . .

I turn to Belinda.

"I think we need to carefully plan what we're going to do and how we're going to do it. And I think we need to see what Martin has been hiding in the boiler room."

She stares at me, with no idea of what I am talking about.

"Come with me." I hurry out of the room and Belinda follows me. We cross the foyer into the kitchen, and there is sweet Kat at the butler's table by the window, drawing pictures of birds and butterflies and coloring them with her wax crayons. *For Baby*, she has written on the tops of the pages.

I smile down on her and squeeze her shoulder. I lack the fortitude to speak to her just now, but she is immersed in her task as a big sister and doesn't seem to notice. I head to the door that opens onto the stairway to the boiler room. I pull it open and lift my skirt as I take the steps.

"Close the door behind you," I quietly instruct Belinda. I don't want Kat following us down.

I flip on the electrical switch for the one incandescent bulb that hangs in the center of the low-ceilinged room. The wooden lid on the vault is closed and padlocked, but I grab the heavy wrench by the boiler that is used to loosen or tighten its valves. I raise it above my head and bring it down on the padlock and hinges, causing Belinda to gasp in surprise. It takes only a few blows for the padlock to skitter away, freed from the wooden planking of the lid, still locked. I lift the lid and rest it against the wall. Ten bottles of what I am sure is not hair tonic rest inside on the shelf Martin made. I reach for one, crack open its seal, and uncork it. I raise the bottle to my nose and catch the strong scent of vinegar.

I let the bottle fall to the ground. It breaks and Belinda startles backward in surprise. In the puddle of broken glass and vinegar are silt and dirt and bits of white rock. And then in the sallow light cast by the one bulb, a shimmering misshapen orb the size of a raisin appears in the spread of liquid and stony mush.

It gleams like the summer sun. Gold.

I look up at Belinda, who is staring wide-eyed at the luminous object on the wet floor.

"This is why he sought you out," I say. "He wanted your father's mine."

Belinda raises her head to look at me. "But there's nothing in the mine. It's been abandoned for decades. There's nothing there! My grandfather and father knew its every inch. There was nothing in it!"

I take out another bottle and drop it to the ground, and it shatters. Two more pea-sized shiny orbs appear in the vinegary puddle of silt and stones, both hugged in the wet embrace of rippling, crumbling white rock. I draw out a third and repeat. Another misshapen lump appears, this one the size of a small, halved lima bean, with bits of stone clinging to it.

I bend down and poke at the creamy white stone wrapping itself around the golden bean. Part of the white stone sloughs off as I touch it. I lift the stone-crusted bean out of the vinegar and stand up straight, holding the golden thing to the light and looking at the strange rocky mush disintegrating all around it. "What is that white stuff?"

Belinda is staring at it, too. "It's quartz. Sometimes . . . sometimes gold ore that is found underground is encased in quartz. My father told me the acid in vinegar can dissolve quartz crystals. It's how he tested rocks he sometimes found in the mine. It's how lots of miners test what they find. Real gold won't be harmed by the acid, but other minerals that look like gold, like . . . like mica or pyrite, will dissolve or become damaged after soaking in vinegar. But not gold."

I look up at her. "Still believe there's nothing in your mine?"

"But . . . but how could I not know? I would've known!"

"You told me earlier you didn't like the mine, that you thought it was dangerous. That you never went down there."

"Because I didn't! I don't! It *is* dangerous!"

"But you also said that on the day your father died he brought you to the mine because he wanted to show you something. But then he fell. What if he found gold after all? What if he'd found something before that day that looked like gold and he'd had someone verify it to be sure? What if *that* was what he'd been going to show you? Quartz in the cave with gold running through it, and which he knew for certain was gold because he'd had it verified?"

Belinda ponders this for a moment. "How would James . . . Martin . . . how would he have known about it?"

"That doesn't matter right now! Maybe somebody talked at an assayer's office about a man from San Rafaela bringing in some freshly mined gold and Martin overheard it. It doesn't matter how he knew. What matters is he was going to steal this from you. It's yours. And he was going to take it right out from under you, using his fake marriage to you as proof he has joint ownership of your property."

I don't mention that Martin might have just as effortlessly decided to kill Belinda when he had tapped into the last of the ore in the cave and was finished with the ruse of being her husband. I also don't mention how easy it is to imagine that Martin was secretly inside the mine the day Belinda's father died, that Martin pushed him into the shaft when the opportunity presented itself, and then dashed away when Belinda ran for help. She perhaps can't see him yet as a heartless beast, but it is getting easier by the minute for me to see him as one.

While Belinda reconciles her mind to the truth of why Martin wooed her into marriage, I break open the rest of the bottles. Each one contains silty, decomposing quartz and golden bits. There were more bottles in the past. I've no idea where they are. Martin made it seem like he had sold them on his route, but now I am certain he has squirreled them away somewhere or cashed them and deposited the money in a bank account in James Bigelow's name or Percy Glover's or someone else's entirely. I grab an empty canning jar off a rack by the boiler and scoop up the nuggets, careful not to cut myself on the shards of glass.

"He'll see the broken bottles when he comes home," Belinda says dazedly. "He'll know we know."

"I hope he does see them. We're leaving here at first light anyway, and he won't know you're with me. He'll arrive home to an empty house and think I opened the bottles and found the gold all on my own. And then he'll come upstairs and unlock his desk and he'll see all his precious papers are gone."

"And then what will he do?" Belinda says, fear in her voice.

"If the police are doing their job, they will be watching for him to return and they'll arrest him. If they aren't, he'll run. He'll have to. I have the papers. He'll know I'll go right to the police. He can't stay here."

"But what if he comes to me?"

"He won't. Your marriage certificate is in that pile of documents, too. He can't risk going back to your place. The police will know all about you and the gold he tried to steal from you and the gold he *did* steal from you. This isn't all there was, Belinda. He'll take what he's already stolen from your mine and he'll run."

Belinda places a hand over her belly. She looks exhausted. "And what do I do then? I just . . . I just go home to have this baby on my own? Am I widowed? An unmarried mother? Abandoned? What am I?"

"You are someone who's been wronged—that's who you are. And don't ever think it's too terrible a thing to bear a child alone. Be grateful you can have one. Not all of us can."

I don't mean to sound hurtful, but I know I do. I thrust the jar of gold toward her.

She doesn't reach out her hand.

"Take it," I say.

Belinda looks at the jar in disgust. "I don't want it."

"Yes, you do."

"No, I don't."

"The gold is yours!"

"I said I don't want it! My father died trying to dig it out, and apparently it's the only reason James wanted me. You take it. You'll need it more than I will. What will you have when you leave this house? Nothing. Take it."

I stare at her for a moment, nearly overcome with the desire to embrace her as a friend, the first I've had since I can't remember when. She is right. I do need it.

"We can discuss this later," I say, as I kick the shards away from our path back to the stairs. "Right now you need to get back home and Kat and I need to pack our bags so we can leave at first light. Martin might be home tomorrow. Kat and I need to be well on our way before he arrives."

"But I've missed the last train," Belinda says as she follows me. "It left the station just after six."

I am surprised to find myself somewhat comforted by this news; it means I won't feel so defeated and alone tonight, with just quiet Kat for company. Kat, the child I love and can't keep.

"Then you'll stay here tonight with Kat and me. We'll all leave together at daybreak."

"There are no trains that early."

"We'll . . . we'll get a carriage to take us to the nearest train station out of the city. You'll go home and Kat and I will continue on to Arizona."

I know this is what I must do. I am obligated by integrity to take Kat to her mother. This is what I would want done for me if our places were reversed.

I make for the stairs, suddenly realizing I haven't fed Kat her supper and the day is gone. I need to make us all something to eat and then pack Kat's and my things. And at some point I need to ring the sanatorium to make sure Candace is indeed still alive and well enough for visitors. And then, somehow, I need to find a way to tell Kat her mother isn't dead after all.

Belinda is still full of questions as she takes the stairs behind me. "When are you going to telephone the police? How will I know when he's been arrested? Will there be a trial? Will I have to come back and testify against him? Am I supposed to tell people back home I am not married? What am I going to tell Elliot?"

"For the love of heaven, we don't know the answers to those questions!" I call out over my shoulder. "No one does. Let us just get through today."

We enter the kitchen. Kat has left her drawings and crayons on the butler's table and I see she has run out of paper. Perhaps she has gone back upstairs to fetch more.

I step out of the kitchen to call up the stairs to her, but as I enter the foyer, I see her in the library at Martin's desk. She has a piece of paper in her hand and is reading it.

Candace's letter.

Kat is sounding out the words in Candace's beautiful hand-writing. The letters are in script, and she doesn't know the cursive letters well. But she does know them.

I rush into the room and she looks up, tears trailing down her stricken face.

"Mama . . . ," she whispers, but not to me.

14

U p until this moment I'd not heard Kat say the word *mama*. I'd called myself Mam to her, and if I instructed her to give Mam something or do something for Mam, she would readily do it for me. I've felt like I was her mother and so I'd been expecting that when I did hear something akin to that word coming from her, she would be talking to me. But she'd been able to parse out the words in Candace's letter, and it was Candace she was referring to now.

Martin told me Candace had died at home in the middle of the night. I'd asked him early on if Kat had seen her mother or had been able to say good-bye, and he'd replied that the body had been taken away by the undertaker while Kat still slept. Martin had thought it unwise for a five-year-old to behold her mother's dead body. Kat had been told when she woke up that her mother had gone to heaven, and then she and Martin left Los Angeles for good five days later. I had imagined Kat's reaction to the news of her mother's passing half a dozen ways: tears, shock, rage, pitiful silence, and also just as I see her now with Candace's letter in her hand. She looks as though she's been put under a spell and will disappear if I don't run to her. I am at her side in seconds and I kneel so that her face and mine are close. I put my hands on her shoulders.

"Kat! Look at me, darling! Look at me!"

She so very slowly turns her gaze to me.

"All will be made right," I tell her. "I'm going to take care of you. I'm going to take care of *this*." I nod toward the letter. "I'm going to take you to her."

"Mama," she whispers again, and she's looking at me but not seeing me, and I feel hot tears sting at my eyes. Oh, how I want to scream at a world that allows someone like Martin Hocking to keep breathing its air.

"I'll take you to her," I say again, and my voice breaks into pieces as I say these words. I draw Kat even closer so that she can rest her head on my shoulder if she wants, but she is stiff and limp at the same time. I could kill Martin for what he's done to this child, for what he's done to all of us. I can hear Belinda sniffling behind me.

"She . . . she . . . I didn't . . . I didn't . . ." But Kat doesn't finish what she wants to say, and I shudder as I recall what Mrs. Lewis told me, that Kat thought it was somehow her fault that her mother had died. I can't help but wonder now if it was Martin who first put that thought in her head.

I hold Kat at arm's length so that I can look into her eyes. She stares back vacantly, as though she, too, is trying to make sense of what her father did to her.

"Listen, love," I tell her. "As soon as the sun is up tomorrow morning we'll be on our way. We're going to send Miss Belinda home and then you and I will go find your mama, all right? I'll take you to her, I promise."

Kat blinks at me.

"Do you understand, my sweet? I'll take you to her."

She grants me a barely perceptible nod.

"I need the letter back, Kat. I need the address."

Kat lets me take the letter out of her hand and I place it back in its envelope. I gather the other documents and the strongbox—which I will try to pry open later—and I hold them to my chest.

"Let's go have a bit of supper, shall we?" I say, as brightly as I can. "And we'll go to bed early so that tomorrow will come quicker."

We head to the kitchen and I heat leftover soup and warm some bread in the oven. No one has much of an appetite. While Belinda and Kat clean up the dishes, I return to the library to use the telephone, and I place the call to Las Palomas. The night nurse tells me that, yes, Mrs. Candace Hocking still resides as a patient there, and, yes, she's able to receive guests for short visits in the afternoons out on the patio. I don't tell her who I am and the woman does not ask. The full confirmation that Candace is still alive doesn't surprise me, and I'm glad there is no small part of me that hoped Candace had died. I don't want that crushing disappointment to fall on Kat. Not now. Not twice. When I am done with the call, I close the library door so that the room will look at first glance just as Martin left it.

Upstairs, Belinda helps me pack Kat's things for our trip and then we head to my bedroom, where I do the same. I choose a few dresses, my mother's old hat, my da's word book. When we are done, we take the travel cases downstairs and set them by the front door. I place the files and the strongbox and the pieces of gold ore—which I have dried off and put into a drawstring bag—onto the entry table by the front door.

When everything is ready for our dawn departure, we head back upstairs.

"We can all sleep in here, in my room," I say. I know Belinda will not want to sleep in Martin's bed, and I certainly do not. And I don't want Kat sleeping alone, either. I pull her mattress off her bed and drag it into my room and place it on the floor next to my bed. And then we change into our nightgowns—I loan Belinda a loose-fitting one of mine—and braid our hair for sleep as if it is just an ordinary day. I sing my grandmother's Gaelic lullaby to Kat until her breathing finally slackens to that of slumber. In the darkness after she is asleep, I hear Belinda begin to softly cry beside me. I have to remind myself that she lost her husband tonight, and, yes, the man she loves does not exist, but she thought he did, and the loss feels the same.

"Will you be all right?" I ask her.

"No. Yes. I don't know," she says in a tired, grieved voice. "I don't feel well. I don't . . ."

She lets her voice trail away.

"There was a time when I felt like my world was ending, too," I tell her after a pause. "But you've reasons to keep living, Belinda. And even if you were able to convince yourself you don't, the sun always comes up the next day. It does. And the next and the next. It just keeps coming up."

She says nothing, and minutes later she falls into an exhausted sleep.

As I lie there in the dark on the mattress where I let Martin touch me and delight me, where I cried out in pleasure at the union of our bodies, I am suddenly overcome with revulsion. I know it was not love between us at those times, but I've been blindly thinking it had been some kind comfort to us both, and I'm sick now that he was only pleasuring me to keep me compliant and content, like a stupid animal. I feel my gorge rising within me and I get myself out of bed as gently as I can so as not to wake Belinda or Kat, and I run into the water closet to heave into the commode what little supper I ate. When I'm done, I turn to run water in the bath as hot as I can stand it to cleanse myself of him, to wash any lingering fragments of his body from me. I cast off my nightgown and lower myself into the steaming water, nearly yelping at the heat, and I scrub myself until my skin is red and nearly raw.

I was stupid to think I could remain so naïve about Martin's comings and goings, and knowing so little about his job. I was stupid to think he grieved his wife when I never saw him shed a single tear over her, never saw him looking at Candace's photograph in Kat's room, never saw him staring off into the distance as if she might emerge from it. I have been stupid, duped by my own desire to have what I wanted. And now I am going to lose it all.

I let the tears fall then.

I don't care about this house and my fine clothes and the little sapphire on my finger and my new last name. I don't care that I'm not married to anyone, legally.

I'd give it all up to keep Kat. Yes, I've long wanted what my mother had, and what I had with her, back when she had it. I wanted a cozy, warm home. A gentle man to share my life with.

Children to raise and love. When I helped Mam care for the wee ones whose mothers worked at the docks, I used to imagine the tots were mine. I loved pretending they were mine.

I know now Kat is what I had wanted most of all.

But Kat is not my child. She never was. She is Candace's little girl.

Why in God's name did Martin bring me out here? He didn't need me. Why bring Kat to San Francisco in the first place when he could have just as easily left her on Candace's father's doorstep when her mother was whisked away to that Arizona sanatorium? Why complicate his appalling endeavors with the annoyance of caring for a child he does not love?

Why, why, why?

The water is cool when I finally pull myself out of it. I towel myself dry and put my nightgown back on. I head back to my bedroom, my head throbbing with unanswered questions. I crawl back into bed and beg for sleep to come. Many minutes later, it finally does.

I wake well before daybreak, and I know slumber will not return to me. My heart is aching as I dress in the dark. I know I am setting out to do a grand thing—reuniting a child with her mother is the grandest thing I could ever do—but my soul is still heavy. I am wondering as I work my buttons if perhaps Candace will let me stay and care for Kat while she convalesces. Surely children are not allowed to live at the sanatorium with their mothers. And yet I can easily see Candace's father sending me away after I return Kat to Candace because he can pay a reputable nanny to watch over his daughter's child. Why would he or Candace trust me to care for Kat? I'm a stranger to them. I am pondering these thoughts when I hear a noise downstairs, the sound of a key in a lock.

Icy dread immediately courses through my body. Only one other person besides myself has a key to the front door lock. Martin.

I hear the door creak open. I hear a footfall on the tiled entry. At the sound of the door's closing, Belinda sits up in bed.

"What was that?" she murmurs.

"It's the front door," I whisper. "Get up!"

I move to the bedroom door, which I left open as we slept. I hear Martin pause in the entryway and I know he is looking at the travel cases and the neat pile of folders and the little drawstring bag.

I step out onto the landing so that he will look up at me and take his eyes away from everything Belinda and Kat and I need to make our escape. When I get close to the stairs, I see that he has the little drawstring bag in his hand. He has opened it and in his palm is a dirty gold nugget. He looks up at me.

Martin flipped on the electrical light that hangs in the foyer because the morning sun has not yet begun to rise, and in that light, his beautiful eyes hold my gaze. I do not see hate or rage or dread in those eyes, because those responses require human emotions, and I no longer think Martin possesses them.

"What is all this?" he says in a tone void of inflection.

I summon courage from some unknown place inside me, because I feel nothing but cold fear. I walk to the edge of the staircase, putting a buffer of space between him and the bedroom behind me. "Kat and I are leaving."

He drops the nugget back into the drawstring bag, pulls it

closed, and places it atop his own valise, which is resting at his feet.

"Going where?" He takes a step toward the stairs. Toward me.

"Stay right there!"

But he takes another step and another and then he places his hand on the banister.

"Stop!" I shout.

"Or what?" he says, but he stops.

"I know," I reply. "I know what you've done. I know Candace is still alive. I'm taking Kat to her, and you're not stopping me."

He is on the first step.

"I have told the police everything!"

"I don't think you have," he says as he takes another step and another.

I look for anything to use as a weapon to defend myself against him if I must, but there's nothing on the landing except a little table and a vase for flowers made of delicate blown glass. I whisk my attention back to him. "The police have seen all the files, Martin," I say, trying to sound bold and confident, but I can hear the uncertainty in my voice. And yet I go on. "You'd be wise to go. Take the gold if you want. Just take it and go and leave us alone."

He takes another step. "I don't think the police have seen anything. I think you just found those documents."

"You're wrong!" I shout as he takes another step and another and another.

"I don't think I am," he says calmly. Martin is nearly at the top of the stairs when Belinda appears dressed and brandishing a letter opener that I had on my dressing table. Kat is right beside her. I shouldn't have shouted at Martin to stop. God, I shouldn't have.

I awakened Kat and she should not be seeing this or hearing this. But I can't think about that now. Between the three of us and the door to freedom is Martin.

The sight of Belinda, however, is enough to cause him to freeze in his ascent.

I expect him to be taken aback in shocked surprise at seeing Belinda standing there, but he merely cocks his head.

"I thought I might find you here," he says to Belinda. "I was in San Rafaela yesterday. Your dear friend Elliot told me you asked for a ride to the train station so that you could go to San Francisco. He said you were looking for me, that you found an address in my coat pocket and that you were worried about me."

It is as he is on the last stair, just inches from me, that I see his coat and shoes are mud spattered and his hair is mussed. He's been traveling by foot to get back here. I can't puzzle out why. Belinda raises the arm that holds the letter opener.

"You!" she says, her voice trembling at the same speed as her shaking hand. "How could you do what you did to me? What you did to your *daughter*? How could you tell your little girl her mother was dead?"

Martin stares at Belinda for a moment, as if her questions are too trivial to answer.

"It was easier," he says finally.

"Easier?" Belinda echoes desolately.

"It is easier to remove obstacles that complicate my endeavors than to tolerate them," he says calmly, evenly. But his eyes narrow a bit, and I can see that right now, in this very moment, Belinda and I are obstacles. I can see, so very clearly, that, yes, he did do something to cause Annabeth to be thrown from her horse, and, yes, he would easily find a way to dispatch Belinda if he no longer

147

needed her, and, yes, he would do the same to me. I mean nothing to him. Neither of us does. Would he harm Kat, though? His own flesh and blood? More than he already has?

As if reading my mind, he tells Kat to come to him.

"Stay where you are, Kat," I say.

"Kat," Martin says coolly, motioning downstairs with his head. "Go into the kitchen and shut the door."

I move to block her from his view. "Kat stays where she is. Go, Martin. Go now."

Martin's mesmerizing eyes turn dark with purpose. I don't think he will harm Kat. He needs her for some reason. It's why he didn't leave her in Los Angeles. But Kat's presence on the landing is what is keeping Belinda and me from harm in this moment. My mind races for a way out, but I am not quick enough to envision one.

In one swift movement, Martin takes the last step to the landing and lunges for Belinda and the letter opener in her hand.

The next moment is a cannonball of shouting, of screaming, and of hands and arms outstretched. We are, all of us, reaching out in all directions for different reasons, and I am stunned for a second by the overwhelming remembrance of a moment very much like this one, when arms had been extended, and hands and fingers had been stretched open like sea stars. I am suddenly back in Donaghadee and time seems to stand still for a second. I hear a whack-whack-whacking sound, but at the same time, I smell the tang of sea air and I feel the cold mist of evening fog.

And then in the next moment, I am back on the landing with Belinda and Kat beside me, and our arms and hands are back at our sides. The three of us are staring at Martin lying at the bottom of the staircase.

There is silence where there had been a rush of noise only seconds earlier. Martin is not moving. A knee is bent at an awkward angle, and blood smears a marble stair where his head smacked it on his tumble down.

Belinda is the first to speak. The letter opener is still tight in her hand.

"Is he . . . is he all right?" she whispers, dread thick in her voice.

For a second I cannot answer. Kat is standing next to me, looking down at her father's crumpled form.

"I'm sure he'll be fine," I say quickly, turning to face Belinda. "He just took a nasty spill because he wasn't being very nice. You take Kat into her room and I'll go down and help him on his way."

"*What?*" Belinda says, as if I am mad.

I fix my gaze on her. "I said, I'll go down and help him on his way. I'm sure he is fine. He just got knocked out when he fell. That's all."

Belinda stares at me, slowly comprehending what I am, without words, trying to tell her.

"Take Kat into her room and see that she is dressed," I say, injecting my voice with an ease I do not feel. "We're still leaving. Just like we said." Then I bend to Kat's height and turn her toward me. She stares at me, glassy-eyed. "It's his own fault that he fell. Do you understand? He fell down the stairs because he was angry and he wasn't watching what he was doing. But he's been mean to us and we don't want to see him right now. We want to go see your mama and we want him to leave. So I am going to help him on his way. All right?"

Kat just stares at me.

"All right, Kat?" I say, in the most authoritative tone I can muster that still rings gentle.

She nods slightly.

"Don't leave Kat's room until I call for you," I murmur to Belinda.

Belinda nods, pale and wide-eyed, and leads the child away. I take to the stairs.

When I reach Martin, his beautiful eyes are open and his breathing shallow. Blood has bloomed at his nose and mouth. I crouch to look at him.

Martin is moving his lips slightly, but no words come. I think perhaps his jaw is broken. Half of me hopes he is dying; the other half knows our situation will be that much more difficult if he is. And yet the question on my mind as I bend to look at him isn't what I shall do if he dies.

"Why in God's name did you marry me?" I whisper to him. "I have no money. I wasn't like Annabeth or Candace or Belinda. Why did you marry me?"

The moving lips produce no answer.

"Why did you take Kat from her mother? Why did you tell her Candace was dead? Why didn't you just leave the child when you left Los Angeles? You don't love her! You don't love anyone."

But he just stares back at me as though surely now that I know everything else, I know the answers to these questions. But I don't.

I glance over at our travel cases. The documents. The gold. I need a different plan. And I need to get Kat out of this house without her seeing Martin lying here like this.

I grab Martin under his arms and drag him across the foyer and into the kitchen to get him out of sight. He moans, but he can hardly open his mouth. I stop at the far end of the kitchen, and I deposit Martin in the corner by the butler's table. He groans softly. Dawn is just beginning to peel back the night. A pale moon peeks at me through the window glass above the table, its pearly light already fading. I stand with my hands on my hips to catch my breath and look down on Martin, who is gazing up at me in surprise. He can hardly believe he is not the one in charge of this moment, that I am. I can see the amazement in his eyes.

"This is not the way I had planned it," I say. "You weren't supposed to be here right now."

He says nothing.

"I need to take Kat to her mother," I continue. "And I need to get Belinda home. 'Tis pretty simple, the way I see it. If luck is on your side, you'll find a way out of this house after we leave. If it's on my side, you'll still be here when I get back. And if you should die before I return I will have kept my promise to Kat. I will have sent you on your way. Straight to hell."

"Don't," he whispers.

"What? Don't leave you? After all that you've done, you think you deserve my help? You killed Annabeth Bigelow, didn't you? I'm not afraid to leave you here like this, Martin. I'm not. Not after what you've done."

I kneel down to close the distance between us so that I can whisper something I didn't think I would ever say to him, not even in the beginning when I thought a time would come when Martin and I might at least be friends. "You don't even know why I'm not afraid to leave you like this, do you?"

"I . . . know . . . ," he murmurs.

Only the slimmest sliver of doubt pierces me. "No, you don't."

He tries to spit. Red foam forms at of the corner of his mouth. "I . . . know," he says in a gasping whisper. "You're running."

I stare down at him.

He returns the stare, daring me to prove he's mistaken. But I do not speak of my secrets. To anyone. Not even to myself.

Besides. I owe Martin nothing. Nothing. What I owe is an easy exit out of this house for Kat.

"You should have left when you had the chance." I stand and turn to the sink. I wet a cloth to wipe up the bloodstain at the bottom of the stairs, my mind spinning. I don't know what I will do with his body if he's dead when I get back. And if Martin is still alive when I return? I look down at him. He is staring up at me and struggling feebly to rise. If he's alive when I come back, perhaps he and I can strike a deal in exchange for my summoning a doctor.

But, no. I don't think Martin is the kind to strike a deal.

It is all too much to consider at once, and I whisper aloud what I told Belinda last night when she was asking too many questions. I've whispered it to myself before. I only need to get through this day. Just this one.

As I wring out the cloth I must push away the image of finding Martin's corpse when I return. A shudder runs through me as I attempt to shake off that repulsive thought. The trembling strangely intensifies, and it's as if the very house is quivering at what might await me when I come back to this house.

But then the floor beneath me begins to tremble, and then heave, and then a deafening roar like a gale over the ocean fills my ears. For one lone second I think the earth is going to open up beneath me and swallow Martin whole to save me the trouble of having to do it later, but in the next second I know it is not just for me the world is shaking.

It's an earthquake, and not just a gentle rocking akin to what I've experienced a few times before. This is like a beast, huge and loud and monstrous, awakening enraged from slumber. The house rumbles angrily and I suddenly remember Kat is on the second floor.

I pitch forward on unsteady feet and run sideways, careering into walls as I stagger away from Martin and out of the kitchen.

I call for Kat as I run, but my voice is lost in the deep groanings of the earth. And then as quick as it started, the roaring stops. The quaking ceases, but everything within me senses that the beast has not yawned and gone back to sleep. The air around me crackles with foreboding.

I see Kat and Belinda at the top of the stairs. Belinda has her arm across her abdomen and another protectively around Kat, whose eyes are wide in terror. Plaster has rained down on them like confetti.

"Come to me!" I shout as I reach for the banister to rush to meet them. Belinda and Kat start down the stairs as I start up. We are halfway to meeting each other when the roaring and pitching and violent twisting start up again, worse this time. The beast tosses us to the wall and I scream for Belinda and Kat to get on their bottoms and scoot as the landing above us splits and the staircase begins to sway.

I can hear dishes breaking, doorframes splitting, floorboards snapping, as Belinda, Kat, and I make our way, half crawling, down the buckling stairs. I throw open the front door and grab our travel cases and the files as Belinda and Kat stumble past me.

The earth is rocking like a ship on a furious sea as we stagger out into the amber light of daybreak. Chimneys from houses up and down the street are crumbling to the street as I pull Kat to me. Belinda cries out, and I turn to her, thinking she's been hit by falling bricks, but she's holding her stomach as blood and water gush to her feet.

The familiar moment returns to me.

I've been here before, too.

15

The world is still writhing as we stumble away from the house and into the street. I remember too late having been instructed by Martin from the very beginning to run to a sturdy inside doorframe in the event of an earthquake, and not to run outside and risk being crushed by toppling buildings. But we are already out on the rippling pavement and I am not going back inside that trembling house. I toss the travel cases down. Clutching the documents in one hand and Kat with the other, I stumble toward Belinda. We could die this way, I'm thinking, having escaped Martin only to be undone by a bigger monster.

When I felt my first temblor months ago and Martin told me it is the nature of the earth to quake from time to time, I looked up what he meant in a book at the library. I read that the world is a spinning ball on a giant dance floor and inside its core are giant slabs of stone that sometimes get too close to one another. When they touch, they must move away. They must. The ballet halts when the slabs collide and as they find their places again. In place of the usual spinning dance is the quaking and shuddering and rumbling, and then the quiet ballet resumes.

But this feels like the slabs have forgotten where they belong. They have forgotten the dance completely. The earth cannot keep itself together without the dance, and I wonder if it will hurt terribly to be swallowed up in the chaos of the danceless world folding in on itself. I bend over Kat to be a cushion for whatever awaits us.

And then, just as before, the quaking stops, and the world above seems to let out the breath it was holding while the world below thrashed. I am afraid to say anything and break the calm, but my mother-heart is still pounding like a hammer and I start saying to Kat, "'Tis all right, it's over. 'Tis all right, it's over," even before I am sure that it is. The sun, low in the sky, now seems hesitant to rise as it peeks at us through a filmy drape of dust. A couple of seconds tick by and the earth beneath us remains steady, like it always is, as if it has no memory of all that just happened.

Belinda cries out, her hands cradling her stomach. She is looking down in terror and disbelief at the rosy pink puddle at her feet.

I know why she sees blood and water.

"When is the baby supposed to come?" I say to her, but she cries out again in either fear or pain, perhaps both, and does not answer me.

"When is your time?" I shout.

She looks up at me with fearful eyes. "Not until next month!"

"We've got to get you to a doctor or hospital." I release Kat for just a moment to grab my travel case. I open it and stuff the documents inside on top of my clothes, Da's word book, and the strongbox. When we made our plans last night, I thought Belinda would be carrying one of the travel cases, but that will be impossible now. I need help. I need a carriage.

The street is now full of neighbors in their nightclothes staggering out of their houses and looking up and down the street. I look to Libby's sturdy brick house, grateful to see that it appears mostly undamaged. Her chimney has partially toppled, but that is the only change I can see.

"Wait here," I tell Belinda and Kat. "Just wait here and I shall be right back. I'm just going to see if Libby can help us. Stay with Belinda, Kat."

I leave them in the middle of the street and run to Libby's front door, pounding on it and trying the knob and only then remembering that Libby and her family are out of town. I dash back to Kat and Belinda, glancing up at my own house. I had forgotten just for a moment that Martin is inside it among the shattered dishes, splintered doorframes, and chunks of fallen ceiling plaster. There is no help for us inside that house, only trouble. I don't care a whit that now Martin must wait, unable to call out for help and surrounded by brokenness. In fact, it's rather fitting, since he is a man who excelled in crushing people.

"Let's start down the hill," I say as I pick up the two travel cases. "We'll find a carriage or something, Belinda. We'll go to the emergency hospital at city hall. It's new. It's nice, I've heard. Hold on to my skirt, Kat."

We start down the hill, passing neighbors in a daze. One is holding a bloodied handkerchief to his head. I ask another if his telephone is working and he says it isn't. No one's is.

We continue down the hill, stopping every few minutes as Belinda doubles over in pain. Every chimney on every house is a pile of bricks on the ground. Windows are broken, pavement is up-ended, and one house leans slightly to the left. As we near a cross street, three men are clawing at the crumbled front entrance of a two-story house. They are calling someone's name—Lila, I think. A little dog with plaster clinging to its fur is barking at the men.

At California Street, where the cable car would stop if the cable car was running, a milkman is trying to calm his spooked horse. Broken milk bottles cover the cart bed, and creamy milk is dripping through the slats onto the twisted rails below. An old man, covered in dust, zips by on a bicycle with a squawking parrot on his shoulder. The horse nickers and starts to rear and the milkman pulls on the reins and says, "Whoa, there, Ginger!"

I approach him. "Please, sir. We need help. My friend is having her baby. Could you take us in your wagon to Central Emergency Hospital? Please?"

At first I think the milkman will refuse. He gapes at Belinda as if to say, *Why on earth would you be having a baby now when the world has just turned itself upside down?* But then his countenance softens and I think perhaps he is a father or a grandfather and knows there is no stopping a baby from coming when it starts to come.

He tells Kat and me to climb into the wagon and sit where his bottles would be if they hadn't all toppled over and been smashed, and that Belinda can ride on the seat up front with him. Belinda looks at me with worried eyes as she grimaces through her pain.

"We'll be right behind you, Belinda. Right behind you. We're not leaving you. Up you go."

The milkman and I help Belinda onto the passenger side of the seat, and then Kat and I find milk-spotted seats in the wagon on wooden shelves where the metal milk crates usually sit. My skirt is made immediately damp. Kat seems unaware of the spilled milk soaking into her dress.

The milkman eases his still-nervous horse away from the twisted rails beneath the wagon wheels and then starts south down Larkin Street, making his way around crumbled bricks and rubble that the quake has tossed into the street. More people are out now. Some are pushing baby prams full of hastily tossed belongings; some are pulling toy wagons loaded with travel bags. All are heading east, toward the ferries I assume, and away from houses they are afraid to stay inside or simply can't. Others, dressed in nice clothes, and whose sturdy mansions surely survived the quake, are standing about, talking to one another, worried looks on their faces.

As the milkman slows to navigate wreckage in the street, I hear one woman dressed in finery ask another if she thinks it is safe to leave their homes unoccupied while they await utilities to be restored, because surely there will be looters. When disaster strikes there are always looters. The other says she doesn't know but she is afraid to go back inside her house. Besides, her maid can't even so much as make her a cup of tea. Her entire set of Royal Doulton is in pieces on the floor, and on top of that, the toilet isn't working. The first woman says she's returning to her house anyway.

We move past them and I hear the clang of a fire brigade as it bursts out of its shed. A man on the street yells that the wharf is on fire, and someone else answers that Market Street is on fire, too, as is a building south of Mission. Broken gas lines are sparking and feeding hungry flames. I look to the east, toward the bay, and it's hard to see past the tallest buildings, a great many of which are still standing. But then I see a plume of slate-colored smoke, and then another farther to the south. The smoke is different from the dust: The dust hovers and then eventually falls; the smoke reaches for the sky like it means to own it. We pass a four-storied building just as it starts to cave in on itself, and the milkman urges Ginger away.

"My family is inside!" a woman yells, and I have to look away as several people rush to pull her back from the trembling building. Seconds later, the structure falls behind us and the horse spooks. Kat and I are tossed to the floor of the wagon as the animal lurches forward in fright. Several tense seconds pass before the milkman again regains control of the horse.

Kat and I are now thoroughly covered in milk and dust and dirt.

"Are you all right, love?" I pull Kat to me and brush broken glass off the skirt of her dress. She doesn't answer, not even to nod yes or no. "We'll be fine, we'll be fine," I coo to her as the wagon returns to a steadier pace. She leans into me, and that movement is almost like an answer to my question, but I don't know which it is. Yes, she is all right, or no, she is not.

The damage from the earthquake is worse the farther south we head. I think I see St. Mary's Cathedral off to my right, but it looks different, smaller, as if emptied of its sacredness. Some buildings have collapsed around it; some are leaning. There are all manner of people in the streets and on the littered walkways, dazed or crying or bloodied. Some are pulling at bricks and planks piled in heaps to rescue those trapped inside partially fallen buildings. I see a woman and man sitting on the crumbled steps of an apartment building with a dead child in the father's arms. I look away from them and pull Kat close to me so that she will see only the front of my dirtied shirtwaist.

And then the massive city hall, that palatial block-long structure where I married Martin, comes into view and it is as though I am looking at drawings in one of Kat's history books of the ruins of the Roman Empire. All those stately columns, massive and thick, are tumbled about like sticks. The dome still stands but has been stripped of its stone. It is skeletal, nearly obscene in its nakedness. Dust floats all around, like flurries of snow. I would not have thought a building of such size and elegance could be brought down by anything.

The Larkin Street entrance to the Central Emergency Hospital, a place I've had no occasion to visit but which I know is located in the basement of city hall, is partially obstructed by piles of stone and rubble. There is activity at the cave-like opening as nurses and people in plain clothes, passersby perhaps, pull out patients on gurneys and stretchers. Some are walking out on the arm of an orderly. Other people are arriving to the hospital, just like us, and are being told the destroyed hospital is being evacuated.

The milkman stops the cart and turns to me. "There isn't no hospital no more!" he says.

Belinda grimaces beside him, her eyes screwed shut.

"Please just take us to wherever they are taking all the other patients." I point to the line of evacuated and incoming injured in the street.

"I've done my part," the milkman says. "I need to see about my own family. I've done my part!"

The sight of all those wounded people has him panicked, and I can see there will be no convincing him. I help Kat out of the wagon and grab hold of the travel cases. The milkman has the decency to help Belinda out of the passenger seat but is gone before I've asked her if she can walk, if she can follow the other patients who are walking on unsteady feet away from the great ruin of city hall. She nods.

I bend to Kat. "We need to help Belinda now, love. She needs us. The baby needs us. Can you carry your travel case, sweets? So that I can help Belinda walk? You hold on to my skirt with one hand and your travel case with the other, all right?"

Kat does not answer me, but she takes the handle of the case when I hand it to her, and when I guide her hand to my skirt, she grabs hold. I pick up my case with one hand and put my other arm around Belinda. We move toward the retreating hospital evacuees. When I am close enough to a nurse who is helping an elderly man in a hospital gown pick his way across the rubble, I ask where the patients are headed.

She looks back at me, and then at Belinda, and she shakes her head in pity.

"Mechanics' Pavilion. Just across the street there."

She points across the wide boulevard to the immense barnlike structure where just the night before costumed skaters competed for a prize. It appears to be undamaged. We took Kat to the pavilion on her birthday the previous summer to see the circus. I'd never seen so many people all in one place; eleven thousand seats ring the exhibition floor. The pavilion is a performance arena, not a hospital. And now, apparently, Belinda will deliver her child inside it.

We make our way across the street with the last of the evacuated patients and all the new incoming wounded.

The floor of the pavilion is being strewn with mattresses that have been brought in from the hospital and nearby hotels. A surgery is taking shape near the entrance with operating tables and trays full of metal instruments, sharp and glaring. Nurses at the door are assessing by sight those of us coming inside.

Belinda is not bleeding from open wounds, nor cradling a broken arm, nor being pulled on a makeshift stretcher with maimed legs. She is a victim not of the earthquake, just of terrifically bad timing.

"Her baby is coming," I tell the nurse who asks where she is injured.

"Is your home still standing? Can you not return and let her have the baby there?" the nurse says, in a frazzled, nearly scolding voice.

"Her baby is coming," I say again. "A month early. And, no, we cannot return home. This woman doesn't even live here in San Francisco."

"All right, all right. I'll see if we've a nurse who can be spared to help her," she says, her tone softening. She calls over her shoulder for an orderly. "Take this woman to where we put the patients from the Female Ward."

The orderly, a thin man whose uniform is spattered with bits of dried blood and dirt, nods and motions for us to follow him.

Belinda grabs me as a labor pain seizes her. "It hurts!" she wails.

"I know," I tell her. I do know how it hurts. I sweep the remembrance away. That was from another life, another time.

We are led past teams of people placing more mattresses on the floor and doctors treating the injured as they get to them in turn. The orderly shows us to a collection of mattresses on the arena floor grouped like a little dormitory. Four on one side and four on the other. Women of various ages, attired in hospital gowns and lying on these beds, watch us arrive. There are no sheets on the mattress Belinda is given. No pillow. No privacy curtain.

I ease Belinda, who is half–doubled over, down onto the makeshift bed. "I'll find some sheets and a blanket. Somewhere."

"Is it her time?" one of the women behind us asks. I turn to her. She is Mam's age but pale and thin.

"Yes."

"Is it terrible out there?" a second woman says. She has a large bandage over one eye. "No one has time to tell us anything. All we saw was what happened to city hall."

"Yes," I say as I loosen the buttons on Belinda's maternity shirtwaist. "'Tis terrible."

"Do you know if Beale Street is all right?" says a woman whose arm is in a sling.

"What about King Street?" says another.

"I don't know. I'm sorry. I don't know those streets."

"South of Mission. How are things south of Mission?" says the woman who looks to be Mam's age.

"I came down Larkin from Polk. It got worse the farther south we came." And then I add because I feel I should, "There are some fires now."

The women are silent as they consider the state of things.

"Here," the woman with the eye bandage says as she extends a bed pillow. "I don't need two."

"And you can have my top sheet," says a second woman.

"And my blanket," says a third. "I'm plenty warm without it."

In less than a minute I have Belinda in bed, and while she is writhing in pain, at least she is in the company of women who have given what help they could.

"I don't want to die," Belinda says to me through clenched teeth. "I don't want to die."

"You shall not be dying today, Belinda," I tell her, as I confidently as I can. "When we see the baby's head, I'll grab the first nurse I see and I'll drag her over here, I swear to you."

"It hurts!"

"I know, I know it does."

I look down at Kat, who is sitting on the floor by the bed, staring at Belinda.

I scoot to sit close to her. "Bringing a baby into the world is hard work, love, but 'tis the way we all come. I came this way, so did you, so did Belinda. So did everybody in the pavilion. All right?"

She nods ever so slightly.

But I know the pains will get worse. And I wish I could take Kat away somewhere where she doesn't have to see how incredibly hard it is to become a mother.

I encourage her to lie at the foot of Belinda's mattress and rest, and she lies down for me, but her eyes do not close. I wonder what she is thinking. Is she thinking about her own mother, who is not dead after all? About her father, who, last she saw, lay in heap at the bottom of the stairs? About the baby she will be a sister to?

I can't tell.

I can't tell if she is thinking at all.

The rush of activity around us continues for the next hour. More mattresses are brought, and more wounded. And now the dead are being brought in, too. The pavilion has been turned into a morgue as well as a hospital. Whenever the doors are opened, a faint odor of smoke wafts inside.

At a little after eight in the morning, the earth starts to tremble again and everyone inside the pavilion gasps. Women scream; some men, too. Belinda gapes at me in utter dismay. Dread for her, for all of us, shoots through me like an arrow. Many who can get up off their mattresses rise and rush for the doors, but policemen stationed there won't let them leave. In the end it doesn't matter. The trembling doesn't intensify and doesn't last, and someone near our collection of mattresses says it was just an aftershock.

As we settle back down into our places, more and more wounded arrive—young children in their mothers' arms, burned and bleeding, and men and women being carried in with broken bones protruding through their flesh. The sounds of misery are all around us and I can't keep Kat from hearing them. I sing to her to attempt to drown them out. But there is no shushing the wails and cries and shouts.

Another hour passes and Belinda starts to make her way into the last stage of childbearing. Perhaps because she is only eight months along, or perhaps because there was blood in her water, everything seems to be moving along a little faster. I look for a nurse or doctor to help her, but I cannot find one before Belinda is crying out that the baby is coming.

All but one of the women in our little group rise off their mattresses and drape their blankets from shoulder to shoulder to offer Belinda the only privacy available to her. I situate Kat in the one-armed embrace of the lady whose other arm is in a sling on the outside of this curtain of women. I tell Kat that as soon as the baby arrives, I will show her the wee thing and won't that be a lovely surprise.

I know enough about the birth process to know what Belinda

needs to do—keep breathing in and out, and bear down with the urge to push, not against it.

At the robust sound of Belinda bringing the child out of the safe confines of her body and into this complicated world, a nurse comes scurrying over with scissors and towels, and I move aside. With deft hands, the nurse massages the tiny infant's chest and cleans out the mouth. She turns the baby upside down to clear the lungs and I see that the little fairy child is a girl. Tiny and perfect. The babe looks nothing like Martin.

"Is she all right?" Belinda gasps as we wait to hear the child's first cry.

And then it comes, sweet and wonderful.

"She's little, but she's a fighter," the nurse says, as she clamps the cord and cuts it. "Not more than five pounds, I'd say. But she's a beauty. The only pretty thing I've seen today."

The nurse wraps the child in one of the towels and hands her to me so that I can show Belinda. And then while the nurse attends Belinda down below, I place the babe in Belinda's arms and motion for Kat to come to us, wanting her to look only at the baby and not at what the nurse is doing. I needn't have worried that Kat's eyes would be drawn to the afterbirth; she only has eyes for her little sister.

"Isn't she a sweet, wee thing?" I say to Kat as I pull her to me.

Kat nods and reaches out to touch one of the infant's tiny, perfect fingers.

The three of us continue to stare at the child as the nurse says she will be back later to check on Belinda. The women who held the blankets move back to their beds and I thank them.

"Is he dead?" Belinda whispers a moment later as she stares down at her child. "Are we going to jail?"

"No and no," I whisper in return. "Everything is going to be fine. You don't need to worry. Don't speak of it now, Belinda."

She says nothing more. An orderly brings us sandwiches and fruit donated by nearby restaurants whose kitchens survived the quake. Belinda is quiet and has no appetite, but I admonish her to eat for the child's sake and she manages to consume half a sandwich. After we eat, I take Kat to a changing area—where in recent days pugilists and acrobats and skaters got ready for their exhibitions—so that we can change out of our soured-milk-smelling dresses and into fresh clothes. From her own case, Kat pulls out the doll who is wearing the frock I made from her old dress. She looks up at me.

"For baby?" Her barely audible words are the first I have heard from her since the night before.

I am about to say her little sister is too young yet for dolls, when I realize she is referring to the dress. She wants to give the new baby, who has nothing to wear, the doll dress made from her own clothes.

Tears prick my eyes and I nod. "That would be lovely."

In our fresh clothes, we return to Belinda and Kat presents her with the tiny dress.

I explain where the material for it came from. Belinda looks down expressionless at the toweled bundle that is her child.

"Here," I say, unwrapping the infant in her arms. "I'll help you." The babe's limbs are tiny and pink, her mouth a perfect rosebud. One of the women in our little group hands me a large white handkerchief.

"It's my husband's. I brought it with me from home. And it's clean, I assure you. You'll need something for a diaper. And the baby's so tiny, this will no doubt do."

I thank her, take the handkerchief, and fold it over and over again into a small triangle. Then I wrap it around the infant's little bottom, tying a loose knot on her small waist. I ease the doll's dress onto her tiny form. She looks like a flower.

"Do you have a name picked out?" I ask.

Belinda just shakes her head. Her listlessness worries me. Maddens me. I keep forgetting she loved her husband. She loved the man I didn't love. I keep forgetting that the husband she loved is gone, never to return, and it's as though he was snatched up in the jaws of a leviathan, here one second and gone the next. A horrifying, violent death.

"Let's think on some names, shall we?" I say. And I begin to list names for girls, starting with good Irish names like Aileen and Fiona and Maeve.

"How about Rosalie?" says the woman with the bandage on her eye.

"Or Helen?" says the woman with her arm in a sling.

"If I'd had a girl I would've named her Margaret," says another. "But I only ever had boys. Six of them."

The women in our set of mattresses continue to suggest names, but Belinda seems not to be interested in any of them.

"There's all those names in the Bible," the woman who looks like Mam says. "Ruth and Esther and Rachel and Sarah."

"Sarah," Kat says. So quietly, but she says it.

"You like the name Sarah?" I ask her, and she nods.

I turn to Belinda. "How about Sarah for now, hmm? You need to call her something, Belinda. She's a beautiful child and she deserves a name." I lean in close. "None of what happened the last few hours is her fault, you know."

Belinda blinks languidly.

"Sarah means 'princess,'" the woman who looks like Mam says.

"There you go. It's a lovely name, isn't it, Belinda?"

Belinda nods slightly.

As if she had been listening, the child opens her perfect mouth and a mewl comes out.

"I think our little princess is hungry," I say.

"I don't know what to do," Belinda says, emotionless.

"I do," says the woman who birthed six boys. She climbs over to Belinda's mattress and we all watch in awe as, with this woman's help, the babe takes to Belinda's breast. For the next few minutes, as injured and dead are brought in and shouts rise for morphine and water, we watch. Belinda seems to soften as she looks down on her nursing infant. They are attached again, mother and child. The look of despair starts to slough off, and in its place is raw wonder. It is not joy yet, but neither is it anguish.

When the child is sated and sleeping, Belinda turns to Kat. "Do you want to hold her?"

Kat nods and I help her sit down on the mattress next to Belinda and position the sleeping infant in her arms.

Belinda is drifting off to sleep as I watch Kat hold her sister. She begins to softly sing to the baby the Gaelic lullaby my grandmother sang to me. The one I sing to her.

The moment is as beautifully perfect as a moment can be. I want it to last forever. And for five or ten blessed minutes it seems like it just might.

But then a shout rings out across the sea of mattresses, across the masses of dead and living.

The roof of the pavilion is on fire.

16

L adies, we're evacuating."

The nurse who helped Belinda earlier has returned, and with her are a policeman and three Sisters of Charity in starched black habits streaked with dust. The nurse is speaking to us in a falsely calm voice. I can see that she is concerned with the enormous task of transporting so many people out of harm's way. There must be four or five hundred injured in the pavilion now. I help Belinda to her feet while the nurse and the others assist the other women in our little group of mattresses. Belinda seems unable to comprehend what is happening. Her face is void of expression, but her eyes tell me she can't believe that again we are fleeing danger. She is also weak from childbearing and not having eaten enough, and she begins to collapse seconds after she stands. One of the sisters reaches for Belinda's baby in Kat's arms and Belinda shouts for me to take her. The sister obliges and hands me the child. A policeman sweeps Belinda up into his arms and begins to head to the exit. With the sleeping baby and Kat to attend to, I make the quick decision to abandon my travel case. After giving Kat the baby to hold for a moment longer, I shove the strongbox, the papers, and Da's word book into Kat's case. I hoist it in one hand and cradle the baby in the crook of my other arm.

"Hold my skirt, Kat," I tell her. "Don't let go!"

Kat looks up at me with fear-filled eyes but obeys. We race to follow the policeman who is carrying Belinda.

We emerge onto the street and into an orange-gold world of smoke and ash. Above us, hundreds of firefly cinders from an approaching blaze we can't yet see are alighting on the roof of the pavilion, which is already heartily aflame in several places. I can't see the other fires—the air all around is a smoldering blanket obscuring everything but what is right in front of me—but I can smell them, feel them, taste them, hear them. Ashes swirl about the ruin of the city hall across the street like snow.

Automobiles and wagons and trucks, every kind of vehicle that can be pressed into service, has been. These are now being loaded with not just the wounded but the bodies of the dead from the pavilion. We are told we will be taking refuge at Golden Gate Park, two miles away. Belinda is placed in a laundry delivery truck along with several other female patients in various stages of ability and health. When Kat and I and the baby reach the back of the truck, we are told we will have to find our own way to the park—there is only room for the wounded and sick in the commandeered vehicles.

"Don't leave me!" Belinda cries out as I hand the baby to a man helping the women get situated inside the truck. The man hands the infant to Belinda as she begs again for me not to leave her.

"We'll find you at the park, I promise!" I call to her. The door is shut on Belinda and my last view of her is her shouting that she wants out of the truck.

Another man raps on the vehicle to alert the driver to get moving.

I can't tell which direction is west; the sun is masked by smoke. I can only follow the trucks and autos and carriages, and the masses of people doing the same. No one is heading east to the ferries now. I hear someone ask why the fire brigades are not putting the fires out and someone else says they have been trying all morning to put them out but the earthquake broke all the water mains belowground. The firemen can access no water. It is nearly laughable that as I hear these words, we are marching west on a peninsula that is surrounded on three sides by the sea. There is water in every direction but one, but no way of getting it to the streets. Those who would put the fires out can do little more than watch them take what they want.

And then I hear a boom off in the distance, and then another. The fire has gotten hold of something explosive, I am thinking, but a man in a military uniform several yards away says the army is dynamiting buildings here and there to create firebreaks and hopefully starve the fire of its food.

I look to the direction that I believe is north and I think of Martin slumped against a kitchen wall. The fires are south and west of my neighborhood. Martin is not in danger, not now at least. I consider for just a moment finding a policeman and alerting him that there is a wounded man inside my house near Russian Hill. But there is no policeman in sight who is not frantically attending to more immediate concerns, and I simply can't have

Martin telling someone how he came to be lying at the bottom of the stairs and then abandoned, injured, in his kitchen, especially if the person he tells is a policeman.

And yet perhaps he would say it was just the earthquake that caused his fall, and then after a doctor patched him up he'd come looking for me. For all of us.

No. I can't think about any of that. My concern right now is for Kat's safety and only that. I only need to get through today. Just today. I look away from the direction of the neighborhoods near Russian Hill and urge Kat to quicken her steps if she can.

She and I have taken long walks before. I know she can manage a two-mile walk, but Kat tires after the first mile. It is no ordinary stroll we are on; everything about it is wrong. A man fleeing with his own family of much older children offers to carry her, and I don't even ask Kat if it is all right. I just let him scoop her up and we continue our trek away from the fires and toward the sand hills surrounding the park.

I've been to Golden Gate Park several times. It is beautiful and immense, bigger than Central Park in New York. But as its eastern entrance comes into view, the park's serene beauty is at once eclipsed by its new purpose as instant refugee camp. And it did not escape damage from the quake, either.

The pillars of the stone gate have toppled from their foundations as if they were made of piecrust. As we move farther onto the grounds, I see that the stately canteen near the children's playground is roofless and its walls have caved in.

And there are so many people. Those dressed in the finest of clothes are wandering onto the same grass as the poorest of souls. The emergency hospital at the pavilion isn't the only entity using the park as a haven from the hell east of us. Someone asks a uniformed man why we aren't being sent to the military compound at the Presidio and he is told that the Presidio is already filling up with other evacuees and injured who are fleeing the fires. We are told to keep moving toward the bowling greens beyond the carousel and children's playground. On our way here, I had imagined we might be taking shelter in the Conservatory of Flowers, provided it is still standing, and it is. But I look to the beautiful greenhouse and I see that no one is opening its doors. And there are too many of us anyway. The man who carried Kat lowers her to the ground as we arrive at the vast lawns.

There is no shelter of any kind. Nothing but trees and grass and flowers. People who arrived before us are sitting or lying on the grass while army soldiers erect a few tents. Kat and I walk among the people on the green, looking for Belinda and the baby.

But I can't find her.

I look down at Kat, whom I've never seen cry before, and two tears are sliding down her cheeks. I drop her travel case to the ground and kneel down.

"We will find Belinda and the baby. They are here. Somewhere they are here. We will find them. All right?"

Several seconds tick by before she nods.

It has been many hours since we've eaten or had anything to drink, so I lead us to a long table of refreshments that have been set up by the military. Soldiers have appropriated food and water from restaurants and grocery stores undamaged by the quake. We wait for a long while in a queue of hungry people, watched over by armed guards who tell us that order will be strictly maintained. There is to be no pushing or shoving or angry words. But everyone is too tired and numb to demand that the queue move faster. When we finally have something to eat, I take Kat to an empty spot on the grass and we eat hard-boiled eggs, dry biscuits, and an apple each. I don't have my lapel watch and I've no concept of what time it is. I just know that when we are done eating, Kat and I both fall asleep on the one blanket a Red Cross nurse gave us.

When I awake sometime later, there are more refugees all around us, and only a few more tents. Most people are sitting or lying on the grass, just like Kat and me, including many of the wounded. I want to continue the search for Belinda and the baby, but Kat is still asleep beside me.

As I wait for her to awaken I listen for snatches of news about the fires from newcomers arriving in the park with bags and baby prams and garden carts loaded with whatever they could grab out of their houses. I learn that the separate fires are joining each other now and have already devoured the downtown blocks closest to the ferry building. Firemen have tried to pump in water from the bay but the blaze has already moved inland a mile. I want so very much to find Belinda and find a carriage going south so I can get her home to San Rafaela and then Kat and I can be on our way to Arizona, but everyone is saying the roads south of downtown are all on fire or that flames block the way to the southern roads.

When at last Kat awakes, I tell her we shall resume our search for Belinda and the baby. I try to make light of our task, calling it a treasure hunt of sorts, but there is no fooling Kat. Searching for Belinda and the baby requires us to look at everyone, and some of the people arriving at the park are hurt or burned or have been separated from loved ones of their own. There is no panic as we make our way through the throngs of people, but the mood is somber.

I return to the entrance to see if there is anyone in charge there who can tell me where the patients from the Mechanics' Pavilion are. I don't find such a person, but I do see a billboard that is at least twenty feet high and that hours earlier had been advertising a brand of beer. It has now been peppered as far as an arm can reach with slips of paper, business cards, and notices asking for information on people or sharing information.

I stop to read the messages. One notice says, *Sylvia and Malcolm Berger are safe. Call for them at Number 120, 28th Ave.* Another reads, *Have you seen our daughter, Eliza Jane Cole? She is eight years old. Dark brown hair, freckles. Red dress. Leave message please!* There are hundreds of little notices on the board, some just tiny scraps of newsprint. The largest sign reads, *Death notices can be left here.*

I set down the travel case, reach inside, and pull out the documents from Martin's desk, wondering which one I can sacrifice a portion of to leave a note. And then I see Da's word book lying atop the strongbox and Kat's clothes. I need the documents. Until I know what has become of Martin, I need them. I take out Da's book and flip to the page where he stopped a few days before his fall with the word *intrepid.* I hesitate and then tear off the bottom half of the opposite page, which he would have filled had he lived longer. I ask an older woman writing a note of her own if I might borrow her pencil when she is finished.

I write, *Belinda Bigelow: Kat and I are here on the bowling green. We are looking for you. Leave a note if you can.* I tack my message at what should be eye level for Belinda, and then Kat and I head to the food tent to stand for an hour to get bread, cheese, bologna, and canned milk. Then we make our way back to the grass to find a new spot to rest, as our original patch has long since been taken by other refugees. I pull Kat to me as we sit down and tell her we will try again tomorrow. Tomorrow we will find Belinda and the baby.

When I say the word *tomorrow*, I realize we are staying the night in this park, on the grass under the stars, with thousands of other people who likewise have nowhere else to sleep tonight. Some people have made makeshift tents out of blankets and rugs, but Kat and I have only the one blanket between us, and I'm glad that as the sun sets the night is not cool, nor is it particularly dark, as the horizon to the east is glowing orange like daybreak.

As we settle in for the night and just as the last light of day leaves us, National Guardsmen walk through the park to announce that a curfew has been set in the park and in the city. No one is to be out and about after sundown or before sunup. No one is allowed to return to areas where the fires have raged nor where the fires are headed. The mayor has declared that any looters will be shot on sight. No candles of any kind are allowed anywhere and no cooking fires inside any structure, as that very thing was the cause of one of the fires now burning out of control. No liquor is to be sold to anyone for any reason. We are also told army tents will arrive early tomorrow morning, but that tonight we must make do with whatever we can. We are not to worry about the fires approaching the park while we sleep. The army has positioned troops outside the park to watch for them.

The guardsmen move on to repeat their announcements over and over to the hundreds upon hundreds of us spread out on the park's lawns.

The last of the sun's warmth is leaving as they walk away. As I wrap Kat in our one blanket and pull her close to me, a Chinese woman who is bedding down next to us with her husband and two sons offers me a quilt. She says something in her language and points to Kat and then to me. I think she is telling me she doesn't want me to be without a blanket, either. I look over at her family and I see that the quilt is extra. I won't be depriving her of warmth. I don't know how to thank her. But she smiles at me as I take the blanket.

Minutes later the ground begins to rumble and tremble, and everyone in the park seems to hold their breath for a moment. But the quaking is only another aftershock that lasts just seconds.

"Are you warm enough, love?" I say to Kat, whispering it into her hair when the park is calm again. I have made the travel case my pillow. Kat is resting her head on my bosom.

She doesn't answer me.

"You were a very brave girl today." And she was. In so many ways.

We are quiet for a few minutes.

"What has happened today hasn't changed anything, love," I say. "I'm still taking you to your mama. It just might take us a few days or so. But I will. I promise. We'll find Belinda and get her and the baby home, and then I'll take you to her. You have my word. All right?"

She grants me the slightest nod against my chest.

Several more seconds pass and then she slowly raises her head, not to look at me but to look outward, toward the sickly orange sky to the east.

"Father?" she whispers tentatively.

My heart knocks against my ribs like a little bird hitting window glass. "He's not here, love," I say calmly, and then I wait to see if it is enough of an answer. I pray that it is.

But it is not.

"Where is he?"

I kiss her head and hug her tight as I eye the sky, forcing any shred of doubt or apprehension out of my voice. I want it to sound as true as true can sound. Because I could very well be telling her the absolute truth.

"I sent him on his way."

17

Our sleep is afforded to us in snatches and spurts as all through the night those fleeing the fires continue to pour into the park. With them comes the latest news. Half of the very heart of the city is gone. Union Square, the Hotel St. Francis, all the little shops I had frequented in that part of downtown—all reduced to ash or to mere skeletons of their former selves. The fires are moving ever closer to Polk Street and the house.

As the morning sun struggles to break through the strange canopy of fog and smoke, Kat and I use makeshift outhouses the army erected overnight, and then we stand in a queue for more than an hour for breakfast. Relief supplies have arrived by ship on the ocean side of the peninsula, and more are expected as word of our unfolding disaster has been sent across working telegraph wires south of San Francisco. The promised army tents arrived during the night, too, and now the troops are attempting to create orderly rows of canvas shelters and assigning them to people via another long and winding queue.

After we eat, I check the bulletin board for any news from Belinda and see nothing, not even my own note. After a bit of searching I see that someone has taken my scrap of paper, turned it over, and written their own desperate message on the back: *Missing! Four-year-old twins! Boy and girl. Worried parents are waiting for them at the canteen. Please help!*

I leave it as is and tear another bit from Da's word book. Again, I borrow a pencil and write a message I can only hope Belinda will see.

We stand in a queue for a tent, but because there are only two of us, Kat and I are quartered with a pair of elderly sisters who are none too happy to share a shelter with strangers. I can tell by their clothing that they have money, or at least they did have money. They are wearing silks and ermine and jewels and an air of importance. The older of the two tells the army sergeant in charge of the tent assignments that she and her sister insist on having their own tent, but the man doesn't even look up at her when he tells her they won't be getting one. The two of them turn up their noses at Kat and me as we step in and stow our few belongings inside. I don't care. At least with a place to put the travel case— which I'm sure the two sisters will have no interest in—Kat and I can look for Belinda without my having to carry it.

But our search for Belinda is again fruitless, even after finding the nurse who delivered Belinda's baby in one of the tents for the injured. She doesn't know where Belinda ended up. Some of the patients were rerouted as we fled the pavilion. I tell the nurse I will keep checking in with her, and that if she learns where Belinda is to please get word to me.

After spending the better part of the afternoon looking for Belinda, we start to walk back to the tent to rest before standing in the queue for supper. The air is heavily tinged with smoke and ash, and I begin to hear in the distance explosion after explosion after explosion. Kat startles with each one and buries her face in my skirt. I hear someone say that the army is blowing up whole blocks of buildings that survived the earthquake with nary any damage at all so that when the fires reach them—and they will reach them—there will be nothing but low-lying rubble to consume.

I hear chatter that the fires are headed toward the mansions on Nob Hill, and I know that means they are headed toward my neighborhood, too, and the house I was living in with my fraud of a husband inside it.

As we make our way back to the tent, it occurs to me that the men setting the charges will surely check the houses they are dynamiting to make sure the occupants have evacuated. If my house has been targeted to be dynamited, soldiers will step inside it to check. They will find Martin. Will he still be alive? Will he say anything? Or will he suppose that I have too much incriminating evidence against him? If he's found, will he be brought here to the park to have his injuries treated? In my search for Belinda, will I find Martin instead?

In the tent as we rest I can't shake the thought of chancing upon him among the rows of wounded.

Kat has said nothing since asking about her father the evening before. She wears a vacant look now that alarms me. It is as if she's evaporating, disappearing into the ashes and smoke. I don't want to take Kat to her mother, and yet I do. I sense an urgency to get her to Candace.

When darkness has fully fallen, and we curl up onto the army bedroll we were given, I pull her close to me and sing to her the Gaelic lullaby she loves. One of the old biddies hisses at me to stop making such a racket. But I pay that woman no mind. I sing until Kat is breathing slow and easy in my arms.

Friday morning dawns cloaked in the same throat-burning smoke as the day before. I can tell without even listening to the talk between soldiers and police presiding over the park that the fires have not abated. The widest boulevard in the city, Van Ness, which is lined up and down with stately homes, has been dynamited on its east side. And not just one block or two or even three, but twenty-two blocks—more than a mile of structures have been sacrificed to stop the inferno. My own street is only one block over from Van Ness, one block east, which means the fire will sweep across it before it reaches this new fire break. Perhaps it already has. Martin is either still inside the house or he isn't.

Kat seems to hover between sleep and wakefulness this morning. She doesn't stir when I try to coax her into getting up for breakfast, even though her eyes are open. I tell her if she doesn't come with me that I'll have to get our breakfast for us, and I'm so certain that she won't want to be alone in the tent—the two sisters have gone in search of coffee—that she will get to her feet. But she just lies there and says nothing, does nothing. I hate to leave her like this, but she needs to eat, so I admonish her to stay in the tent and not to leave for any reason and assure her that I'll be right back.

The talk in the queue for breakfast is whether or not blowing up a mile-long path of buildings and homes on Van Ness will stop the fire's progress. If it does not, the inferno will be headed in our direction. And if that happens, the only thing that will stop it is the ocean.

I am given biscuits and slices of summer sausage wrapped in wax paper to bring back to our tent. I'm not looking forward to another day like yesterday, of mindless traipsing through a sea of bedraggled refugees and injured souls, but what else can we do today except look for Belinda and the baby?

I walk past the bulletin board on my way back to the tent, and again my note is gone—this time nowhere to be found. I don't know that I'll ever find Belinda in this mess, and I don't know how much longer I can wait. I am thinking that as soon as we are given the all clear to leave the park and find our way out of the ruined city, I will take Kat to Arizona as I promised and assume Belinda will find her own way home. I'll have to find a way to open that strongbox to see if there's anything inside it I can pawn for cash to buy a train ticket.

As I'm walking back to Kat, pondering my options, I hear a woman call out and at first I don't turn. I don't recognize the name being shouted as my own or the voice that calls it. But then it is as if a clockwork bit slides into place and I remember why I'm there and who I have been looking for and why, and I turn toward the sound.

"Sophie!"

It is Belinda. She's getting out of a carriage with the baby in her arms and wearing a dress I don't recognize. A nurse is handing her a bag made from a pillowcase but Belinda hasn't grabbed it; she is instead calling out to me. I pick up my skirt, holding tight to the summer sausage and biscuits in my other hand, and for the first time in many hours I am running toward something instead of away from it.

Even though I have known her only four days, it is the most natural thing in the world to envelop Belinda and that baby into a tight embrace as though we are sisters. She is crying and I find that I am also shedding tears of happiness and relief that something good can still happen in this upside-down world.

"They took me somewhere else!" she is saying. "And they wouldn't bring me here to the park where I knew you were! They wouldn't bring me and there were no carriages, and then the fire was headed toward us. I begged them to take me here instead of the Presidio with the others!"

"I'm so glad," I tell her. "So glad. Kat and I have been looking for you in every corner of the park. I was beginning to think . . ." But I do not finish. I don't want to say I was beginning to think about abandoning her in San Francisco. I pull back from her to look at the infant in her arms. She is absolutely beautiful. I don't see a hint of the man who helped create her and I am glad I don't.

"You're all right, then?" I say instead. "You were well taken care of?"

"Of course we took good care of her." The nurse still in the carriage is now extending the pillowcase bag to me. "There's extra diapers in there and a few things for the little one—just what we could scrounge up. I think Mrs. Bigelow should be staying in a proper shelter tonight at the Presidio, but she was adamant that she join you here."

I take the bag. "Thank you so much for bringing her." I guide Belinda away from the carriage and the entrance with its broken gates and trodden-down grass and that horrible bulletin board.

"Where is Kat?" Belinda says as we clear the entrance.

"In our tent. She's been worried for you and the baby, I think. I hope that's all it is. She's . . . she's different this morning."

Belinda looks at me, concern etched across her face. "Does she . . . does she blame me for what happened on the stairs?"

"She does not. And don't be asking her about it, please, Belinda."

"Have you . . . has he . . . ?"

But Belinda cannot finish her question.

"I haven't heard from Martin. I don't think I will."

Her eyes widen.

"He was still in the house when we ran out of it," I tell her, though surely she must know this. She saw Martin's crumpled form, the blood on the stair, the leg bent in an impossible angle. "In the kitchen. I had to get him away from the front door so that Kat wouldn't see him. She thinks I sent him away. But he didn't look good, Belinda. He was breathing strange."

"And he's still there? In the house?" Belinda asks softly.

I lower my voice, too. "I'm fairly certain the house burned down last night. And I'm thinking he was either dead inside or still alive inside it, which means he won't be troubling us anymore."

Belinda stops and looks up at me in dread. "But if that's true that means . . . that means we killed him!" she whispers.

"No. No, it does not," I say, as softly but as firmly as I can. "It was gravity and the earthquake and the fire and the limits of the human body that killed him. All the forces of nature. Not us. Do you hear me? And don't forget it was only me that left him. Me. I could have told a policeman or soldier about him, but I didn't. I didn't save him, and that's not the same thing as killing. It's not."

It's not.

Belinda looks unconvinced. She stares at me and I want to assure her I've had time to ponder this. Far more time than she has had.

"You're sure?" she asks.

"Yes."

"What if he got out of the house?"

"He didn't." Surely he didn't. They dynamited Van Ness, not Polk. Not Polk. Nobody checked the house to see if anyone was still inside. Not the houses on Polk.

Tears as shiny as polished silver form in Belinda's eyes. She blinks and they slide down her cheeks. I know why.

"There was no James Bigelow," I tell her gently.

She smiles mournfully. "But there was." She looks down at the cherub in her arms.

"And Martin killed him. That's who was doing the killing, Belinda."

"Was he going to hurt us?" Belinda murmurs, her eyes still on her sleeping child.

My mind takes me back to the seconds before Martin was sailing down the stairs, his arms and legs akimbo. I see in those beautiful eyes a glittering purpose, cold and hard as ice.

"Yes, I think he was."

We are quiet for a few moments as all around, refugees and soldiers and Red Cross nurses and priests and firemen move past us in all directions.

Then Belinda sniffs hard and blinks back tears that threaten to continue falling. She turns toward the sea of tents, signaling that she is ready to move again. We resume walking.

"Where will you live now?" Belinda asks a moment later.

"I don't know. I don't know what I will do after I take Kat to her mother."

"You can come live with me. At the inn. I have plenty of rooms. You can help me run it. Help me take care of the baby."

She doesn't say it, but I think I hear in her voice the words, *Help me let go of what was never mine.*

Her offer fills my hurting soul with tiny seeds of comfort and hope. I don't know yet what lies ahead. I don't know what will happen to me when I meet Candace or what my options will be, if indeed I will have any. "Thank you. I'll think on it. Thank you, Belinda. It's quite kind of you."

I am grateful when we arrive at the tent that the two sisters are still out and about and that Kat is alone on our bedroll. She glances at me first with disinterest, but then she sees Belinda coming in through the flap behind me and her eyes narrow a fraction in disbelief.

"Look, love!" I say to her. "Look who I found!"

Kat just stares, unblinking.

For a moment it seems Belinda isn't sure how to respond to this reaction, but then she closes the distance to Kat.

"I had a hard time getting here, Kat," Belinda says tentatively. "I hear you were looking for me and the baby. I'm sorry we weren't here. I couldn't get a carriage and they didn't bring me to the park at first."

Kat is still looking at Belinda as if she cannot trust that she and the baby are there.

Belinda kneels down onto the bedroll.

"Would you like to hold the baby, Kat?"

Kat slowly raises herself up to a sitting position, her face still awash with fear and doubt. When she is sitting cross-legged,

189

Belinda moves to sit beside her and places the tiny bundle in Kat's arms. It is only then, when she can feel the tiny weight of her half sister, that the veil of distrust begins to fall away. The infant emits a sad little mewl, and Kat begins to rock ever so slightly and the babe quiets. Through the folds of the blanket the baby is wrapped in, I can see that she is still wearing the little dress made from Kat's old frock.

"I chose the name you like," Belinda continues. "I've been calling her Sarah. It's such a pretty name, and she is such a sweet little princess, isn't she?"

Kat does not look at Belinda, but she nods once in agreement.

The moment is wonderful and beautiful, and my heart feels as though it might burst. I hand Belinda the summer sausage and biscuits wrapped in wax paper and leave the two of them to go ask for another bedroll and for Belinda's name to be added to our tent assignment, the spinsters be damned.

And then for the rest of the day we coo over Sarah and ignore the sisters and their disapproving glances and wait for our deliverance.

We wake on Saturday morning to the blessed news that the fires have been put out at last and that only a few hot spots to the north are giving the weary firemen trouble. Those who can get to the ferries via ruined Market Street will be given free passage across the bay to Oakland, and from there, the Southern Pacific Railroad will grant a free one-way ticket to wherever any refugee wants to go. We only have to somehow get ourselves to the Embarcadero—a four-and-a-half-mile trek from the park to the ferry landing, and half of it through the smoldering wreck of downtown. The closest railway station to Belinda's home in San Rafaela is south of us at Townsend Street, but no one can tell me if that train station has survived the horrible fires in the Mission District. I do not want to walk all the way to Townsend to find out the station is a heap of ashes. Somehow I have to get the four of us to the ferry nearly five miles away.

"I can walk it," Belinda says when I worry aloud that walking such a long distance with her having just given birth seems unthinkable.

"You've just had a baby!" I reply. "We need a horse and buggy."

But there is no getting a horse. I know this. The ones still alive are all being used for more important purposes than transporting women and children to ferries. Some autos are being used for hire, but only the rich can afford the prices opportunistic people are charging for such services. One vehicle parked outside the park bears a sign saying the driver will take anyone out of the city for the exorbitant fee of fifty dollars. I've heard it's not just transportation that has soared in price. Bread is apparently going for a dollar a loaf outside the refugee camp.

"I can do it," Belinda says. "We can go slow. I can do it. Please, Sophie! I want to go home."

She says the word *home* in that way we do when home is more than just an address. Belinda has been on an odyssey; we both have been, and not for just the last five days. We've been on it since Martin Hocking came into our lives and changed them. And now she just wants to go back home.

I am happy for her that she has a home to go to after this soul-crushing journey. I am envious she does.

And so we ask for passes—the only way you are legally allowed to be out among the ruins of the city—and begin the walk along with thousands of others east to the bay. Tens of thousands remain at the park as we leave it. We have somewhere to go; countless others do not.

I carry the travel case containing Kat's clothes, the strongbox—which I still have not found a way to open—and all the documents that prove who Martin Hocking is, or was. Kat carries the pillowcase bag with the diapers and baby blankets. Belinda carries Sarah. We are told there is no safe water anywhere to drink on the way, and we are each given one can of milk to last us until we reach the ferry building.

The first two miles we walk in silence, as if in preparation for what we will see when we cross Van Ness. Our throats and eyes burn with the acrid smell of smoke and fluttering ash, but there is no damage from the fires here. Not yet. The dynamiting of all the houses and buildings on the east side of Van Ness stopped the fire's westward progress, and we are only seeing damage here and there from the earthquake. Toppled chimneys, leaning walls, cracks in the street. We pass people whose houses are still standing and who ask if we have any food. They don't want to leave their homes unguarded and go to the overcrowded refugee camps at the park and Presidio, where relief supplies are available. We have no food to give them.

Belinda, Kat, and I take our time and reach Van Ness an hour and a half after setting out. Up and down the street on its eastern side is a long vista of ruin and rubble, black and gray and smoking. We cross Van Ness into what had been the fire's domain and make our way to Market Street, passing Polk first, which is a black ribbon of devastation as far as I can see. For one blink of a moment I see in my mind the image of Martin wrapped in flames as he sits slumped and broken and bleeding in the kitchen. I see him with his eyes open and I can't tell if he is dead or alive as the damnation he deserves overtakes him. I don't want to know which it is. I don't. Perhaps he got out. Perhaps. At some point I'll have to return to what's left of the house if I want to know for sure. But I can't think about that. Not right now. Not today.

We walk past the wreckage of the once massive city hall. What the earthquake did not dismantle the fire consumed. The dome still stands, but it is purposeless and naked against the low gray sky. The Mechanics' Pavilion, where Sarah was born only three days earlier, is completely gone. It was made of wood, and there is nothing left to mark its former existence but ash and soot. We walk past piles of still-hot bricks and twisted iron and the skeletal, blackened shells of buildings that were constructed of heartier materials than wood. Automobiles flying the Red Cross flag and with soldiers in the front seat bearing rifles pass us. Chinatown off in the distance to our left is gone. All of it. Swept off the face of San Francisco as if it had never been there.

The tall ferry building at the foot of Market Street begins to come into view blocks before we reach it, and I'm amazed that it still stands. The waterfront was saved by the navy, which means the docks can be used not only for our exodus but for relief supplies to be delivered as well. It is the first sign of life I have seen since we crossed Van Ness. The sight of the ferry building's clock tower reaches up into the smoky haze as if to beckon us toward freedom.

I hang on to this thought as we make our way to the ferries, and as we wait and wait and wait for our turn to board one.

When we are finally standing on the deck of a ship just like the one that brought me to Martin a year ago, I turn to face the city as we steam away from it. I see the vast open fields of ash beyond the stubborn brick and stone skeletons. There was life in all those empty spaces, and now there isn't. What was there is gone. Erased. Something else can take its place, though. Something else will.

Something new.

Something different than what was there before.

Better maybe, stronger. But certainly not the exact same thing.

This is how we make ourselves over when calamity strikes, isn't it? I should know.

The ground cools; we sweep away the ash and envision the new life. And then wait for it to take its first breath.

Martin was wrong about me. I wasn't running when I married him. I was making something new. Starting over.

Beginning again.

18

INTERVIEW WITH MRS. SOPHIE HOCKING
CONDUCTED BY AMBROSE LOGAN, U.S. MARSHAL
CASE NUMBER 069308
Official transcript

San Francisco, CA
November 6, 1906

QUESTION: Can you clarify for me what you mean when you say using a false identity is not the worst thing Mr. Hocking has done?

ANSWER: I . . . I don't have any proof of what I think he did. I just have . . . a notion about it.

QUESTION: I'd still like to hear about it.

ANSWER: I don't think that's a good idea. I told you. I don't have any proof.

QUESTION: I am not asking you to provide any proof. I want to know what you think he may have done.

ANSWER: I found some papers in his desk the day before the earthquake. And a photograph. He had been married before, under another name, to a woman in Colorado. This woman had inherited her father's ranch. I think Martin married her to get that inheritance. She died, and I don't think her death was an accident.

QUESTION: Why is that?

ANSWER: Because she was the daughter of a cattle rancher and she died in a riding accident.

QUESTION: And that seems suspicious to you?

ANSWER: Yes, it does. She had surely grown up around horses.

QUESTION: But even an experienced rider can be thrown from a horse. Hard ground is unforgiving.

ANSWER: Yes, but . . .

QUESTION: But what, Mrs. Hocking?

Interviewee doesn't respond.

QUESTION: What were you going to say?

Interviewee doesn't respond.

QUESTION: Were you going to say, yes, but when you look at Martin Hocking's pattern of behavior of marrying women who possess something he wants, this woman's death looks suspicious? He also married Belinda Bigelow because she had something that he wanted, yes? I'm wondering if you know what that was, Mrs. Hocking.

ANSWER: How would I know that?

QUESTION: Because the two of you are closely acquainted now, I gather. Isn't that correct? You are presently living at her inn?

ANSWER: I lost my home in the quake and fire. She offered me a place to live. It was kind of her.

QUESTION: Indeed it was. You've been kind to her as well, though. A nurse on staff at the Central Emergency Hospital told me you brought her in labor to the pavilion on the morning of the earthquake and stayed with her, nearly delivering her baby yourself, and that you relentlessly searched for her at the refugee camp at the park until you found her.

Interviewee doesn't respond.

QUESTION: I am wondering why you did all of that for a woman your husband was sharing a bed with?

ANSWER: Martin treated her cruelly. Belinda loved him. She loved the man she thought he was. I don't. I don't love Martin Hocking. I never have.

QUESTION: Mrs. Hocking, calm yourself. I am merely asking—

ANSWER: Now, you listen to me. I married Martin Hocking because I wanted out of New York. I was tired of being cold and hungry and alone. I wanted hot food and warm clothes and a soft bed. And a child to love. I didn't marry Martin because I loved him, but Belinda did. She loved the ghost of a man Martin had concocted to woo her. He didn't care that at some point James Bigelow would probably vanish out of her life and his child's life. He took gold from her father's old mine. That's why he married her. For some gold in an abandoned mine. He didn't care about Belinda or his unborn child. I could not abandon her, in labor no less, in a city destroyed. I'm not like him.

QUESTION: I am not suggesting you are. I—

ANSWER: But you are suggesting it. You question why I helped Belinda, stayed with her, searched for her. She was grieving the loss of a man who never existed, and she gave birth to his child, all while fleeing fires and destruction just like the rest of us. How could I not help her? How could I not?

QUESTION: I apologize, Mrs. Hocking. Please retake your seat. Please.

ANSWER: No. I am done. I don't have to be here. You said it at the beginning. I am done with this. I don't care if you have found him. I don't care. I'm done.

QUESTION: Mrs. Hocking, it is better for you if you stay and finish the interview. Please. I advise you to finish the interview.

ANSWER: Why should I?

QUESTION: Because I, too, have my doubts as to the so-called accidental death of Annabeth Grover.

Interviewee retakes seat.

ANSWER: You . . . you know about her?

QUESTION: I do. I know about Candace Howell, too. I know she was raised in a wealthy home and had considerable wealth of her own, bequeathed to her by her grandmother. I am fairly certain Martin Hocking married her to get to it. I know when he married you, he was still married to her.

ANSWER: I didn't know Candace was still living when I married Martin. He told me she was dead. He told his own daughter she was dead. I didn't know.

QUESTION: Mrs. Hocking, can you tell me please if you are also an heiress? Are you positioned to come into money? Do you have wealthy relatives back home in Ireland? Distant ones, perhaps?

ANSWER: No, I do not.

QUESTION: So you do not have wealth and you are not in line to inherit wealth or property?

ANSWER: No.

QUESTION: Do you see my problem, Mrs. Hocking? The man you unlawfully wedded is in the habit of marrying women for their wealth and then, in at least one case that we know of, perhaps disposing of them. But you are not like the others. These other women cared for the man they thought they were marrying. You do not. They had wealth. You do not. You know who he is. They did not. Do you see the predicament I am in?

ANSWER: I told you already. I am not like him. I wondered, too, why he married me. He said it was to appear to be a successful insurance man blessed with a wife and child. But I soon knew that couldn't be true, because no one related to his business ever saw me. For a long time I didn't know the true reason, either. But I figured it out when I took Kat to Candace. And you listen to me, sir, about that. I took Kat to her mother because it was the right thing to do. It was also the hardest thing I've ever had to do, because I love that child. I love her as if she is my own flesh and blood. But I did it. I brought her to her real mother. Candace thought she would die without seeing her child again. I cried with Candace and I held her and I cared for her just like I did with Belinda, because *that's* the kind of person I am.

QUESTION: One moment. You just said, for a time you didn't know why Martin Hocking married you, but then you met Candace and it became clear, that you figured it out. Does that mean that now you do know why he married you?

ANSWER: Yes.

19

Oakland has become a teeming city of refuge, akin to Golden Gate Park on the first day of the fires. Boats of every shape and size have been ferrying people across the bay for the last three days. As we make our way from the landing to the street, I hear someone remark that hundreds upon hundreds of Chinese men and women and their children have flooded Oakland's Chinatown. The place is swarmed; it can absorb no more. Other displaced San Franciscans have gone on to Berkeley, where the gymnasium at the university has been turned into a lodging house. Dozens of homeless slept on university grounds last night under the oaks.

Multitudes of others have headed to the telegraph offices, the doors of which are now being guarded by soldiers to keep people in line and in some semblance of order. Stacks of messages to be sent are piled high in the one telegraph office we can get to on foot. Belinda had thought she would send a telegram to her friend Elliot to let him know we are coming, but I don't see how we will get that message to him before boarding a train that will take us first south along the bay to San Jose and then north again to San Mateo.

"But there will be no one there to meet us at the station," Belinda tells me when we turn from the long queue outside the telegraph office nearest the pier.

I assure her that after all that we have come through the last few days, we will surely find a way to get to San Rafaela from the station, which she says is three miles away.

We leave, only to stand in an equally long line for three train tickets. By the time we get to the counter, though, there are no more seats available on south-going trains for the day. We are given tickets for a train leaving midmorning tomorrow. We are told by a kind woman at the door that if we wish, we can take shelter in the First Presbyterian Church tonight, as they have turned their pews into beds and the women of the church are preparing food for as many as the church can hold. So this is what we do.

There is little privacy inside the church sanctuary, but we find a back-row pew that offers the most we can expect. I can't help but watch as Belinda nurses the child once we settle in. It is such a beautiful sight. My own breasts ache with how beautiful it is. All around is chaos, but the baby simply does what babies do. She nurses in her mother's arms while Belinda sits on a hard pew in a crowded church full of displaced people. The baby would do the same if she were in a palace. Everything is just fine in her tiny little universe, and she will have no memory of all this. While Belinda, Kat, and the baby rest, I wash out the few diapers we have under a spigot outside and set them to dry on the limbs of a squat hawthorn bush. Supper is stew and dumplings and apple brown betty for dessert, and, oh, how wonderful the simple meal tastes.

We awaken in the morning, where, on any other Sunday, the room would be filled with parishioners dressed in their finest, but today the reverend simply moves through the pews of grime-covered refugees, greeting us and offering a prayer over those who ask for it. We head to the train station an hour after breakfast and wait in the crowded terminal for our train to San Jose. I have never boarded a train looking like I know I must look. I've not bathed in a week or attended my hair. I am wearing the same dirty clothes I wore four days ago when we fled the pavilion. But I look around at the other passengers, and most look the same as me. Some look worse. There are a few paying customers who are clean and kempt, and they look upon the rest of us with pity.

We take our seats aboard the train car and I notice that someone has left a copy of the Oakland morning paper on the cushion. The front page contains story after story of the San Francisco quake and fire. More than six hundred persons are either known to be dead or missing. At least a thousand are injured. Most of these have been transported to hospitals outside the fire section, but some are still being treated at refugee camps like Golden Gate Park and the Presidio. Tens upon tens of thousands of evacuees do not have homes to return to, and five hundred city blocks—four and a half square miles—have been destroyed. I also read that San Francisco is not the only city damaged. North of the peninsula in Santa Rosa there is as much damage relative to the size of the city as in San Francisco, perhaps more. And at Stanford University the roof and ceiling at the memorial church collapsed. More than one hundred patients and hospital staff died inside the destroyed Agnews State Hospital closer to San Jose. The movement of the earth was felt by people as far north as Oregon and as far south as Los Angeles.

I set the newspaper aside as the train chuffs away from the station. I don't want to read any more about how terrible the quake and fires were. I know well enough what they did, and what I hope they did. The upholstered seats are far more comfortable than the pews we lay upon last night, and in no time at all, the four of us have fallen asleep.

An hour later I awaken as we are pulling into San Jose. There is evidence in its downtown of crumbled buildings and structure fires, no doubt caused by broken gas lines. But the burned-out sections are contained and small. San Jose's firemen clearly had access to water. We change trains to head back up the peninsula to San Mateo, some thirty miles away. As we ease out of the city, the view outside our window changes from cityscape to rolling hills and pastureland. The sight of such simple, natural beauty is almost too much for the eyes after so many days looking at ruin and loss. I was annoyed that our only way to get to Belinda's home was such a meandering, complicated process, but the pastoral sights outside the glass as we get ever nearer to her inn are calming.

When we enter San Mateo, I can see bits of crushed brick and stone at the foot of some buildings from fallen chimneys and fascia, and as we pull into the station, there is a wooden building off to the side of the depot that has caved in. All of this is evidence that the earthquake shook this town, too. Still, I am reminded a bit of Donaghadee as we step out onto the small platform. There isn't the salty tang of the Irish Sea, but the feel of the town—peaceful and unhurried—is the same. Belinda told me minutes before that she went to secondary school here, and that it's where everyone in San Rafaela goes to shop if not within the pages of the Sears, Roebuck and Company catalog. We step inside the none-too-large station, and out again to the street to see about hiring a carriage. Belinda has money at the inn to pay a driver, if he will just get us there. I still have found no implement with which to pry open the strongbox to see if there is cash inside.

Again we are reminded of how we must look as we approach a gray-haired carriage driver for hire. His eyes widen a bit, just like everyone else's have as we've walked through the station, but he seems to quickly figure out where we've come from.

"Fled the fires in San Francisco, did you?" he says when he takes the travel case from me.

"Yes," I tell him, grateful not to have to explain anything.

"More of you have been coming this way yesterday and today. No trains out of the Townsend station, I hear," he says as he assists Belinda onto the seat. "We had a bit of damage here, too. Not like you had, of course. The jail and the railroad freight depot over yonder came down, and the orphanage is a heap. All the young ones got out, though. City hall and the library are gone."

"What about San Rafaela?" Belinda says. "Was it bad in San Rafaela?"

Good Lord, don't let anything have happened to her inn, I mutter to myself. Not after everything else she's lost.

"Well," the driver says, "I hear people lost their chimneys and some folks' houses wobbled off their groundings. No one died there, though, I don't think. Is that where you're headed?"

"Yes, please," I tell him as I help Kat in and climb in beside her. "The Loralei Inn."

We set off, making our way quickly out of the little city and into the countryside. We pass farms and orchards and country mansions that appear undamaged, at least from this distance. All is serene and calm, but I know Belinda is straining to see her home come into view.

San Rafaela is a small former mining town, with a mercantile, a feed store, a post office, a primary school, and a handful of other businesses on its single main street, and then houses large and small on side streets and out among groves of trees. After we pass the school, I see a carpentry shop and I wonder if it's Elliot's. Then off to our left is the road sign for the Loralei Inn. It's painted white with tiny blue flowers and trailing vines and it's swinging slightly on its hinges in a breeze. It's not until we pass a huge sycamore blocking the full view that we can see that the structure is still standing.

Beside me, Belinda lets out the breath she'd been holding. I don't think either one of us had considered that the earthquake might've wrecked the inn until we saw the damage in nearby San Mateo. I know without even asking her that the inn is more to her than just her livelihood, and I'm surprised anew that she has asked me to come live with her here. The inn is part stone and part wood; the stone no doubt played a role in its survival. The window frames are painted forest green and the rest of the trim and beams are polished redwood. It is three stories high and surrounded by trees except for a fenced patch of sunlight off to the side—Belinda's herb garden. Two large clay pots of lobelia and white alyssum are stationed at the bottom of the porch stairs; one of them is cracked wide, a result of the quake, I am guessing.

We have no sooner pulled into the gravel approach than the screened front door opens and a young man steps out. He is tall and slender, with curly reddish brown hair. He is not handsome, but he has a kind face and gentle features. He stands there for a moment, head cocked, wondering, I suppose, if we've come about a room. I know without Belinda saying it that this is Elliot. I step out with Kat, and the driver assists Belinda and the baby out the other side. Belinda comes around the back of the carriage and I behold the second Elliot recognizes her.

The man is at Belinda's side in seconds.

"Thank God!" he says, wrapping her in a gentle embrace so as not to crush the infant. "I was so worried when you and James didn't come home! I told him where you'd gone, and he went looking for you. I expected you both back from San Francisco that night. And you've delivered the baby!" he says. "What happened? Where is James? Why isn't he with you?"

Belinda opens her mouth to answer him, but even I would have trouble answering these questions, though I know all the answers to them. Her friend seems to sense she doesn't know where to begin.

"Are you all right?" he says in a less agitated voice. "Are you hurt? Is the baby all right?"

"Yes," she says. "I am all right and so is the baby. Sarah came nearly a month early but she's strong and she's healthy even though she's small. We're all right."

"What happened? Did James find you?"

"I . . . I missed the train Tuesday night and I stayed with . . ." She pauses and then nods at me. "My good friend Sophie here. At her house in San Francisco. We . . . we were awakened before dawn by the quake, and then the baby started coming and there was no way to stop it. We . . . couldn't get out of the city and the fires were everywhere. If it wasn't for Sophie I don't know what I would've done."

Elliot seems to notice me for the first time. He extends his right hand in greeting. "Elliot Chapman. Pleased to meet you."

I shake his hand. "Sophie Hocking. Likewise."

"Sophie got me to the hospital, Elliot, when all the world was caving in around us, and nearly delivered the baby herself. She looked for me after we were evacuated. And she brought me here. Brought me home even after she herself lost everything." She turns to me and there is so much she is saying to me without words. Her eyes are shining as she looks at Kat standing next to me and continues. "And this is her—" Belinda struggles for a moment and then the word slips out. "Her daughter, Kat." I hear the catch of emotion in her voice as she says this while holding her own child close to her breast. Tears pluck at my own eyes and I blink them away.

Elliot reaches out to clasp my hand again. "Thank you so much for helping Belinda, and for bringing her home." He turns back to Belinda. "Where is James?"

I clear my throat. "Perhaps we should all go inside and let the driver be on his way?"

Elliot turns to the man. "Allow me." He starts to reach into his pocket, but the driver, who has been watching us, perhaps a bit taken with the emotional reunion, says there will be no charge today.

He sets my travel case down by my feet, and the pillowcase bag. "Good day to you all."

"Thank you. That's very kind," Elliot says quickly, picking up my case and the pillowcase bag in one hand.

The driver tips his hat and steps back up into the cab. With a flick of the reins he is off.

"Come," Elliot says. With one arm around Belinda he leads us inside the inn.

The interior of the Loralei is as welcoming as the outside, although paintings and pictures thrown crooked have only partly been straightened to their right places, and I see a wastebin full of shards of glass and porcelain near the front door. The Loralei has lost some of its serving ware, I'm thinking. Elliot sets the travel case and pillowcase bag down in a large common room where there are sofas and armchairs and a stone fireplace that is dark and cold: the only dark and cold thing in the room. Belinda settles onto a sofa, the baby still in her arms.

"Everything is all right at the inn, except for those dishes?" Belinda says, nodding toward the bin near the entryway.

"Yes, yes. Aside from those and a few lamps and vases, most everything else is fine."

"Thank you so much for watching the inn for me all this time, Elliot. I thought it was going to be just for an afternoon," Belinda says wearily.

"No more talk of that," Elliot says. "Tell me what happened. Where is James?"

Belinda turns to me. Without a word I rise from my chair and walk over to her. "How about if Kat and I take Sarah and go take a peek at your lovely garden, Belinda."

Belinda looks up at me in both gratitude and trepidation as she hands me her child. What she must tell Elliot about the man she married she surely wants to say in private, but it won't be easy.

"The back door is just off the kitchen, through there." She nods toward a dining room with a long table and a breakfront empty of its dishes.

We make our way, Kat and I and the baby, through this room and into the sunny kitchen. It is large and cheery. Breakfast dishes and pots and pans are in the sink. There were no doubt guests here last night, and it must have fallen to Elliot to cook for them.

As we move toward the back door I hear Belinda say to Elliot, "I need to tell you something."

Since our clothes are already grime covered it doesn't matter much that we sit down on the grassy dirt under a peach tree at the edge of the herb garden. I place Sarah in Kat's arms because Kat seems to be most at peace when she is holding her sister, and the baby soon falls asleep in that tender cradle of young arms. Belinda will tell Elliot everything, I'm guessing, even what happened on the stairs. Probably what happened after, too. I'm not sure how I feel about that. I do not know the man.

But I do know what she has told me of him. She trusts him, and I can tell that he loves her. Still. I imagine she will also tell him Kat is not truly my daughter and that I will leave this place with her, and that when I come back—for I've decided I will come back to the inn to live, at least for a while—I will likely return alone. As I imagine her telling him this, I decide at that precise moment that I shall keep the surname Martin gave me even though I know it isn't truly mine. If Candace and her father don't insist I take back my maiden name, I don't see the harm in keeping it. I've a marriage license that looks official enough. I shall ask this favor of Candace. It's nothing compared to what I am giving her in return. This thought oddly comforts me, that I can keep it. It's the only thing of Martin's that I still want.

Kat and the baby and I sit in that beautiful, calm place for what seems a long while. I revel in the sun dappling our faces and the clean air and the buzz of honeybees in the blossoms above our heads. I chase off any thought of transporting Kat to Candace tomorrow so that I can simply enjoy an hour with no ash or queues or troubling realities.

When Belinda emerges from the inn some time later, she sits beside us on the ground and puts Sarah—who is awake now and starting to get restless—to her breast. I want to ask her how much Elliot now knows, but we can't have that conversation with Kat sitting between us. I will have to wait to ask her after Kat goes to bed.

"Where is he?" I say instead.

"I insisted he go home. I know he's got business of his own that has gone unattended while he's been running the inn for me. There aren't any guests at the moment. The four who were here left this morning, but I'm guessing more refugees will be arriving in the days ahead as the southern roads out of the city become accessible. Let's go inside, wash and rest up, and change our clothes."

I look down at my soiled shirtwaist. "I don't have any other clothes. I had to abandon my bag when we evacuated the pavilion."

"I have plenty of dresses that you can choose from and which I won't fit into for a while yet. I owe you everything, Sophie. Everything I have is yours."

"You don't owe me anything."

"But I do. Of all the people in San Francisco who might've helped me at the worst moment of my life, that it was you . . ."

She is thinking of the man we both unwittingly married. She is thinking maybe that should make us enemies. But in truth, it has bound us together like family. Like kindred souls.

We are both quiet for a moment. A cool breeze kicks around us and I get a good whiff of how I smell.

"So how about that bath?" I say.

We spend the rest of the afternoon cleansing ourselves of the filth and grime clinging to our skin and hair. It feels so good to put on a clean dress, even one that isn't mine. I don't care that it's a wee bit short on me and the buttons are tight. By early evening we are all of us rested and sweetly smelling of lemon verbena, and the horrible clothes we were wearing before are soaking in a tub of hot water and suds. While Kat and I take care of the baby, Belinda makes us a quick supper of sausages, fried potatoes, and pickled carrots she'd preserved last summer. Elliot brings by freshly cut wood for the stove for tomorrow and makes sure there's nothing else we need before we retire for the night. He eyes me carefully when he comes, but I don't see suspicion there; it's more like gratitude, perhaps even admiration.

Before he leaves he pries open the strongbox for me. Inside is a woman's wedding ring—Annabeth's, perhaps?—forty dollars in cash, and a key for a safe-deposit box for a San Francisco bank that I know for certain is now a hulking, burned-out skeleton of a building. I don't know if boxes like these can survive a devastating fire. I don't know if I care.

When the girls are at last tucked in bed and Belinda and I are sitting in the large common room with cups of tea, she tells me about the conversation with Elliot hours before.

"James—I mean Martin—had come home hours after I left, just before twilight," Belinda tells me. "When he found Elliot here instead of me, he asked where I was and Elliot told him that I had gone to San Francisco in search of him. Elliot explained I'd found the address in the coat pocket and that I was going to see if the person at the address could help me find James. Martin had left immediately, even though it was getting dark, to head back to

San Francisco because he knew I was going to find *you*. I don't know why he arrived at your house so many hours later and looking the way he did with his boots and trousers all muddy. Elliot feels badly that he sent Martin in our direction, Sophie. He feels so badly about it."

"He couldn't have known not to tell Martin where you'd gone."

"Yes, I told him that, but he's angry with himself nonetheless. He never liked Martin; I told you that before. He wishes very much he'd told him nothing. Martin would've stayed here, most likely waiting for me to come home. And we could've gone to the police and they would have come here and arrested him."

"We wouldn't have been able to go to the police," I remind her. "The next day was the earthquake."

"Still, things would be different."

I see a flash of an image of Belinda, the girls, and me arriving here at the inn today and finding Martin instead of Elliot. Because if Elliot had told Martin nothing, that's what could very well have happened. "They could be worse," I tell her.

A few seconds of silence pass between us.

"Did you tell him what happened?" I ask.

"Yes."

"Everything?"

"Yes."

"And you trust him?"

"I do. He still cares for me, Sophie. Even after all of this, he still loves me. He would never do anything to hurt me or those I care about."

A few more quiet seconds pass.

"He knows about Kat? And he knows where I have to go? What I have to do?"

"Yes. He . . . he said he'd accompany you if you don't want to go alone. I told him how hard this will be for you. He'll take you if you want him to."

I find the notion touching, a generous gesture from an obviously kind man. But I'll not be taking anyone with me on the journey to Arizona. I want the last hours I have Kat all to myself.

I tell her this, and Belinda nods in understanding. She knows the depths of mother-love now.

"But you are coming back here, aren't you?" she asks.

"Yes."

She reaches across the sofa to squeeze my arm. This makes her happy, the idea that I shall return, that she can give me a home and a child to sing lullabies to, that she can give me versions of what has been taken from me.

"I'll need to go back to San Francisco at some point," I say, and she frowns.

"Why?"

"I must see what's left of the house. And I need to see the lists of the dead and injured. I need to make sure. I need to make sure he's gone."

She leaves her hand on my arm and says nothing.

And then she nods. She needs to know, too.

We need to be sure.

20

Morning birdsong is drifting over my head through the half-open window as I awaken. I lie in the most comfortable bed ever with Kat next to me, still asleep, lips slightly parted. A quilt that has been dried in the fresh country air is tucked up to our chins. It would be so easy to just stay at the Loralei with Kat and never leave. So easy to pretend I don't know that Candace still lives. So, so easy, if only Kat didn't know.

But surely the ease would in time give way to guilt and shame.

I need to leave today for Arizona. The longer I wait to do what I must, I know the harder it will be. I must go while I still have the resolve to do the right thing.

I try to keep my tone cheerful as I tell Kat before we head downstairs for breakfast half an hour later that today we will at last be on our way to see her mama. She has not said but a word or two since the tent at Golden Gate Park, and when I tell her this now I am met with silence. But I see in her eyes a mix of conflicting thoughts. She loves little Sarah, that is obvious, and I even think she loves me. Part of her wants to stay here; part of her wants to see her mother. Her heart is painfully torn in two, and it occurs to me that surely it has been a long time since this poor child has been truly happy. Maybe she can't even remember the last time she was truly happy. I think back to Candace's letter and how she wrote that she'd not been a good mother to Kat when she had the chance. I recall her writing that she took the losses of her infant sons far too hard and I wonder if Candace was neglectful, withdrawn, or impassive toward her daughter. Did she withhold love from Kat the way I know Martin did, the way her grandparents apparently did? Martin told me Candace had been sick for a long while before she died, but I'm thinking now only half of that statement is true. She'd indeed been bedridden for months, but not before she died. It was rather before her father whisked her away to that sanatorium. Candace hadn't been well enough to care for her daughter, nor had she the will to. This is why I ponder if there was ever a time when Kat remembers feeling loved and cherished. Perhaps with me she did. Perhaps with me she does. Perhaps she does not trust this love I have for her, because with everything that has been stolen from her, why should she?

And now I am taking her away from her half sister, who is precious to her.

"I know how jumbled you must feel inside." I pull her to me as we sit on the bed. "I want to stay here, too. But your mama longs to see you, and I know you ache to see her, too. It's all jumbled, isn't it?"

Kat sighs lightly against my chest. She nods.

"I'll find a way to come visit you," I tell her. "I'll bring Belinda and the baby, all right? We'll all come. I'll find a way. Don't you worry about that."

We stay there, saying nothing to each other, for a long while. It's a heavenly moment for me nonetheless, sitting in silence with the child I love as close to me as my own skin.

At the breakfast table the mood is solemn. Belinda has obviously also grown fond of Kat and is sad to see her go, even though she has known her less than a week. When people are thrown into an abyss and together find their way out of it, they are not the same people. They are bound to one another ever after, linked together at the core of who they are because it was together that they escaped a terrible fate. It doesn't seem like Kat and I met Belinda only last Tuesday. It seems we have always known her.

Kat holds Sarah while I help Belinda with the breakfast dishes. Then I bring down the travel case we brought, which now holds Kat's clothes as well as one of Belinda's nightgowns and a couple of her shirtwaists and skirts.

Elliot is taking Kat and me to the train station in San Mateo, where we will board a train that will stop first in San Jose and then continue on to Los Angeles, with stops in between. From Los Angeles we will board another train to Tucson. I'm grateful for the ride to the station, but I'm not looking forward to sitting with Elliot, with Kat between us, for twenty minutes.

"He can't ask me about Martin," I told Belinda when she said he'd be at the house at nine o'clock to fetch Kat and me. "He can't say one word about him. Not with Kat there in the buggy."

"He knows he can't, Sophie," she assured me. "He won't."

And she is right. After our good-byes—Kat, already protecting her wounded heart, barely acknowledges Belinda and the baby as we bid farewell—we take off in the buggy and Elliot fills the silence with talk of the land and his shop and how his father and grandfather were carpenters before him.

It seems in no time at all we are back at the train station in San Mateo.

"You have everything?" Elliot says after Kat and I are standing on the pavement in front of the depot.

I have money for the train tickets, the travel case, Candace's letter and the other documents I took from Martin's desk, the rest of the cash from the strongbox in a borrowed handbag. Kat.

"Yes."

Elliot and I stand and look at each other. So much could be said; so much won't be.

"Thank you for your help," I finally say.

"I did nothing. You are the one who did everything. I can never repay you for it. You saved her life. In more ways than one."

"You still love her?" I am sure of this, but I ask anyway.

"Always. I will never love anyone else."

This man perplexes and amazes me. I eye Kat, a few feet away from us. She is staring off in the distance, detached from the moment and my conversation with Elliot. I turn back to him.

"Even though she married another man?" I ask quietly.

He shrugs. "I don't think love is something you can start and stop by choosing. Our hearts tell us who we will love, not the other way."

"You must've wanted him to disappear from the moment she met him."

Elliot considers my words for a moment. "Am I glad he's gone? Yes. Did I wish him gone? No. She cared for him."

"She won't always, Elliot."

"I know," he says. "I can wait."

"That baby is a sweet little thing. She takes after her mother, I think."

He smiles. "You are no doubt right." He then hands me a piece of paper with the address of his carpentry shop written on it and a telephone number. "If anything happens and you need help right away, send me a telegram, or if you can get to a telephone, place a call to me. I'll pay for the charges."

"Thank you." I take the piece of paper and place it inside my handbag. As I do, a thought occurs to me. "That old mine of Belinda's has been visited, you know. It needs to be secured. Do you understand?"

He nods like he's already thought of this. "I'll take care of it."

Elliot seems made of all the best attributes a person could have.

"You are a true friend," I say. "She's lucky to have you in her life."

He says nothing to this, perhaps because he believes not in luck but rather something deeper and truer and hallowed.

For the first time in many, many months, I wonder where my own life would have taken me if I had known and loved a man like Elliot Chapman.

"I can escort you to the platform if you want help with the luggage," he says.

This thought makes me laugh, and he smiles wide, too, at my needing help with a travel case I dragged across the peninsula with Kat in tow, all while being chased by fire and uncertainty.

"Thank you again for the ride," I answer as I pick up the case and take Kat's hand.

Together my girl and I make our way through the depot and onto the platform, where our train is waiting for us.

. . .

The day is long and uneventful as we steam ever farther south. I get out Da's word book after we leave San Jose, but my many attempts to have Kat choose a word for the day go unrewarded. I finally choose one for us. It's a French word. *Ménage.* It means all the persons who make up a household.

We sleep a little, watch the world go by—most of it farmland opening up to desertlike terrain—and eat sandwiches Belinda made for us. When we finally reach the Los Angeles depot, a large structure with skylights and an arched roof that soars above the station's platforms, it is near nightfall. I find us a little hotel a block away from the station so that we can easily get to our early-morning train to Tucson. The buildings here are not as tall as those in San Francisco were, and the feel of the place is different, too. The sun seems closer somehow. And the sky bigger.

If Kat finds this corner of California familiar to her, I can't tell. I'm sure she was at this train station when she and Martin left Los Angeles, but I see no evidence on her face that this place has any meaning to her. There is only the slight sheen of anxious expectation in her eyes; at least that's what I think it is. I am tempted only for a few seconds to ask the hotel manager if I might use their telephone and pay whatever it will cost to call the sanatorium in Tucson and tell the nurse in charge that we are coming. Right now Kat is still mine, and when I hand her over tomorrow to Candace she won't be.

The next morning, a little after sunrise, we board the train that will take us to Arizona. I don't know how well Kat slept, but I slept poorly, and as we ease away from Los Angeles and toward golden mountains the color of toast and honey, the clacking of the train soon lulls us both to sleep. When I awaken we are in the middle of a barren wasteland dotted with towering, multiarmed cacti that look as though they are beings from a fantasy world. We head to the dining car for lunch, and then finally at a little after one in the afternoon we pull into the Tucson station, a wooden depot with deeply set eaves and windows that are shaded by colorful awnings. It is only late April, but it is already ninety summerlike degrees. I can see why people who suffer from consumption move to this part of the country. The heat is intense and bone-dry. I am no expert on the disease ravaging Candace's body, but I do know consumption turns the lungs into a wet soup before it kills you. Anything wet here is surely soon dry.

I hire a carriage to take us to a hotel near the station. The two-story building is plastered in creamy white stucco with arches and a red-tiled roof. The inside of the hotel is only slightly cooler than outside, but I want to freshen up—as best I can—before I take Kat to her mother. And I want Kat to look well cared for, too.

I change and apply fresh toilet water. I rebraid Kat's hair and retie the ribbons on her dress.

Then I sit her down with her hands folded in mine.

"I don't know what's going to happen today, love," I tell her. "I don't know if you'll be coming back with me to this hotel tonight or if I will see you again before I'm asked to return to where I came from." I watch her face to see if these words are affecting her.

She blinks. She breathes. She says nothing. But I feel her hand stiffen the tiniest bit under my palm.

"Whatever happens, I will come back to visit. I will bring Belinda and the baby with me. I promise you that, Kat. I promise."

Her eyes take on a silvery luster.

"And I want you to know that I love you as if you were my own daughter. I always will. Will you remember that?"

I wait for her to answer me. Several seconds later she nods. Once.

"All right, then. Now, you know your mama's been very sick. She may not be able to see us today or she might not be able to put her arms around you or the nurses might not let us get too close because they don't want us to get sick. So we need to be ready for whatever we might see when we get there, all right?"

Another nod. I wish I knew what she was thinking. I wish I could hear her voice just one more time.

I hire a second carriage to take us to the sanatorium, which I learn is located two miles outside of town. Las Palomas, where Candace resides, is not the only sanatorium here, the carriage driver tells us; there are many others. It's a booming business these days, he says, with consumptive men and women coming from everywhere to avail themselves of the hot, dry climate in Arizona.

"Do the people who come here get better?" I ask him. "Does the heat cure them?"

"I don't rightly know. Maybe," he replies. "I've never heard of anyone leaving a sanatorium here because they're completely cured. I wager the heat slows the illness down. You can live longer here, but I don't think very many go back home to where they were before. Some probably do."

"And how does the rest of the town feel about so many ill people coming here?" I ask.

"Business is always a good thing, I reckon, and as long as the facilities are outside the city, I don't suppose people are going to complain. We just don't want the sick folks in town."

It appears as if he's about to tell me why no one wants the sick in town, but I already know why and I don't want Kat to have to hear those reasons, so before he can say anything else I ask him about the tall, multiarmed cacti I've been seeing everywhere. He tells me they are saguaro and that they can grow to a height of sixty feet and live to be two hundred years old.

"They're slow growers. They don't do anything in a hurry." He spends the rest of the time we are in his carriage telling us everything he knows about the saguaro.

We soon arrive at the sanatorium. It is a long, one-story structure surrounded by desert sand, acacia trees, and mesquite. It is plastered in the same white stucco and roofed with the same red tile as many of the buildings in town. A covered patio in the back and off to the side is partially visible from the gravel carriageway. A few residents in white cotton shifts are reclining there on wheeled lounges while a large electric fan stirs up the air. One woman is reading, one is napping, and two men are playing cards with each other. Neither of the women looks like Candace from this distance.

On a smaller patio in front of the entrance, a man in street clothes is talking with a beautiful but pale woman who is sitting in a wicker chair several feet away from him. I can tell without even hearing them speak to each other that the man loves the woman, and that he is sitting as close to her as he can without endangering himself.

In the courtyard of the entrance, and not too far from where the couple is visiting, is a large statue of the Virgin Mary. Her hands are open and inviting, as if to welcome any who might cross the threshold. A wooden sign next to her cautions visitors, however, that Las Palomas is for the treatment of tuberculosis— the scientific name for consumption—and that those who enter do so at their own risk. As we climb out of the carriage I ask the driver to come back for me just before sundown or so. I can wait on the front patio if it only takes a little while to do what I must and then am dismissed.

The pale woman watches Kat as we make our way to the large wooden front door.

The inside of Las Palomas is surprisingly cool considering the heat outside. Ceiling fans on a low revolution speed twirl the air above our heads. The floor is tiled in terra-cotta squares, and brightly colored pots of palms grace all the corners. The large room resembles the inside of someone's house, not a hospital. A nurse looks up from a writing desk.

"How can I help you?" She has kind eyes and a wrinkled face from perhaps many years in the Arizona sun.

I tell her that we've come to see Candace Hocking.

The nurse smiles and casts a glance at Kat. "We restrict visits from children, I'm afraid."

"I thought as much," I tell her. "But Kat here isn't an ordinary visitor."

Before I can explain why, the nurse says, "This is Kat? This is Mrs. Hocking's daughter?"

It hurts to hear her say that. It shouldn't but it does. "Yes. This is her daughter."

"Mrs. Hocking did not say you were coming," the nurse says, her tone a mix of alarm and delight.

"Mrs. Hocking does not know we are coming. I thought it best to wait until we arrived. Perhaps you could let her know we are here?"

"And is Mr. Hocking also coming?" she says, looking beyond me to see if Martin is hovering just inside the door.

"He is not."

"And your name, miss?"

"Just call me Sophie."

She invites us to please have a seat. When she returns ten minutes later I can't tell from her face what kind of reaction Candace had to the news that Kat is here.

"Mrs. Hocking is waiting for you on the patio," the nurse says. "She is most anxious to see you. You will both be safe if you keep your distance. The disease is only catching if you breathe the air she coughs, and our residents work very hard to limit their coughs. I will take you back in a moment, but first may I have a word with you, Miss . . . ?"

"Sophie will do."

She smiles politely, but with puzzlement, and I follow her a few yards away from where Kat sits on a sofa gazing down at her lap, at the doll with the cracked cheek.

"Mrs. Hocking is very weak," the nurse says. "I don't want Kat to be frightened of how her mother looks. She had been doing so well, too, but she took a turn after hearing of the death of her father—"

"Candace's father is dead?" I blurt.

The nurse blinks at me. "Why, yes. You didn't know?"

"I didn't. When did he die?"

"Well, I would say it was about a month ago now."

I can't help but wonder how Candace's father met his end. Martin told me Candace's father wasn't in good health, but not that he was near death. I search my mind to recall if Martin was home with me in late March or away. I wouldn't put anything past him. Not now.

"What happened?" I ask.

"There was an automobile accident. In Los Angeles. His car

225

went off the road and overturned. He perished underneath it, I'm afraid."

"Was there another vehicle involved?"

She raises an eyebrow. Why would I immediately want to know that? I could see she was wondering.

Why, indeed.

"What I mean is, does anyone know what caused the accident?" I add.

She shakes her head. In the end it perhaps doesn't matter now if Martin had a hand in this. What does matter is that with Candace's father dead, there is now one less person who will take Kat to raise if Candace cannot. I sense an arrow of hope shooting through me. Candace can't raise Kat alone in her condition. She will need help.

"So you'll tell the child? About her mother? About how she looks?"

"Yes." I turn and walk back to Kat.

I kneel down so that I am looking up at her. "We're going to see your mama, love. She's been sick, you know, and sometimes when we're sick it makes us look tired and it's hard to laugh and smile and look happy. But she's very glad you're here. All right? She's very glad."

I stand and hold out my hand. Kat grasps her doll tight with one hand and me with the other.

The nurse opens a door that leads to a long hallway that goes both right and left, and we head down the one that ends at an open door and sunshine.

And I feel my heart tearing in two.

21

've heard that tuberculosis has long been called consumption because it slowly consumes you until you are nothing but skin and bones, a living soul trapped inside a body that is wasting away. Not only that, but the disease, which lives inside your lungs, seeks to infect those close to you by crawling inside your spit and your breath so that when you cough, it might also consume them. Those who can afford the fresh air and care of a sanatorium might live with the disease for a stretch of years; a few may even beat it. But those without wealth are almost always devoured by it. I witnessed the ravages of untreated consumption often enough in the tenements and in Ireland before I left.

When I see Candace, I see why the older name for tuberculosis lingers. She is lying on a wheeled lounge chair at the edge of the patio, still in shade but as close to the brilliant sun beyond as she can be. She is pale, gaunt, and hollowed out. Her blond hair, which in the photograph that Kat has is golden and luxurious, is now dull and thin. Still, I see hints of her former beauty as Kat and I close the distance, in the swanlike shape of her neck, in her porcelain-doll lips, and in the grass green hue of her eyes. She tries to rise out of her lounge as we near her but falls back against her pillows. She instead stretches out an arm for Kat as tears begin to trickle down her face.

"My girl!" she says in a still-lovely voice. "My baby girl! You're here! You're here."

Kat has stopped next to me, still some distance from her mother, and she is staring at the figure on the lounge. I cannot read Kat's thoughts, but I am sure she is wondering how this withered waif can be her mother, how the voice she still remembers could be coming from a skeleton of a woman who has stolen her mother's body. Despite the talk we had, Kat is unprepared to see her mother like this. How could any child not be?

I take Kat's hand and we take a step forward before she stops again.

"Kat!" Candace says wearily, unable to keep her arm aloft. "It's me, darling. It's me. It's Mama."

Kat looks up at me and then at her mother. Candace tips her head to study me for a moment, as if seeing me for the first time.

"'Twill be all right, love," I murmur to the child. "Remember what I told you?"

Kat's grip on my hand tightens as we take another step toward the lounge chair. Candace reaches out again with one hand. The child is close enough now that if she just takes one more step, her mother could touch her. But she turns to me instead and leans in close to my body. Candace looks up at me again, her lovely eyes pools of sadness.

I look into those eyes, which are full of mother-love, and I say the same thing to Candace that I said to Kat. "'Twill be all right," I say. "Give her just a moment."

Candace seems to hang on to my words as she brings her gaze back to her daughter. She lets her hand rest again on her abdomen. "I'm so glad you came, Kat," she says, injecting artificial calm into her tone. I can hear the falseness clear as day. "I've missed you so much. I've prayed every day since I came here to see you. I'm so sorry it has been so long. I . . . I didn't know where you were. I kept hoping I would get well enough to come looking for you. But I . . . I'm so sorry that I didn't. I'm so sorry, Kitty Kat."

It is when Candace says this pet name, a name that surely she's called her daughter many times before, that Kat's grasp on my fingers lessens and I feel her edge away from me. God, it feels all wrong and all right, how she is leaning away from me now and toward her mother.

Candace sees the shift and lifts her hand wearily again. This time, Kat takes it, and when she does Candace starts to pull her close.

The nurse who showed us to the patio and who has been standing next to me the whole time also moves forward. "That's close enough, Mrs. Hocking. We don't want your little girl to get sick, do we?"

Candace freezes, her hand still holding Kat's. Their arms are bent into a triangle, as though they might arm wrestle.

Tears are cascading down Candace's face. "I would hold you in my arms, if I could, Kitty Kat. If it was safe, I would hold you."

Kat suddenly bends forward to rest her head in her mother's lap. With her other hand, Candace begins to stroke her daughter's hair. They have found a way to embrace.

229

A second nurse brings me a chair, setting it close to the lounge, and I gratefully slip into it. It is beautiful to watch mother and daughter holding each other, and it is dreadful. For many long moments no one says anything. When Kat finally lifts her head, she turns to look at me and I can see that she has been exhausted by the emotional weight of the reunion. I hold my own hand out and she comes to me so that I can pull her into my lap. I position her so that she can still hold her mother's hand but can rest against my bosom.

Candace looks up at me in both relief and anguish. "Do I know you?" she whispers.

"No."

"Did Martin send you? Is . . . is he coming?"

Kat stiffens slightly in my lap when she hears her father's name. I pat her knee gently. Candace notices.

"Martin is not coming."

"What is your name again?"

"Please just call me Sophie."

A few seconds of silence pass between us.

"How . . . why . . ." But Candace's voice drops away. She surely can sense that I cannot answer all her questions with Kat sitting there listening. I nod to assure her that I do have the answers she seeks.

I begin to share with Candace all about our train trip, the views we saw out our window, the stop in Los Angeles, seeing the tall saguaro cactus for the first time. I keep the chatter light and cheery, sharing with this woman what Kat would tell her if Kat had been living a normal life up until now. Candace is smiling at my descriptions but looking nervously from me to her daughter, surely concerned that I am doing all the talking.

I silently plead with Candace not to ask why, and she must sense this. As I chatter away, I begin to rock slightly in my chair, lulling Kat—I hope—to slumber. Candace watches me in fascination and distress. I think she can tell that I love this child and maybe even that this child loves me. It is disconcerting to her, as it would be to me. When Kat is in deep sleep, at my request the first nurse brings large sofa pillows from the visitors' lounge and makes a bed for her on the patio stones a few yards away. I lay the child down and return to my seat. Then the nurse leaves us, taking all but one resident inside. Only an older gentleman remains, and he is nodding off.

"Who are you?" Candace says to me, wearily, but with keen interest. "Where is Martin? Why isn't Kat saying anything?"

I have known this moment was coming, but even so, now that it is here, I fumble for a place to start. So much of what I have to say is terrible.

"I don't know how to tell you everything you need to know," I finally say.

Perhaps she can hear it in my voice, that Martin is gone, for she asks me before I continue, "Is . . . is he dead?" Her voice is bereft of strength.

"I think so, yes."

I wait a moment for this news to settle. She looks away from me, toward the desert and its desolate horizon beyond the patio stones. When she turns back to face me, her eyes are glistening.

"What happened to him?"

"Did you know he was living in San Francisco?"

"No."

"Do you know what happened there? Do you know about the earthquake?"

"Y-yes. Is that where Kat was, too?" Fear injects itself into her voice.

"Yes. But she's all right. We . . . we had a few rough days, she and I. Scary days. But she's all right."

This both comforts and alarms her. "And Martin?" she says a second later.

"We . . . were all in the house before the earthquake struck. He . . . he fell down a flight of stairs just before. And then came the awful fires. He . . . he likely didn't get out of the house before it burned."

"Why? Why didn't he?" Candace says, horrified. Obviously Kat and I got out.

I hesitate. There are so many reasons Martin Hocking very likely perished inside that house.

"Why didn't he get out?" Candace whispers.

I inhale deep and then let the breath out. "I have so much to tell you. So much. 'Twill be hard to hear, and I'm sorry for that. I truly am. I trust you will be able to bear it?"

She nods slowly, her wide-eyed gaze tight on me.

"I think I need to start at the beginning, well before the earthquake, or none of this will make sense."

Candace says nothing for a moment. She looks past me to where Kat is sleeping atop sofa pillows. Then she turns back to me. "All right."

"I was living in New York City until a bit more than a year ago," I begin. "I had emigrated from Ireland but I . . . I wasn't happy there. I was hungry and cold and living in a hovel of a tenement because I couldn't afford anything else. I saw an advertisement in the paper. A man out west was looking for a new wife for himself and a new mother for his little girl. I answered that advertisement. Your husband placed it. Martin told me you were dead, and that he was a widower and that Kat didn't have a mother. I didn't know you were alive. I only just found out. I swear to you I didn't know. He told Kat you were dead, too, and she thought it was her fault. Martin had found a way to blame her somehow; he made it seem that mothering her had made you weak and sick and that it was her fault you had gotten ill and died. She stopped talking when she thought you had been taken from her and that it was her fault."

I stop for a moment to gauge Candace's ability to hear more, because there is so much more to say. She swallows hard as more tears slide down her cheeks, but unlike before, these are tears of anger and profound regret.

"He told her I was dead?" she whispers.

I nod. She closes her eyes, breathes in and out with whatever strength is left to her to do such a thing, and I wait. When she opens her eyes, the sadness has been replaced with bafflement.

"But . . . but wait. Why would you do that? Why would you marry someone you don't know?" Her tone is accusatory, and for a moment I think she is as angry with me as she must be with Martin. I tell her the answer I've been telling myself: I had to get out of New York. I didn't care that I was marrying a man I didn't love. I had made the mistake of giving my heart to someone before and had been crushed, and I was none too keen to do it again. I wanted a warm home and food to eat and a child to love. I wanted more than what I had. I wanted more than what I had been left with.

"I believed in time I would come to have affection for him, maybe even love," I say. "But I never did. And I am quite sure he never had any affection for me."

Candace sighs and closes her eyes tight again for a moment, as if to wish me and my horrible news away. I wait a few seconds for her to look at me again. When she does, I continue. "Martin told me he traveled about for an insurance company assessing risk, and that for appearance's sake he needed to be seen as a successful married man with a family rather than an unlucky widower and father to a motherless child. That is why he married me, he said, and I believed him. At first."

She swallows hard again and waits for me to go on.

"He told me his parents had died when he was six, in a carriage accident back east, and that he had been raised by an aunt and uncle who made his life difficult and that there was a cousin named Belinda who now lived south of San Francisco. He was helping her sell hair tonic that she made from herbs in her garden. He had the bottles in the boiler room of our house in San Francisco. But the bottles were not filled with hair tonic. And Belinda was not his cousin."

Candace dabs at her eyes with a handkerchief. "Who was she?" she says a moment later.

"She was someone who had inherited an abandoned gold mine. Martin had married her under another name to get to it. He had found out somehow that there was, in fact, gold inside it. Four months after marrying me, he married her. All while still married to you."

Candace seems to dissolve for a moment into her pillows, and her face becomes a mask of the worst kind of sadness. She brings a hand up to her forehead, and many moments pass before she removes the hand to look back at me.

"How do you know all this?" she asks, misery etched into her face. "How do you know this is all true?"

"Because Belinda came to my house looking for her husband. The man she knew as James had my San Francisco address on some letters she saw. He had told her he was a land surveyor and that he traveled for his job; that is how he explained his absences from her. He'd been gone longer than expected and she'd been worried. Belinda came to my house the day before the earthquake. She was pregnant, far along. And she saw my wedding photograph on the mantel in the living room. She saw that Martin was the husband she knew as James. We pieced it together, and we found all the documents that prove it in Martin's desk. I have those documents right here in my bag. And that's not all. There was someone else before you. He married a girl in Colorado under another, different name. She was set to inherit a cattle ranch. Her mother died suddenly after she and Martin married, and that young wife died a year later in a riding accident."

My voice is catching in my throat as I think about Annabeth, and that perhaps a similar fate had been awaiting me and Belinda. "Only I don't think it was an accident," I continue, tears stinging my own eyes. "I think Martin killed her for the ranch. He sold it when she died and then came to Los Angeles with the money and got hired as a stable hand, where he met you. An heiress."

What little color remains in Candace's face suddenly drains.

"Sweet Jesus," she whispers, as though something monumental and devastating has just been made clear to her.

"What?" I say. "What is it?"

"Father was right," she whispers, but not to me. She is inside a moment of her own between herself and a parent who I know has recently died.

"About what?" I can't help asking.

She slowly turns her head back to face me. "My father said all along Martin married me to get my grandmother's inheritance. I didn't believe him. I believed Martin loved me, and it hurt to my very soul that my father thought he didn't. God, what a fool I was. An utter fool!"

"Don't be too hard on yourself," I quickly interject, thinking back to what Belinda told me about how she'd been wooed. "I think Martin knew how to charm women into falling in love with him. I think he had made it his life's work."

"But how could I have not seen it? I knew enough about men and what they wanted. I knew what my father's rich friends' sons were like underneath their airs and bravado. I knew!"

"I don't know any rich young men, but I'd wager Martin was not like those wealthy sons. He wasn't one to put on airs. He put on masks."

Candace is quiet for a second. "Yes," she says vacantly, looking past me as if to gaze upon the years before. "He *was* different. I'd forgotten that's what I had liked best about him."

"That he was not like your other beaux?"

Candace sighs lightly, remembering a happier time, perhaps. "Yes. He hadn't come from money. He was just a stable hand, and he worked hard and took good care of my horse. He was quiet and polite and didn't strut about like a peacock. He was so handsome, but he never acted like he knew he was."

Now Candace turns her head to face the desert landscape. "Martin was the first man I ever lay with," she says softly. "Being with him in that way was like . . . like touching starlight. Like being made of starlight. When I found myself carrying his child and I told him, his first response wasn't 'What are you going to do?' but 'What can I do for you?' I said, 'You can marry me.' He just smiled and said, 'It would be my honor.'"

She pauses a moment in happy reverie.

"How old were you?" I ask.

Candace turns back to me. "I was eighteen, old enough. We went before a justice of the peace and didn't tell anyone for a month. He kept saying we should tell my parents, and I kept saying I wanted to wait for the right time. And he finally said, 'That time will never come, Candace.' He was right. We told them and my father exploded like a stick of dynamite. He accused Martin right then of only marrying me for my grandmother's trust, which I was set to come into on my twenty-first birthday. I told my father he was wrong, that Martin married me because he loved me and his child that I was carrying. They were devastated when I said that. Oh, the looks on their faces. And then my father accused Martin of getting me pregnant on purpose because he'd learned my grandmother's inheritance only passes to my offspring and not to a spouse. Father told Martin he wouldn't see a penny of that money, nor any of his money, either. He said he'd disinherit me before he'd see the likes of Martin getting one cent."

Candace looks off again into the golden horizon.

"I am so sorry that happened to you," I say. I don't know what other words to offer her.

"My mother just sat there weeping," Candace continues in a faraway voice. "Martin said very quietly that we should go, so we did. The whole time we were walking away from them, my father was shouting at me that I had ruined my life, and their lives, and that I wasn't welcome in that house. I didn't hear from my parents for a long time. Not even when I lost that baby at six months."

Candace turns to me and her cheeks are wet. "It was a little boy. So tiny. I don't know why he came too early. I wanted to shove him back inside me when he slipped out. He was so tiny. So beautiful."

"I'm so very sorry," I say, because I am. Because I know. I know what it's like to hold a miniature life in your hands, one that was knit together inside your own body. And I know what it's like to feel it grow cold in your embrace. I reach out to hold her hand. In compassion. In solidarity.

"I was so sad after that," Candace says, a moment later. "I loved that little baby. Martin thought I would grieve less if we had another child. We were living in his little cottage on the stable grounds and I was watching all my old friends in their beautiful clothes having riding parties and laughing and being happy. I didn't think I could ever smile again. I had only one person who seemed to care about me. Martin. So I believed him that another baby would fill the horrible emptiness inside me. I was overjoyed when I was with child again. I carried my second little boy until the very end, but he never took one breath. Not one."

I squeeze Candace's hand to remind her I am there, as she seems to be reliving the moment again, that abysmal moment when she realized another baby she'd labored to bring into the world had already left it. I can hear in her cracking voice this ache that does not lessen with time but rather hides in the shadows, this relentless specter that is always right there, just over your shoulder. One little twist and you're staring at it again. It is an ache that is as heavy as marble, as cold, as colorless.

"I am so sorry for your losses. Truly, I am," I say.

In the next moment Candace seems to pull away from the ter-

rible memory. She continues as if distanced from what she is telling me, as though it happened to someone else.

"I fell into an abyss then," she says tonelessly. "I didn't care
about anything. I didn't care that we finally had money every
month from my grandmother's trust and could move to a nicer
house. I didn't even care when I became pregnant again, and God
help me I didn't care when I gave birth and this time the child
lived. I didn't care that I had a beautiful little girl. I didn't care. I
didn't care that Martin often didn't come home at night. I didn't
care that I smelled other women's perfume on him." She looks
over at Kat sleeping like an angel across from us. "I was a terrible
mother to my little Kitty Kat."

I stroke her hand. "Surely you weren't."

"No. I was. All she wanted from me was love, but I felt like I
had nothing to give, so that is what she got."

"She knows you love her. She's always known. I am sure of it."

"I don't see how. I left them. I left them both. Just before Kat's
fourth birthday. I . . . I just . . . I wanted to disappear. I went to
the beach at the Venice Midway and I was going to step into the
ocean and just keep walking until it took me . . ."

Her voice falls away. I can almost believe she let the sea have
its way except that here she is next to me.

"And then?" I gently ask.

She blinks, long and slow, as if she's being pulled back from
the frothing surf. "There were some people on the beach who had
opium, and they invited me to . . . to be with them. Share their
pipe. Share everything. So I did. And I let whoever wanted to
touch me touch me, and I lay with whoever wanted to lie with
me. It seemed an easier way to dissolve than walking into the

ocean and drowning. And it was working. I was disappearing, a little more each day. It almost worked."

"But something happened?" I ask, because something surely did.

She is slow to answer.

"My father had heard from one of his club friends that I had been seen down there, in the company of scum, as he said," she finally replies. "He found me and brought me home. Home to Martin, that is. Martin hadn't even been looking for me."

Candace sighs heavily. I can see how exhausting this is for her. "I picked it up there in the alleys near the Venice Midway, this disease that is killing me." She laughs lightly, and it is a laugh empty of all mirth. "So, you see, I am disappearing after all. I am getting what I thought I wanted."

Again I squeeze her hand. It is all I can do. I cannot undo what has been done. I cannot give her back her husband or her dead children or her health or the wasted years with Kat.

"It was all—too much—for my mother," Candace says, a sob cracking her words into pieces. "She couldn't bear to see me the way I was. She died less than six months later. I'd broken her heart."

"I'm sure you didn't."

"No. I did."

Candace is quiet for several moments. She closes her eyes against the anguish of having lost her mother and feeling responsible for that loss. "It makes perfect sense now," she says many seconds later, eyes still closed and her voice void of strength.

"What does?"

She opens her eyes and looks across the patio to Kat's sleeping form. "Martin had *wanted* me to take my own life. It was good enough for him that I came down with consumption instead. That's why he was against my coming here. He wanted me dead because he had Kat. And Kat would inherit the trust."

I know she is right about that, but it doesn't explain everything. It doesn't explain why Martin left Los Angeles. Why he placed that advertisement. "Why, then, do you suppose he fled with her to San Francisco?"

Candace ponders this for only a moment. "It can only be because Father threatened to expose him. He'd found out that before me, Martin had trifled with other wealthy young women at the riding club in hopes of winning their affections. I didn't want to believe him. He told me this when he whisked me away to this sanatorium. Father said he was going to inform the police that Martin had wanted the consumption to kill me and that they should look into all of Martin's past activities."

"So Martin came to San Francisco and placed the ad . . ." I let the observation trail away as I contemplate this. It still makes no sense why he sought me out. I don't fit his pattern in any shape or form. "Why would he marry *me*, then?" I wonder out loud. I am little more than a pauper without Martin.

"You don't have money?" Candace says, a look of wearied puzzlement on her face.

"I don't have anything," I say, and even as the words leave my mouth, clarity falls over me. Of course. My poverty was the reason. If the police had caught up with Martin in San Francisco, his marriage to me would have been evidence only that he is a polygamist, not that he seduces women for their money and then plans for their demise after he marries them. "That's why he married me, Candace. He wanted proof that he's not a man who tricks wealthy women into marrying him. I'm the proof."

And that's why Martin took Kat with him, I muse to myself. Not to torture Candace. He doesn't care about Candace. He took Kat because she will inherit Candace's trust. Kat was money to Martin, the only thing he did care about.

We sit there with sweat trickling down our necks for several long moments while I wait for Candace to ask me again how Kat and I got out of the house but Martin did not.

She will ask.

And I must tell her.

We sit quietly for a long time, Candace's forehead lowered in her hand. Just when I think she has instead nodded off to sleep, she slowly tilts her head to look at me.

"What happened to Martin?"

I look about the patio to see who else is braving the worst heat of the day. The elderly man on the far side of the paving stones is snoring as he sleeps. The nurses are inside. Kat still slumbers.

I turn back to Candace.

"You need to know something before I tell you the rest. What I did, I did for Kat. It's important that you keep that in mind. I'm . . . I'm asking for your trust with what I am about to tell you."

Candace just stares at me and doesn't say anything.

"Do I have it? Do I have your trust?"

"I . . . I don't know you," she finally says.

"I brought Kat to you when I could've kept her. You owe me your trust."

She glances at her daughter and then shifts her gaze back to me. "All right," she says. "You have it."

I want to believe she means it. I will have to likewise trust that she does. *Here we go*, I tell myself.

"Do you remember when I said earlier that Belinda had come

to San Francisco looking for the husband she knew as James?" I ask. "And that she saw my wedding portrait with Martin?"

Candace nods, and I begin with that moment in the sitting room, when the portrait frame hit the rug as the kettle screamed in the kitchen. I tell her nearly everything from that moment to our arrival at the Loralei five days later.

I am vague about how Martin fell, telling Candace only that when he lunged at us there had been a struggle and he lost his footing. I don't tell her about the oddly familiar snippet of time when my arms were outstretched in those seconds as Martin reached for Belinda and I reached to stop him, and I don't tell her of the paired moment when I looked at Belinda and saw the rush of water and blood spill from between her legs—those memories belong to another time, another place, another girl. They have no place here on this sweltering patio.

And then I ask her again if I have her trust. She says I do.

"Then I'll tell you exactly what happened at the top of stairs. Everything you and I decide to do next hinges on what truly happened, and whether we report Martin Hocking as a polygamist and possibly the murderer of a rancher's daughter or whether we don't."

She stares at me, wide-eyed. "What do you mean? I don't understand."

"If we report Martin to the police, they will begin an investigation. They will ask when was the last time I saw him and many other questions. We can't have them asking questions, Candace."

When I say this I glance over at the sleeping child we both love. And when I look back at Candace, I see the exact moment she recalls that I told her that everything I did, I did for Kat.

"What are you telling me?" she says, anger and disbelief and dread thick in her voice. "What happened on those stairs?"

"He was going after Belinda," I answer quietly, mindful of the sleeping man and the open windows of the hacienda. "Kat already loved her little sister. She already loved her even though she hadn't been born yet. And Martin, this man who had lied to her about you, was lunging for Belinda. To harm her."

I see the scene again in my mind. Martin's arms outstretched to grab Belinda, mine to stop him, Belinda's to raise the letter opener.

And Kat's to protect the baby.

"Are you saying Kat *pushed* him?" Candace whispers.

I hesitate only a second before answering her.

"With every ounce of strength she had."

22

don't believe you," Candace says as a hot breeze kicks up a swirl of sand a few yards beyond the patio. "Kat wouldn't do that. She's not like him!"

But I can tell by the trembling in her voice that she does believe me. "You're right, she's not anything like Martin." I reach for her hand. Candace pulls it away. "She is not. Kat only meant to protect Belinda and the baby, I'm sure of it. She couldn't have known what that fall would do to him."

"How do I know it wasn't you who killed him?"

"It *was* me who killed him," I say, willing her to hear me. It matters what Kat thinks about how he died. And what others will think. "I am the one who left him in that house, unable to get out, unable to call for help. He was gravely injured when I left him, but it was I who left him! I couldn't let Kat see him like that, can't you see? I couldn't have Kat thinking again that she was responsible for the death of a parent, even the likes of him. She had to leave the house thinking he was alive. And everyone else must think it, too, that the last time Martin Hocking was in that house, he was alive and well."

"What was he going to do?" Candace says, not much more than a whisper. "What was he going to do to Belinda? To you?"

I shake my head at the thought of it and the echo of Martin's cold words. "We knew too much. We were obstacles to his plans. He said as much."

"And . . . Kat? What would he have done to her?" Candace's face is awash in fresh tears.

"He wouldn't have harmed her. She was financial security if and when the gold ran out. He wouldn't have harmed her. I think he knew how to keep her intimidated into silence."

"If everything you're saying is true, why didn't he just kill me?" Candace asks in a quiet but brusque voice.

"Because he didn't have to. You were already dying. Killing someone is messy business. With you, he didn't have to do anything."

We are quiet for a span of seconds as the worst truths about Martin settle about us.

"You believe she was saving the life of that baby?" Candace says a moment or two later.

"I know she was."

"Then . . . then it was a brave thing she did." Awe now laces Candace's words. "And selfless. She isn't like him, but she's not like me, either. It's my fault she doesn't speak."

"I don't think that's entirely true. Kat was starting to talk more and more before Belinda came, before the earthquake. She was beginning to trust the world to hear her voice again. I think she was too young to lose you the way she did, and she found a way to live with that loss by holding in all her words. But I think Martin was glad of her silence. I think he used his coldness and his lies to keep her too despondent and heartbroken to speak. I think she's gone quiet again now because she is bewildered and afraid. The earthquake and all those days afterward, they were days no child should have to see. I think she will find her voice again. Love brought it out before."

"Love from you?" Candace asks, and this time I cannot read her tone.

"Yes. I do love Kat. I love her as though she were my own child."

"And yet you brought her to me."

"She is your daughter, from your own body. And she knew you were alive. I'd be no better than Martin if I kept her from you."

"So you brought her even though this disease I have will probably kill me?"

This gives me pause for a moment. "Especially because of that."

Again we are quiet for a few moments.

"I know . . . I know she can't stay here at the sanatorium with you," I continue. "I had supposed your father would be here and that perhaps he would insist on taking her. I'm sorry for your loss. The nurse told me your father died recently."

"Yes," Candace says tonelessly.

"And as for Kat, she can stay with me in town for as long as you like. I have a little room at an inn near the train station. I can bring Kat in to see you every day that you are allowed visitors, if you want."

"You would do that?" she asks, bemused disbelief cloaking her tone. "You would do that for a sick woman you don't know?"

"I would do it for Kat. You're her mother and she loves you. I know she does. She wanted so much to come to you."

"I suppose that would suffice until I can make other arrangements."

I clear my throat nervously and for no good reason. "You don't have to make other arrangements. I am perfectly able and willing to care for her. Now and . . . later."

Across from us, Kat stirs on the cushions. Candace and I say nothing else as we watch her awaken. She sits up on the makeshift bed and looks first to me in puzzlement and then to Candace, as though she's just been dreaming and in that dream there was only one of us.

"Come, sweets," I tell her. Kat climbs up off the cushions and comes to me, and again I pull her into my lap so that she can be as close to her mother as the illness will allow.

Candace reaches out a weary arm and lays it across Kat's lap.

The unfinished conversation Candace and I were having hangs between us like a heavy chain, but we sit in the baking silence, a trio of wounded souls, until a nurse comes for Candace and tells her it is time for her rest before supper.

"Which inn are you staying at?" Candace asks as the nurse releases the brake on her lounge chair.

"The Desert Rose."

She nods and then looks to Kat. "I'll see you tomorrow, Kitty Kat. All right?"

Kat nods once.

And then Candace is wheeled away from us.

We ride in silence back to the inn. I want to ask Kat what she's thinking, but I know she will not answer me. She does not seem upset to leave her mother after having been with her for only a little while, nor does she seem anxious about our plans to return to the sanatorium the next day. We eat a supper of roasted chicken, pinto beans, and warm tortillas at a restaurant across the street from the hotel, and then we head up to our room and spend an hour before bed looking at Da's word book.

In the morning when we go downstairs for breakfast, the hotel owner informs us that a Mrs. Candace Hocking has paid for our stay and has secured the room for as long as she will require me to have it. She has also paid for our meals and the daily travel to and from the sanatorium. I am both relieved and a little miffed that Candace is meeting my expenses. I don't want to be paid to care for Kat—as though I am an employee—and that is what this seems like. But the cash from the strongbox won't last forever and I don't know how long I will be here. It seems this is a time when I will have to take each day as it comes.

Before we head out to the sanatorium, I take Kat to a little stationer's store a few blocks from the inn, where I purchase a tablet of paper and some wax crayons so that she can draw pictures. I have learned that this is one of the ways Kat can communicate. On the carriage drive to the sanatorium she draws a picture of a baby wearing a pink ruffled dress. It is as good a likeness of an infant as one could expect from a nearly seven-year-old, perhaps better. I know without asking that Kat has drawn a picture of Sarah. She misses the little one. I find that I do, too, strange as it may sound. I miss the baby and I miss having Belinda to talk to. When we return to town today I will need to send Belinda a telegram letting her know that I might not be leaving Tucson for a while.

Truth be told, I am hoping I am here indefinitely. Though I long for the calm beauty of the Loralei and the fragrance of the country air and the new home waiting for me away from the echoes of what happened in San Francisco, it won't be near as sweet without Kat. I don't want to return to that idyllic place if it means leaving Kat.

When we arrive at the sanatorium, the residents have just had their lunch. Several, including Candace, are on the patio awaiting their afternoon visitors. She seems less pale today, almost rosy-cheeked. Being reunited with her daughter seems to have invigorated her.

Today, there is a little boy with his mother visiting an older man who appears to be the boy's grandfather or uncle. The two children eye each other for a while before the lad finally comes over to Kat and asks if she wants to come play with him and his toy soldiers. By this time we have been visiting with Candace for close to an hour. Kat has already shown her the picture of Sarah, and now she is interested in the boy's miniature armies. The little boy, whose name is Randolph, looks to be about Kat's age, and he doesn't ask why she doesn't speak. Indeed, as Kat sits down in silence several yards away to look at the tiny brigade, I wonder if he is the youngest in his family and happy to dominate the conversation for a change.

With Kat out of earshot, Candace and I have the first chance to speak openly again about our situation. I first thank her for taking care of the hotel, the meals, and the transportation. She seems surprised at my gratitude.

"Of course I would pay the expenses of you minding Kat for me," she says. "I will pay you an hourly wage, as well."

I swallow back the sting of those words. "I don't need a wage."

"Nonsense. You are providing a service to me. Of course you need a wage."

I let the observation fall away. I won't take a penny for loving Kat, but I don't say this.

"Did she . . . talk about me last night? Did she say anything?" Candace asks.

I shake my head.

"Does she ever say anything about what happened to Martin? Does she ever ask about him? Does she wonder why you've not heard from him?"

My mind takes me to the first night in the park, when Kat and I slept under moonlight and she asked where her father was and I told her I'd sent him on his way. It was the last time she spoke of him.

"She hasn't said much of anything since the day Belinda came," I answer.

"Maybe she doesn't remember what happened."

"Maybe."

"What will I tell her if she starts talking again and she asks why her father hasn't come back?"

I bristle at the thought of Kat asking Candace this a year or two or three from now, and not me. "I think you can wait to decide what to tell her when and if she asks. Don't borrow tomorrow's burdens, my gram used to say."

"Yes, I suppose you're right."

Candace is quiet for a moment. "What was Kat like when you were with her in San Francisco? Was she happy? Did she have favorite toys? Little friends to play with?"

I tell Candace about the lovely house Martin had secured and our neighbor Libby and her little boy. I tell her about teaching Kat her letters and how brilliant she is at jigsaw puzzles and reading. I tell her about the back garden and our flowers, and the time Martin and I took her to the circus and to the seashore to collect shells.

Talking exhausts Candace, I know this from yesterday, so when she asks me next to tell her about Ireland, I fill the next hour with the happiest memories I have before everything changed for me, both to fill the silence and so that I won't seem like such a stranger. I tell her about the fishing boats and the pewter gray Irish Sea, and my gram's cottage with the curtains made from her wedding dress. I tell her about helping my mother watch the wee ones in the lane while their mams helped their fathers at the docks, and about my father, who wanted to go to university and was told he was not smart enough nor was there the money for it, so he took it upon himself to become a learned man. I tell her about the word book he made and how every time he read a book he collected all the words inside he did not know, found out what they meant, and wrote them down, and that he shared those words with me so that I, too, could know what he knew.

"Your father loved you," Candace says, and it must pain her to say this.

"Yes, he did. He was a kind and gentle man. Everyone in the village liked him. He was good to my brothers and my mam, and he wasn't bitter or resentful that he'd wanted to be a teacher and was instead a roofer. And he might have liked me best, being the youngest and the only girl." I laugh lightly and Candace smiles.

"It must have been difficult, then, to leave your parents when you came to America," she says.

I hesitate for a moment. I will be heading into dangerous waters if this conversation continues in this direction. "My father died when I was sixteen," I answer a second later. "He fell from a roof and struck his head. He never woke up afterward and died a few days later."

"That's so sad."

I nod and say nothing. Emotion as thick as taffy is wedged in my throat. I swallow against it.

"Your brothers were there to help you and your mother?" Candace asks.

"The older ones were married and on their own already. My brother Mason, who was nineteen, had already been set to come to America, and my mam told him not to stay back when he'd worked so hard to save to go. So then it was just Mam and me at the house."

"And?"

"And it was difficult for us without my father's income, to be sure. My two older brothers had their own families to provide for and I think their wives resented Mam's and my need. It was not a good time."

"But you left, too."

"I . . . I did. A few years later."

"You left your mother?"

I feel again the lapping of waters that I will not step into.

"She wanted me to go," I say, and nothing else.

Candace stares at me for a moment. "Are you close with your mother? Do you miss her?"

The image of Mam crying as she helps me pack my bag, and then pressing into my hand money she can't afford to give, fills my head; the ache of it fills my heart.

"Yes. I miss her very much."

"I miss my mother, too. You are lucky you can perhaps see yours again someday. I wish I could see mine. I would tell her how sorry I am."

I flick a stray tear away, smile at Candace, and say nothing.

"Do you think I will see her when I die? Will I see my mother in heaven?" Candace asks, holding my gaze as if she truly believes I know the answer.

"I can't imagine God keeping mothers from their children in that beautiful place," I venture.

She rests her head against the pillowed back of her lounge chair. "Yes. How could it be heaven if you were sad there?"

Kat strolls back to us and hovers between her mother's bed and my chair. Candace lifts her hand. "Come sit on my bed, Kitty Kat."

The child goes to her. Candace is tired from our visit, and Kat is giving away no words today. As I have nothing else to add, we sit in silence as the fan circulates the air above our heads and sweat beads on our brows and necks.

When we leave a little while later, Candace tells us she'll see us tomorrow. A hint of a smile tugs at Kat's mouth.

The next afternoon Candace wants Kat to herself during the visiting hours on the patio and I am asked to wait inside in the reception area. I watch with hesitation as Kat is led back. She turns once to look at me and I assume she wants assurance I'll be waiting for her, so this is what I tell her.

The next day it happens again, and the next. I ask the nurse who has been escorting Kat if Mrs. Hocking and her daughter are enjoying their visits, but what I truly want to know is if Kat is speaking to Candace.

The nurse smiles and shrugs. "They spend most of their time looking at nature books Mrs. Hocking has borrowed from the sanatorium library. You know how the child is. She doesn't talk."

On the fifth day, when Kat is collected to be taken back to Candace, she grabs my hand as if to take me along.

"I'm not sure I'm invited to go onto the patio with you," I tell her.

Kat stares at me for a few seconds before frowning and whispering the first word I've heard from her in days. "Come," she says.

I look to the nurse for confirmation that I am also being asked to come to the patio and she again shrugs; this was apparently Kat's idea.

"I see no harm in your going back with her," the nurse says. "You can always sit off to the side."

When we arrive on the patio Candace looks up in surprise at my approach; the smile she had been wearing for Kat diminishes a bit.

"She wanted me to come," I say softly.

"How do you know she did?" Candace asks, brow furrowed.

"Because she said it."

This seems to silence Candace for a moment. The visit commences then with Candace asking Kat about how we spent our morning. Perhaps this is one reason why Kat wanted me here, to answer what is probably a daily question. I tell Candace about the walk Kat and I took after breakfast and the lizard that crossed our path and the nice invitation from the innkeeper's wife when we returned to let Kat help her make empanadas, which are tiny little turnovers filled with meat, onions, and spices. After we share about our morning, Kat heads to the shadiest part of the patio to draw pictures on her tablet.

"Do you want me to go back into the waiting area?" I ask Candace.

"No."

We watch Kat for a few minutes.

"So. Your father's word book," Candace says. "Do you have it with you?"

"It's back at the inn."

"Would you bring it with you next time? Would you let me see it?"

"Of course." I can't help but smile. I'm hoping this means my days of waiting alone in the visitors' lounge are over.

The next day I do in fact bring Da's word book. I enjoy watching Candace look at my father's neat script and read aloud the words he found interesting and didn't want to forget. We laugh over some of them, like *flatulence*, which my father had described as meaning *those nasty pops of stink out the arse*, and *uppity*, which he defined as *bigheaded folks apt to scrape their noses on the ceiling*. When Candace comes across the word *redamancy*, which Da had defined as *loving someone deeply and having that love returned in full*, she looks up at me from the page.

"That first day, when you told me who you were, you said that you didn't care that you'd married a man you didn't love because you'd given your heart before and it had been crushed."

I look down at my father's handwriting, the comforting swirls and flourishes of the ink. "Yes."

"What happened?"

Kat is a few feet away working a puzzle that I bought at a five-and-ten in town—one hundred intricate pieces—and she is thoughtfully engaged in her task.

I decide in that moment that I will tell Candace a portion of what I never tell anyone. I want her to know that I understand what it's like to be betrayed by someone you thought you could trust. I want her to know that I know some of the hard road she's had to travel.

"There was a young man in my village," I begin. "A fisherman like his father and grandfather and brother. He was more a friend of Mason's than mine, but I fancied him. He was tall and strong and all the girls in the village had their eye on him. Da hadn't thought much of Colm. He wanted me to marry someone genteel and educated, a learned man. Colm wasn't like that. But Da was already gone when Colm started showing interest in me, coming round the cottage to visit, bringing Mam and me choice catches of fish, telling me I was pretty. Mam and I were struggling to get by, and when Colm asked me to marry him a few months before my eighteenth birthday, I said yes. Mam didn't try to talk me out of it even though she knew if Da were alive he'd say no. She thought at least I would have plenty to eat, married to a fisherman, and she wouldn't have to worry about how cold the house got at night, because she would be the only one in it. And I thought by marrying Colm I could make sure she had plenty to eat, too. I said yes partly for her, and she did the same thing."

"But you loved him?"

"I thought I did. I think it was more that I loved that he chose me, that of all the girls in the village he chose me."

"And you were happy at first, weren't you?" Candace says, and it's not a question. She knows there was bliss in the beginning, because the same was true for her.

"I was. At first."

I stop for a moment as I parcel out in my head what I will share with her and what I won't, what I will allow myself to relive in front of her and what I won't.

"When did you stop being happy?" she asks, when I don't continue.

"When I realized he could be as violent as he was loving," I answer. "Colm was a man of strong feelings, which means he could be extremely happy one moment and extremely unhappy the next. He did not take well to disappointment, and life is unfortunately full of disappointments."

"Did he hurt you? Did he strike you?" Candace's eyes are full of concern but also curiosity.

"He would throw things about when he was angry. Sometimes at me. Sometimes what he threw about were his fists."

"Did you tell anyone?"

I shrug, as much to shake off the hard weight of these memories as to ask, *What good would that have done?* "Even if I told someone, how could that person have helped me? Colm was my husband."

"So you just let him have his way?"

"I thought he would outgrow it. He was only a few years older than I was. I thought he would learn to bridle his anger and that he would learn to trust me. He couldn't stand to have another man so much as wish me a good day, and I thought in time he would realize that it was my full intent to be faithful to him and that I didn't see other men the way he thought men saw me. And I mistakenly thought that when I told him I was expecting a child, that would also soften him. But it didn't."

Candace is holding on to my every word, despite their awful weight. "What happened?" she asks, nearly breathless.

"I lost that baby much like you lost your first son," I say, and that is all I will say. "My child came too soon."

Candace's eyes are rimmed with silver now. "Was he angry at you for losing the child?"

My silence at her question allows her to think that he was.

"Did you leave him?" she asks. "Is that why you came to America? To get away from him?"

"No. Sadly, he died." My tone is flat and I cannot help it. "He had too much to drink one night on his boat and got clumsy. When it was discovered he had fallen overboard it was too late. He'd drowned."

Candace seems to need a moment to take this in. And I am glad for the seconds of silence.

"Did you mourn him?" she finally asks.

"I mourned the death of a life I might've had," I say. "If things had been different."

"So you came to America to start a new life."

"You could say that."

"And it turned out to be a terrible one?"

"Life in the tenements and the factory was very . . . difficult," I reply. "After everything I'd already had to bear, Martin's advertisement seemed quite inviting."

"And his bed?"

I ponder this for a moment. "Colm was at times a gentle lover and at times a beast. But I wasn't missing a man in that way. At some point I thought I would be ready again for the marriage bed and so I asked Martin from the very first if he would wait for affection to grow between us. He didn't seem to care one way or the other. He didn't even ask why."

"Because he didn't need you for that."

"No. He didn't. And then when I thought I was ready for such things, he didn't put up a fuss. But he never kissed my mouth, never told me I was beautiful, never looked at me the next morning like he couldn't wait to do again what we had done the night before. I realized in time he wasn't ever going to love me. I had decided that having Kat was enough and that I didn't need love from a man if I could have love from a child."

"It's not the same thing," Candace says, almost scolding me.

"No. It's not. But it's as grand in its own way."

She leans back into her pillows, satisfied. And I am glad.

I can see now she views me as perhaps a sister of sorts, rather than a contender.

I have told her the truth about who I am, and how I am like her, and it has bonded us.

It isn't the whole truth, but my words included no lies.

23

A week passes in Tucson, and then another. Our days are the same from one sunrise to the next. Kat and I spend the mornings in town, sometimes reading or doing puzzles or taking a walk or plucking out notes on the piano in the hotel lobby. We spend the latter part of the afternoon with Candace.

At first Kat seems happy with our slow-paced daily routine. She is as relaxed as I have seen her in quite a while, and she has even started to grace us with a few words, here and there. Thankfully Candace does not make a big show when Kat answers one of her questions with her voice instead of a nod.

But as the hot yet tranquil days pile on, I nevertheless begin to sense a restlessness in Kat, a tendency to stare off into the distance as though she's heard her name being called from somewhere far away. Candace notices it, too, after a few days and asks me out of Kat's hearing if I think the child is remembering what happened on the stairs. But I don't think that is what is occupying Kat's thoughts. She seems a bit troubled in her spirit, true, but not anguished. It is something else, some other concern she has. I begin to wonder if she's sensing that at some point she's going to have to choose between her mother and me. Even if the real choice is made for her, which it likely will be, she will have to choose how she will accept it.

On one of our trips back to the hotel, on a particularly burning-hot afternoon, I ask Kat if there's anything I can do for her. I want to help her feel comfortable with the transition that we can all sense is coming. Candace and I both know living in a hotel is no life for a child and that at some point a more permanent arrangement has to be made. We are living in limbo every day we are here. It is so disconcerting that I sometimes find myself staring off into the distance.

"Do you want to talk about anything?" I ask her. "Do you want to tell me what's bothering you?"

And to my surprise she leans into me and murmurs, "I want . . . to go home."

It is a giant of a sentence for a girl who hardly ever speaks, and such a surprising one; so surprising that for a moment I am speechless.

"Home?" I finally echo.

"I want to go home."

I don't know how to respond to her. What is she thinking of when she thinks of home? It can't be here in Tucson with her mother or she wouldn't have uttered these words. Is it the house in San Francisco? Did that place, with me there as her second mother, feel like home to her? The thought that this might be true is dizzyingly sweet one moment but achingly disquieting the next. I haven't even shared with her that the house we lived in is most likely gone.

"I have something I need to tell you about our house in San Francisco," I say. "I probably should have told you sooner, but we've been so busy with . . . all the changes."

She tips her head up to look at me, her questioning eyes inviting me to continue.

"The fire that was so terrible when we were sleeping in the park? It came to our street, Kat, and I'm pretty sure that it took the house. The clothes and toys and drawings that were in your room . . . I'm sorry to tell you, poppet, but I believe they are gone. I think all the houses in our neighborhood are gone."

Her eyes widen but she says nothing.

"But I want you to know that if the fire did take our house, what was inside it can be replaced," I say. "You can get new clothes and new toys and new books, all right?"

She stares at me, taking in this news silently. And then she whispers, "Timmy's house, too?"

"I don't know for sure, love. Timmy's house was made of bricks so maybe it did not burn all the way. But he wasn't home then, remember? He and his parents were gone the morning the earth shook. They weren't there. I'm sure he's fine."

"My house is burnt?"

"Yes, love, I think it is."

She ponders this silently for a moment, as she looks out the carriage window. I can't tell what she is thinking. I am about to ask her if this news is upsetting her when she turns her face upward toward mine again.

"Are you sad?" she asks.

"A little," I answer. "I was happy living there with you. Are you sad?"

Kat is quiet a moment. "A little."

"But I am so very happy that even though the house might be gone, you and I are safe."

"And Mama and Belinda and baby Sarah, too," she adds, as though they had all been with us the whole time and I forgot to mention them.

I realize at this moment that what she's missing is not so much the house itself but something else, something a fire cannot touch. It's that sacred place where your soul is at rest because all the people you love most are there. I know the place. I knew it in Donaghadee, a long time ago, and I've stumbled upon it again, in my own strange way, with Kat.

"Yes." I kiss the top of her head. "Mama and Belinda and baby Sarah, too."

"But not Father," she says, and I lift my head from hers with a slight start.

"What was that, love?" I say, and I can feel the calm of the previous moment bleeding away like water in a drain.

"Not Father."

I want her to continue, to tell me what she means, but I don't know how to coax thoughts out in a way that will keep her thinking of home and everything wonderful. I pull away just enough to be able to see her expression. She is staring at the floor of the carriage, a pensive look on her face.

I fold my arms tighter about her. "It's all right to feel topsy-turvy about your father, love. It's all right."

"He lied."

"Yes. He did."

"He's not nice."

I lay my head against hers and a tear that I am very glad she cannot see falls on her hair. I say nothing.

"He went away?" Her tone is questioning, as though she requires assurance that a return to home does not equal a return to him.

"Yes. I think he's gone. Maybe for a very long time. Maybe for always." And because I do not want Kat to live a life of bitterness, I offer her the only advice I can in this moment. "Your father didn't know how to love, sweets. He didn't know. But you do. You *do*. Promise me that you will remember that whenever you think of him, Kat. He did not know the way of love. But you do. Promise me?"

She nods and says nothing more, not on the rest of the carriage ride and not for the rest of the day. But as we lie in our sweltering room that night I think of what she said to me about wanting home, and a solution presents itself to me. It is far from perfect, but this is not a perfect world, is it?

Even so, it is a solution I don't have the courage yet to suggest. I must wait until the timing seems right.

By the end of the third week in Tucson, the calendar has leaned into mid-May and the scorching heat is feeling more and more like a hot poker needling at me to tell Candace my idea.

On one hot and breezy afternoon, we go to visit Candace as usual, and after a while, Kat does what she usually does and heads to the coolest corner of the patio to draw pictures.

A letter bearing a Texas postmark is resting in Candace's lap; it has been there for the entirety of our visit. I can feel the weight of it between us. That letter is important or Candace would not have brought it out to the patio with her. Candace sees me looking at it and fingers the edges of the envelope.

"I've heard from my cousin Lucinda," she says, her voice already sounding tired and weak even though we've only been with her an hour.

"Oh?"

"She's the youngest daughter of my mother's sister and a few years older than me. She lives in Texas. I wrote to her just after you arrived. Lucinda has invited Kat and me to come live with her and her husband and her two young sons."

My heart starts to pound inside me and words of response can't find their way to my tongue. When I say nothing, Candace continues.

"My father left the bulk of his estate to worthy causes. He disinherited me just like he said he would so that Martin would receive nothing when I die. But he left a substantial amount to this facility. I can stay here in Tucson for the next twenty years if I want to. But I don't want to. And I don't have twenty years. My condition is worsening. The doctor and nurses here have told me as much."

Tears prick my eyes and I fight them back. "I'm sorry." I am indeed truly sad for her, but I also don't want her taking Kat to Texas. I don't know if the tears are for me or for her.

"Lucinda says she and her husband are willing to raise Kat. If we went now, Kat would have a chance to get to know them before I . . . before I go."

But even as these words sting, I sense a hesitancy in Candace's voice.

"Is that what you want?" I ask, my voice sounding feeble in my ears.

Candace sighs and gazes at Kat on the other side of the patio. "I don't know what I want, other than I want my Kitty Kat to be happy and cared for. Not just now but after I am gone."

The tears I'm holding at bay begin to slip down my face because this is what I want most, too, for Kat to be happy and cared for, now and always. I must have taken leave of my senses to think I was the suitable choice to make it so. I am not her family. I am not even legally her stepmother. I am someone who has known her for less than two years. I am someone who answered an advertisement to marry a stranger. I am someone with a past that I never allow myself to revisit.

I love Kat, I do. But who am I to think I should be the one to mother her after Candace passes?

Candace shifts her gaze back to me. "Lucinda said they are willing to raise her," she whispers.

I nod but do not trust myself to say, *I heard you.*

"She didn't say they are wanting to, though. I fear they are merely offering what family should offer."

"Don't go," I blurt, surprising myself with how these two words explode off my tongue. "Please, don't take her there."

Candace stares at me for a moment. "She's my daughter," she says quietly but with authority.

"I know she is. But she . . . she loves her little sister so much. I know that might be hard for you to imagine because of who Sarah is, but Kat loves her just the same. She would never see her again if you took her to Texas. And Kat . . . Kat loves me, too, Candace. I'm so sorry if that's hard to hear, but she does. And I love her. Doesn't love make a home? Doesn't love make a family? She's been through so much in her young life. I'm the only one besides you who knows just how much she's had to shoulder. Your cousin doesn't know. Your cousin would never know!"

The tears continue to fall, and I blot them with my sleeve.

Candace is staring hard at me. "You would have me hand over my child to you while I am still living? You would have me go to Texas without her?"

"No! No, I would not have you do that."

"I cannot have her stay here with you in that hotel for who knows how long. A hotel is not a home."

"I'm not asking you to do that, either."

"Then what would you have me do?"

I lean forward and reach for one of her bone-thin hands. "Kat wants us to all be together—you, me, her baby sister, and Belinda. She told me this in the carriage a few days ago."

Candace furrows an eyebrow. "She said that?"

"In her own way, yes. She said she wanted to go home and she mentioned all of us being there, including you, wherever that home may be. She knows it's not here in Tucson. She's knows it's not in San Francisco. I think she means the inn in San Rafaela where Belinda and Sarah are."

Candace stares at me, shakes her head slightly. "I don't understand what you are suggesting."

"We are the people who she loves, Candace. We are the people that make up her home, her world. It's a fragile world, but it's the only one she has, and she is just learning to trust it again. I would have you come to San Rafaela and live with us at the Loralei. I would have you spend your remaining days, however many you are destined to have, in that beautiful place surrounded by people who will care for you and your daughter; people who want to be in Kat's life and who are not just merely willing to be. I would have you know that when you breathe your last your daughter will have everything you want for her. It's what Kat wants. She wants us all to be together."

Candace's eyes have turned silver just imagining being in a place of beauty, but the imperfection of this plan is so clear. "You know what you are asking of me," she whispers, staring at me with her hollowed eyes.

I nod. I do know. San Rafaela is not Tucson. The air on the Pacific coast is not oven hot; it is cool and fragrant and sometimes the morning fog is as moist and damp as a blanket made of rain. It is not the place for someone with consumption.

I squeeze her hand. "If your doctor thinks your condition is indeed worsening, even here, then where do you want to spend the rest of your mortal life?" I ask. "I know where I would want to spend mine. And I know who will give Kat the kind of home you want her to have, not just for now but always. *I* will."

Candace and I sit that way for several long minutes, I imploring her silently to ponder my audacious solution and she bravely considering it. I am most likely asking her to cut her life shorter than if she were to relocate to Texas, and if that isn't enough, I'm asking her to trust me with the raising of her child.

"I need to think about this." Candace withdraws her hand from mine. "I'm tired."

As I rise from my chair, I can see that she is exhausted in every way. I have laid too much on her.

In the carriage back to the hotel, Kat is more withdrawn than she has been in several days, and I wonder if she heard some of Candace's and my conversation. Even though she was absorbed in her artwork several yards away, there is nothing wrong with Kat's hearing, and we were the only ones out on the patio today. Candace and I kept our voices low, but Kat might've heard enough to understand that life is full of difficult choices.

The next day when we return to Las Palomas, the nurse comes out to the reception area and tells me Mrs. Hocking would like to speak to her daughter alone for a little while. There is nothing I can say except that I shall wait.

Many minutes pass before the nurse returns and says that I am also now welcome out on the patio. When I reach Candace at her lounge, Kat is sitting in the chair that I often sit in and I see what appears to be a look of satisfaction on her young face. Candace looks weary today, and yet there is a look of contentment on her face as well.

"Kat and I would like to come live at the Loralei with you," she says.

A smile spreads itself across my face and I go to them, scooping Kat onto my lap as I take the chair, and then I lean in to Candace as close as I dare. "When would you like to go?"

Candace surveys the monochrome landscape on the other side of the shade, and a bouncing tumbleweed skips by. "The sooner the better. I'll have my lawyer make all the arrangements. It will only take a phone call. I'll take care of it."

As we head back to the inn, I want to ask Kat what she and her mother talked about those long minutes before I was brought back to them, but I'm not sure Kat will have the words to tell me, and in the end it doesn't seem to matter.

"I'm so glad we're all going home together," I say instead.

Kat leans against me and nods.

"This is what you wanted, isn't it, Kat? For us all to be in one house?"

"Yes," she says. "Home."

When we get back to town, I pop into the Western Union office to send Belinda a telegram letting her know that Kat and I are returning to the Loralei and that we are bringing Candace with us.

Two days later we board a train car that Candace has arranged to be solely ours so that no one need be worried about being exposed to tuberculosis. Despite being pale and wearing a lace mask, Candace looks beautiful in a lemon-yellow shirtwaist trimmed in yards of white lace. She has had her hair professionally coiffed, and while she leans heavily on me as we make our way across the platform, she still looks every inch a well-bred woman of influence.

Not long after we settle in to our well-appointed private car, the train begins to ease away from the depot, and toward everything that lies beyond the desert's blistering reach.

24

When we arrive at the San Mateo train station two days later, Belinda, Elliot, and the baby are there to greet us. It is such a happy reunion and, oh, the sweet changes in baby Sarah in the month that Kat and I have been gone. She is smiling and cooing and it's hard to believe Martin had a part in creating something so wonderful.

Introducing Candace to Belinda is not as awkward as I thought it might be; the three of us have all traveled the same journey—along different paths, of course—and we've a kinship that strangely unites us. As we make our way home to the Loralei through the peaceful countryside, Candace keeps remarking how beautiful and green the view out the carriage window is. She is equally taken with the Loralei, as I'd hoped she would be. It is surely nothing like the fancy hotels she probably stayed in as a girl growing up in a wealthy family, but there is a quaint beauty at the Loralei that I would guess no opulent palace can match.

Belinda gives Candace her bedroom on the main floor. Belinda and Sarah join Kat and me on the second floor. Candace, Kat, and I are taking up three of the inn's guestrooms and Candace insists on paying Belinda the room rate for all of them.

Belinda at first attempts to refuse, but Candace says, "The inn is your livelihood, and I must have a part in making this solution work for all of us. Let me have my part."

Belinda relents.

Candace is exhausted by the time we unpack her things, and Belinda suggests she rest before dinner. But Candace does not want to be inside; she wants to be out by the garden under that peach tree. Elliot hauls out a sofa and positions it so that Candace can nap among the shady boughs and buzzing bees. The picture of her on that sofa with Kat sitting next to her on a blanket with Sarah in her lap is a beautiful image I know I will always remember.

What a beautiful family Martin has made of us, despite himself.

For a full week I allow myself to enjoy the serenity of the Loralei and the treasure of having Kat there and knowing that it is the beginning of her always being with me. Candace spends as much time outside as the weather will allow, and even though the intense Tucson heat is no longer aiding to keep her tuberculosis at bay, she seems rejuvenated in her spirit if not in her body. I think she's happy for the first time in years.

We spend many of our afternoons out under the peach tree, sitting on a blanket and listening to her tell us stories from her childhood, a pastime I encourage so that Kat will always feel a connection to her first mother.

I find I very much enjoy helping Belinda run the inn. With Sarah still waking at nights to nurse, I quickly settle in to being in charge of making breakfast for us and any inn guests. Belinda also hands over all the laundry duties to me when I ask her to. I like doing the washing. It reminds me of what is possible to clean away with just water, soap, and effort.

Elliot is at the inn nearly every day; it's plain to see how very much he loves Belinda, and it is also clear that Belinda's perspective of what romantic love looks like is also changing. Time will ease the distress of the mistake she made in choosing Martin over Elliot, I am sure. When it does, Elliot will be there.

When I have a moment alone with Elliot I ask him what he has done about the mine. He tells me the earthquake caved in the entrance. There may be gold to be had yet inside, but getting to it now will be near impossible without immense labor and probably dynamite.

"No one will be going back inside for a long time, if at all, but I set out a sign to remind any passersby that it is private property," he tells me. "Belinda has not been out there, and it is far enough away on the property that she doesn't need to see it. That mine has brought her nothing but heartache."

I ask Elliot if he knows how Martin was able to mine the gold without Belinda knowing, and he answers that he suspects Martin had enlisted a couple of paid laborers to dig it out. Two Chinese men dressed in filthy clothes had been seen multiple times in Martin's company in San Mateo. Elliot had been asked by a longtime friend of Belinda's father if he knew who those Chinese men were who'd been with Belinda's new husband.

"I never saw the two men myself," Elliot says. "And no one has seen them lately."

I walk out to the mine's entrance after this conversation to see its destruction for myself. There is no longer an opening to the cave. Instead, there is an immense pile of boulders and a NO TRESPASSING sign. I am very glad the mine sits on the farthest edge of Belinda's property, such that none of us need ever stand again where I am standing.

As the first of June approaches, I know I can no longer put off going back to San Francisco to see the ruins of the house for myself. I have checked the final tallies of the dead and injured from the quake and fire. Martin Hocking's name is not listed anywhere, which means either he didn't get out of the house and no one has identified his remains, or somehow he did get out but he didn't use the name Martin Hocking while getting treatment for his injuries. I must know which it is.

The four of us—Belinda, Candace, Elliot, and I—sit in the common area one evening after the children are in bed, and on a night when there are no guests, to discuss what my next steps should be. It is nice to have Elliot a part of the conversation, as he is levelheaded and somewhat outside the situation. Not only that, but he made a trip to the county recorder's office in Redwood City to look into the legalities of getting out from underneath a marriage when a spouse has vanished.

We already decided earlier that my reporting Martin as a polygamist to the San Francisco Police no longer seems wise. Neither Belinda nor Candace wants me going to prison for having abandoned Martin to die in that house, nor do we want blame to fall on Kat for having caused his terrible injuries in the first place. A full investigation into his polygamist activities would surely lead to the police to discover that Martin *had* come back to San Francisco on the day of the earthquake. I would be asked too many questions.

It does, however, seem to be in Belinda's best interest to report one James Bigelow as having deserted her. Elliot tells us Belinda cannot file for a dissolution of her marriage based on desertion if she does not report that her husband has done so. We decide she will tell the authorities that she and James had grown distant since their rather impulsive nuptials, that he wasn't keen on the responsibilities of being a father, and that he'd threatened to leave Belinda. The authorities may or may not exert any effort in looking for James Bigelow, but even if they do, what will they find of him? James Bigelow is a ghost. He will be seen as a scoundrel who truly abandoned his wife, leaving no trace of where he ran off to.

But it is not as clear to me what I should do. "If I go back to San Francisco and report Martin as missing, will they look for him?" I wonder aloud. "With everything needing to be done to recover from the earthquake, I wonder if they will."

"Then the same will be true for you as it is for me," Belinda says. "You, too, can be free to marry again. They will eventually declare Martin dead, won't they?"

"After seven years," Elliot says. "That's a long time, Sophie."

"What else can I do? I can't change how long it takes," I reply. "If it takes seven years, it takes seven years. I would have to wait."

"You could report Martin as having abandoned you like I am going to do. You could have your marriage dissolved, too," Belinda says.

But I don't want my marriage dissolved. I'd rather be viewed as Martin's widow than an unmarried woman. I don't want to go back to being Sophie Whalen.

"I would never be able to prove Martin abandoned me," I say instead. "He was good to Kat and me. And he owned that beautiful house and all the furniture inside it. Plus he had three thousand dollars in a bank account. He wouldn't just leave all of that as your James would have left you and your inn. I could never prove that he would do that."

The three of us are quiet for a moment. I don't want to report that Martin has deserted me, but I'm not convinced I should report him missing, either.

"What if I report him missing, and in their search for him, the police go to what's left of the house and find his remains?" I ask. "Won't they wonder why I didn't know he was in the house when it burned? Won't they wonder why he didn't get out? The police and firemen and army soldiers were going up and down the neighborhood streets, shouting for people to evacuate. I read that in the papers. Won't they wonder why Martin didn't heed their command?"

"Some people don't listen to authority," Belinda replies. "They will probably think he was a foolish man who didn't listen to them. He will be a casualty of the earthquake and fire. They will declare him deceased, won't they?"

I ponder this for a moment. Perhaps Belinda is right. But what if she is wrong? What if going to the police to report that Martin is missing leads to a deeper look at Martin's life? A deeper look at mine?

"I could just quietly disappear," I say. "Nobody is going to miss me in San Francisco. No one is looking for me there, and no one's going to find me here. And I don't need Martin to be missing and then declared dead for me to be free to marry another. I am already not legally married to him."

The others around the table are quiet while they consider my words.

"Would you still call yourself Sophie Hocking, then?" Elliot finally asks. "Is that the name you would go by?"

"I don't see why not." I turn to Candace. "If anyone here in San Rafaela asks, I can say that I am your sister-in-law. It will seem natural then for me to be the person who takes Kat if and when your disease claims you." I do not mention that in due time, people would surely forget that I wasn't Kat's real mother, because we would have the same surname. There is another reason why I would like to keep Martin's name, but I don't need to share it with Candace; I don't even need to think about it. It has nothing to do with any of this.

Candace holds my gaze, her brow a wee bit furrowed. "But you're not my sister-in-law. Martin doesn't have a brother."

"I know. It's just an answer for anyone who asks. How many even will?"

"Or," Candace says slowly, as though she is still puzzling out a solution. "Or we can just tell anyone around here who asks that Kat is Sophie's daughter and that I am the relative. And if locals ask where Sophie's husband is, and if she feels so inclined to answer, she can tell them that he sadly perished in the earthquake and fire, which is true."

There isn't a sound around the table at this suggestion.

"I . . . I would never ask you to do that," I finally sputter.

"You aren't. I am saying it makes the most sense. We need to keep alive the ruse of Martin's marriage to you to protect you and

Kat from any kind of criminal prosecution—and you, too, Belinda; you were there; you knew what happened and did nothing—then it makes the most sense. You know it does. I'll soon be gone. It makes the most sense."

"But . . . Kat's inheritance. Don't you want her to have the money your grandmother left you? You told me it can only be bequeathed to your child," I counter.

"Kat will still receive the inheritance," Candace says wearily. The length of this conversation is exhausting her. "We'll just tell people here she is your daughter. My lawyer in Los Angeles knows Kat is my child. He also knows I am dying. I'll instruct him to draw up a document appointing you as my daughter's legal guardian, Sophie, so that if you should ever need to prove you are the rightful person to raise her, you will have it."

"Won't your lawyer wonder who I am?"

"I'll tell him you *are* my sister-in-law, just like you said, that you married Martin's brother. That's why your last name is also Hocking. He won't know Martin didn't have a brother."

"But, Candace—," Belinda begins, and Candace cuts her off.

"Look. I know she's *my* Kitty Kat. I know it, and that's all that matters. The rest is how we keep her safe and the rest of you able to care for her. And this is how we do it."

The next day, the first Friday in June, Elliot arrives at the inn to take me to the depot to board the first train of the day for San Francisco. My plan is to do what I need to do and return by evening, as staying overnight in a city of refugees is out of the question. From what I have read in the *San Francisco Examiner*, which Elliot has been able to procure for me a time or two, Golden Gate

Park is still a tent city of thousands upon thousands of homeless. Kat and I were lucky to have the Loralei to escape to. Too many others don't have such a place.

On my way out the door, I tell Kat that she gets to spend the day with her mama and Belinda and the baby while I see to affairs in need of attending.

"Where?" she says, her head cocked in puzzlement. I have never said such a thing to her before.

"Out and about," I say cheerfully. "I'll bring you back a sweet." And I kiss her head and leave with Elliot before she can decide that is not a good enough answer.

We are less than a mile down the lane when Elliot offers to accompany me to San Francisco to help me survey the ruin of my house.

To help with whatever I might find there.

"It's kind of you, to be sure, but I will be fine. I can manage this," I answer. "And you have your own business to run."

"But how will you get out to where your house was? I doubt the streetcars are running, and what if you can't hail a carriage?"

"I'll be all right. I've walked a long stretch before. I can do it again."

"And if there are remains of a body to be dealt with? What will you do then?" His tone is abrupt and blunt, as though he means to surprise and nauseate me into accepting his offer of assistance.

But I am not afraid to come upon the burnt remains of Martin Hocking. I feel nothing but disgust for him. I've already considered this, imagined it. Practiced it in my head. I've already visualized the pile of ashes or the blackened corpse or the grisly mixture of both. I shall not be undone by it. I am ready to see what the fires of judgment did to Martin.

"I'll bury anything I find in the backyard," I reply to Elliot.

"With what? And in broad daylight?"

"I'll find a way. And I'll do it after sundown if I must. You forget what I've already had to do."

He is quiet for a few seconds. "Let me come with you," he says a moment later. "Let me help you . . . do this."

"And be responsible for implicating another person in my offenses? No. I won't let you be part of this. This is my mess to clean up. Besides, I'll be fine."

He shakes his head and looks away from me. He either doesn't believe I will be fine or is sickened that I will be. "If you're there after sundown, you'll miss the last train."

"I very much hope that does not happen. I'll sleep on a bench in the train station if I do miss it, and I'll ask you to please tell Kat that the trains are running off schedule and I'll catch another one tomorrow. I've had to sleep in worse places than a train station, Elliot. I appreciate your concern, I do. But you don't need to worry about me. I'll be fine."

He is quiet after this and we say little the rest of the way.

"I'll come back for you at seven thirty tonight," Elliot says, when he drops me off at the depot twenty minutes later.

"If I'm detained, I'll find a way to send a telegram to your shop," I reply. "Please make sure Kat understands that I am all right."

"If it comes to that, I will." He tips his hat in farewell and I turn for the platform and the train that will take me to what is left of San Francisco and the life that I tried to make for myself there.

25

With the Southern Pacific train station on Townsend Street operational again, it takes less than an hour to return to San Francisco, as opposed to the hours-long trek we had to make after the quake. I step out onto streets that have been stripped bare of their burned buildings. I remember that the inferno that scorched this area south of Mission Street had swept its way north to join a second fire in those first few hours after Belinda gave birth. The worst burns we saw at the pavilion came from the blaze that consumed these neighborhoods. There is little left of these city blocks now to suggest what stood here before; I see only scraped slabs, oddly shaped lumps of charred metal, flattened piles of ash, and men and women with shovels and wagons, working to cart it all away. On a few scraped lots, lumber has been delivered and the framing of new structures has begun.

Street signs that might have told me where I am are gone now, and I have to ask in which direction I might find the neighborhoods near Russian Hill. A man in utility worker coveralls takes pity on me when I tell him I've come to see what is left of my house near there. He offers to take me in his wagon as far as Union Square. It is less than half the distance; I will still have a combination of a dozen blocks north and about that many west to get to the house, but I take him up on his offer. Twenty blocks isn't so bad to walk, not when you have a purpose. He sets off at a slow pace and I notice his horse is a tired-looking creature whose ribs are showing through its flanks. The man sees me looking with compassion at the animal.

"We've had to work the horses too hard," he says. "They all look like this. Some worse. It can't be helped. There is too much to haul away."

We travel through the ruin of the neighborhoods south of Market and arrive ten burned-out blocks later at what is left of Union Square. What had been so familiar to me only a few months before is now a foreign landscape. The Dewey Monument—a tall obelisk topped with the lithe goddess of victory to honor Admiral Dewey's bravery in the Spanish-American War—still stands in the center of the square, but I recognize little else. At the base of the victory statue is a hastily constructed hotel in the shadow of its wounded parent, the looming but heavily damaged Hotel St. Francis. But all around that bit of makeshift new construction is dead grass and soot that spreads out on all four sides toward shells of buildings or single walls or open spaces cleared clean of what once stood there.

I thank the man who gave me the ride and I start north up Powell, a street I know. I pass men of all ages laboring to clear away debris or lay new cable-car track. I know that at first, men were pressed into service because there was so much work to be done. In the early weeks after the fires, any able-bodied man still in the city was told he would assist in the cleanup efforts or leave. Only those with special tags reading DO NOT PRESS had been able to escape the call to help, and these were only doctors and others whose special abilities had been needed elsewhere. I'd wager most of these workers are now getting paid for their efforts; they are heartily laboring at the task and dressed appropriately for the work.

I turn on California Street to head west again, and I pass signs for food distribution tents and announcements for the locations of community kitchens that have been set up. I walk past one such place with long tables where soot-covered workers and mothers with little children and even men in suits are seated and eating a meal. I'd read earlier in the *Chronicle*—which is using the *Oakland Enquirer*'s printing presses—that the city has been divided into sections for relief supplies, and each one is run by a chairman aided by an army officer. Within the sections are numbered food stations distributing supplies that have been sent from everywhere in the country and that are guarded by armed military so that nothing can be stolen and then black-marketed. A few automobiles rumble past me, all of them being driven by uniformed soldiers—apparently privately owned vehicles are still much under the command of the military. Most of the traffic in the street is comprised of wagons being pulled by thin, overburdened horses.

Some folks walking the streets along with me seem to be there only to view the grim austerity of this once golden city. I can tell by their clothes and manner that they've come from Oakland or some other place to sightsee. There are even vendors on the street selling these people trinkets pulled from the ashes as souvenirs.

I don't understand the desire to view this cataclysmic destruction or to carry home a memento of it. I suppose some people simply need to see what could have happened to them but didn't, and to have a visual reminder of it.

Eight blocks later when I at last turn to start up Polk, the immediate view up the street is an incline of alternating flatness and scattered stalwart chimneys. It is like a desert landscape lacking any hue or definition except for scattered cacti made of brick that are reaching for the sky with wounded arms. Houses and buildings that were constructed of brick and stone are the exception. Some of these still stand, but they are hollowed out, as though the home or building had been begun but then never completed. Off in the distance on the top of Russian Hill I see a small clutch of houses that somehow escaped the flames. They stand as if to remind everyone who looks at them of all the beautiful homes that stood on these streets.

A few people are out and about. Some are raking through debris in the continued search, I suppose, for the odd gem or coin that the flames did not devour. Others are sweeping, pushing, and piling the remains of their houses into piles to be hauled away and dumped in large open spaces by the marina. I continue up the street, remembering how it was to escape down it the morning of the quake.

As I ascend the last block, I can't get a good look at where my house should be, as the home directly next door is a brick structure that is partially still standing and obstructing my view. I can see that Libby's house across the street still stands as well, but it is missing half its roof and every window frame is charred. My breath is coming in short gasps as I close the distance and step ever nearer to the house I lived in. When the hulk of the house next door is no longer impeding my view, I behold what remains. It is as though a giant hand of flame had reached down and grabbed the contents of my house, held it in its blazing fingers, and then flung to the ground its ashes. There are no walls, no floors, no roof.

There is no part of the house that is recognizable except for half the chimney, the misshapen shell of the cookstove in what had been the kitchen, and twisted pipes here and there. Large chunks of blackened onyx and marble from the fallen fireplaces on the second story litter the ground floor like ancient ruins. The space the house occupied looks smaller somehow, reduced now to just its footprint on the charred ground.

There are no timbers to have to push past to get to what had been the kitchen, no heaping piles of burnt plaster, no ceiling tiles or skeletal frames of bedroom furniture. I read in the newspaper before I came that the fires had burned at one thousand degrees Fahrenheit—an unbelievably intense heat that I couldn't imagine until now. This fire did not just burn; it consumed.

I pick my way across the pocked ground and around the fallen fireplaces, crunching down on unrecognizable charred bits, to stand at the iron cookstove. I look down at the spot where I left Martin. He was by the butler's table and the back window, both of which are now gone, and near the door to the boiler room, now a sunken receptacle of ash and blackened metal. I bend down to poke at the gray powder at my feet with a shard of marble, but I find not a trace of Martin's body. Not his wedding ring, not a tooth, not a fragment of bone.

I cast my gaze back across what had been the dining room,

searching for a skull, a torso of blackened ribs. Shouldn't there be a scrap of something if Martin crawled across the kitchen floor in an attempt to escape? I stand and pick my way back among the second-story fireplaces, all of them heavy enough to fall on a burning body and crush it.

As I stare at the bizarre detritus at my feet, a mix of melancholy and uncertainty overcomes me.

I wanted there to be something left of Martin. I needed there to be a recognizable shred of who he was to bury, not because he deserves it but because I do, and so does Kat. It was never my design to hurt him, nor had it been Kat's. Still, I chose not to save him. I chose not to run back into the house and drag his broken body out. I chose to deceive Kat so that I could protect her. I chose to let her imagine her terrible father being shooed out of the house after I'd helped him to his feet rather than have her see what pushing him down the stairs had truly done to him.

It seemed the right thing to do in that moment. And when Belinda's waters splashed down at her feet onto the heaved ground, it seemed the right thing to leave Martin and get her and Kat to safety.

When it started to feel wrong was when I knew the fire was storming its way to this neighborhood, and I was safe at Golden Gate Park and able to alert someone that my husband was hurt inside our house and I said nothing. Perhaps I could have saved Martin if I'd told someone. But I didn't.

Martin had been a cruel man, in both big and little ways.

To me, to Kat, to Belinda and Candace, and to poor Annabeth. Perhaps to others. It was not my responsibility to punish Martin Hocking for his crimes, but neither was it my responsibility to rescue him.

It wasn't. It wasn't.

This I know.

And yet I can't shrug off the needling truth that Martin might have been able to get to safety somehow.

But . . . but how could he? He'd been gasping for breath as if at death's door. I saw it in his beautiful eyes, and I know that look, don't I?

I didn't kill Martin Hocking. I just didn't save him.

For the first time since it happened, I see the quake as an ally, not an enemy.

The earthquake and its blaze have surely covered what I did with a mantle of absolving fire. It was kind to me and Belinda and Kat in this way.

Perhaps it was the only kind thing it could do. Perhaps all during the catastrophe that began at dawn on the eighteenth of April, this was the only kind thing it could do. The earth can't help its nature to shift from time to time as it settles itself back into its proper place. The earth did not build the city here, nor pipe it with gas, nor construct its bowels with water mains that couldn't withstand the natural movement of the planet. People did that. It is the nature of the earth to shift. It is the nature of fragile things to break. It is the nature of fire to burn.

And just as it is the nature of men and women to build, it is also in our nature to begin again after disaster. This I know, too.

There is nothing left of the life I had here in San Francisco. I stand in the ashes of that life. And I realize with sudden relief that this is a gift to me as well. An amazing, wonderful gift. I can walk away and begin again, a step I have already mastered. I can do this. I have already done it. I am not some delicate thing that has been broken too many times. I am strong, I am resilient, and

I refuse to be haunted by any ghost of Martin Hocking, dead or alive. I can walk back to the Townsend station, get on a south-bound train to San Mateo, and never look back.

And then into this quiet and empowering meditation I hear a voice I recognize. I turn involuntarily toward the sound.

Libby from across the street is running toward me, calling my name.

26

INTERVIEW WITH MRS. SOPHIE HOCKING
CONDUCTED BY AMBROSE LOGAN, U.S. MARSHAL
CASE NUMBER 069308
Official transcript

San Francisco, CA
November 6, 1906

QUESTION: So it's your belief, then, that Martin Hocking wed you to throw off suspicion that he marries women for their wealth?

ANSWER: That and he wanted a nanny and housekeeper for free. This is not just my belief, sir. It is fact.

QUESTION: And you say you arrived at this conclusion after meeting Candace Hocking?

ANSWER: Yes. Her father had reported Martin to the Los Angeles Police. Martin knew they'd be looking into his affairs. At what he does.

QUESTION: It is not against the law to marry a rich woman.

ANSWER: But Martin wasn't taking care of Candace when she got sick. He was *letting* her die. Surely that is illegal. Contact the Los Angeles Police and they'll tell you. Candace's father reported him.

QUESTION: I have already been in contact with the Los Angeles Police.

ANSWER: So you know that what I'm telling you is true.

QUESTION: Candace's father did in fact ask a detective in Los Angeles to look into Martin Hocking's activities.

ANSWER: And?

QUESTION: And I am not convinced that proves Martin Hocking married you merely to throw off an investigation.

ANSWER: What other possible reason could he have for marrying me if not for that? I told you. I don't fit his pattern. I don't have any money. I don't have anything.

QUESTION: But you have surrounded yourself with people who do have resources.

ANSWER: What . . . what do you mean?

QUESTION: You are the legal guardian of seven-year-old Katharine Hocking, heiress to Candace Hocking's estate, and therefore you are guardian of the child's substantial income, correct?

Interviewee doesn't respond.

QUESTION: And you removed Candace Hocking from the Las Palomas Sanatorium in Tucson, where she was under a doctor's care, and brought her to San Rafaela, where she was under *your* care. And not long after, she died. Isn't that correct?

ANSWER: I did no such thing. I did not take her from that sanatorium. She wanted to come to San Rafaela. She signed herself out. She was dying already. Ask her doctor at Las Palomas. Ring him up and ask him. He will tell you. She was dying. And she didn't want to die there in the godforsaken desert. And, yes, she made me Kat's legal guardian, because she knows I love her daughter. How dare you suggest I had anything but the best of intentions for Candace and for Kat?

QUESTION: Mrs. Hocking, as I said earlier, I am only after the truth. That is what I am seeking here.

ANSWER: And that is what I am telling you.

QUESTION: Are you, though? Tell me again why you waited six weeks to report Martin Hocking missing.

ANSWER: He travels for his business. I didn't know he was missing.

QUESTION: Are you saying he habitually travels for extended periods of time for his job?

ANSWER: Some of his times away are longer than others.

QUESTION: Has he ever been away for six weeks?

Interviewee doesn't respond.

QUESTION: Mrs. Hocking, was your husband ever away from home for his job for six weeks?

ANSWER: No.

QUESTION: Five weeks? Four?

ANSWER: No.

QUESTION: Was he ever away from home for three weeks?

ANSWER: No.

QUESTION: Two?

ANSWER: No.

QUESTION: I want the truth, Mrs. Hocking. Why did you wait six weeks to report your husband missing?

ANSWER: Because I didn't care that he was missing, all right? I didn't care. He is a horrible person. I have documents at home that prove what a horrible person he is. He abandoned Candace, stole her child from her, told Kat her mother was dead, married me falsely, married Belinda under a bogus name, stole from her mine, and he murdered that woman in Colorado. I know he did. Maybe her mother, too. Look into that, if you want to see the kind of person Martin is. Look into how Candace's father died while you're at it. Look into why that man's automobile went off the road. I didn't report that Martin had gone missing because I was in Tucson with Kat, reuniting her with her mother. That's what I was doing instead of worrying about where Martin Hocking was. I didn't give a damn where he was. And I still don't.

QUESTION: Thank you for telling me the truth. That is all I want from you.

ANSWER: That isn't all you want from me. You want me to confess to you that I've been a partner to Martin's crimes and offenses.

QUESTION: Only if it's the truth.

ANSWER: Well, it's not.

QUESTION: And yet how can I believe you, Mrs. Hocking, when I know for a fact you have lied to me with regard to other matters?

ANSWER: I haven't.

QUESTION: But you have. You've been lying to me since the moment you sat down.

ANSWER: That's not true. I—

QUESTION: Since the moment you told me your name.

27

When Libby reaches me, she flings her arms around me and presses us into a fierce embrace.

"I have been so worried about all of you," she exclaims. "I was afraid something terrible had happened when all the neighbors started returning to the street to clean up and no one had seen you or knew where you all were. Are you all right? Are Mr. Hocking and little Kat quite well? Is everyone all right?"

She steps back to assess me. I still can't quite believe that there will be no vanishing act on my part now, and I fail to answer her questions. Libby mistakes my numbness for inability to share with her some kind of devastating news.

"Oh, my dear! What has happened? Tell me! Where are Kat and Mr. Hocking?"

"They, uh . . . ," I begin, and then falter. "Kat . . . Kat is with a friend. She and I made it out of the house and . . . we were evacuated to Golden Gate Park and then we . . . we've been . . . staying with a friend south of the city."

"Oh, thank goodness! And Mr. Hocking?"

"I . . . we don't . . . I don't know where he is."

Libby's eyes widen. "What do you mean you don't know where he is?"

"He . . . uh, he didn't return from his last business trip before the earthquake."

"Do you mean you haven't seen or heard from him since?" Libby's eyes widen even more.

I shake my head. My thoughts are racing. I don't know how much to say. It seems everything I am telling her is too much. Too much if I want to just disappear.

"Oh, you poor darling," Libby exclaims. "You poor, poor thing. And what has anyone been doing about it?"

I shrug. I don't know what to tell her, so I tell her nothing.

"Are you saying no one has done anything to help you find him?"

Again I shake my head. Oh, for the love of God, why can she not just leave me? Why can't she just waltz back across the street and forget she saw me?

"And you've checked all the hospitals and—oh, I have to say it, dear—the morgues? You've checked with them?"

"Yes."

"And you told the police he is missing?"

"No. This is the first day I've been able to get back. I thought . . . I thought maybe I'd find him here." I almost let out a laugh. I *had* thought I'd find him here. In blackened pieces.

Libby turns to face her own house with her arm still around

me and begins to propel us toward it. "Chester! Chester!" she shouts, and I can see that her husband is standing outside the wreck of their home staring up at it. Another man is standing next to him.

"Don't you worry, now," Libby soothes in a voice I've heard her use with her little boy. "We'll help you."

"I . . . I don't . . . You don't need to trouble yourselves," I say.

"Nonsense!" she replies. "Look at you! You're distraught." Again she yells to Chester. "Darling, Mrs. Hocking's husband is missing and no one's been able to help her!"

"It's all right." I try to pull away, but she has her arm firmly across my back as we make our way across the cracked street.

When we get closer, I can see that the man with Chester is a policeman.

"We've had looters inside. Can you believe it?" Libby says. "We had to call the police to get them to understand they need to patrol the streets. Officer! Officer! You simply must help my neighbor here. Her husband is missing!"

The policeman turns to me. He looks weary and older than his years.

"Is that true, madam?"

"Of course it's true!" Libby says.

"Let Mrs. Hocking answer, pet," Chester says gently.

"Yes," I reply. "He's missing."

"How long?" the officer says.

I pause.

"Since before the earthquake!" Libby blurts. "Tell him, Sophie."

Oh, how I wish I could just evaporate into nothing.

"He travels for his job," I finally answer. And then it suddenly occurs to me that I can just tell the police that Martin was expected home on the day of the earthquake rather than a day or two after it. Maybe they will more readily assume then that he was one of its victims. Declare him dead. "I expected him home around the time of the quake. But then of course there were those terrible fires. I . . . I've heard nothing from him."

"And have you checked with the hospitals?" the policeman says. "The morgue?"

"She has!" Libby says woefully.

"Then you should come down to our temporary station and fill out a report," the policeman says, shaking his head and looking at me with pity. "I can't promise you we will find him, but we can keep a lookout."

"We can bring her down to the station, can't we, Chester?" Libby says, rubbing my arms as if she thinks I am cold.

I gently extricate myself from her. "You don't have to do that. I can manage. Truly."

"No, you cannot! You are in no shape to deal with this! You don't even know where that temporary police station is. We're nearly done here, aren't we? Chester can finish boarding up the doorways and Officer Nichols and I will go down with you to the station. Chester can meet us when he's finished here."

"It's not far," the policeman assures me, "and I'll be happy to take down the details, Mrs. . . . ?"

"Hocking," Libby says, surely thinking I am too distressed to even remember my own name. "Sophie Hocking."

Any chance that I might've slipped out of Libby's clutches and out of San Francisco without visiting the police station is gone now. We turn to walk down the hill.

"I'm so terribly sorry about your house," Libby says, linking her arm through mine. "So very sorry. We lost a great deal, too, but not like you. All your beautiful fireplaces lying there burned and broken like that."

I cast a glance back toward the hulking shapes of marble and onyx and granite, and I wonder what they cover, what they crushed.

"Do you suppose Mr. Hocking will build again?" Libby says. "That is, if he can be found. Oh, but of course he will be found. Of course he will!" She leans into me and squeezes my arm. "We are going to rebuild," she continues optimistically. "The outside brick is all right, but everything inside needs to be redone, and oh! I'm expecting a baby! I never got a chance to tell you! So we'll be building a new nursery. I'm hoping for a little girl this time."

I let Libby chatter away as we walk. There's nothing I wish to contribute to the conversation, and my silence seems to be provoking sympathy from the policeman. He keeps glancing at me with eyes full of compassion. I will hopefully be more likely believed if I appear to be so distraught about my missing husband I can barely speak.

We arrive some blocks later at a temporary police station on Washington Street. It appears to have been an office building of some kind prior to the disaster. There are adding machines piled in a corner and more desks than the police officers probably need. There is a hum of activity in the large open space as other officers and men in plain clothes speak with one another. There are a few other women in the room, most seated at typewriters, tapping away. The officer politely asks if Libby can wait for me in a sitting area by the front door while I provide the officer with the details of my missing husband. He then sets me down in a chair at the far end of the busy room and hands me a glass of water.

"She likes to talk, that one," the officer says, nodding toward Libby.

"She . . . she likes to be helpful."

The officer takes a seat at a desk across from me and pulls a sheet of paper from out of its top drawer. "Now, then. I just need to get all the pertinent details."

I provide all the information about my husband, his name, our address on Polk, his age, what he looks like, any distinguishing marks, what he was wearing when I last saw him. I tell him that Martin left San Francisco in his vehicle—which I have never seen but which Martin has told me is a Ford Model T painted dark blue and which he keeps garaged down by the Embarcadero.

When the officer asks when I last saw Martin, the lie comes off my tongue easily. I tell him that I last saw my husband three days before the earthquake and that I expected him home the day of.

"And this is the first time you have reported that he's missing?" the policeman says, cocking his head.

"I wasn't aware he was missing until now. I didn't know how to get back into the city. It wasn't easy to get out, you know, and it was hard to get back in. My daughter and I were evacuated to Golden Gate Park and left the city as soon as the fires were put out. She and I have been staying with a friend. I didn't think Martin was missing until I got back to San Francisco and could not find him here. I thought perhaps he would be at the house. I didn't know it had burned." So many lies, so easy to say. "I thought maybe he was worried our daughter and I were the ones who were missing."

"And you've inquired of his employer?"

I think up a serviceable fib in seconds. "Martin had been doing business with insurance companies, but he came upon a new venture with hair tonic. He was selling it. On the road."

"Any friends here in the city we can ask? Any clubs your husband belongs to? Places he frequented?"

I shake my head. "Martin is a private person. When he's not on the road he likes to be home. And we've been in San Francisco less than two years. He didn't have close friends here."

"All right, then," the officer says. "I'll just need the address where you are staying and we'll be done here."

I give him the address of the Loralei, glad to be finished, eager to leave.

He stands and points toward Libby. "If you'll just take a seat with your friend, I'll see if Detective Morris wants to chat with you."

"Detective Morris?" I stand as well, and my heart takes a stutter step.

"He's handling most of the cases like this. If your husband is truly missing, and not just wounded or deceased, he could have been the victim of foul play, especially since you expected him home. There were a great many unsavory types out and about after the quake, I'm sorry to say."

"Oh, but the detective needn't take up my burden today if there are so many others."

The officer's brows furrow themselves into a crinkle. "I would think you'd want him to hop right on it."

"Y-yes! I do," I stammer. "I am just mindful of others who came in before me."

He smiles and pats my arm. "If Detective Morris is not busy, he'll want to talk with you. Especially since you're not staying in the city."

He leads me back to Libby, and I sit down next her. The officer walks away with all the information I gave him in his hand.

"I have to stay for a bit," I tell her. "You don't need to wait here with me. I don't know how long it will take. It's so busy in here."

Libby reaches for my hand and squeezes it. "Of course I will stay. Chester hasn't even come for me yet. I'll stay."

"But Timmy—"

"Timmy is with a nanny. We're renting a house near the Whittier Mansion over by the academy—which didn't burn, thank heaven. It's a sweet little place and the nanny lives with us. He'll be fine. I wouldn't dream of leaving you here alone, Sophie. What of kind of neighbor would I be?"

A smile forms at the corners of my mouth. I am thinking how little she understands what I am capable of handling, and she is thinking how grateful I am that she is staying with me.

"Do the police know something?" she asks. "Is that why they've asked you to wait?"

"No. The detective looking into cases of missing people might want to speak with me because I live outside the city now."

"Oh," she says, as if she understands all that this means. "So . . . is it terribly worrisome with Mr. Hocking being missing? With the way you two . . . met? I was just wondering if love has blossomed between you and if this is now a very tragic thing not knowing where he is."

I can see that Libby very much wants me to be brokenhearted at Martin's absence and what a sweet, romantic image that would be for her. I'm also thinking that it would do me well for people to think I miss my husband and want him found. I reward her with another little smile.

"I have indeed grown to have feelings for him," I say, and it's not a lie. I do have feelings for Martin; they are just not ones of affection.

"You poor thing!" Libby says. "I do hope he can be found quickly. Perhaps he's lying in a hospital bed somewhere and for some reason he's unable to speak or maybe he's forgotten his own name and you'll find him and when he sees you he'll remember you and he'll know that he has feelings for you now, too!"

"Oh, I'm sure he has mutual feelings for me," I reply, also not a lie. Libby beams and we are quiet for a few moments, which allows me time to wonder what this detective might ask me. I was not expecting this. I was expecting to file a report that nobody would care about. Again I wonder what lies beneath the crush of the fallen fireplaces. I turn to Libby.

"I feel badly for the neighbors on our street that our place hasn't been cleaned up at all. I see everyone clearing away the remains of their burned houses. I don't want people thinking that we're not going to be taking care of that."

"Oh, I suppose they will understand with the situation being as it is," she says. "Still. The place *is* a sore sight."

"I wouldn't know where to begin to hire someone to clear it all the way," I say, knowing that Libby, ever the fountain of service to her pathetic neighbor, will want to help me.

"Let Chester and me find someone to do that for you. There are so many men out of work and wanting to earn money. It's not hard to find the workmen. Getting wagons to haul away the rubbish is the hard part. But then you don't have much left of your house to haul away." She gives me a sympathetic look. "I shouldn't have said that."

"It's quite all right. It's primarily the few things that didn't burn entirely," I say. "The cookstove. And the slabs from the fallen fireplaces. Some piping. You've seen it. And I would be so grateful if you could line up the labor for me. I have some money back at the house where I'm staying to pay for it."

"Not to worry, not to worry. We can take care of that later. Now, you're sure there's nothing of value there? Nothing you'd want the workers to try to save for you?"

"No, but I would like to be there when they come, just in case they . . . they do find something."

"Chester can do that for you. Watch over those men while they scoop it all up. The academy is not in session."

"No! It's . . . it's all that's left of my life in that house. I want to be there."

Libby pats my hand. "You know all those things can be replaced. All of them."

I nod as if she's giving me sage advice I had not thought of before. "You're so right. Thank you for looking into that for me."

"It might take a day or two to schedule it," she says. "Everything is moving so slowly. It took us days to get our debris carried away. It's better now that more time has passed."

"I'm so grateful."

"Say! Why don't you stay with us for a few days, hmm? It would be much easier for you to come back this way to check on the workers, and you'll be here if the police have news for you."

Despite Libby's being the one to have gotten me inside this police station, I am grateful to know what is left of the house will soon be swept clean. I accept her offer, provided we can stop at a Western Union office so that I can send a telegram alerting my friends and Kat of my whereabouts.

As she begins to tell me she has a number of extra nightgowns, since they'd been traveling when the earthquake struck, a man in a button-down shirt, dotted necktie, and brown slacks approaches. He sits down in the empty chair next to me, and I can see that he has the piece of paper with all my answers to the officer's questions in his hand.

"Mrs. Hocking, my name is Detective Morris. I am so sorry to hear that your husband is missing and I trust we will be able to help you locate him."

"Thank you. I am very grateful for any help you can give me," I say, with as much of a convincing tone as I can muster.

"I wish we could give it our full attention," he continues, "but we are still dealing with a number of other pressing issues since the disaster here."

"I understand. I do."

"You're Irish," he says with a half smile.

"Most people mistake me for a Scot," I reply.

"I've a friend from college who is Irish. How long have you been in the United States?"

"Not quite four years."

"And where was home for you?"

"The North," I say, and that is all I will say.

"And you met your husband here in San Francisco?"

"Oh my, you should hear how they met!" Libby interrupts enthusiastically, and I want to kick her. Detective Morris turns to her, realizing that she isn't just some random woman sitting next to me.

"I'm Libby Reynolds. I'm Sophie's neighbor across the street," Libby says happily.

"Pleased to meet you," the detective says.

I open my mouth to regain control of the conversation, but Libby is too quick.

"She was a mail-order bride!" she continues, and I close my eyes in disbelief that she can be so helpful one minute and so unhelpful the next.

"Is that so?" Detective Morris says, smiling at me.

"It's not quite like that," I say.

"But it is!" Libby gushes. "Mr. Hocking was a sad, lonely widower with a sweet little girl and he put an advertisement in a New York paper for a new wife and new mother for his child. Sophie answered the ad and he chose her. And she came out on the train and married him the same day. And they had never met!"

"When was this?" the detective says, still smiling.

"March of last year," I answer, rubbing a temple in mock embarrassment.

"That's quite the story," the detective says, cocking his head and watching me carefully.

"And guess what?" Libby says "They've grown to care for each other! Isn't that the most romantic thing? It's just like a love story in a book."

"Indeed it is."

"Libby," I say.

"What? It's nothing to be embarrassed about. It's perfectly lovely."

"So you were in New York when you answered this ad?" Detective Morris asks.

"Yes. I wasn't happy there. I lived in a dreadful tenement, I worked for pennies, and I was cold and hungry most of the time. I thought I could be happy here with Martin and his little girl. I knew I could love his child and I thought it was certainly possible that I would grow to care for him and that he might in turn come to care for me."

"And that's exactly what happened!" Libby exclaims.

Detective Morris is still looking at me intently. "Would you say that's what happened, Mrs. Hocking?"

"I would. I would indeed," I say, and I am surprised at how self-assured I sound.

"So, then—and I'm sorry to have to ask this—you have no reason to believe Mr. Hocking has deserted you?"

"Of course he didn't do that!" Libby says.

Detective Morris ignores her. He is looking only at me.

"No. No, he wouldn't leave us. He certainly wouldn't abandon his child. He wouldn't do that."

The detective consults the sheet of paper. "And your husband is a salesman? Selling . . . hair tonic?"

Libby laughs. "That's not right. He works in insurance!"

The detective looks up at me.

"He . . . he does both, actually," I say quickly. "But he was out selling the tonic the last time I saw him."

Libby turns to me. "You never told me he was doing that!"

"It was a new venture. He was giving it a go." I can feel beads of sweat forming on my brow.

"And it was going well?" the detective says.

"As I said, it was a new venture. He was taking it south of the city to try to sell. To druggists and mercantiles and five-and-tens and the like."

"Do you know from where he would have been returning?" the detective asks.

I don't want the police anywhere near San Rafaela. Nowhere near it. "Daly City, I believe."

The detective makes a note on the sheet with a slim pencil that he pulls from a pants pocket. "All right. I'll have one of the officers make a call down to Daly City to see if anyone remembers seeing him."

"Thank you so much," I manage to say.

The detective stands. Thank God he is finished with me. "We will be in touch if we have any news for you, Mrs. Hocking. And if you should hear from your husband or think of anything else that would be of assistance in finding him, please let us know."

"Yes. Of course."

The detective smiles politely. "Good day to you both."

The man walks away from us and disappears into an office whose broken glass-paned walls have been replaced with sheets of plywood.

"Well, he was very nice, wasn't he?" Libby says.

"He didn't need to know all that about Martin and me."

"And you needn't be so ashamed of it. I was shocked at first when you told me, but look how everything turned out."

"Indeed," I mutter as I stand.

Libby rises as well and again links her arm through mine. "Let's go find Chester and then head over to our new place. And then Chester can see about getting some men to clean up your old house."

"Yes," I answer.

Yes. The sooner the remains of my house are buried, the sooner the police will conclude that Martin Hocking, who was on his way home the morning of the quake, instead fell victim to it.

And the sooner I will be done here and can remake myself elsewhere.

Again.

28

Libby and Chester's rented house near Lafayette Park is ten blocks away and on the other side of Van Ness, the side that did not burn. Chester apologizes that he was unable to secure a carriage, and I assure him that walking, even when it's uphill, is not troublesome to me. After a quick stop at a Western Union office near the makeshift police station, we head west to reenter neighborhoods that I walked through weeks before when smoke and despair hung heavy in the air. But now it is June and the sun is out and homes and businesses that needed repair are being repaired. It does not feel hopeless here.

Libby's new place is situated two blocks across from the beautiful Whittier Mansion, a massive structure of Arizona sandstone that apparently the earthquake could not wobble. Their rented cottage is far smaller than their home on Polk was, but it's quaint and well-appointed, and I'm sure thousands of other homeless San Franciscans would be happy to occupy it.

"This house belongs to a tutor friend of Chester's who's in Seattle for a spell, taking care of his mother," Libby says as she gives me a tour of the inside. It is fully furnished, two stories, with three bedrooms upstairs and a guest room off the kitchen that might have been the housekeeper's bedroom in the home's earlier life.

Chester leaves us to find a work crew for me that can, I hope, start in the morning. Libby and I settle in first to tea—the nanny is also her maid—and then playtime with Timmy, who has indeed grown taller in the couple of months since I've seen him. Libby fills the time with talk of their travels, of discovering she was with child when she vomited all over a banqueting table in Boston, and of how hard it was to hear of the disaster that had befallen San Francisco while they were away and to know her home had most likely been destroyed.

"It wasn't completely destroyed, of course, but everything inside that didn't burn reeked of smoke afterward. We were hardly able to salvage anything," she says, as we sit on the floor with Timmy and a basket full of new toys. "And yet looters are still sneaking their way into the house at night to comb through the ashes looking for valuables. It's so ruthless, isn't it?"

"Yes." People can indeed be ruthless.

She asks about the friends I am staying with and how I made it out of the city and what I've been doing all this time.

I keep my answers short and simple and vaguely truthful. "Kat and I took a ferry to Oakland several days after the quake and then a train down to San Jose to get to my friend's place near San Mateo. We've just been recovering from the shock of the last few weeks. It was hard on Kat, as I'm sure you can imagine. And my friend just had a baby, so we've been helping."

311

"I am surprised you've made a friend who lives elsewhere than in the city," Libby says, curiosity clinging to her words.

"Belinda and I have a mutual friend in San Francisco. Kat and I were fortunate to have somewhere else to stay besides here. So tell me. How will you decorate the new nursery?"

Libby spends the rest of the time until Chester returns telling me every detail of her plans, not just for the nursery but for the inside of her soon-to-be-repaired house. She stops twice to ask if she should stop, if sharing her ideas is making me grieve too much the loss of my own house, and I tell her to keep talking. It is therapeutic to hear talk about all the new things that will emerge out of the dust of the destruction.

And it helps pass the time.

When Chester arrives, he tells me luck shone on him today; he found a four-man crew that was finishing up hauling away debris from the remains of a business on Leavenworth and who can be at the site of my house at nine o'clock tomorrow morning.

"It's not necessary for you to be there, Mrs. Hocking," Chester says. "If you think someone needs to watch over the workmen, I can be there. The academy is on a term break right now for the summer. I'm happy to do it."

"Thank you so kindly," I reply with forced calmness. "But I want to be there. They might find my grandmother's lapel watch or something else of sentimental value. I just want to be there."

He nods and tells me he will see if in the morning he can find a carriage to take me there. The rest of the evening passes too slowly for me. I awaken the following morning at sunrise, well before the rest of the house. Chester is in fact able to locate trans-portation for me. When a carriage comes at half past eight, I bid Libby good-bye and thank her for her kind hospitality but explain that if all goes well, I will catch an afternoon train back to San Mateo and will no doubt see her again soon.

"I need to get back to Kat," I tell her, knowing she will understand this. We do have that in common, she and I. We love our children.

"I'm so very glad I saw you standing there yesterday," she says as she hugs me good-bye. "And we were very nearly finished at our own place, and I would have missed you. It is so fortunate that we were both there at the same time."

"Quite so" is all I can say in return, but then I think maybe it is fortunate that Libby saw me. Maybe it is good that I didn't just attempt to disappear, but that now the police think Martin Hocking did not come home as expected the day of the earthquake and is perhaps missing within the disaster, as are many others. Rather than feeling like I need to be invisible, I feel that I will instead soon be liberated. It is only a matter of time.

"You will let us know the minute Mr. Hocking is found, won't you?" Libby says, releasing me.

"I promise."

"Don't give up hope, dear Sophie. I'm sure he will turn up."

"Of course."

"And do please tell Mr. Hocking to rebuild. Almost everyone on the street is going to. You will tell him, won't you? I want you for a neighbor again!"

I smile, nod. I think I understand why Libby would like me to return to San Francisco. I am the kind of friend to whom she can count on feeling sweetly superior. Her affluent friends probably make her too often fear that she doesn't quite measure up. But not me.

"I'll tell him," I say.

She sends me out to the carriage with a boxed lunch and a parasol because, she says, there are no more leafy trees on our street to provide shade. She stands at the door to her cottage, waving good-bye with one hand and the other holding the tiniest mound at her waist.

I arrive at the ruined house just as the workmen pull up.

It is no small feat hoisting up the slabs and chunks of broken fireplaces and placing them onto flatbed wagons. Each time the workmen lift another section I stand as close as I can to see if Martin's crushed body is lying underneath. There are indeed charred remains beneath the heavy stone, but I don't know what any of it is and no one shouts that they have found human remains. While they are dragging away a piece of marble from what had been the dining room, and where Martin could have possibly dragged himself if he had tried to crawl out of the house, I see a blackened shard sticking up out of the mess and I'm thinking it could be bone. I kick at the rest of the debris and I see another sliver of something that resembles the first, but surely no one else would think it was bone—only someone who thought there'd been a body there before the fires would think that. The workmen come back from the wagon to find me poking about the piles of ashes and spreading them thin, and they're no doubt thinking I'm looking for something precious. I look up at them and shrug as if to say that I can't find what I'm looking for when in fact I think I have. I pocket the first shard to bring home with me and show to Belinda and Candace. I toss the other one.

It takes the rest of the morning and half the afternoon to clear and haul away the shattered, burned remains. When the workmen are done, there is nothing left of my old house except for the foundation and the stone steps leading up to where the front door used to be, which one of the men says he'd like to come back later to remove and take to a salvage yard to sell, if I am amenable to that. I am. I send a telegram to Elliot's shop from a Western Union office that I pass on the long walk back down to Townsend Street that I will be returning before dark.

It is late afternoon when I get to the station and buy a ticket for the next train south. When I arrive at the San Mateo station at dusk, it is Belinda who has come for me with Elliot's carriage. She waits until I am inside the cab and we're pulling away to ask me if I found Martin.

"There wasn't much left of the house or what had been inside it," I answer. I explain to her about the intense heat and how the second story's heavy fireplaces fell to the first floor as the house burned, crushing whatever lay beneath. I pull from my pocket the shard, and she glances at it.

"Is that him?" Her voice is tinged with an emotion that I don't recognize, a variant of grief, perhaps.

"I don't know. Maybe." And then I tell her about Libby seeing me poking about the ashes and my unplanned trip to the police station and then Libby and Chester offering to help me clear away the remains of my house.

"That's not the way you wanted to take care of this," she says when I am finished.

"I know, but perhaps it was unrealistic for me to think I could disappear completely from San Francisco and never be missed. At least now I have gone on record as saying my husband is missing."

She nods once and we are quiet for a while. "Kat asked about you," Belinda finally says.

"I'm glad to hear you say that."

"It was nice to hear her voice." Belinda nods toward the shard in my hand. "I suppose you are not going to be telling her about any of this."

"No."

"She might be thinking that at some point he will come back into her life, you know. To hurt her or you or me—or to take her away from you. I can't help wondering about that, too."

"I know. I'll wait until Martin is officially declared a casualty of the earthquake and then I'll just tell her he probably died. That might not happen for a year or so. I don't know when exactly. But I do know Candace will die first. And soon. Kat doesn't need to lose both parents so close to each other."

"What if he did get out, though? What if he does come looking for us? For her?"

"He won't. Why would he? I have all those documents. He can't risk it. And, besides, he . . . he couldn't have gotten out. Not the way he looked when I left him."

I have to believe I am right about that. Martin is dead to me. Dead.

"So we just wait, then, for this to truly be over?" Belinda asks a moment later.

"I think we check in with the authorities from time to time to see if there's any word on our husbands—you with the San Mateo County Sheriff and me with the San Francisco Police. That is what concerned wives would do if their husbands went missing. And while we wait, we get up each morning and take care of our children and the inn, and we go to bed each night. We live."

All of us except for Candace.

When we get back to the Loralei, I have to wait until Kat is in bed to tell Candace what I told Belinda on the way home. I show her the shard I brought back with me. She reaches out with one hand to hold it.

"You think this is bone?" she says.

"Could be. Might be."

"It's lighter than I thought it would be," she replies. And then she hands it back.

"What do you want me to do with it?" I ask. "He was your husband."

"I don't care. Bury it. Burn it. Throw it into the sea. I don't care."

The next day I make the long trek to the mine and I shove the shard in between two large boulders blocking the entrance. A fragment of the shard splits off and falls into the dirt. I grab a rock at my feet and hammer the shard farther in. Fragments continue to fly off, but I continue until the diminished shard is firmly embedded in between the boulders. I don't tell the others what I've done when I return to the inn; I just tell Belinda and Candace that what I brought home from San Francisco has been properly disposed of.

A week later I use Elliot's telephone and I ring up the San Francisco Police Department and ask to speak to Detective Morris. I ask if there is any news on the whereabouts of my husband. There isn't.

Belinda rings the county sheriff and officially reports her husband as having deserted her. For the next month and a half we inquire about our missing husbands on a regular basis. In those six weeks Sarah grows cuter and fatter, Belinda looks less and less like a grieving widow and more like a woman in love with Elliot, and Kat begins to say a word or two every hour. As the weeks pass

I find that I no longer startle when an automobile pulls up outside the inn or when the door to the inn opens and the first thing I hear is a man's footfall. Martin would be a fool to come back if he's somehow still alive.

And Martin is no fool.

I write my mother that Martin—the quiet man I married for convenience—was sadly a victim of the terrible quake and fire, but that Kat and I are safe and now living south of the city with friends. I tell her that she needn't worry about a thing, that everything she'd wanted me to have and sacrificed for me to have, I have.

Candace is the only one of us who seems to be waning rather than gaining strength. When the first day of August approaches, she calls me to her bed, which she rarely leaves now. She is as pale and thin as she was when I first met her, perhaps more so. We have had the doctor from the village to see her twice, and both times he has told us she needs to be sent to a warmer, drier climate. Both times Candace declined to follow his advice.

When I arrive at her bedside, she reaches for me with a weak arm and takes my hand. I sit down next to her.

"I want to go to my cousin's in Texas," she whispers.

The words hit me hard. "But . . . you said you wanted to be here! You said you wanted for you and Kat to be here. With me!"

"I do want Kat to be here with you," she murmurs. "But I don't want to be here. I don't want Kat to watch me die. I want to say good-bye to her while I'm alive. I want her to remember me alive."

Relief and concern immediately twist themselves inside me. Candace doesn't want to take Kat. But still. How can she possibly travel in her condition? "You are too weak to go such a great distance by train, Candace."

"I have the money to hire a private coach and a nurse."

"But it's so far and . . . and what if you die along the way?"

"What if I do? It would be a blessing to go so quickly. I want to go. I'm ready to go."

"Candace—"

"Let me go to my family. Let them see to it that I'm buried next to my mother and father. Please, Sophie. I've asked you for nothing. Please help me to do this."

Hot tears are sliding down my face. "But Kat . . ."

"Kat will be happy here. She already is happy here. She has you and Belinda and her sister. She already has more than I ever gave her. You can't stop what is happening to me. I will die. Let me choose where."

When I say nothing, she goes on. "I've already taken care of the documents appointing you as Kat's legal guardian when I am deceased. I will make sure my family understands no one is to contest it, not that I think anyone will. My lawyer has already contacted the bank in Los Angeles that disperses the money from the trust. The monthly amount is substantial, Sophie. Kat will never want for anything. And I expect you to use that money in whatever way will secure for her a good home. Do you promise me you will do that?"

I nod as more tears trickle down my face.

"Say it," she breathes.

"I promise."

Candace leaves by private coach two weeks later, on the thirteenth of August. Belinda and I stand back from the four-horse carriage to give her as much time alone with Kat as she wants to say her final good-bye, but Candace keeps her last words to her daughter brief. I hear her tell Kat through the open carriage door that she is soon going to heaven to be with her mama and papa, just like she told her, but that she will watch over Kat all the years of her life, and that if she ever needs to talk to her or touch her, she need only go to Belinda's peach tree and put her arms around it, and Candace will whisper to her through the branches that all is well.

Candace then motions for me to come to the open carriage door to stand by Kat.

"Miss Sophie is your mama now," Candace says from where she reclines on the seat inside. She nods to me and I put my arm around our little girl.

"I am so proud of you, Kitty Kat. You're such a brave girl," Candace says to Kat. "Be happy. I love you."

Next to me I feel Kat shudder. No words are coming out of her mouth, though. Not one. I start to bend down to encourage Kat to say farewell, but Candace interrupts my movement with three words to the nurse sitting across from her that stop me.

"Close the door."

The nurse leans forward and pulls on the handle, and the carriage door clicks shut.

Candace doesn't say good-bye, and I know 'tis so our dear Kat won't ever regret not saying it, either.

The driver slaps the reins. We watch as the carriage heads down the gravel drive and then turns south. When we can no longer hear the jingle of the harnesses and the clopping of the hooves, Belinda, Kat, and I turn to go back inside the inn.

Over the next two weeks, I can see Kat retreating into silence to work out her mother's absence; I have learned this is her way of coming to terms with events she cannot control. We all have to find a way to do that, don't we? She has found this one. Who of us can say it isn't a good way? We imagine together each night before bed—me with words and she with thoughts—where Candace's carriage might be. We picture her on the desolate landscape of Arizona and New Mexico and then maybe finding the gateway to heaven on her journey. I think it brings Kat comfort to think of her mother as skyward bound, like Elijah in a chariot. She has drawn several pictures of a carriage pulled by winged horses flying into the sun.

I don't know if she fully understands she will not see Candace again, but I find her often at the peach tree, looking up at its branches and listening to the rustle of its leaves.

On the tenth of September we receive a telegram from Texas and learn that Candace died three days after arriving.

29

September slips into October like it did the previous autumn in this part of California—subtly and with nowhere near the kind of fanfare as in New York or northern Ireland.

I enroll Kat in the little primary school in San Rafaela with some trepidation; she is silent most days, still puzzling out the loss of her mother through the absence of words. I tell her teacher, a Miss Reeves, that my daughter has had to suffer much in her young life and to please, if she could, adjust her expectations. I'm expecting her to tell me to take Kat home like that headmistress did back in San Francisco, but Miss Reeves says Kat is more than welcome in class, and it will be nice for a change to have a child who doesn't interrupt instruction time with out-of-turn talking. Kat seems neither eager nor hesitant to attend school. She is interested in learning—she has always been—and after the first few days the other children seem to accept the quiet new girl; at least this is what Miss Reeves tells me.

Our new life at the Loralei is tranquil in so many ways. I know I should be more distressed at Candace's passing, but the fact that she is gone has loosened fetters that had been bound around my heart. Kat is thoroughly mine now, the way I thought she was when I married Martin.

The trust checks from the Los Angeles bank begin to arrive—one a month—in the middle of September. It is more money than Kat and I need to contribute to our board and lodging at the inn, and it occurs to me that in a year or so there might be enough surplus for me to pay Elliot to build Kat and me a cottage on the property, if Belinda will allow it, and I am almost certain she will. Belinda would then have back two of her rooms for inn guests and Kat will have her own home always, no matter where life might take me.

When I share this idea with Belinda and Elliot, they're both in favor of it, Belinda because she has come to think of me as her big sister and Kat as a niece and she wants us near, and Elliot because he feels he owes me so much for bringing Belinda safely home to him. It is enjoyable in the evenings after the children are in bed to imagine what the little house might look like and where to situate it. It is at one of these impromptu idea sessions over tea and cake after supper that Elliot asks me if I will always want to live here in San Rafaela and, more specifically, at the Loralei. What will happen to the proposed little house if I want to marry again, maybe have other children?

There is so much I could say in answer to this question. I have told Belinda so very little about my life before—a fraction of what I told Candace to gain her trust—and I myself am starting to feel detached from it. I've wondered if that would happen someday, and I've pondered what it would feel like to see the person I was as a stranger I no longer know. It is not necessary for Elliot to know that I can't have children, but I can address the rest of his question truthfully enough and without having to revisit a past that feels less and less like it belongs to me.

"I am in no great hurry to marry again," I reply in a gently sincere tone. "And the house will always be Kat's to do with as she will. You'll let her stay here in it even into her adult years, yes?" I ask Belinda.

"Of course," Belinda says.

"She may want to marry and move on herself," Elliot adds.

"She might. She probably will," I answer. "And if she does, I imagine she would let me stay in the little house that her trust money built. But that's further into the future than we need to look. Right now I just like the idea of having our own little home, right here, at the Loralei."

We settle on a drawing of the proposed cottage that I share with Kat a few days later.

"It . . . will . . . be ours?" she murmurs. The four words are stitched loosely together, but they still sound as beautiful as a song to me.

"Yes, love."

"Here?"

"Right here. See, there's the peach tree." I point to the tree crudely drawn to the right of the floor plan of the two-bedroom, one-story cottage.

She looks up at me. "Our old house?"

"The fire took our old house, remember? It's gone and we don't have to go back there."

"Father?"

I swallow back a bit of fear that she worries about him finding us, taking her back. Or hurting her for what she did to him.

"He's gone, too."

She blinks at me, long and slow, and her eyes are glistening when they open. She is feeling something deep and painful at these words of mine, and I realize I've been a fool to think she could cast away any longing for Martin's affection as easily as I did. She doesn't know all that he has done, all that he might have done if he had reached Belinda that morning instead of falling down the stairs.

I pull her close to me. "He would have loved you better if he had known how, poppet. You are easy to love. He didn't know how. Some people just don't know how to love. But you do. And I do. Belinda does. Elliot does. Sarah does. Your mother did. There are people who love you, Kat. Who will always love you. You and I can make a home for ourselves in the circle of that love if we want to. Shall we?"

She leans into me and nods. I will have to remind her of this when she thinks of Martin. I will have to remind myself that she likely will think of him, even though I will not.

By the end of October, I've already saved a hundred dollars beyond what I have kept aside in a savings account at a bank in San Mateo. When the trust was set up years ago, it was to fund Candace's lifestyle as a well-bred woman, but I spend very little of Kat's money each week on our livelihood. Much of it goes into a savings account that will be hers when she's older. I'm starting to think we will have our own little house in less than a year's time.

In early November Elliot asks a friend of his to help clear a level spot by the peach tree so that when I am ready for the building to start, the location will be waiting.

It is when I am watching the two men work the ground to lay stakes that Belinda brings a letter to me that has come in the day's mail. It is addressed to me and it's from the San Francisco Police Department.

I open it hastily as Belinda stands over me. We are both surely hoping the police have decided my husband was likely a victim of the earthquake and fire seven months ago and that they regret to inform me that he has been declared dead. I know I'm wishing it.

But that is not what the letter says.

"They are asking me to please return to the station to supply them with additional information about my missing husband," I say to Belinda.

"What additional information?" Belinda says, brows furrowed.

"I don't know."

"You already told them everything you know."

"You mean I already told them everything I want them to know."

Belinda takes the letter from me and reads it. "Can you decline to come?"

"I don't think that would look good. I should want to be of assistance, shouldn't I?"

She hands the letter back to me. "Maybe they are ready to declare him dead but they don't want to say that in a letter. Maybe they think it would be kinder to tell you personally."

"Maybe."

But neither one of us truly thinks that's what this request is about. It is something else. And it's unsettling to us both.

The letter asks if I would be so kind as to come by the newly constructed station at eleven o'clock on Tuesday, the sixth of November, four days from now.

What can I do but go?

I choose carefully what I will wear to the police station. I dress in a tastefully subdued gray shirtwaist with black piped trim and eyelet lace at the neck and cuffs. I haven't worn my wedding ring in many weeks, but I slip it on now before I go. Kat doesn't ask where I am going, but I can see that she wants to know.

"Just some business to take care of in the city," I tell her. "I'll be home later today, I promise."

Elliot drives me to the train station, and again, as before, offers to accompany me.

"Now, how would I explain you? You are unexplainable."

"I suppose I am."

"I'll be fine."

"I don't know," he says, frowning. "Maybe it's time to prepare yourself for learning that he is not dead after all," Elliot says. "Maybe they found him and he's alive. Maybe that fall down the stairs wasn't that bad."

"It was bad. He could barely breathe when I left him. And if he'd been found alive they would've said so; they wouldn't ask me to come in to provide additional information. I don't want to talk about this anymore, Elliot. It's making me nervous."

We ride the rest of the way to San Mateo in silence.

The city has improved greatly in the months I have been away. Everywhere there is the aroma of fresh lumber and paint and the sounds of hammers and saws. New buildings have risen, most of the piles of ash are gone, and the landscape has gone from desolate wasteland to reborn city. It is much easier to get a carriage from the train station this time, and I am at the new police station many minutes before eleven o'clock.

I am told to wait after I give my name to the uniformed officer seated at a tall desk in the tiled lobby. I spend the minutes before anyone comes for me calming my thumping heart. When at last my name is called I am taken to a room with an oaken table and chairs that are new and that smell of tung oil. There's a woman seated there with a stenography machine that also looks new. Next to her is a man I do not know. It is not Detective Morris.

"Thank you so much for coming in, Mrs. Hocking," this man says, his voice cordial, his smile polite. "I'm Deputy Ambrose Logan." He is a little older than me, perhaps thirty, and he reminds me a little of my brother Mason with his dark hair and eyes. When I ask where Detective Morris is, I am told that the case of my missing husband has been referred to the U.S. Marshal's Office. I have to ask this Deputy Logan what that is. He tells me the U.S. Marshal's Office deals with cases that are federal in nature. I don't know what that means, either, but I do not ask. The deputy reaches down to the seat of the empty chair on his other side and lifts up a file thick with papers and sets it in front of him. A photograph of Martin slides out when he opens it and lands askew between us.

"May we begin?" he says.

At first the questions are the same as those I answered when I first reported Martin missing. But as the minutes go by and as the woman in the room taps out everything I say, the deputy's questions become more and more about me. He keeps looking at the papers in that file. So many papers.

He asks me if I saw Martin the day of the quake, if I knew that Martin was traveling back to San Francisco that day or that his automobile had been found outside San Rafaela on the road to San Francisco.

He knows about Belinda.

He knows Belinda was in my house the morning of the quake and he knows Martin was married to Belinda all the while being married to me.

He knows about Candace.

God in heaven, he knows about Annabeth.

My head is spinning. Deputy Logan has so many papers. What else does he know? The room is getting warm and I want to leave.

I rise to go because we are no longer talking about the whereabouts of Martin Hocking. He is instead accusing me of being an accomplice of Martin's, of being a part of his terrible schemes. Of collaborating with him to get to Belinda's gold and Kat's inheritance.

But the deputy bids me to please retake my seat, that it will be better for me if I finish the interview.

Better for me? How can anything he is saying be better for me? This man thinks I am like Martin Hocking. I am nothing like Martin. How dare he suggest I am?

The deputy just wants the truth, that's all he wants, he says, and I tell him I *have* been telling him the truth.

But, no, he says. I've not been telling him the truth. I tell him I have. And he says I have been lying to him since the moment I sat down and told him my name.

30

B eads of sweat break out on my forehead and on the back of
my neck, even though the room has suddenly gone cold.

"My name is Sophie Hocking." I force myself to look
Deputy Logan straight in the eye. I say it again. "My name is
Sophie Hocking."

The deputy says nothing. He doesn't pull out a sheet of paper
from that bulging file of his, and he doesn't contradict me. He
just continues to look at me, studying my face.

"I have done nothing wrong," I continue, as a strange calm fills
my bosom. I don't know where this quiet resolve is coming from,
but I hold fast to it. "I wed a man who I thought was free to
marry. I love his child. I have done all I can to give that little girl
everything she needs for a happy life, including taking her to her
real mother when it would've been far easier for me to keep her
for myself. I cared for Belinda, I practically delivered her child,

and I searched for her day and night after we got separated. I have taken no gold of hers. None. And, yes, I manage Kat's trust, but I can show you every receipt of everything I have bought since I became her guardian. I have paid for our room and board. I have bought her clothes for school and crayons and paper and I've replaced puzzles and dolls and books that the fire stole from her. I've put money into a savings account that will be Kat's when she is older, and I'm saving some each week to build a house for her so that no matter what happens to me she will always have a home in which to live. What does it matter what my name is, I ask you? A name is nothing. It is just words on a piece of paper. This is who I am. Despite everything that has happened to me, despite everything that's been done to me, I am still a person who knows how to love people. This is who I am."

Deputy Logan continues to stare at me. I cannot tell what he's thinking other than he is contemplating what I have just said.

"You would maintain this under oath if it came to it?" he asks. "That you have done nothing wrong?"

"I would." By all that is good, I would.

He pauses for a moment and then turns to the woman. "I think it is time we give Mrs. Hocking a break, Mrs. Fielding. I will call you back in when I resume my questioning."

Mrs. Fielding's fingers become still over the funny-shaped keys on her machine. She seems a bit surprised, but then she stands and walks from the room, closing the door behind her.

"I don't want a break," I tell him. "I want to go. I have nothing else to say."

Deputy Logan regards me silently for a moment. "I want to believe you, I do," he says, "but I think you know what happened to Martin Hocking, despite you having told me that you don't. I think you know where he is. And considering what you and I both know about him, I want to know why you won't tell me."

I swallow hard and say nothing.

"I've got quite the predicament," he continues. "I think Martin Hocking well deserves whatever fate might have befallen him, because, like you, I think he killed Annabeth Bigelow Grover. I think he killed her mother. I think he forced Candace's father's car off the road."

He pauses for a minute, studying me. Then he continues. "And I know things about Martin Hocking that you do not. I know that his parents are not dead, as he no doubt told you. I know that when he was a child he hurt animals just to see them suffer, and I know that when he was sent away to a boarding school he was expelled for insubordination and verbal abuse against his fellow classmates. I know that when he was sixteen and his older sister confided in him that she wanted to kill herself because she'd had her heart broken, he offered to help her do it. I know that he swung the rope over the barn rafter, made the noose, and helped her into it. I know he watched her hang and did not try to help her when she regretted her decision immediately and tried to pull the rope off. She was saved at the last moment by their father."

My heart is pounding and I feel nausea rising from the very core of me as I picture Martin doing this terrible thing. I see a young woman—his own sister—hanging and her feet wildly kicking and her hands grasping at her throat and Martin just standing there. Just standing there watching her die. I see their father rushing in, screaming at Martin, *What have you done!* I can't stop seeing it. I made for Martin a cozy home and tasty meals, and I laundered his clothes and brought him tea. I shared his bed. I let him share mine. I did all of this for a monster. I put my hand to my mouth to quell the queasiness, and the marshal just barrels on.

"I know that he was banished from the home after this and that he rode the rails west for several years, learning how to fool unsuspecting people into trusting him. I know that during these years he was itinerant he collected birth certificates and death certificates that he could use to create false identities. I know his name isn't even Martin Hocking. It is Clyde Merriman."

The deputy stops for a moment as I struggle to take it all in. The room now seems to lack sufficient air. I feel light-headed and afraid.

"I didn't know," I whisper, and I taste bile in my mouth.

"I know you didn't," Deputy Logan says.

He waits for a moment so that I will hear those words fully.

"I'm aware that you didn't know we've had our eye on the man you knew as Martin Hocking for a long time," he continues several seconds later. "And I know you are not in possession of Belinda's gold. I know which assayer's office Clyde Merriman took the gold to. I know which identity he used to convert the gold to cash. I know he has a safe-deposit box in a San Francisco bank with said cash tucked inside it. I know he was a terrible person who has killed perhaps as many as ten people."

"*Ten?*" The word is a gasp off my tongue. Ten people dead by Martin's hand. Ten!

"Yes, I'm afraid so."

Belinda and I could have been numbers eleven and twelve. Easily. Hot tears spring to my eyes and I squeeze them back in as best I can. Two slip out anyway. Beneath my shirtwaist and corset my lungs are heaving. I cannot still the rapid rising and falling of my chest. Surely the marshal can see I knew none of this.

"That's horrific!" I whisper.

"Indeed. As I said, he was a terrible person. But I am a servant of the law, not of my own opinion, and it does not matter what I think about Clyde Merriman," he says. "What matters is what can be proven in a court of law, and because I have more suspicion than I have hard evidence, you may have done the world a favor if harm has befallen him and you are the person you say you are."

"I am," I say, and my voice sounds like a child's, weak and naïve.

"So you say. But I have a problem." He opens up the file, reaches in, and pulls out a document. He pushes it toward me.

It is a certified copy of a death certificate from County Down in Ireland for a Sophie Clare Whalen.

My vision is suddenly blurred. The room seems to sway; the whole world seems to sway, just like it did the morning of the quake.

"Where did you get this?" I hear myself ask.

"I told you. We've been investigating this man for a long while. We've looked into his activities. All of them. We've looked into the women he has married. It wasn't difficult to follow your immigration trail back to where you started. You left Ireland as Sophie Whalen. You obtained a passport with Sophie Whalen's birth certificate. But that's not who you are. Because Sophie Whalen is dead."

"What do you want from me?" My voice is not much more than a whisper.

"I want the truth," the deputy says.

"I can't tell you," I murmur, my eyes shut tight. I can't. I can't.

"You can. And you will." His words are hard, but they are spoken gently, as though to empower me to say what he wants to hear.

I open my eyes.

He is looking at me with a gentler gaze than when I first sat down with him. It's almost as if we are no longer officer of the law and suspected accomplice. We are two people who know the world harbors cruel people who often go unpunished.

But I say nothing.

He points to the death certificate that rests between us. "Sophie Whalen was your sister, fifteen months younger than you. She died of a fever when she was three. You assumed her identity when you left Ireland. I want to know why."

He doesn't know. He doesn't know. He has that thick file with all those papers and he still wants to know why I took my sister's name. I want to press my hands to my ears to shut out his question and the roar of fear, but my arms won't move.

What answer shall I give him? What answer can I concoct that will satisfy him and ring true? What can I say that will keep me safe and still sound believable?

What do I say?

But I can't think. I can't!

When I remain silent, the deputy reaches into the file and pulls out another document and pushes it toward me. I close my eyes so that I don't have to see it. He says nothing as he waits, supposing that I will in fact look at it after all.

He is right. When I open my eyes, I see a copy of a birth certificate for Saoirse Colleen Whalen.

The girl I was.

"Where did you get these?" I whisper.

"They are public records. Anyone can access them."

He pulls out another document. And another. And another.

A marriage certificate uniting Saoirse Whalen and Colm Mc-Gough.

A death certificate for the infant daughter of Colm and Saoirse McGough, born too soon.

Colm McGough's death certificate, dated three months before I immigrated to America. Cause of death? Accidental drowning.

"I wrote to the authorities in County Down and inquired about the drowning death of Colm McGough in Donaghadee. I received a notice by return post that the ruling was accidental but that there was doubt among his family members that it was truly an accident. He wasn't at sea; his boat was tied up at the pier when he fell overboard. He knew how to swim. The police had wanted to talk to his widow but she left soon after he was buried and no one has seen her since."

I can only stare at the documents laid out in front of me. More tears slip down my cheeks.

Kat.

My little girl. I have failed her.

The deputy waits until I look up at him.

"It is just you and me in this room," he says. "Mrs. Fielding is not here. This is your one and only chance to convince me to let you go and be done here. Tell me the truth."

31

The few memories I have of my little sister are as delicate and thin as tissue. I was only four and a half when the sickness took Sophie from us. I remember her being a happy child, mischievous sometimes, and afraid of the dark—she would cuddle close to me in the bed we shared at night. I remember her sitting on my grandmother's lap and my being jealous because I wanted Gram's lap to be only mine. I remember her taking one of my shoes once and throwing it into the well just to hear it splash. I remember her golden brown curls and the yellow hair ribbons she liked to wear that at one time had been mine. I remember her lying in our bed burning with fever and how I had to sleep at Gram's cottage while she was sick and I liked it. I remember Gram telling me between sobs that the angels had come for her and I remember the tiny coffin. I remember the sound of my mother's wailing and my father carrying the coffin up the hill to the cemetery with other men from the village.

After Sophie's death my parents seemed unable or unwilling to talk about her, and so her presence lifted and she became like a vapor to me, a dream. A dream of a sister whom I might have had but never did. As the years went on, my parents learned to laugh and smile again, and I know they loved again because I would hear them in their room next to mine. But there were never any more babies and I don't think they grieved that. Losing Sophie had changed them, made them fearful of having more children who could also be taken from them.

My father brought out his word book again when I was eight or nine; I didn't even know he had it, because he had put it away when Sophie died. But he was ready, I suppose, to continue to learn all that the world had to teach. I was the only one of the children interested in Da's word book. My brothers weren't curious and didn't value schooling like my father did. None of them wanted to be learned men who taught at university or performed important work in an important office building dressed in an important-looking suit.

So it was me with whom Da shared his word book. The book kept us close even as I became a young woman and started to be more and more interested in Mason's friends. My two older brothers, Niall and Ross, both married at age twenty, and since they were eight and ten years older than me, they were out of the house and creating families of their own well before I knew where babies even came from. Mason, only three years older than me, didn't mind my company, especially after the older brothers moved out, and he let me follow him and his friends almost anywhere they went. He had a group of chums and most of them were unremarkable fellows.

Colm McGough was the exception. He was a year and half or

so older than Mason and tall and handsome. He was the boy in the village all the young girls wanted to impress. He came from a family of fishermen by trade, the second-born of two sons, and the rumor was his father, Gerard, was an authoritative figure who showered little affection on his boys. His mother was a meek little creature who seemed to be afraid of Gerard McGough's very shadow. I don't think I ever heard that woman give an opinion of her own volition or contradict Mr. McGough. Still, Colm seemed a cheerful sort, easygoing, and he surely knew he had the eye of every young girl in the village. I would daydream of him, and I was content enough with that. I had no illusions that Colm McGough fancied me. I was Mason Whalen's little sister; that's all I was. That's what I thought, anyway.

The day my father fell from the roof was an ordinary day. I was still going to classes at sixteen, although many of my schoolmates had stopped at fourteen and were working or learning a trade. I was walking home from school, the long way by the docks, and keeping my eye out for Colm's fishing boat, when I heard someone calling my name. A neighbor was running toward me, holding her skirts up so that she wouldn't trip. My father had fallen and hit his head, the doctor had been summoned to my house, and my mother needed me.

I ran home expecting my father to be sitting in his favorite chair with a chunk of ice to his head, laughing about his clumsiness. But when I came into the house I saw that my da was not in his chair. He was in his bed with a bandage around his head that was seeping blood, and his skin looked pale and slack. The doctor was there and he was telling my mother that it was quite possible Da would not awaken, that my father's eyes were fixed when the doctor had shone his light in them and that was never a good sign.

The doctor told us he could do nothing for him. Prayer was the only thing that could save my da. So we prayed. For four days we prayed. But the doctor was right. Da did not awaken. My mother had been sitting up with Da at night for fear of missing the moment he opened his eyes, but she had fallen asleep holding his hand, and when she startled awake at dawn on the fifth day, the hand in hers was stiff and cold.

Up to that point what I knew of death was the loss of Sophie, which I could barely remember, and the loss of my gram, who had died three years previous. My grandmother had seemed old to me and it seemed natural when she passed. I didn't like it one bit, but other people's grandmothers had died. It didn't seem odd, just sad. My father's death, however, seemed wrong, as if a giant mistake had been made. I could not fathom that my da was gone.

I remember very little of his passing or his funeral or burying him next to my sister and my grandmother. I was in a fog of numbness that I didn't want to emerge from. Mason had already been set to emigrate to America. A second cousin on my mother's side had offered to sponsor him, and he already had his passage booked. He made it clear that he didn't want to stay in Donaghadee; he wanted to make his own way in the world even more so now that our father was dead. He did not want to be a roofer, and that's what his lot would've been had he stayed. My mother told him to go, even while I begged him to stay. My two older brothers who lived nearby—but not in Donaghadee—offered to help as best they could, but they had children of their own to provide for. It would have made sense if one of them had offered to take in Mam and me, but neither one did. I wonder to this day if Niall and Ross were jealous of the love Da had lavished on me.

At first the neighbors would bring us warm dishes of food or a freshly plucked chicken or jars of preserves. But as the months went on and everyone returned to their own lives, Mam and I began to feel the loss of my father's income. There wasn't enough to eat in the house, little coal for the fireplace, and no extra money for gifts or a cake for my seventeenth birthday four months after my father's fall.

Colm began to show up on our doorstep from time to time with extra fish from his day's catch. We had heard from Mason by this point and we knew he was safely in New York, had found work, and was going to be sending us some money as soon as he found a better job. I believe Mason had asked Colm to check on my mother and me in his absence, as his happiness with his new life in America was making him feel guilty. Colm had obliged.

The more Colm came over, the more he found solace at my house, I think. Mam was a good cook and a good conversationalist and his mother was neither. Colm could share his opinion about something, whether it be politics in the village or the world at large, and my mother would engage with him. At some point he began to see me no longer as just Mason's little sister. I remember with utter clarity the day he told me I wasn't a little girl anymore and that I was pretty.

"Stop your teasing," I'd said to him with a laugh, because I was sure he was. "It's not nice."

"I'm not teasing," he replied. "You're the prettiest girl in the village. And the truest. You're not like the other girls, all full of giggles and fancies and flirtations. I wouldn't trust a one of them."

It was a compliment of some kind, but even then I wasn't sure what he meant by it. *Trust those other girls with what?* I thought.

"You're the kind of girl every man wants for his own, you are," he said.

I had never had a boy say anything like this to me before. And I had never dreamed Colm McGough would ever say such a thing to me.

He was good-looking, somehow didn't smell of rotting fish, was congenial, laughed a lot, drank too much sometimes with his brother and friends, and sometimes told bawdy stories that made me blush.

Most of the time he came by the house to see me, but occasionally he'd take me down to the docks and I'd watch as he and his friends passed around a flask of whisky. The other girls in the village, none of whom I was close to—my closest friends had moved away for work—were jealous, I suppose, that Colm had chosen me and distanced themselves from me. After a while Colm seemed to be the only friend I had. A few months before my eighteenth birthday he asked me to marry him.

We were on his boat at the docks, and we were alone. We'd been kissing and Colm had his hands everywhere on me. I hadn't let him have his way fully with me. I had made a promise to my da years before that I wouldn't give my body to a man who hadn't first given me his pledge in marriage. Once you've given a man your body, Da had told me, he doesn't need anything else from you. I didn't want to break my promise to my da. So I kept telling Colm no and he kept whispering things and caressing me, trying to get me to change my mind. I think he thought that he could; I think he had with other girls.

I pushed myself away from him and said, "I'll not be giving you what isn't yours! I'm not your wife, Colm."

He smiled wide. He liked it that I hadn't been with anyone else, and that I wouldn't consider being with anyone I wasn't married to. "Then, be my wife, Saoirse," he said. "Marry me."

I didn't know if it was love I felt for Colm or just immense attraction, but I knew if I did marry Colm, I would always be able to look out for Mam and there would always be food for us both. The fishermen in the village weren't rich, but they never starved. When I told her that Colm asked me to marry him, she as much said the same thing to me: that it would be a relief to her to know that I would always have food to eat and a warm bed and a strong man to protect me. She gave her permission and we were married a few weeks later.

I knew enough from what Colm and I had done when no one was watching to know there were pleasures to be had that I had yet to experience. The first time I lay with him was indeed magical even though painful, and I was happy, truly happy, for the first time since my father had died. This was a pleasure that seemed to have the power to mask every other kind of disappointment, even grief. Even if just for a little while.

The first time Colm struck me I lay on the kitchen floor with my hand on my cheek too stunned to move. We'd been married for only four months and we had just come back from a walk into the village from our little seaside home at the end of a long lane. A man whom we both knew well had tipped his hat to me in greeting and I had wished him a good day. This was the reason Colm had hit me when we returned to our cottage, though at first I didn't understand why and I had to ask him. I could not grasp what the offense had been. Colm yelled that it was not that I had said hello to the man; it was how I had said it and how I had looked at the man, but I didn't know what Colm meant. I hadn't looked at the man in any particular kind of way.

It happened again a few weeks later, and then again a few weeks after that. I realized I could not return the greeting of any man in the village when Colm was nearby, as he mistook every cordial interaction as coquettishness on my part. I began to look forward to the times when he was out at sea because then I could relax and not worry about the grocer or the cobbler or the milkman talking to me.

Colm didn't hit me when he was drunk. Strangely enough he was lazily cheerful when he had too much drink. It was when he was sober that he was the most dangerous, and I never knew when something I would do would set him off. Sometimes he'd get angry if I took too long making supper or if I had it ready before he was wanting to eat. Sometimes he would not come home at night, and if I asked him where he'd been, he would go into a rage, saying it was not my place to question him. He would usually apologize hours or days later, but he'd never say he'd try to change. I wanted to reach out to Mam to ask her how to have the kind of marriage she had with Da, but I couldn't bring myself to tell her what Colm was truly like. My friends from my school days were living their own lives now in other villages, or they'd gone to Belfast to secretarial school or nursing school. I had no one to confide in.

A year passed and then I found myself pregnant. I foolishly believed that my being with child would make a better man of my husband and he would begin to see anew his role as loving provider. But Colm took the news strangely that we were to have a child, and in bed that night he was savage toward me, hurting me as he lay on top of me. It was as if he wanted to yank out the new life he had put in. But weeks later he was happy about it and he put his hand on my growing stomach and talked to the child, calling him a little boy and telling him what it would be like to teach him the ways of the sea.

I was six months along when Colm came home angry after a fight he'd had with his father. I had never seen him so livid. I could tell it was not safe for me to be in the house and I wanted to escape to my mother's while he settled down. When I mentioned that I needed to take something up to Mam's, he took great offense, yelling at me that he had just gotten home, and when I tried to move past him and go anyway, he yanked me by the hair, threw me to the floor, and began to kick.

I tried to protect my child. I tried to crawl away, and when I could not, I curled into a ball and put my arms around my stomach. But the kicks from his heavy boots kept coming and coming until he finally tired of it. He stood over me for few seconds, breathing heavily.

"You're a useless slag," he said, nearly spitting the words on me. Then he grabbed his coat off its peg. "And don't even think of going to your mam's." A second later he was out the door and on his way to the pub.

As soon as he was gone, the childbearing pains began to come. I struggled to my feet and out of the cottage. I got as far as halfway to the neighbor's house before collapsing in water and blood. My tiny blossom of a girl was born that night as blue as a summer moon. I held her dead body as my vision went cloudy and as the blood continued to pour from inside me, and then I knew no more.

When I awoke two days later I was in a hospital bed in Belfast. I was not a mother. I would never be a mother. Everything within me that could make and hold a new life had been torn out of me.

I was in hospital for ten days. Colm did not come to Belfast to visit me. My mother came every day to sit with me and cry with me. I told her what Colm had done even though I knew it would hurt her.

"You'll not be going home to him," Mam said. "You'll not."

But I did. It was Colm who came for me the day I was discharged. He told me he couldn't bring himself to come visit, and he felt bad for what had happened. But he did not seem sad that he had killed our baby girl and nearly killed me. When we arrived home, my mother came to the cottage and Colm sent her away. I watched her at the window crying as she went back to the house I had been born in, too weak to run after her.

I had cried my eyes dry, and I now felt nothing except for a cold, hard rumbling that was lurking deep within me, like water just about to boil. I didn't know what to make of it. It didn't feel like hatred; it felt stronger than that. The first time that Colm reached for me in bed after I miscarried our child, I just let him have his way. I felt nothing except that cold boil at the core of me. It was as if there was another person inside me with a plan, but I didn't know what it was other than I wanted Colm to pay for what he had done. He had killed our daughter.

I knew that if he were to strike me again, I would hit him back. I was looking forward to it. I started looking for things around the house that I could use to pummel him. I began practicing with the fireplace poker, but in the end I needn't have practiced with anything at all.

Four months after our baby girl died I walked to the docks where his boat was tied up because he'd asked me to bring down his supper. He had too much repair work to do to come up to the cottage. He was in a foul mood and I could tell there was going to be trouble. He and his father had had another fight and I was going to be bearing the brunt of it if I didn't leave.

So I said nothing, placed the covered iron skillet that held his dinner on an overturned crate, and turned to go. He grabbed my arm and twirled me back around and asked where the hell was I going. We were close to the railing and there were ropes and nets and pipes littering the deck and I started to slip on them. I tried to wrench my arm free to regain my balance, which made him begin to lose his. He raised his hand to hit me and I ducked and grabbed the skillet. I lifted it and then brought it around with all the strength I had. The pan connected with his head and he pitched backward and over the railing.

There was a splash as he hit the water. I looked over the side to see him under the surface holding his head, with ribbons of red swirling through his fingers. His eyes were scrunched shut, but as he realized where he was, he opened them wide and looked up at me. He shot one hand out of the water toward me—his fingers splayed like limbs on a sea star. I stood there and did nothing.

His eyes widened and he shot up the other hand, the one that had been holding his head. He surfaced for a second and tried to say my name, but he was struggling to tread water and his head was bleeding, turning the water red around him. And I stood and did nothing.

He began to drift downward, still looking at me, still reaching one hand toward me. He was losing consciousness, and I did nothing.

I did not save him.

I waited until I could not see him any longer. I wiped the skillet with the cover I had brought and replaced the sausages and potatoes that had fallen from it. Then I ran, yelling for help.

It came too late, of course. I told the other fishermen who came in answer to my cries that Colm had been drinking and had stumbled and fallen overboard. I had been coming to the boat with his dinner when I saw him fall, and I ran but I couldn't get to him in time.

He was pulled from the water, dead. The gash on his forehead looked so small compared to the amount of blood that had flowed from it.

I wasn't sad that he was dead.

I wasn't ashamed of what I had done.

He had killed my little girl. He was slowly killing me.

And now I was free of him. Or so I thought.

His brother and father could not believe that Colm had not been able to swim to shore after he fell, even with a gash on his head. He was a good swimmer. They wondered why I hadn't jumped in after him or thrown him a life vest. They wondered what he had hit his head on when he fell. They'd been with him only a short time before and he'd not been drinking then. How was it that he was drunk—as I had claimed he was—so soon after they'd left him? They began to talk with others after the funeral and after I'd returned to Mam's house. It was just talk at the pub, but Mam heard of it and began to worry for me, because I had told her the truth of what had happened. She knew how Colm ended up in the water.

It was Mam's idea for me to go to America to be with Mason, her idea to use Sophie's birth certificate to get a passport in Dublin, far away from home. It was her idea for me to have a fresh beginning with a name she still loved so very much and which would ensure no authorities in Donaghadee or County Down would ever know where to find me. It would also give me what she felt I deserved and what she had been unable to give me—a new and happy life.

I went to Dublin with my dead sister's birth certificate. I worked in a restaurant there for two months as Sophie Whalen, and then I got a passport and booked a passage to America. My letters to Mam I sent to my brother Niall in Bangor so that the postmaster in Donaghadee wouldn't know an S. Whalen was writing to her from New York.

I wasn't anxious to get out of Manhattan because the tenement I was living in was appalling. It was, but that is not the reason I answered Martin's advertisement. The tenements were full of other Irish girls like me, and a young woman I knew and who knew me had arrived from the village next to Donaghadee. She was living on my block. If I had stayed, she would've recognized me. I couldn't take the chance that she would write home and that word would get out where I was. So I left and became Sophie Hocking. I became her. That's who I am now.

Sophie Hocking.

There is no Saoirse Whalen McGough.

32

When I'm finished telling Deputy Logan what he insisted on knowing, my only thought is that I will not return home to Kat tonight and I promised I would.

This deputy sitting across the table will surely arrest me for killing Colm, even though I know it was not I who took his life. The ocean took him, as surely as the fire took Martin. Forces of nature stepped in to balance what had been set off-kilter. But how in heaven can I convince him of that?

Worse, I have not made arrangements for Kat if anything should happen to me. I will want her to stay with Belinda, but will that lawyer of hers let her? Might he contact Candace's cousin in Texas? Is that who will take Kat when I am sent to prison? Or will I be hanged for what I've done? Will I be sent back to Ireland first to face my judgment?

All of these thoughts are zipping around in my head like flashes of lightning, each one quick and hard and blazing. I wish it had been me who fell overboard that night in Donaghadee. I wish I'd been the one who'd been hit in the head and plunged into the frigid water. I wish the water had taken me instead, embraced me like a lost soul and carried me far away from this world of sorrows.

Into this cyclone of thoughts I hear a voice. Deputy Logan has asked me a question. I look up at him and he can see that I did not hear it. His arm is extended toward me and in his hand is a clutch of white fabric.

"Would you like a handkerchief?" he says.

A stream of tears has coursed down my cheeks, down my neck, and into my lap.

"It's not for Colm that I am crying," I blurt. "It's not because of what I did."

"Yes, I know."

The handkerchief is still extended.

"He killed my daughter."

Deputy Logan says nothing, but a second later I take the handkerchief. It smells of cedar and lime and pipe tobacco. Such comforting fragrances. They remind me of Da. I press the fabric to my cheeks and I breathe in deep.

And I wait for the deputy to tell me what my fate will be.

He doesn't say anything for several long moments.

"My concern is the whereabouts of Clyde Merriman, the man you know as Martin Hocking," he finally says.

I can form no words for a second. "Did . . . did you not hear what I just told you?" I finally ask.

"I heard every word."

Silence hovers between us.

"Where is he?" the deputy asks seconds later.

"I think . . . I think he might be dead."

"Did you do something to him?"

The words slip easily off my lips. "I did not save him."

"Where is he?" the deputy says again.

"I'm not entirely sure anymore."

"Then why do you think he is dead?"

"Because I saw . . . him." I refold the handkerchief and place it on the table. He does not reach to take it.

"I want to know everything that happened," he says. "I want to know how Belinda Bigelow found her way to your house. I want to know why she stayed the night and how you knew Candace was still alive. And I want to know what happened to the man you know as Martin Hocking."

A welcome but bizarre calm wraps itself around me as I begin to tell the deputy all about the events of the last seven months, starting with the day before the earthquake. I tell him everything that happened on the stairs. And everything that happened afterward. When I am finished, the deputy says nothing for several tense seconds.

"So you do not have proof that the man you know as Martin Hocking is dead?" he finally asks.

"No."

"Then it's possible your husband is still missing," he says, not taking his eyes off mine. And I can see so very clearly that he is not going to be arresting me today. A second or two passes as I ponder why.

"I suppose that's true."

He's still staring at me, as though he is formulating a plan in his head. He is deciding something. I cannot discern his thoughts.

Then he leans forward and pushes the certified copies from the

County Down records office toward me. Sophie's death certificate. My birth certificate. My marriage certificate. Colm's death certificate.

I look at the papers and then I raise my gaze. I don't know what this action of his means. I have already confessed. I have already acknowledged what these documents mean.

"Take them," he says softly, looking down at the papers.

"Pardon?" I whisper.

His gaze travels back up to mine. "I am the only one who knows you are Saoirse Whalen. I am the only one who knows who you truly are. I have not yet shared these documents with my superiors. It was premature to say anything until I talked to you. If you take these documents now, they will be out of this file and out of my investigation."

"But . . . but you corresponded with officials in Ireland at the county offices. They know about me! Won't they come for me now?"

"I requested copies of public records related to Sophie Whalen and Saoirse Whalen McGough of Donaghadee. It was not necessary to supply a reason. I said nothing about how these documents relate to an Irish immigrant named Sophie Hocking."

"But . . . but what if the public records people mention it to the magistrate? What if they tell him that a U.S. marshal was asking for these records?"

"Do you think they will?"

"People like to talk."

The deputy leans back in his chair. "You may someday have to answer for what happened on that boat in Donaghadee as you had to answer for what happened at your house here in San Francisco. All of us at some point, either in this life or the next, have to answer for our actions, Mrs. McGough. I will surely have to answer for mine in this moment. Take the documents."

He lets this sit between us for a moment, this notion that we choose our actions at the moment when we must and he is choosing to let me go free. He is going to pretend he doesn't know my true identity, or what I did. He could get fired for this. Perhaps arrested and sentenced to prison for it. But he is doing it anyway.

"Why are you letting me go?" My voice is no louder than a whisper.

"Because I believe you. I believe in justice, too, but I know that sometimes it is not delivered in the way it should be. Sometimes it is not delivered at all, and the evil man walks free."

A vein in his neck is pulsing faintly and I detect a slight sheen misting over his eyes. Deputy Logan has been wronged by evil, as I have been. He lost someone he loved because of it, as I have. Perhaps more than one person.

But his loss was not vindicated by the forces of nature, as twice mine were.

"Take them," he says, and the glistening in his eyes is blinked away.

I reach for the papers. I place them atop one another, quarter-fold them, and place them in my handbag.

"Take the handkerchief, too."

I look up from the handbag. "What?"

He nods toward his handkerchief, which smells of him and is wet with my tears.

"Why?"

"So that you do not forget."

He says nothing else and I realize that he is asking me to remember this transaction we are making, he and I. I am to take the handkerchief and keep it as a token of our covenant of silence. He will never reveal what I did, and I likewise will never expose him for letting me go. I reach for the handkerchief and place it in my handbag next to the folded papers.

"I am going to ask Mrs. Fielding to return so that we can finish. I will be quick. You will answer as if I had shown you none of those documents. Agreed?"

"Yes."

"I am going to file a report stating that Clyde Merriman was in San Francisco on April 18, went missing during the earthquake and fire, and is quite likely a casualty of the disaster. The police here will likely declare him dead in time. The name Clyde Merriman is surely dead. If he is indeed still alive, he will take advantage of being declared deceased and will likely resurface as someone else and I will have to start over. You, on the other hand, surely have nothing to worry about. He will think you've done him a favor if he indeed survived."

The thought of that disgusts me. "He didn't. He couldn't have!" I say.

"I hope you are right."

I say nothing as I push past any doubts that Martin didn't crawl out of that house alive.

"Are you ready for me to bring Mrs. Fielding back in?" Deputy Logan says a second later.

I rub away lingering remnants of tears, pinch my cheeks for a bit of color, and smooth my hair. "Yes."

The deputy stands, walks over to the door, and opens it. He calls for the recorder to return, and Mrs. Fielding enters the room and takes her chair again.

"Mrs. Fielding, can you tell us please where we left off?"

The woman looks at the little scroll of paper in her strange machine. "Question: And yet how can I believe you, Mrs. Hocking, when I know for a fact you have lied to me with regard to other matters? Answer: I haven't. Question: But you have. You've been lying to me since the moment you sat down. Answer: That's not true. I— Question: Since the moment you told me your name."

"Thank you, Mrs. Fielding." Deputy Logan turns his attention to me. "Now, then. You state that you have been answering my questions truthfully. I ask you now, if you were under oath, would you maintain that your name is in fact Sophie Hocking?"

His gaze is tight on mine.

"I would," I reply.

"And if you were under oath, would you maintain that you do not know the whereabouts of the man you know as Martin Hocking?"

"I would."

"And if you were under oath, Mrs. Hocking, would you still maintain that you waited to report your husband missing until six weeks after the earthquake because you were unconcerned about his whereabouts?"

"Yes, I would."

"Why were you unconcerned?"

"Because I do not love him. I married him for convenience."

"Is there anything you wish to add or amend to what you have told me today?"

I shake my head. "No, sir."

The deputy regards me for a moment. "So be it. I think we are done here. Again, Mrs. Hocking, thank you for coming in. If there is any news of your husband, we will let you know, and I trust you will do the same if you hear from him."

My mouth drops open a little. We are finished. He is done with me. "Of . . . of course."

He stands. "I'll walk you out."

I rise from my chair, holding my handbag close to me. Deputy Logan opens the door for me. We walk out of the station and he continues to follow me out onto the pavement and into the mellow autumn sunshine.

We stop a few feet from the station entrance.

"I meant what I said, Saoirse McGough," he says softly. "I believe in justice, but I believe it is best administered by those commissioned by the rest of humanity to give it. Do you understand what I'm saying?"

"I never intended to take matters into my hands. I only wanted—"

"Do you understand what I'm saying, Saoirse?"

I nod. "Yes."

He breathes in deeply and then exhales. "Go home and raise your daughter."

Gratitude fills my soul that he is letting me do both. "Thank you." I wish I had better words.

He nods, and I see the vein in his neck pulse again. I can go home to my daughter and make a life for her and me, but he cannot do the same. Someone beloved was stolen from him by a wicked man who walks this earth free. I can see it as plain as day.

"Who was it that was taken from you?" I ask.

He is surprised at first but hesitates for only a moment. "My wife and son."

"What happened to them?"

He inhales and then lets the breath out slowly. "It was made to look like a robbery gone wrong, but it was a retaliatory act by the brother of a convicted man I sent to the gallows. I could not prove it."

"I am so sorry."

He shakes his head as if to deflect my sympathy, because to accept it would open a wound still struggling to heal, I'm guessing.

"I . . . I hope happiness returns to you someday," I say as respectfully as I can.

I want him to know that I understand too well how hard it is to walk the path of loss. And even as I say such words to him, I see my life being given back to me by this man who has also known injustice. I see my little house at the Loralei as a hope-filled place where quiet Kat can fully find her voice again within the great circle of affection for her there. I see Belinda and Elliot marrying and adding to their family little brothers and sisters for Sarah. I see myself learning to trust in humanity again, and maybe even in the love of a good man. I have been reminded today that truly good men do exist.

I see myself atoning for the mistakes I have made by doing good whenever I can, for whomever I can. I see my mam emigrating to America with the promise of a job at the Loralei and Kat being wrapped in her grandmotherly embrace. I see myself keeping the handkerchief that sealed my pardon close to my bosom, to remind me that I am still the girl my da loved, still the sister Sophie clung to at night when she was afraid, still the mother of the blossom baby I would have named Juliet. I am that person and more. I am Mam to Kat. Auntie to Sarah. Friend to Belinda and Elliot. Confidante of a benevolent U.S. marshal, a good man I know I shall never see again.

"Good-bye." Ambrose Logan starts to leave, but I touch his arm to stop him.

He turns.

"It's pronounced 'Seer-sha,'" I tell him.

He tips his head slightly. "What is?"

"My name."

A glimmer of a smile tugs at the corners of his mouth. "Good-bye, Mrs. Hocking."

He opens the door to the police department, and I turn from him to face the wide horizon of so many lives rising from ashes.

Epilogue

Carson City, Nevada
1926

The courtroom brims with family members of the victim, journalists, and—like the woman in the third row—the curious. A verdict has been reached, and those in the gallery are eager for the jury to return to their seats.

The man accused of murder is sitting with his back to the spectators. The woman can see that his hair is graying now and that it has lost some of its wave. She wouldn't have recognized him from this angle. She has not yet seen his face.

It was the photograph in a Nevada newspaper of a man charged with poisoning his wife that caught her eye. She is in Carson City only to attend a wedding. She wouldn't have known of the Clayton Sharpe trial concluding today if she had not glanced at the newspaper at the hotel's breakfast table. She had known it was him the instant she saw the photograph. She would know those eyes anywhere.

All through the years, she had wondered if he was still alive. Mam told her when she was still a young girl that the San Francisco Police had long ago believed him to be dead. But there had been no body. They had held no funeral. He didn't feel dead to her. He didn't feel alive, either. She hasn't spoken of him in as long as she can remember.

When she was twelve, Mam married a man from San Rafaela who owned a vineyard and who asked her to call him by any name she wanted. She has always called him Da because it makes Mam and Gram smile when she does and because she loves Sam like a father. He has always loved her like a daughter. She never thinks about this other man anymore. But she wonders now why he is still using names that do not belong to him, and why he lies, and why he likes to hurt people.

She's not sure if she should tell anyone about this when she returns home. Perhaps she will tell Victor, who is at home with their eighteen-month-old son. Perhaps only him.

If Clayton Sharpe is convicted, he will be executed. The newspaper stated it is what the prosecutors have asked for. He will hang. In that case, nothing will change for her and Mam and Belinda, will it? Perhaps if he is found not guilty she will have a decision to make, because then he will be free. She contemplates what she will do if the jury does not convict him. She contemplates how she will feel if it does.

The room is called to order as the judge takes his seat, and then the jury is brought in. The bailiff hands the jury's decision to the judge. He looks at the piece of paper and then hands it back. The accused man is ordered to stand. She watches him rise from his chair unsteadily, using a cane for balance. One leg appears to be slightly shorter than the other.

The decision is read aloud.

Clayton Sharpe has been found guilty of first-degree murder in the death of Bernice Templeton Sharpe and is sentenced therefore to death by hanging.

Cries of elation and relief erupt in the gallery. She feels nothing more than a pinch of sadness for what could have been if this man had been someone else. But he was who he was.

She watches as the condemned man is prepared to be escorted out of the courtroom. As he turns, he casts his gaze across the gallery and their eyes meet. It's been twenty years, but it appears he would know her eyes anywhere, too.

A crooked jawline produces a lopsided grin that is disturbingly attractive. "Kitty Kat," he murmurs.

She does not smile back. She holds up her left hand as if to adjust her collar but it is so that he can see the wedding band around her ring finger. It is the only way she can think of to tell him that despite all that he did to her, she's been loved every day since she last saw him. Every day. They all have.

He furrows his brow like he doesn't understand.

Because he doesn't.

Mam told her this. Ages ago. Before he disappeared from their lives like a phantom.

He doesn't know the way of love.

And then he is gone from the room and people begin to stand and talk to one another.

The journalist sitting next to her turns to her. "Did he just say 'kitty cat' to you? Do you know him?" His tone is incredulous and his notepad is open for her answer.

"I've never met Clayton Sharpe," she replies with a start.

"But he said 'kitty cat' to you just now. I heard him."

She is about to answer that she does not know the man when the older gentleman sitting next to her on her other side says, "The lady has kindly told you she has never met Clayton Sharpe."

The journalist shakes his head, and as he stands to leave, he shoves his tablet and pencil in his pocket.

Kat turns in her seat to face the man who came to her aid. He is a bit older than Sam—early fifties, she thinks. His brown hair is flecked with gray, and he is wearing plain clothes, but a law enforcement badge of some kind is pinned to his vest pocket and is peeking out from under his suit coat.

"Thank you," she says.

"I, too, have never met Clayton Sharpe, but I've been looking forward to seeing him in a court of law for a long time."

Kat says nothing.

"I am a U.S. marshal," the man says, opening one side of his coat briefly and showing her the badge. "I knew this man by a different name many years ago. I was in San Francisco then, several months after that terrible earthquake." His kind gaze is intent on her now, and the room suddenly feels too small, the walls too close.

He is looking at her with a gaze that speaks words she is meant to understand. And she does.

"I'm afraid I must go," Kat says, rising to her feet, the blood in her veins rushing. "I've a friend's wedding to attend."

He rises as well. Quickly. "Will you be all right?" he says gently, and he nods ever so slightly toward the door where Clayton Sharpe exited the courtroom. Kat stares at the U.S. marshal for a long moment. Somehow this man knows why Clayton Sharpe called her "Kitty Kat." But there's something about the fatherly way the marshal is looking at her that makes her want to answer him rather than abruptly take her leave. The marshal knows what the convicted man did to her all those years ago, and to people she loves.

He knows.

"I will be fine," she replies, matching his soothing tone. "I *am* fine. I don't know Clayton Sharpe. He is a stranger to me."

The marshal smiles. He looks relieved. Satisfied. "Good day to you, then, madam."

She moves away from him and the gallery chairs and steps out into the aisle. She pauses a second, and then turns toward the marshal. "And a good day to you, too, sir." Then she faces the oak doors that lead to the world outside.

Kat walks briskly out of the courthouse and into the golden afternoon.

Acknowledgments

I am indebted to these wonderful people with regard to the writing of this book: Jeanne Dickson and Hayley Dickson for the walking tours of San Francisco; Sylvia Rowan, a gracious and helpful librarian at the San Francisco History Center; John Privara, a volunteer with the California State Railroad Museum; Michael McCurdy, law librarian at California State Library; and Malcolm E. Barker, whose book *Three Fearful Days*—a compilation of firsthand accounts of the 1906 earthquake and fire—was indispensable to me. As always, I'm grateful beyond words for my editor at Berkley, Claire Zion, who sent me back to the drawing board twice with this one, and I'm so glad she did; for my entire team at Berkley—including Craig Burke, Danielle Keir, Tara O'Connor, and Fareeda Bullert; and for my agent extraordinaire, Elisabeth Weed. Many thanks, too, to my mom, Judy Horning, for careful proofreading, and to my sweet husband, Bob, for cheering me on on my hardest days.

Acknowledgments

I endeavored to present all the details of the 1906 earthquake and fire as accurately as possible. I confess I did take liberty with fictional San Rafaela, as I wanted to control every aspect of the town where the Loralei Inn was located and the placement of the abandoned and also fictional mine. San Rafaela *could* exist a few miles from San Mateo, but it does not. All the other cities and towns mentioned in the book are real places, as are the chilling details of the three days San Francisco burned. It is believed the great San Francisco earthquake of 1906 would have registered a magnitude 7.9 on the Richter scale. As I have described in the pages of this novel, it struck in two immediately successive rounds, starting just before daybreak on Wednesday, April 18. The first round lasted only a few breaths' time; the second, a terrifying forty-five seconds. The quake broke apart major water mains in the heart of San Francisco and burst open gas lines, which then started dozens of fires almost instantaneously. Roughly five square miles of San Francisco burned over the next three days—five hundred city blocks. An estimated twenty-eight thousand buildings were destroyed and half the city's four hundred thousand inhabitants were made homeless. The official death toll in San Francisco from both the quake and the resulting fires is estimated to have exceeded three thousand people.

Since then the study of earthquakes has come a long way. With state-of-the-art equipment, today's seismologists have been able to create detailed diagrams of California's renowned San Andreas Fault, a 750-mile-long line that marks the boundary between the North American and Pacific tectonic plates. The movement of the earth can now be charted with amazing accuracy, but no one can adequately predict when that movement will occur. The San Andreas Fault is famous for major earthquakes, including this one

366

in 1906 and another in 1989. A 100-mile section of the fault, running from San Bernardino south to San Diego, has remained unnervingly quiet for nearly three hundred years. It is expected that someday it will awaken from its slumber, but no one can say when that day will come. There is always that gnawing question, even among those of us who live in the Golden State, if the Big One will strike in our lifetime.

If you get the chance to visit San Francisco, I encourage a visit to the California Academy of Sciences in Golden Gate Park, where you can physically experience the sustained tremors of the great quake of 1906—all from inside a simulator built to look like the dining room of a Victorian-era "Painted Lady" house.